HITLER, THE WAR LORD, SPEAKS:

"War is eternal, war is universal...Let us go back to primitive life: the life of the savages. What is war but cunning, deception, delusion, attack and surprise?...When the enemy is demoralised from within, that is the right moment. A single blow must destroy him. Aerial attacks, stupendous in their mass-effect, surprise, terror, sabotage, assassination from within, the murder of leading men...sudden attacks, all in the same second, that is the war of the future. A gigantic, all destroying blow...I shall make war. I shall determine the correct moment for attack. Gentlemen, let us not play at being heroes, but let us destroy the enemy...My motto is: Destroy him by all and any means. I am the one who will wage the war."

— Adolf Hitler, 1933

THE GERMAN ARMY
1933-1945
Volume I
By Matthew Cooper

ZEBRA BOOKS
KENSINGTON PUBLISHING CORP.

ZEBRA BOOKS
are published by
KENSINGTON PUBLISHING CORP.
21 East 40th Street
New York, N.Y. 10016

Copyright © 1978 by Cooper and Lucas, Ltd.

All rights reserved. No part of this book may be reproduced in any form or by any means without the prior written consent of the Publisher, excepting brief quotes used in reviews.

First Printing: April, 1979

Printed in the United States of America

Introduction

Things and actions are what they are, and the consequences of them will be what they will be: why, then, should we desire to be deceived?
BISHOP JOSEPH BUTLER
1692–1752

'My hands are done for, and have been ever since the beginning of December. The little finger of my left hand is missing and—what's even worse—the three middle fingers of my right one are frozen. I can only hold my mug with my thumb and little finger. I'm pretty hopeless; only when a man has lost any fingers does he see how much he needs them for the very smallest jobs. The best thing I can do with the finger is to shoot with it. My hands are finished. After all, even if I'm not fit for anything else, I can't go on shooting for the rest of my life.' Thus, in January 1943, an anonymous German soldier wrote of his condition during the battle of Stalingrad; it is not known whether he survived, but it was unlikely. His suffering was not unique. In the German Army alone, in the five and a half years of the Second World War, more than 2,500,000 soldiers were killed and 5,000,000 wounded in the pursuit of an empty cause.

Although no further direct mention of the suffering of individual fighting soldiers will be made, it is as well to remember from the outset that this, in the final analysis, is what this book is all about. For the political and military failure of the German Army, both in the corridors of power and on the field of battle in the years from 1933 to 1945, had one result: the unnecessary death of two and a half million of its men, and untold suffering for countless others. For the world at large, the victim of Hitler's aggression, this was a cause for great relief; for the German Army, it was a tragedy.

The Army of the Third Reich was a failure. Certainly, it won many victories: it conquered Poland in twenty-seven days, Denmark in one, Norway in twenty-three, Holland in five, Belgium in eighteen, France in thirty-nine, Yugoslavia in twelve, and Greece in twenty-one. In the vast spaces of the Soviet Union and the North African desert, although final success was to elude it, its feats have remained remarkable to this day. Indeed, the myth quickly developed that the German Army of the Second World War was an excellent fighting machine, one of history's best, and that its defeat was mainly, even solely, due to Hitler burdening it with tasks far beyond its material resources. But this is to mistake appearance for reality; from the beginning there were evident beneath the façade of easy victory the seeds of later defeat, both in the headquarters of the high commands and on the field of battle. The first transient victories should not obscure this. The German Army was the prisoner of its heritage, both political and military, from which it never succeeded in breaking free. Had it not been for one man—Adolf Hitler—this need not have been so disastrous, for contemporary foreign armies were, after all, suffering the same disability. But the moment this dictator entered the European scene as Führer of the Third German Reich, the fate of the Army was sealed, and an irreversible destiny appears to have determined its descent to ultimate failure.

To understand the reasons for this failure, this book concentrates on two themes: the relationship between Hitler and the senior generals, and the strategic development of the Army. It is argued, firstly, that in their political relationship with Hitler, the generals were largely innocent of the blame that has so often been laid at their door, but that, at the same time, they inexcusably surrendered up their military responsibility and, knowingly, allowed an ungifted amateur to gain operational control of the Army, pervert its strategy and lead it to disaster; and, secondly, that the commonly accepted idea of the German Army having been well-equipped and well-trained, and having practised a revolutionary form of warfare known as *Blitzkrieg*, is a myth. Throughout, I have attempted to look at the ideas and events of 1933 to 1945 as the Army leaders themselves would have seen them, rather than as historians have tended to understand them with the advantage of hindsight. Thirty years after the end of the Second World War we may be able to see clearly where, from the beginning of his dictatorship, Hitler was leading Germany; from the relative security of contemporary western society, we find it easy to condemn all those who condoned or ignored the evils of National Socialism; and, having seen the potential of modern weapons, we believe that we discern their use in a revolutionary strategy during the early years of the war. But are we right to expect the German generals to have done so? I think not. Their background, their heritage of political and strategic thought, was very different from ours, as was the society and age in which they lived. Only when this is realised, do the failures of the German Army under Adolf Hitler become understandable; and only when these failures are recognised, do we see how fortunate were its enemies. It is easy to believe that it was not the Germans who won the early campaigns, but the Allies who lost them, just as it was not the Allies who finally won the war, but the Germans who lost it. For the failings of the German Army under Hitler may we all be thankful; without them, the world today would be a far different place.

Those looking for a detailed, chronological account of the many campaigns undertaken by the German Army from 1939 to 1945 will be disappointed. This, they can find elsewhere. Here, I deal solely with the themes outlined above. In Part One, the reader will find portrayed the political relations between Hitler and the Army leaders from 1933 to 1939; in Part Two, the strategic basis of the Army until 1939 is analysed; in Part Three, the political and military developments in the years of victory are described, covering the campaigns in Poland, Norway, western Europe, the Balkans and the Soviet Union until early 1942; and, in Part Four, the events of the years of defeat are dealt with, showing how the German Army failed to gain victory in the Mediterranean, the east and the west, and how Hitler gained final, total, control over its operation.

This book may be likened, although, alas, not too closely, to the broad brush-sweeps of the Impressionist painters rather than to the detail of the Pre-Raphaelites. It attempts to provide for all readers, whether specialist or general, a fresh interpretation of the fortunes of the German Army from 1933 to 1945, so long overdue for revaluation; but, within the physical constraints of one book, much has had to be left out. Some may believe that my choice of subjects has been at fault, and that important aspects have been omitted; others may think that my selection of facts and quotations has been too subjective, designed only to support my own view of events. Perhaps; but, from the beginning, Napoleon's admonition was always with me: 'It is easier for the ordinary historian to build upon suppositions and to weave hypotheses together than to tell a simple story and stick to the facts. But man, and especially the historian, is all vanity; he must give full rein to his imagination, and he must hold the reader's interest, even if truth be sacrificed in the process.' Whether I have avoided this pitfall, the reader alone can judge.

No man is an island, and no author is entire in himself. The writing of this book owes much to many. Foremost among them is Miss Elaine Austin, who has given much time to reading and correcting the manuscript; her knowledge of the English language and her patience have been invaluable. Lady Liddell Hart, whose hospitality I shall always remember with gratitude, has been of great help in allowing me to work in her husband's library and among his papers; this has been of inestimable value. I should also like to thank James Lucas of the Imperial

War Museum, who has been of considerable help in many ways. My editor, Michael Stevens, together with Graeme Wright, has patiently given his great experience to the production of this book; they have my warmest appreciation. Others who have made valuable contributions are Dr. Anthony Clayton, of the Royal Military Academy, Sandhurst, Anthony Shadrake, of King's College, London, Terry Charman, of the Imperial War Museum, Paul Silk, of the House of Commons, Douglas Dales, Miss Elizabeth Malone-Lee, Nigel Carnelley, John Calder, Otto Kuhn and Herr L. Klein, who has been to many institutions in Germany on my behalf. Particular thanks must also go to David Henson, who occasionally let me work! Then there is the army of women who typed the manuscript: Miss Beatrix Hawkins, Miss Susan Banks, Mrs. Annabelle Egremont, Miss Jane Howard, Miss Ann Power, Mrs. Diana Faires, and, last but not least, Miss Julia Burn; to them all, my thanks. I should also like to express my gratitude to Brian L. Davis for the loan from his collection of the uniform and helmet for the jacket, and to all those at Macdonald and Jane's who have put so much effort into producing this book. Mention must also be made of institutions that I have used: the Library of the House of Commons, the Library of King's College, London, the War Office Library, the Department of Documents and the Library of the Imperial War Museum, and the Public Record Office. Again, may I express my gratitude to all who have helped me.

Matthew Cooper
LONDON, JUNE 1977

PART ONE

The Political Destiny of the German Army 1933-1939

Must helpless man, in ignorance sedate
Roll darkling down the torrent of his fate?

DR. JOHNSON
Vanity of Human Wishes

1

Political Heritage

Every people is the child of its history, its past, and can no more break away from it than a man can separate himself from his youth.
    HANS DELBRUCK
    Krieg und Politik

'It will be up to the generals to see that the Army does not in the end kiss Herr Schicklgruber's hands like hysterical women.'[1] So wrote General Wilhelm Gröner in 1932, two days after leaving his post as Reich Defence Minister and eight months before the National Socialists assumed power in Germany. It was to take just six years for his worst fears to be justified: the generals had failed; the Army had become Hitler's.

For this, the verdict of history has been harsh. The International Military Tribunal instituted by the victorious Allies immediately after the war, although it acquitted the German Army General Staff and High Command of the charge of being criminal organisations, nevertheless delivered the opinion that 'They have been responsible in large measure for the miseries and sufferings that have fallen upon millions of men, women, and children. They have been a disgrace to the honourable profession of arms. Without their military guidance the aggressive ambitions of Hitler and his fellow Nazis would have been academic and sterile. . . . they were certainly a ruthless military caste. The contemporary German militarism flourished briefly with its recent ally, National Socialism, as well or better than it had in the generations of the past.'[2]

Why, historians wonder, did the once-proud, independently minded Prusso-German Army transform itself into nothing more than the subservient military instrument of a dictator's megalomaniac will? Why, they ask, did the generals allow Hitler to take power in 1933, and then stand passively by while he proceeded to subject both Germany and her Armed Forces to his control? Surely, many argue, the Army leaders must have been aware of the enormity of the political ideas they were prepared to tolerate; and why, they moralise, did they seek to exploit this regime of unparalleled evil for their own ends, thereby allowing a reign of terror to degrade the German people and inflict on the world a war, and a genocide, of cataclysmic proportions? In answering these questions, most historians have accused Hitler of a base desire to subvert the independence of the Army, and of using every known method of guile and deceit to realise it. Moreover, they have judged the military leaders to have been, at best, moral cowards, and, at worst, calculating opportunists. One historian, a senior officer who participated in the actions of the Armed Forces High Command, believed 'that the fateful goddesses of the ancients cast over them [the German generals] their shadow and their spell: Chores, who dazzled with success, Hybris, who threatened the victims with loss of moral and intellectual equilibrium, and, finally, the Atae, who made those under the spell believe that they could achieve the impossible.'[3] Another, a famous British military historian and theorist, has compared the German officer of 1933 to 1945 to 'a modern Pontius Pilate, washing his hands of all responsibility for the orders he executed.'[4] Some have thought the Army's leaders to be vain, weak men, exemplifying the saying of the French Field-Marshal, MacMahon: 'Of all the people in the world, the generals are those who have the least courage to act,'[5] while still more have seen fit to apply to them the old Latin proverb: *Quem Deus vult perdere, prius dementat* (Those whom God would damn, he first makes mad).

These judgements echo the belief of Ludwig Beck, onetime Chief of the Army General Staff, who remarked in 1937: 'The Armed Forces enjoy among our military-minded nation almost unlimited trust. The responsibility for what is to come rests almost exclusively with the Army. There is no avoiding that fact.'[6] But Beck was mistaken. Care must be taken neither to allow moral indignation to cloud vision, nor to enable emotion to take the place of cool detachment; nor to let the compulsive desire to apportion blame to distort the facts.

The question that should be asked is not, did the generals do the best for their Army and for their country, but, simply, could they have acted other than they did? If it can be proved that not only were they fully aware of the implications of the régime with which they were forced to deal, but that they also possessed the freedom to act as their individual and collective consciences dictated, then indeed they were guilty of a moral failing the like of which history has seen few parallels. If, on the other hand, it can be shown that these men were not the masters of their own destiny, that they were not capable of taking any other political path, then their innocence is assured. If choice was not theirs, history cannot condemn; it can only record their tragic failure.

The generals who were faced with National Socialism were the prisoners of their own proud heritage. The tradition bestowed on them by their predecessors was one of unconditional personal obedience to, and identification with, the autocratic Head of State, coupled with a self-imposed isolation from the world of politics—an isolation which, although elevated to the status of a military virtue, took the form of a political naïvety and ineptitude. This tradition extended back over several centuries, during which time it served both Germany and her Army well, and even after the collaspe in 1918 of the social order on which it had been based, the officer corps, still fairly representative of the middle and upper classes of society, maintained a fundamental belief in its continuing relevance. This was to prove disastrous. It ensured that Germany's military caste became trapped within an ivory tower of its own making, isolated from, and incompatible with, the ever-changing, and always confusing, political realities of the twentieth century. Unconditional obedience and political inexperience were not the best of qualifications for entering the power struggle that was the dynamic of the Third Reich.

Nevertheless, they were the traditions of a force in which the senior generals from 1933 to 1939 had served, on average, thirty-six years of their lives.

The German Army had long been accustomed to following an autocratic ruler. The political system of the Reich after 1871, known by the special name of Prusso-German Constitutionalism, was based on a ruling class of great landowners, and centred on the person of the Prussian King and German Emperor—The Kaiser. His power, though in theory circumscribed by the Bundesrat and the Reichstag, was in fact absolute: it was his exclusive privilege to conduct foreign affairs, hold supreme command of the Armed Forces, and declare war. In periods of acute internal dissension, he could also assume a military dictatorship. Furthermore, in his hands lay the appointment and dismissal of all senior officers. It was to such a man that the Imperial Army gave its loyalty. Article 64 of the 1871 Constitution declared: 'All German troops are obliged to obey unconditionally the commands of the Emperor. This obligation is to be incorporated in the military oath.'[7] The Prusso-German Army was the living embodiment of Plato's rule expressed through the mouth of the Athenian in *Laws XII:* 'Now, for expeditions of war much consideration and many laws are required; the great principle of all is that no one should be without a commander; nor should the mind of anyone be accustomed to do anything, either in jest or earnest, of his own motion, but in war and in peace he should look to, and follow, his leader, even in the last things being under his guidance; . . . he should . . . not teach the soul, or accustom her, to know or understand how to do anything apart from others.'[8]

The personal bond that was deemed to exist between each soldier and his Emperor was a matter of considerable pride to the Army, and it served to underline the deep commitment of the officer corps to the idea of monarchy and to the social order it represented. It became a heinous offence, punishable before a military Court of Honour, to give expression in terms contrary to the crown, reminders constantly being given that 'it is an intolerable state of affairs for officers publicly to express opinions that conflict with those which His Majesty has approved.'[9] But such regulations were totally unnecessary for the vast majority of officers, for they believed implicitly in the established order of autocratic society, and possessed, in common with their ruler, a dogged, instinctive opposition to the ideas of socialism and democracy, which threatened all they held dear. It was only among the other ranks that active Social-Democratic supporters were found.

If the Army was to remain 'a sharp, reliable weapon in the hands of its kings,'[10] it was essential that disruptive influences be kept out of it. For example, although recruits were given lectures of patriotic content, the Emperor in 1907 issued an order prohibiting the discussion of political and social questions. As a result, politics became a much-neglected, even despised, subject, associated with the Social-Democrats who continually beset the authority of the Kaiser. During his interrogation by the Gestapo in 1944, Hans Oster, one of the few officers to take direct action against Hitler's dictatorship, remarked: 'During the monarchy it was really a sort of boyish enthusiasm for soldiering that sent us into the Army. It never even crossed our minds that the whole régime might collapse one day. Politics meant nothing to us. We were in uniform and that was all that mattered.'[11] In his memoirs General Gröner, Defence Minister from 1928 to 1932, commented that 'Even the senior officers [in the Army] had no political sense. . . . In the Navy it was different. Foreign travel had left the naval officers better equipped to judge political events. In the Army the only people who took an interest in politics were the military attachés.'[12]

Then came total and crushing defeat in the First World War. As Oster recorded: 'It was like being hit on the head with a hammer—the collapse in 1918 and the way the monarchy ended in a rickety affair of political parties.'[13] For a short while the distracted and divided German soldiery indulged in suicidal political strife, centred around their crudely formed anti-democratic, anti-republican, and anti-socialist beliefs. *Freikorps* (Free Corps), formed by unemployed officers, ranged the country, and crisis after crisis culminated in 1920 in the Kapp putsch, a right-wing attempt, supported by part of the Army, to overthrow the new republic. Then, in an effort to save the Army from itself, its Commander, Hans von Seeckt, firmly re-established the grand tradition of political disinterest, confirming and emphasising its status as a military necessity; with that, the Army was withdrawn from the political arena. In place of political intrigue, von Seeckt sought to foster the 'old spirit of silent, self-effacing devotion in the service of the Army.'[14] The soldiers were now ordered to ignore current politics, which most of them did with alacrity, only too glad to leave the unfamiliar uncertain environment of Machiavellian cunning, stratagem, and guile for the sure, uncomplicated profession of soldiering, even though this might imply acceptance of the hated Weimar Republic—

the democratic, republican interlude between the absolutism of the Kaiser and the dictatorship of the Führer. Unconditional obedience was reaffirmed as a fundamental of military service by Wilhelm Gröner, who announced in 1930: 'The soundness of any armed force rests upon unreserved, unlimited obedience. Soldiers who want to see whether an order suits their own ideas before they carry it out are absolutely worthless. Thoughts of that kind lead to mutiny, to the dissolution of the Reichswehr and eventually to a war of all against all.'[15] Politics were outlawed. Von Seeckt had no doubt that the Army 'certainly must not be "political" in the party sense. "Hands off the Army!" is my cry to all parties. The Army serves the state and the state alone.'[16] Although concerned that the troops should understand what was happening around them, he refused to allow radically minded elements into the service, whatever their military prowess. He denied the soldier the right to vote, and he prohibited absolutely any connexion with political parties. As Oster said: 'We were all quite sure that under the political conditions of the times this was the only road to our objective, viz., getting the troops under discipline again, and making them the foundation and preparation for building up the Army. . . . The words "party" and "playing politics" had an unpleasant ting for us.'[17] General Siegfried Westphal recorded: 'The result was an indifferent and even uncritical attitude to political questions among the higher officers.'[18]

In such a way the small but highly influential Army became a reliable, if unthinking, pillar of the state, isolated entirely from allegiance to political creed or party. Certainly, Hitler had no cause to thank it for any assistance during his *Kampfzeit* (period of struggle) in the years leading up to his assumption of the chancellorship. Indeed, before 1933 he experienced little but opposition from its leaders: from such men as von Lossow, the Reichsheer commander in Bavaria, von Seeckt, Gröner, the Minister's successor, von Schleicher, and the Army Commander, von Hammerstein. This was demonstrated not only in November 1923, during the abortive Munich putsch when the military leaders in Bavaria refused to support Hitler's attempted coup, but also in 1930, when four young lieutenants of Leipzig were imprisoned for the dissemination of National Socialist propaganda in defiance of the ban on political action After this last incident General Gröner felt it necessary to issue a special circular to senior officers; the action of the lieutenants, he asserted, had shattered 'faith in the Reichswehr as an unshakable rock of obedience and devotion to duty, on which is founded the whole edifice of the state.'[19] In another on the same subject, this time addressed to all officers, the Defence Minister emphasised that 'the Reichswehr is above all parties, and it serves the state alone. It must hold itself absolutely clear of party strife and of day-to-day political pressures. . . . All military measures and regulations are governed by this consideration alone.'[20] Should any officer feel unable to abide by them, resignation was his only honourable alternative. Removal was also resorted to; for example, General von Epp was dismissed because of his association with the NSDAP (he was later appointed a *Reichsleiter* [national leader] of the Party), as was Colonel Hierl (later to become Head of the Reich Labour Service), and Captain Röhm (the future SA leader). After the putsch in 1923, several officers were dismissed, and the staff of the Infantry School, who had supported Hitler, came under considerable disfavour; von Seeckt, who was given constitutional dictatorial powers during the emergency, even banned the National Socialist Party. Such was the attitude that made the Army, in Westphal's words, 'a bulwark against threats to the republic either from the left or the right.'[21] The Reichsheer was, in short, the ideal of the non-political Army held so dear by western society.

Mighty though this principle of political independence might appear, however, it contained considerable weaknesses, the main being that isolation from politics brought with it a lack of understanding. As Hans Oster remarked: 'We were not born into the world of politics; we are not political fanatics fighting to get power in the state for one party. That is not what we were taught to do.'[22] One of the saddest victims of this political disability was Field-Marshal Wilhelm Keitel, Chief of the Armed Forces High Command from 1938 until the end of the Second World War. In the quiet, introspective atmosphere of his cell at Nuremberg in 1945, he was to write:

> 'Although the education of a professional officer is thorough, it is only one-sided; the intellectual and political education . . . is as a rule less complete. This has nothing to do with a question of intelligence . . . but I want to stress the fact that the training of a good soldier was fundamentally different from an education for a purely liberal or academic profession. The officer's profession is not a liberal profession: a soldier's cardinal virtue is obedience . . . the very opposite of criticism. . . . The consequence of all this is that . . . the one-

sided education of the professional soldier described above results in a lack of ability to make a stand against theses which are not part of his real territory. Nothing is more convincing to a soldier than success.'[23]

Political ignorance resulted in a further, related, symptom: a lack of political balance. It was this that Dr. Julius Leber, a leading Social-Democrat, understood when he wrote:

'I fear the Reichswehr has been built up on a colossal mistake of von Seeckt. He believed that discipline was enough, and that obedience to the commander's will was a sufficient guarantee for the proper functioning of the Army. But no unit in these times will place itself unreservedly in the hands of its commander. The links between the soldiers and the public are far too intimate for that.... It is not enough to give a soldier orders. He must have a mental image of what his task consists of.... He needs not only discipline but other kinds of incentive.... It is axiomatic nowadays that rulers and ruled, their ideas and their arms, form a single whole with a common purpose and must be sustained by common ideals.... If these ideals and symbols are withheld from young men in the Army, they will run after other ideals and find themselves other symbols—subsitutues such as the recollection of imperial glories and patriotic language'[24]

But it was not just the young men who possessed an

emotional yearning, so typical of political naïveté, for something more than was offered by the republican régime; the whole Army, including the senior generals, suffered from this lack of political balance, a loss which caused it to live in the imperial past and for a new future, but not for the republican present. The historian, Herbert Rosinski, summed this up in 1939, when he wrote:

'To those who did not themselves experience it, it is almost impossible to convey what the First World War meant to the German people. The peaceful and prosperous development enjoyed without any serious interruption for nearly half a century was suddenly shattered and the German nation found itself overnight at war with half the world; it threw all its strength, wealth, and faith into that struggle—to wake up, after four years of unparalleled exertion and brilliant victories, not only defeated, but outlawed and branded by a world whose triumph it could not understand and who made no effort to understand it. The result was that it lost its mental balance; the economic distress after the war increased the disease and defeated all attempts at internal consolidation, until the Nazi movement, playing with considerable skill upon the psychological and material distress of the masses, rose on the ruins of the Weimar Republic and offered to the distracted nation the quack remedy of its emotional creed.'[25]

Thus, while the vast majority of soldiers within the Army held fast to the Seecktian doctrine of *Überparteilichkeit*, considering their profession to be apart from, and above, politics, they found the emergence of National Socialism, together with other nationalist creeds within Germany, not entirely unwelcome. The social composition of the Army was, after all, one that had traditionally leaned towards the right in politics. The officers came mainly either from established military families, from the nobility, or from the professional middle classes; the other ranks were recruited from the country rather than the towns, from that part of the population that was conservative rather than radical. To such men, the new movement was, at the very least, tolerable; it provided for the politically uneducated some kind of substitute for the vacuum left by the disappearance of the monarchy. It appeared to exemplify the autocratic Germanic spirit, the return of which was eagerly awaited by so many, and to provide an alternative to the decline in the fortunes of the nation and the Army. It stood against the terms of the Versailles Treaty and for general rearmament; against the atmosphere of Marxism, socialism, and pacificism, and for the respect and glory of the Reich and its Army; against the democratic 'Government of the November Criminals,' and for the concepts of authority, discipline, and national regeneration. It was easy to ignore Hitler's ill-defined socialist doctrines; there were few officers who could not but feel some sympathy for a politician who promised: 'We will see to it that, when we have come to power, out of the present Reichswehr shall rise the great Army of the German people.'[26] The individual motives of those who looked favourably on the new creed ranged from ambition and pragmatism to idealism, but the general feeling was summed up by Oster, who, when under interrogation, said: 'With the upheaval of 1933 . . .

the soldiers felt released from the strain which the "System" had laid on their consciences. The return to a vigorous patriotic policy, the rearmament, the reintroduction of military service—to the officers, this all meant a return to older traditions. Under the "System" soldiers had done their work because it was their duty; but these features of the National Socialists' work of reconstruction had warmed their hearts.'[27]

However, for a tiny minority of German officers, those at the very top of the military leadership, this loss of political balance was not simply a naïve sympathy for right-wing, nationalist ideas, but a desire for direct interference in the government of the nation. These men were unrepresentative of their heritage and caste, a product peculiar to the extraordinary times in which they lived. Under Bismarck, the General Staff, influential though it was, possessed no control over either the domestic or the foreign policy of Germany, the Iron Chancellor being little-inclined to allow the military to meddle in his jealously guarded province. Von Moltke's idea of a preventive war against Russia in 1887 received short shrift, while the intrigues of his deputy, von Waldersee, were purely of a personal nature and not in the tradition of the General Staff (as a result, he lasted in his post only for two years). Under Wilhelm II, this position remained unaltered, as evidenced by the relative neglect of the Army in favour of the Navy during peacetime, and it was only during the First World War that, in the absence of strong, coordinated political and military direction, the generals first took an active hand in the machinery of government. Behind the constitution of Imperial Germany there grew, from 1916, a military dictatorship of the General Staff dominated by two giants, Generals von Hindenburg and Ludendorff; only national collapse in 1918 was to bring this to an end.

After the war, following this new precedent, a few officers of no political experience, but of the highest military seniority, took the principle of *Überparteilichkeit* one stage further. In their eyes, the soldiers role was not that of passive onlookers, standing by while the various political parties wrought what they would with the fortunes of the nation; rather, their duty was to save Germany from the ravages of the politicians, whether of left or right-wing persuasion, and to assist it to regain its former greatness. Von Seeckt first propounded this idea in his attempt to influence national policy. He believed that 'the Army and its leaders must be assured of their rightful position in public life. . . .'[28] In the pursuance of this aim he set his eyes on nothing less than the presidency of the Reich. But his ineptitude, together with his ill-concealed contempt for politicians, led to his downfall. The next arch-proponent of this thesis was General Kurt von Schleicher, who was appointed Reich Defence Minister on 2 June 1932. Politically ambitious, he advocated the dissolution of the despised democratic institutions of the Republic and the creation of a virtual military dictatorship. This, he intended, would govern the nation under the authority of the President, the revered Field-Marshal von Hindenburg, by virtue of Article 48 of the Constitution, which allowed for rule by emergency decree. The idea behind this policy was explained by von Schleicher's devotee, General Curt Freiherr von Hammerstein-Equord, who wrote in 1929, one year before his elevation to command the Army: 'The revolution has taught the German Army officer to discriminate between the provisional régime of the state and its permanent identity, and to serve the latter, which is symbolised by the Reich President, elevated above ephemeral ministries and incoherent governmental bodies.'[29]

It was with such justification that a handful of the most senior generals took upon themselves the right of determining the political course of the nation. It inevitably brought them into opposition with the National Socialists: not only did they, the aristocrats, feel an instinctive dislike for the violent methods of the NSDAP and for the bombast and crudity of its leaders, but they also abhorred its challenge to von Hindenburg's authority represented by Hitler's candidature for the presidency in 1932, and the clear threat to the Army's military supremacy manifested by the party's paramilitary force, the SA, the *Sturm Abteilung*, (Storm Detachment), which, by 1933, numbered some 400,000 men. Gröner, appointed Reich Minister for the Interior in late 1931 in addition to his post as Defence Minister, warned the Army that the National Socialists 'are to be distinguished from the Communists only by the national base on which they take their footing. . . . In order to use it [the Army] for the political aims of their party, they attempt to dazzle us. . . .'[30] In opposing National Socialism, Gröner's and von Schleicher's cooperation with the government could hardly have been greater, and in order to preserve Germany from Hitler and his followers they had no hesitation in advocating the restoration of the monarchy, as well as the expansion of the Reichswehr to rival the right-wing paramilitary organisations, especially the SA.

The political machinations of the Army's leaders in the last years of the Weimar Republic have no place here; suffice it to say that by the beginning of 1933 they had come to occupy, however uncertainly, the highest offices of state. Von Schleicher, in addition to his post as Reich Defence Minister, had been appointed Reich Chancellor and Reich Commissioner for Prussia on 2 December 1932, and he was faithfully supported by the two most important men in the Army—von Hammerstein, the Commander-in-Chief, and Wilhelm Adam, Chief of the Troop Office (General Staff). The Bendlerstrasse, where the military commands were situated, and the Wilhelmstrasse, Berlin's 'Whitehall,' were now as one.

Yet, within one month, von Schleicher had met his downfall, von Hammerstein had been isolated, and Hitler had been offered, and had accepted, the office of Reich Chancellor. Von Schleicher had failed in his attempt to split the National Socialist Party and suppress the SA, and, worse still, he had lost the confidence of von Hindenburg, who was disillusioned by his constant, devious, and inconsistent *politiking*. Von Hammerstein, too, had aroused the suspicions of the President, who rejected all his efforts to proffer advice. The initiative passed from the generals, and the politicians immediately made it theirs. On 28 January 1933, von Schleicher resigned together with his cabinet; within thirty-six hours Hitler had been invited to become Chancellor by von Hindenburg. The generals' brief and unsuccessful flirtation with political power was over.

This, many historians argue, was when the Army should have acted. That it failed to do so, thereby ignoring von Hammerstein's promise that 'the Reichswehr will never allow them [The National Socialists] to come to power,'[31] has been seen as the first occasion on which the Army failed in its duty towards the German nation. It is claimed that, in permitting the National

Socialists to take the reins of government, the generals were acting purely from their own short-term, selfish interests. Sir John Wheeler-Bennett has alleged that they:

> '... wished to secure for the benefit of the Reichswehr, all that could be gained to advantage from the Nazi movement, while dominating and controlling it in policy. They were still dreaming in their blindness of a martial state in which the masses, galvanised and inspired by modified National Socialism, would be directed and disciplined by the Army. They may well have had it within their power in those fateful January days to combat successfully the final consummation of that National Socialist rise to power, which they, by their own equivocal policy, had helped to promote; but they did not wish to do so.'[32]

This is to misunderstand the dilemma that confronted, and entrapped, the military leaders. Isolated from the centre of power around the President, they lacked unanimity of aim and organisation, and were troubled by the thought of breaking their traditional allegiance to the legally constituted political executive. Moreover, aware that a large part of the Army would be not unsympathetic to the triumph of National Socialism, they held strong fears that, as a result, the troops would refuse to obey orders to take action against the new regime. After all, no support could now be expected from von Hindenburg, their Supreme Commander. Nor did the Army leaders look on Hitler's legal assumption of power as the worst of the political alternatives then facing the country. Von

Hindenburg was still President and Head of the Reichswehr, and was thought to be able to keep his Chancellor in check. Furthermore, only three of the eleven members in the new cabinet were National Socialists, and it might have been assumed they would be swamped by the eight conservatives. For this reason, it was considered safer to have Hitler in the government than out of it. Both von Schleicher and von Hammerstein believed that a National Socialist/Communist revolt would follow the creation of a right-wing nationalist government under the two main contenders, von Papen and von Hugenberg, and that the resulting civil war would leave Germany defenceless against any attack launched by Poland, an eventuality which at that time was considered to be far from remote. Moreover, the generals saw no apparent reason why Hitler would retain power any more successfully than previous chancellors, especially as the splits and factions within the NSDAP, together with its waning public support, were increasingly apparent.

Had the Army and its leaders been united in opposition to Hitler, could they at that time have prevented his accession to power? The senior generals were aware of the considerable risk of worsening the internal situation in Germany through direct military intervention; studies had shown that there existed the distinct possibility of the 100,000 strong Army, devoid of heavy artillery and tanks, being defeated in civil war by the SA, already four times its numerical strength, supported by other right-wing parties, and possibly the Communists. Even had the soldiers triumphed, there was no guarantee that the nation would return to a government and a political order any better than that which previously existed. Indeed, the reverse might have been the case: the bitterness and divisions caused within society by the Army's intervention could so easily have created an even worse situation. And, whatever the possible outcome, the fact remained that it was neither legal, not the practice in western countries for the military to interfere in the proper constitutional workings of the nation—certainly not without the specific orders of the Head of State and Supreme Commander. The National Socialists' accession to power was entirely legal, and, moreover, was allowed and ratified by von Hindenburg. Where the Supreme Commander led, the Army was to follow.

Such was the position of the generals in January 1933. They had before them no room for manoeuvre. It would have been a matter of some surprise had the Army moved to prevent Hitler's chancellorship, and its failure to do so provides no basis for condemnation. The generals could only stand to one side of the political arena, adopt the air of interested spectators, and await events. The once-influential German Army was powerless to intervene; as a political creature, it was impotent.

2
First Years

We cannot change politics; we must do our duty silently.
GENERAL WERNER VON FRITSCH
Commander-in-Chief of the German
Army, 1934–38

In 1933 there began the curious and tragic relationship between Hitler and his senior military advisers, which, within little more than five years, led to the subjection of the Army to the dictator's will, and, within a further seven, to its complete destruction on the field of battle. About this process there was an air of inevitability, as if, from the moment Hitler took office, the soldiers' fate was sealed. But it should not be thought that, in the years leading to 1938, the dictator was the coldly calculating, devious politician so often portrayed by historians, that his sole constancy lay in a deep contempt for the generals and a burning desire to subvert their independence. The opposite is nearer the truth, as Hitler's summary of his early guiding principle illustrates: 'It has always been my view that we can achieve our goals only with the Reichswehr, and never against it.'[1]

Only after 1938, in the middle and later years of the Third Reich, did Hitler turn sharply from his *laissez-faire* policy towards the Army to one of strict control and, ultimately, of complete subjection. This arose simply out of his frustration at his generals' ever-increasing opposition to his policies, an opposition which struck at the very basis of his long-term aims: rearmament and foreign expansion. His faith in his military advisers weakened, he found himself forced to render them impotent and to transform their successors into mere executors of his will—a not unnatural action, and one achieved with far less suffering than by other dictators.

Leaving aside his social, economic, racial, and foreign policies, Hitler's overriding political philosophy was unequivocal: he, and he alone, would determine the direction of the Reich, and, by so doing, would select the goals to be attained and the methods to be used. By August 1934 he had acquired total power within the state: as Chancellor he possessed supreme executive authority; through the Enabling Act of 1933 he was given supreme legislative authority; and, from the merger of the office of Chancellor with that of President on the death of von Hindenburg, he assumed supreme command of the Armed Forces. Furthermore, the Reich Defence Law of 21 May 1935 gave him the right to declare states of emergency, mobilisation, and war. All the major decisions between 1933 and 1945 were Hitler's, and his alone; the views of Party associates, cabinet ministers, industrial magnates, Junker landowners, and generals counting for nothing if not in accord with his own ideas. Indeed, their advice was often not even sought. Reich ministers were reduced to the role of departmental heads, Party leaders to organisers. In the Byzantine power politics that characterised the Third Reich, only one law was inviolate: the Führer's authority was unchallengeable, his decision supreme. Hitler may have acknowledged his need for professional advisers to provide the Army with superior military qualities, but he nevertheless stated his intention of not allowing himself 'to be ordered about by the commanders-in-chief. I shall make war.'[3] In his opinion the generals were sterile . . . imprisoned in the coils of their technical knowledge,'[4] and, 'in spite of the lessons of the war, they want to behave like chivalrous knights. . . . I have no use for knights. I need revolution.'[5]

From the very beginning of his chancellorship, Hitler displayed his intention to brook no interference in his policies from his military advisers. In his determination to eliminate political opposition, he engineered, with the active support of some of the more senior generals, the isolation and then the resignation of von Hammerstein, who left his post on 1 February 1934; and in his ambition to exercise control over Germany's rearmament and foreign policy, he created the Reich Defence Council on 4 April 1933, a body entrusted with the task of planning and coordinating the nation's activities for war. Composed of the Ministers for the Interior, Foreign Affairs, Finance, Propaganda, and Defence under the chairmanship of the Chancellor, the Council had the effect of bringing the Armed Forces more closely under the control of the government, and, therefore, of Hitler, while at the same time ending the traditional position of the military as the sole advisers to the Head of State on such matters. Satisfied with this, he took no further steps to bring the Army under his control until 1938. Until then, the position remained as Guderian summed it up: 'Any attempt to widen the General Staff corps officers' appreciation of the political situation was prevented, first by the traditional limitation of their interests to purely military matters and, secondly, by Hitler's principle according to which every fragment of the machinery which controlled the state was kept in a sort of specialised, water-tight compartment and no man might know more than was essential for the performance of his own particular job.'[6] The days of power, of Ludendorff, von Hindenburg, Gröner, von Seeckt, and von Schleicher, were now no more. This restriction of interests was met with relief by the Army, the great majority of officers believing, with Guderian, that 'policy is not laid down by soldiers, but by politicians';[7] and expressing their thanks, with General von Choltitz, for entrusting the soldier once again with the 'purely objective tasks of the service.'[8] These men understood something that historians, in their anxiety to accredit to Hitler nothing but evil intent, have overlooked: that the Führer's actions were but those of a determined politician, desirous simply of exerting his influence over national policy; that, until 1938, his attitude towards the Army and its leaders was unequivocally one of harmonious cooperation, even of friendship, the product of convenience rather than of single-minded ambition.

On assuming power, Hitler possessed not the least desire to add the running of the Army to the already onerous task of governing the nation, and, doubting their abilities as much as he feared their ambitions, he had not the slightest intention of placing the military under the control of his political subordinates. Hitler's requirement was for an Army loyal to his person, responsive to his policies, and, in common with all other organisations within the Third Reich, receptive to the idealogy of National Socialism. For the rest, he intended it to be the sole bearer of arms in the defence of the nation, his chief, although not sole, adviser on military affairs, completely independent of, and impervious to, Party interference, and fully capable of ordering its own affairs as it alone thought fit. As such, Hitler's intentions were no different from those of most other political leaders. Although he recognised the importance of the Army in the political structure of the nation, he was anxious, nevertheless, to ensure that it provided no damaging opposition to his own policies. As in democracies, alike with dictatorships, the Army of the Third Reich was to be seen, not heard; its leaders, while retaining primacy over military matters, prevented from taking part in purely political debate and decision. In his attitude towards its ideological outlook, Hitler differed little from national leaders throughout history. Even in liberal parliamentary democracies with small, professional armies, the soldiers have been expected to reflect the general political and social outlook of the time, being condemned and derided should they remain hide-bound or caste-ridden. National Socialism after 1933 became not merely a party programme but a national creed, its tenets characterising the Germany of that age. It would have been strange indeed had the Army remained isolated from, or unreceptive to, its dogma.

Hitler's spirit of friendship towards the Army was evident from the moment he assumed office. Just twenty-four hours after his appointment as Chancellor, he addressed, without awaiting an invitation, troops of the Berlin garrison on the spirit of the new Germany. A few days later, on 3 February 1933, he delivered a speech of more than two hours' duration to a gathering of the leading officers of the services, in which he promised them rearmament and the 'strengthening of the will to defence by all possible means,'[9] reasserted their key position within the state against the rival claims of the SA, and confirmed that they were to remain 'unpolitical and above parties.'[10] At its conclusion, as the generals emerged from the room, their suspicions radically undermined, one was overheard saying: 'At any rate, no Chancellor has ever expressed himself so warmly in favour of defence.'[11] The opening of the new Reichstag on 21 March provided Hitler with a further opportunity to display his respectful recognition of the Army's position. The ceremony was held at the old garrison church at Potsdam, the home of Prussian militarism, and Hitler made a favourable impression by bowing low before the aged Field-Marshal von Hindenburg. This occasion was seen as a symbol of the unification of the new movement with the old Prusso-German tradition, confirming the extinction of the Weimar Republic. Field-Marshal von Mackensen commented: 'We German officers used to be called representatives of reaction, whereas we were really bearers of tradition. It is in the sense of that tradition that Hitler spoke to us, so wonderfully and so directly from the heart, at Potsdam.'[12]

But it was to be Hitler's lack of interference in internal

Army affairs that made the greatest impact on the soldiers. He refused to nominate his SA leader, and former Army captain, to succeed von Hammerstein, as many feared he might do; he yielded gracefully when his nominee for the post of Army Commander, von Reichenau, was rejected by the President; he made no attempt to influence the basis of promotion for officers, or to alter the judgements of courts-martial; he offered no criticisms during briefings and exercises; he usually signed unread the documents presented to him by Friedrich Hossbach, his military adjutant; he more often than not accepted unquestioningly the advice of his military subordinates; and he took no part in the planning of operations. He always gave the appearance of complete trust in his generals, and treated the new Army Commander-in-Chief, von Fritsch, with 'respectful discretion.'[13] The generals were shown only the charming side of his character, and were unaware that when necessary he made a conscious effort to adapt his chaotic working routine to their needs.

Such was Hitler's praise of his servicemen that, at a meeting of senior officers and Party officials on 3 January 1935, he declared: 'The Army and the Party are the two pillars of state. . . . Then someone from the Party may come to me and say "All right, my Führer, but General So-and-So both speaks and works against you." Then I shall say "I don't believe it." And if the man says "But I can show you written evidence, my Führer," then I shall tear the scrap of paper up, for my faith in the Armed Forces is unshakable.'[14] On one occasion Hitler went so far as to admit to the generals certain feelings within his own National Socialist movement: 'I know that you accuse me of many wrong things which exist in the Party. I admit that you are one hundred per cent correct, but you must remember . . . I still have to work primarily with persons of low quality.'[15] He constantly emphasised the debt he and his Party owed to the Army. At the Nuremberg rally in 1936, for example, he declared: 'The Army educated us. We have all come from the Army, those of us who became the Party storm-troops and the motor corps.'[16] He even found it within himself to ascribe to the Army a decisive role in his own success, such was his desire to court its friendship, when he remarked, quite wrongly: 'If the Reichswehr had not stood at our side during the days of the revolution, then we should not be standing here today.'[17]

Positive proof of Hitler's good intentions towards the Army came on 30 June 1934, with his eradication of the SA leadership in what has come to be known as the Night of the Long Knives. The *Sturm Abteilung*, under the command of SA *Stabschef* (Chief of Staff) Ernest Röhm, had become potentially the most powerful organisation in Germany, by 1934 numbering some three million uniformed members. As the paramilitary formation of the National Socialist Party, it had been indispensable to Hitler's rise to power, the dictator recognising this when he told his storm-troopers on 7 May 1933: 'You have been till now the Guard of the National Revolution; you have carried this revolution to victory; with your name it will be associated for all time.'[18] But the success of the SA, coupled with the beliefs and actions of its more prominent and politically extreme members, ensured its ultimate downfall. The storm-troopers had by then come to arouse considerable uneasiness, even fear, in the rest of the Party, seeming to threaten Hitler's position as effective leader of the German nation. The SA leadership saw itself as 'the incorruptible guarantors of the fulfilment of the German revolution,'[19] and believed that Hitler and his supporters were betraying its basic principles. At the same time the SA was regarded by its leaders as the future German Army, a people's militia based on new principles of organisation, discipline, service, and political commitment.

Röhm, who liked to see himself as 'the new army's Scharnhorst,'[20] expressed it thus: 'We have to produce something new, don't you see? . . . The generals are a lot of old fogeys. They never have a new idea.'[21] In February 1934 he felt so confident of his position that he sent a letter to the Head of the Defence Minister's Office, von Reichenau, with the pronouncement: 'I regard the Reichswehr now only as a training school for the German people. The conduct of war, and therefore of mobilisation as well, in future is the task of the SA.'[22] Armed SA headquarter guard formations were formed, and Röhm even went as far as to initiate discussions with the French military attaché in Berlin.

The Army, understandably, was deeply alarmed. So, too, was Hitler, although his concern was not entirely for his own fate. Many had been expecting Hitler to make the choice between the SA and the Army in a manner favourable to his political storm-troopers; he was, after all, the Supreme Commander of the SA. As von Fritsch was to record: 'Every thoughtful soldier, I suppose, shared my belief that the storm-troops were meant to take the Army's place. . . . I myself should have thought it perfectly natural if this had been the Führer's intention. All the same, it was frightening to think of the consequences—the total destruction of the Army's foundations. . . .'[23] In the event, Hitler unhesitatingly supported the Reichswehr in its claim to be the rightful, and sole, bearer of arms in the defence of the Reich. This was not simply a move of convenience which would serve the double aim of reassuring the generals while curtailing Röhm's power; it was a conscious choice of principle arising from his belief in maintaining the Army's traditional role. His position was made so unequivocal, and devoid of any reciprocal conditions, for it to be anything else. Had he wished, it was not beyond Hitler's political skill at least to attempt to remove the danger to his own position posed by the SA leadership, while retaining the capacity of the SA organisation to develop into a National Socialist people's army. That he did not contemplate such a course is evidence enough that he saw nothing but impracticabilities and disaster, military as well as political, in his storm-troopers' plans. There can be little doubt that the relative levels of military expertise in the Army and the SA, and the latter's reputation as an ill-disciplined street-fighting outfit, made Hitler prefer that German youth was trained in a field-grey uniform rather than in a brownshirt.

In May 1933, after strong warnings from his Defence Minister, von Blomberg, Hitler sanctioned an agreement in military matters reached between the Reichswehr and the SA, which provided for the Army's unquestioned superiority. This he followed by a series of five speeches, each giving clear support to his soldiers. On 28 February 1934, before a conference of the Reichswehr and SA leaders in the Great Hall of the War Ministry, and in response to a plea from the Defence Minister for a ruling, Hitler, in the words of one of those present, stated:

'... his decision to reject the suggestions of Röhm

to form a SA militia and to affirm his resolution to build a people's army on the lines of the old army out of the Reichswehr. He based this on examples from military history, to prove that a militia, such as Röhm suggested, was not efficient for national defence. The SA would have to limit itself to political tasks. For the transitional period, he declared himself to be in agreement with the suggestion of the War Minister to employ the SA for tasks of frontier protection and for pre-military training. . . . Otherwise the Armed Forces must be the only bearer of arms of the nation. . . . After this address, the feeling of contentment reigned amongst the military audience that the Army High Command had scored a notable success over the Party organisation, and that it appeared as if Hitler wished to rely first and foremost on the Army.'[24]

Von Blomberg and Röhm were then asked to sign an agreement to confirm Hitler's policy statement. The SA leader was so furious at this, that he exclaimed to his colleagues a short while later: 'What that ridiculous corporal [Hitler] says means nothing to us. . . . I have not the slightest intention of keeping this agreement. Hitler is a traitor and at the very least must go on leave. . . . If we can't get there with him, we'll get there without him.'[25]

This comment was quickly relayed to the 'ridiculous corporal,' whose reaction was: 'We must allow this affair to ripen fully.'[26]

Despite Hitler's assurances, however, the Army remained apprehensive of the SA's intentions. Friction continued, especially at local level, and certain

Wehrkreise (area commands) began preparations to meet an unspecified emergency, which was in reality the feared storm-troopers' coup. The Army dismissed Röhm, whose known homosexuality was an anathema to the military, from the officers' league, and rifles were placed by the side of desks in the Bendlerstrasse. Although most officers did not believe events would come to a fight, some actively plotted for such an outcome, believing it to be the only method of ridding themselves of the danger from the SA. From the end of April the storm-troopers' enemies had begun to prepare, and combine, their forces, while at the same time bringing increased pressure to bear on a still-reluctant Führer to act decisively. This was no easy task, for Hitler remained loyal to his old friend Röhm, and there was no truth in the suggestion that he coldly and dispassionately engineered the downfall of the man and the organisation to whom he owed so much. But, by rumour and falsehood, Heydrich, Himmler, and Göring managed at last to persuade the Führer that Röhm and his subordinates were actively planning a putsch to overthrow the new régime. On 29 June 1934, Hitler finally decided to take action. In the early hours of the following day, units of the SS, with arms and transport provided by the Army, went into action against their former comrades; by 4:00 a.m. on 2 July, when the killings ended, more than a hundred men lay dead.

The events of 30 June achieved many goals. The SA, although it remained a large Party organisation, was rendered politically and militarily impotent; Hitler's authority was extended; Göring was satisfied at the removal of a rival; Himmler was left free to develop his SS empire; and the Army was confirmed in its position as sole arms-bearer in the defence of the nation. On 13 July

Hitler announced: 'My promise to him [von Hindenburg] to preserve the Army as a non-political instrument of the nation is as binding for me from innermost conviction as from my pledged word.'[27]

So much for the attitude of Hitler towards the military, but what of the Army leadership which, in January 1933, had been so antipathetic towards the National Socialists? Within a year it underwent a considerable transformation. The 'big four'—the Defence Minister, the Head of the Minister's Office, the Chief of the Army Leadership, and the Head of the Troop Office—in whose hands the direction of the Armed Forces and the Army lay, had changed. In place of von Schleicher had come von Blomberg; instead of von Bredow, there was von Reichenau; von Hammerstein had been replaced by von Fritsch; and in Adam's former post was Beck.

At the head of the German Armed Forces stood Werner Eduard Fritz von Blomberg, appointed Reich Defence Minister with the rank of *General der Infanterie* at the age of fifty-four, one day before Hitler gained the chancellorship. Von Blomberg was a strange mixture of a man. Tall, erect, blue-eyed, and radiating presence wherever he went, he was nicknamed 'the Siegfried with the monocle' because of his physical appearance, 'the Rubber Lion,' because of the insubstantial personality that seemed to lie beneath his vital exterior, and 'Hitler Youth Quex,' after the character of a famous propaganda film, because he idolised the Führer. Ironically, one of von Hindenburg's reasons for appointing von Blomberg to serve in the Reich Cabinet had been his belief that he, in contrast with von Schleicher, typified 'the soldier above politics.'

Frank, open, and well-liked, von Blomberg revealed considerable energy in, and dedication to, his work. His military career was impeccable: he had been awarded the much-coveted Pour le Mérite (the highest decoration of the Prussian Armed Forces) for his brilliant planning work during the First World War, and, in 1927 as a staff officer, he had reached the highest position of Chief of the Troop Office. Falling out with von Schleicher, he was transferred to command Wehrkreis I, East Prussia, in 1930, and it was while there that he was appointed leader of the German military delegation to the disarmament conference at Geneva in 1932.

Able professional soldier he might have been, but politically von Blomberg was naïve, and much restricted in his outlook. By temperament he leant towards totalitarianism, albeit for the best of motives—stability in society, the improvement in living standards, and the greatness of the nation. Lacking mental balance, von Blomberg was a combination of many strong drives; an emotional man, moody, enthusiastic and impulsive, he was at the same time vacillating and easily influenced. On a trip to the Soviet Union in 1928 he was impressed deeply by what he thought to be the qualities of its régime, so much so that he later confessed he was near to becoming a Communist. But, like so many in Germany, he found those aspects of Communism he considered so praiseworthy to be present also in National Socialism; he saw Hitler as the saviour of the nation, a man of strength and authority whom he could respect, one who propounded an ideal with which he could identify. Von Blomberg's idolisation of the man and the message was that of a romantic fantasist rather than of a hard-headed political realist. He initially gave Hitler willing and unhesitating support, fully believing that by doing so he was acting in the best interests of both the country and the Army; his reply to objections on this score was: 'The Führer is cleverer than we are, he will plan and do everything correctly.'[28]

For this, Blomberg has incurred the censure of many, including a large number of former German officers. In his memoirs, Hossbach was particularly damning:

> 'The fund of trust which the German people, since earliest times, and since, and despite, the loss of the war in 1918, placed in the soldier involved for Blomberg the moral obligation of being the advocate of reason and of forming a barrier against totalitarian claims on the part of the state. It is the tragedy of modern German history that Blomberg was, neither as soldier nor as statesman, a strong personality, forceful and creative, guiding and leading. His intelligence lacked the foundation of a firm character.'[29]

But this is to over-emphasise the Defence Minister's weaknesses. In Nuremberg prison he wrote: 'Had I been a spineless tool in the hands of Hitler, as some generals now assume, then he probably would have dealt differently with me [in 1938].... The other generals heard nothing of my protests and showdowns with Hitler.'[30] Certainly, if von Blomberg had been the tame executor of Hitler's wishes, the dictator would have had no reason to dismiss him in 1938. The importance of von Blomberg in preserving not only the Army's independence of the Party machine but also its voice in the affairs of state should not be neglected, for, as General

Warlimont stated: '. . . be it remembered that, well on into the war, Hitler was apt to give vent to his recurring dislike of generals, the General Staff and its training, and the mental outlook of the Army as a whole, in these words: "All that goes back to the time when Blomberg's broad shoulders came between me and the Wehrmacht."'[31]

Initially, however, the man who, on 29 January 1933, took charge of the Bendlerstrasse, could not have suited Hitler better. Indeed, he was every political leader's dream: an able professional soldier, totally loyal to the régime, and concerned that those under his authority should be likewise. Von Blomberg immediately embarked on a reformation of the Defence Ministry, replacing von Schleicher's men with his own. His first and most important appointment was von Reichenau, who, on 1 February 1933 at the age of forty-eight, became the new Head of the Minister's Office. Formerly von Blomberg's Chief of Staff in Wehrkreis I, von Reichenau was now to be his principal assistant and deputy, and was thus chosen as much for his political beliefs as for his military and organisational abilities.

Like his chief, von Reichenau was a first-class soldier, but, in contrast, he was also an individualist, who, brimming with life, was unable to accept constraints on his actions. Although an aristocrat by birth, he had lost faith in the destiny of his own class, and, although a senior officer through well-deserved promotion, he possessed little respect for the conventions of rigid discipline and strict order that characterised the old Army. He invariably treated his men with a familiarity that did not breed contempt, and his superiors with an irreverence that aroused resentment. An anglophile, a lover of fast cars, and an athlete of considerable ability, von Reichenau was a member of the International Olympic Committee. Lacking the emotionalism of his superior, he possessed a sober, forceful personality of drive, determination, and considerable ambition, his hard exterior accurately representing an intelligent, calculating mind that delighted in making considered decisions. Highly critical, unable to suffer fools gladly, von Reichenau was saved from isolation from the world by a magnanimity, a sense of humour, and a regard for his men which earned him high respect.

Von Reichenau's character was reflected in his political beliefs. If von Blomberg was the apotheosis of the political romantic, von Reichenau was the archetype of the political realist. Although initially an adherent of National Socialism, a frequent guest at Hitler's table, and constantly accused of being a 'Party general,' he was no blind, subservient follower of the Führer. What had first attracted him to the new creed was its revolutionary outlook, with the prospect of throwing off the deadweight of the past and substituting in its place effective action beneficial to both the Army and the nation. But he always detested the cruder aspects of National Socialist philosophy and its personalities, among whom he included the SS leaders; and, in time, he came ever more to disagree fundamentally with Hitler's policies. He attended dinners for Jewish front-fighters of the First World War; he expressed dislike for the excesses of nationalism; he explored the possibilities of instituting a youth movement to rival the Hitler Youth; he contradicted Hitler's foreign policy; and, by the beginning of the Second World War, he had become so disillusioned that he had entered into subversive opposition to the régime he once supported so ardently. For the Army, it was a tragedy that he never fulfilled his erstwhile ambition to become its Commander-in-Chief; although not recognised at the time, he, alone among the generals, possessed that combination of political insight, courage, drive, and conviction necessary to halt the progress of the later years of Hitler's dictatorship.

Those selected for the posts of Army Commander and Chief of Staff were men of a different stamp, relationships between the two groups often being strained as a result. Werner Thomas Ludwig von Fritsch, who, on 1 February 1934 at the age of fifty-three, was made Chief of the Army Leadership with the rank of *General der Artillerie*, was a man of exceptional military ability, but possessing no political skill or interest whatsoever. Such qualifications, in fact, suited Hitler and von Blomberg, who, although they had pressed for von Reichenau's elevation to the post, had been forced to accept von Fritsch owing to the strenuous advocacy of von Hindenburg, whose appointment it was. In the President's eyes, von Fritsch possessed everything von Reichenau lacked: no political sympathies, a long experience of command, and the general respect of his colleagues.

Of von Fritsch, the French ambassador recorded that his 'haughty and surly exterior covered a human wit and a more amicable nature than appeared.'[32] Indeed the new Army Commander was an humanitarian with a deep, undemonstrative religious piety of a strict Protestant nature, a high personal morality, popular, and with an authority in the Army greater even than that of von Seeckt, whose friend and pupil he was. A self-contained man, von Fritsch admitted: 'I have never spoken to others about myself. I simply cannot do that.'[33]

Nevertheless he exhibited considerable personal charm. Apart from his intense love of horses, von Fritsch's only other interest lay in his work, into which he sometimes appeared to retreat from the unpalatable realities of the political world around him. His monocle, needed to correct a serious weakness in his left eye, was also a feature of his personal defences. He himself said: 'I wear a monocle so that my face remains stiff, especially when I confront that man [Hitler].'[34]

Politically, von Fritsch was inadequately equipped to meet the challenges of the new National Socialist state. His belief in the ideal of the 'soldier above politics' was implicit. In 1937 he wrote: 'I have made it my guiding rule to limit myself to the military field alone, and to keep myself apart from any political acitivity. I lack everything necessary for politics. Furthermore, I am convinced that the less I speak in public, the more speedily I can fulfill my military task.'[35] As events were to show, von Fritsch was no easy lapdog of the politicians, shrinking from any connexion with them, so much so that he sent back the golden Party badge presented to him by Hitler as a singular honour. He made no attempt to disguise his contempt for the National Socialists, soon becoming renowned for making loud, uncomplimentary comments whenever he felt inclined. In his directives, von Fritsch avoided the clichés of National Socialism so beloved of von Blomberg, and his uncompromising attitude to the introduction of ideology into service life was well-known. Many were the soldiers he protected when they became embroiled in political scraps, his sole disciplinary action often being to warn them not to speak so loud in public again.

Like his chief, Ludwig Beck, the new Head of the Troop

Office, was regarded favourably by all, even by those who sought good relations with the new régime. Appointed by von Hammerstein on 1 October 1933 during a routine reshuffle, he, too, was an excellent soldier and military thinker, his outstanding reputation coming in part from his brilliant planning of the withdrawal, under the most difficult circumstances, of German forces totalling some ninety divisions at the end of the First World War; and from his authorship of *Die Truppenführung*, the standard Army tactical manual, in which his clarity of thought and expression made a great impact on all who read it. The same age as von Fritsch, Beck also was a shy, cautious, retiring man of great honour, personal charm, and austere Christian morality. Unlike the Army Commander, with whom he nonetheless got on well and formed a strong partnership, he was a highly cultured man of poise and deliberate manner, possessing little of the stiffness traditionally associated with the German officer. Experiencing the pleasures of married life for only a brief period in 1916, before his wife died the following year, Beck led a simple existence, totally immersing himself in his chosen profession, often working up to fifteen hours a day, and experiencing his greatest pleasure in the practice of horsemanship.

Beck's political attitude has long been misunderstood; too often the charge of opportunism has been levelled against him. Welcoming the advent of National Socialism for the promise it held for the future, he nevertheless remained true to his deeply held belief in the traditional position of the Army within the state. For a time, he was able to reconcile both these views quite happily, but the moment he felt that Hitler was pursuing damaging, even destructive policies, his conscience forced him to oppose them. Westphal recorded Beck's admonition in 1938 to a brother officer who failed in this duty:

> '... at a recent concert Hitler had spoken to one of the commanding generals about the attack [on Czechoslovakia]. Beck asked the latter: "Did you express your misgivings openly?" The general answered that in view of the large number of listeners he had not thought the moment to be opportune and had been non-committal. Beck rose and said sharply: "Herr General, you were yourself once a General Staff officer. As such you should know it is the duty of a German General Staff officer to speak his mind openly and without reservation to everyone, even to the Chief of State. It is a thousand pities that you did not do so."'[36]

However, his lack of success in speaking out forced Beck into more covert opposition to National Socialism, and thence into a full-scale conspiracy which ultimately led to his death. Such an evolution was not achieved without intense moral suffering. While he remained Chief of Staff, the doctrine of political independence, the traditional loyalty to the legally constituted executive, together with his political inexperience, had served to render his opposition ineffective. It was only his well-developed honour, integrity, and courage that enabled him to escape from these binding restrictions and attempt his Führer's overthrow—an escape which few of his brother officers found possible to effect.

3
Alliance

The whole period from 1933 to 1939 was a revolutionary one, full of internal tension in all the spheres of political, international, and economic life, and it was clear that the Wehrmacht, and, above all, the old Army, was being drawn into the vortex. Every army is but a part of its own people.
GENERAL GUNTHER VON BLUMENTRITT

With the possible exception of von Reichenau, none of the military leaders in those critical years from 1933 to 1938 possessed any political ability, and all were ill-suited by their experience to meet the new conditions of the 1930s. All accepted the new régime, albeit for different reasons, and all, at the outset, served their political master faithfully. Perhaps even more important, all were condemned by fate to work in an environment that was continually, and rapidly, developing in favour of the National Socialists; for, by mid-1934, the overwhelming majority of officers had at least come to accept the new régime, even if they did not actively support it. And why should they not have done so? Von Blomberg reasoned in 1945:

> 'Hitler emphasised the *Soldatentum*, the selection of capable men, and the re-establishment of German sovereignty within the German frontiers. These were aims to which any healthy nation would give its approval after a defeat, as France had done with great success after 1870–71.... The German people agreed with the Hitler of those days. The masses obtained tangible advantages in the matter of social justice, the labour market, and above all an increasing importance of Germany as a political body. How could we soldiers, who had continually to deal with the masses, think otherwise?'[1]

And were not the majority of Germans of all classes at that time also blind to the logical consequences of National Socialism? The plebiscite of 12 November 1933 on Hitler's home and foreign policies had resulted in a resounding ninety-five per cent 'Yes' vote for the new Chancellor; the generals themselves, on the other hand, coming as they did from a privileged background, were regarded as reactionary by the great mass of the population, and had little or no following in the country. And had not most of the political parties come to terms with Hitler and his movement? When Hitler assumed power in 1933, he was opposed only by the Communists, and even they had flirted for a time with an alliance with the National Socialists. The Conservatives were his allies, albeit uneasily, the Centre voted with his government and suppressed its mental reservations, while the Social-Democrats, although condemning his internal programme, nevertheless supported his foreign policy. Thus, as Westphal notes, the Army leaders 'had to carry through their struggles of conscience quite alone, without being able to seek advice from members of a parliament, from a free press, or from any other responsible and independent men.'[2] Furthermore, the Army, for so long a devout believer in autocracy, had never been the champion of civil liberties, Jews, socialism, or democracy; there was, then, no reason why it should greatly perturb itself over the censorship of the press and radio, the destruction of the trades unions, the imprisonment of Communists, the emasculation of the Reichstag, the prohibition of anti-state political activity, the restrictions placed on the Jews by the Nuremburg Laws, and the dragooning of the Catholic church, although there is no doubt that these did disturb individual officers.

What of the concentration camps? As yet, they were seen as nothing but rather tough internment centres necessary for the protective custody of Communists and 'socially disruptive elements,' from which people were regularly released; their more ominous role was yet to come, during the war, as centres for genocide. Germany was experiencing unusual times, and these warranted unusual measures. As von Reichenau told a council of commanding officers in February 1933: 'We must recognise that we are in the midst of a revolution; what is rotten in the state must fall and it can only be brought down by terror. The Party will proceed ruthlessly against

Marxism. The Army's task is to order arms. No succour if any of the persecuted seek refuge with the troops.'³ At the same time, there was abroad a strong belief that Hitler either did not condone, or was not aware of, the worst excesses of his followers; he was only waiting for the establishment of internal stability before relaxing the strict measures he had taken in the interests of security. Distressing events though there were, they were largely unreported within Germany and, certainly, represented only a very small part of life in those early years of the Third Reich. Terror was to develop only later. The Führer, it was argued, had just taken decisive action against his SA associates, to whom he owed so much, precisely because of their excesses. Even General Halder, a future leader of the conspiracy against Hitler, could write in August 1934: 'The Chancellor's intentions are pure and inspired by idealism; but they are being abused and sometimes actually reversed in practice by the swarm of utterly incompetent—often downright useless—Party organisations . . . the Führer [wants] to build on existing values. . . .'⁴

Furthermore, was it not a fact that many of Hitler's promises were being fulfilled? Not only was the economy improving, but, most important of all, the interests of the soldiers were being respected, their autonomy preserved. Hitler had given proof of his oft-repeated assurances that the Armed Forces were to be the sole bearers of arms in the nation, and he had begun his policy of rearmament and the destruction of the Versailles Treaty. Therefore, why should the Army not acknowledge the Führer? Certainly, as events have shown, the soldiers were wrong in their political judgement, and tragically so, but this was true of almost the whole of the German nation.

Indeed, it was so with much of the world.

This, then, was the situation in which the Army's leaders found themselves in the early years of Hitler's dictatorship. None of them, not even von Blomberg, was the spineless creature so often described by historians, and, certainly, none had any intention of abdicating the Army's traditional autonomy within the state. All shared the belief, seldom consciously defined and never commonly agreed on, that the only way to maintain their traditional role within the National Socialist state was to establish a close relationship between the Army and the ideals of its government, while remaining apart from its sole political party. Beck was one of the few to give expression to this; in 1938 he wrote: 'Quite apart from the fact that the Army's basis today is National Socialist, as it must be, the Party's influence must not be allowed to penetrate the Army, for it could only have a destructive effect.'[5] Such a delicately balanced policy, however, demanded a political expertise, a unity of action, and room for manoeuvre on the part of the Army leaders that were lacking completely. Without them, the generals' attempts were likely to fail, precisely because, in maintaining their independence and influence in military matters, they were brought inevitably into opposition with Hitler's rearmament and foreign policies which, in their view, were becoming increasingly dangerous to both the nation and the Army. Such opposition the Führer was not prepared to tolerate. Independence from his Party was one thing; obstruction of his aims, another.

The first outward sign of the Armed Services' acceptance of the new national creed of National Socialism was von

Blomberg's order of 19 September 1933, which directed servicemen to salute uniformed members of the Party and its organisations (the SA, SS, etc.). This was followed, on 25 February 1934, by the order for the wearing of the *Wehrmachtsadler* (Armed Forces eagle) on uniforms, the bird clutching in its claws a swastika, the symbol of the National Socialist Party. It would be wrong, though, to exaggerate the importance of this: the spread-eagle was an old German symbol used extensively by the Imperial Army, and the form now adopted, although with the swastika, was by then considered to be a national, rather than a purely Party, emblem, distinct from that worn by political formations, as, indeed, was its position on the uniform. Neither von Fritsch nor Beck dissented from the order, the former expressing the hope that its introduction would give the necessary impetus to Hitler to deal with the SA. More significant than this purely outward formality was the Army's acceptance of the Aryan Paragraph in the regulations governing the appointment of state officials. As from 28 February 1934, and at the suggestion of von Blomberg, the Armed Forces accepted the imposition of racial restrictions on military appointments. Serving officers and men not of Aryan descent were to be retired, and henceforth none was to be allowed into the Armed Forces. However, relatively few Jews were dismissed, as a clause was inserted to enable those who were also war veterans to remain in service. Furthermore, the regulations of the Aryan Paragraph were not fully enforced, and they were used primarily as a device for ridding the Army of troublemakers who happened to have Jewish ancestry. In the event, only thirty-nine soldiers and eleven sailors were affected, and the affair attracted relatively little attention, few officers taking the matter as far as Colonel von Manstein, who wrote to von Reichenau complaining of the cowardly way in which the Army had surrendered to the Party. The Head of the Minister's Office was angered by this effrontery, but von Fritsch took the matter out of his hands and did nothing more about it. The whole issue was promptly forgotten.

The Army's support for Hitler during the period preceding 30 June 1934, and on the fateful Night of the Long Knives itself, was considerable, for the generals were as keen as anyone else to see the pretensions of the SA curbed. The military had no reason to take other than the most stern measures necessary to counter any threat to their autonomy—a threat which, in the case of the SA, brought into question nothing less than the continued existence of the Army. A close alliance with their protector, Adolf Hitler, was, therefore, vital. Von Blomberg announced in the Party's newpaper, *Völkischer Beobachter*, the day before the purge: 'The Armed Forces stand in close unity with the whole nation, wearing with pride the symbol of the rebirth of Germany on habit and uniform, standing in discipline and loyalty behind the leadership of the state—the Field-Marshal of the Great War, Reich President von Hindenburg, its Supreme Commander, and the Führer of the Reich, Adolf Hitler, who once came out of our ranks and who will always remain one of ours.'[6] Just four days earlier, on 25 June, von Fritsch had placed the Army on a country-wide alert and was preparing to resist any attempted putsch by Röhm and his associates. And on the 30th, despite the reluctance of some generals, including the Army Commander and Chief of General Staff, to mount an offensive rather than a defensive action against the storm-troopers, the soldiers took an active part in the capture and killing of the SA leaders. Although they did not pull the triggers, they gave rifles and ammunition to the SS men who did, provided transport and refuge for the murder squads, and were even sent by themselves to disarm certain SA units. But, most important of all, by word and deed the soldiers gave Hitler the assurance that, if the worst came to the worst, the German Army was on his side.

The climax to the Army's identification with Hitler came with the death of the Reich President and Supreme Commander, Field-Marshal von Hindenburg, on 2 August 1934. Hitler and his associates were not unprepared for this event; it had been apparent for the previous six months that the old man's life was drawing to a close, and within one hour of his death came the announcement that the office of Chancellor would henceforth be merged with the office of President. Hitler was now the undisputed head of the German Reich.

The leaders of the Armed Forces were also ready to exploit the new situation. The soldiers had always disliked the form of the oath taken under the Weimar Republic, by which they swore allegiance not to the Head of State, as in the traditional German military oath, but to the hated democratic and republican constitution. Thus, seizing the opportunity that von Hindenburg's death presented, von Reichenau, on his own initiative and without any influence being brought to bear by Hitler, composed a new oath to the Head of State which could be sworn the moment he took office. Hitler, naturally enough, was happy to agree with the change, von Blomberg was enthusiastic about it, and von Fritsch accepted it, as did Beck, but with deep foreboding. Consequently, in the afternoon and late evening of 2 August, the anniversary of the first day of German mobilisation for the First World War, at ceremonies throughout Germany, soldiers and sailors took their oath of allegiance to the new Head of State and Supreme Commander. The oath ran simply:

I swear by God this holy oath, that I will render to Adolf Hitler, Führer of the German Reich and People, Supreme Commander of the Armed Forces, unconditional obedience, and that I am ready, as a brave soldier, to risk my life at any time for this oath.

By this oath, every individual serviceman of the German Armed Forces placed himself at the sole disposal of one man, Adolf Hitler, in his position as Reich Chancellor and President, the power of whose offices had been extended by the Enabling Law that swept away all legal or constitutional constraints. As a result, Hitler had to render account to no man for the use to which his soldiers were put.

The generals have been strongly criticised for having placed themselves and the Armed Forces in this position. Wheeler-Bennett has pronounced: '. . . the pledge which he [Hitler] exacted on 2 August 1934 was one of personal and binding loyalty and, at least in his interpretation, of blind and unreasoning obedience.'[7] Certainly a number of German officers since the Second World War have attempted to use as an excuse the point of honour that the oath entailed, so as to rid themselves of all responsibility for their actions. General Jodl was to plead, shortly after his capture in 1945: 'As a soldier I obeyed, and I believed my honour required me to maintain the obedience I had sworn. . . . I have spent these five years working in silence although I often entirely disagreed and thought the orders I got were absurd and impossible. I have known since the spring of 1942 that we could not win the war.'[8] A very few recognised at the time of its introduction the possible dangers inherent in the form of the oath. Beck described 2 August as 'the blackest day of my life,'[9] and his first instinct was to resign. However, as his brother later wrote, 'He appears to have let von Fritsch talk him into believing that, as things were, such a step was impossible and that the Armed Forces would not have understood it. A large number of senior generals had already thrown in their lot with Hitler, and they, at any rate, must have known what an oath to Hitler's person could bring in its wake.'[10] But if a man of Beck's intelligence and integrity could come to accept the oath, how much more possible was it for the rest of the Army?

Was the taking of this oath the criminally foolish action that is so often suggested? As has been indicated, the oath sworn personally to the Head of State was the traditional form used by the German Army throughout its history. It was the oath pledging to uphold the much-despised constitution of the Weimar Republic that was the exception. The soldiers had always preferred this personal link with their Head of State, a link they saw as the essence of their military honour, and it was a matter of great pride to them that they had publicly indicated their willingness to lay down their lives in his service. To him they pledged unconditional obedience, simply because conditional obedience was the antithesis of the discipline that formed the basis of military life. Moreover, the Weimar oath was largely meaningless because it was sworn to a little-understood and much-disliked constitution, and, owing to the legal loopholes it offered to sharp-minded soldiers to disobey orders, it had proved positively detrimental to discipline. Furthermore, the Weimar oath, although it gave 'loyalty to the constitution' and demanded services 'to protect the German nation and its lawful establishments,' did specify obedience 'to the President and to . . . superiors.' Who was the final arbiter of what the constitution was, and what it demanded? One man: the President. Foreign military oaths, too, provided for personal loyalty and obedience to Heads of State and governments: the British soldier swore 'to observe and obey all orders of His Majesty, His Heirs and Successors,' which, in reality, meant the government of the day; the American pledged himself 'to support and defend the constitution,' but also promised 'to obey the orders of the President'; while the Soviet would 'remain obedient, unto my last breath, to my People, to my Soviet Homeland, and to the Soviet Government.' Should the fact that personal loyalty was sworn to a Head of State who was also a dictator have caused any misgiving to the German soldiers? Democracy was alien to German historical development and thought, their political beliefs having always tended towards autocracy. Up to that time, few envisaged even a part of the terrible fate that lay ahead under Hitler; the vast majority of those with any form of political awareness, even if they did not see the Führer as Germany's salvation, certainly saw him as a catalyst for improvement. Finally, those, like Beck, who feared for the consequences of such an oath but could take no immediate action, at least had the comfort of knowing that, however hard it might be, their conscience could override their oath and, if necessary, enable them to disobey or even to overthrow their Head of State. After all, an oath is but an empty form of words if the substance, the idea that lies behind it, is dead.

Hitler was unhesitating in his expression of gratitude to the Armed Forces for the manner in which they had manifested their acceptance of him as Head of State. In a letter addressed to von Blomberg he wrote:

> '... I wish to express my thanks to you, and through you, to the Armed Forces, for the oath of loyalty which has been sworn to me. Just as the officers and men of the Armed Forces have obligated themselves to the new state in my person, so shall I always regard it as my highest duty to intercede for the existence and inviolability of the Armed Forces, in fulfilment of the testament of the late Field-Marshal, and in accord with my own will, to establish the Army formally as the sole bearer of arms of the nation.'[11]

The Army and the Führer now appeared as one. As Supreme Comander, Hitler ordered it to appear at the Party rally at Nuremberg in September 1934, where it performed its displays of drill, tactics, and equipment to the delight of the audience. On 9 November 1936, von Blomberg even marched in the front rank of National Socialist dignitaries through the streets of Munich to commemorate the abortive 1923 putsch. On both occasions the Army lent its weight of authority and prestige to the government and to National Socialism.

Not only did the Army identify itself with the outward

expression of the new régime, it also adapted itself to the ideals of the 'Germany reborn'—the ideals of National Socialism. Just as these were established in all sectors of German society, so were they extended to the Army. But the importance of this should not be exaggerated, for the Army was not turned into a political formation along the lines of the armed SS as a result. Throughout its history, the military had always shared the political outlook of the nation's rulers, and, in that respect, the Army of the 1930s was no different; traditionally, German youth had completed their education in the Armed Forces, so now it was only natural that the Army should train the young manhood in the spirit of the new Germany. Hitler, the war veteran, fully appreciated the 'system of values and decency'[12] of the front-line soldier, and it flattered the serviceman to know that in *Mein Kampf* he had written: 'Thus in the main, the period of military service shall serve as the conclusion of the normal education of the average German.'[13] This is the theme that runs throughout the political directives issued by von Blomberg. In April 1935 he decreed: 'The educational goal . . . is not only the basically trained soldier and master of a weapon, but also the man who is aware of his nationality and of his general duties towards the State. . . .'[14] In addition, Hitler saw the soldiers' acceptance of National Socialism as an insurance of their loyalty to him and to his aims during the bitter life-or-death struggle he believed lay ahead. He reasoned that political determination brought such strength to the soldier's sword as to render it invincible. For von Blomberg, National Socialism was to form the basis of the military virtues that, in his romanticism, he believed to play such an important role in the conduct of war.

The ideological infiltration of National Socialism into the Army, although inevitable, was not of itself destructive of its independence. Nor, indeed, did it on its own threaten the autonomy of the Army any more than that of the Armed Forces of other nations which also shared the general constitutional and political outlook of their governments, be they democratic, fascist, communist, or national socialist. Even in the United Kingdom today, the British Army owes loyalty to a system of political values, and unqualified allegiance to the sovereign and his or her duly elected ministers is basic to its undertaking to defend the constitutional and territorial integrity of the nation. Furthermore, the very fact that the leaders of the German Armed Forces themselves had introduced the new ideology into the ranks insured that Hitler and the Party possessed little reasonable cause for intervention.

In a series of directives, von Blomberg set out to establish the position of the Armed Forces within the newly organised structure of the Third Reich. On 25 May 1934, in a proclamation on the 'Duties of the German Soldier,' signed by von Hindenburg, he defined its role as 'the bearer of arms of the German nation. It protects the German Reich and the Fatherland, as well as the people united in National Socialism, and their living space.'[15] The same day, in a decree entitled 'The Armed Forces and National Socialism,' he specified the bond between the serviceman and the new ideology:

> 'National thought is the natural basis of all soldierly efforts. However, we do not wish to forget that the philosophy which fills the new state is not only national, but National Socialist. National Socialism

draws its rule of conduct from the necessities of the life of the whole people, and from the duty to work in concert for the entire nation. It embraces the idea of the fellowship of blood, of the fate of all German people. It is indubitable that this principle is, and also must remain, the foundation of the duty of the German soldier, for the principles of soldierness and of National Socialism arise out of the same experiences in the Great War.'[16]

On 22 July 1935, in a secret order, the Defence Minister stipulated:

'As regards the state, it goes without saying that the Armed Forces accept the National Socialist view. It therefore becomes necessary to convert officers of the Reserve to the same way of thinking. In consequence no one is to be trained for, or commissioned in, the Reserve of Officers unless he sincerely accepts the National Socialist state and stands up for it in public instead of adopting an attitude of indifference or even hostility towards it.'[17]

The following year, on 16 April 1936, von Blomberg issued a further decree which explained the relationship of the Armed Forces to the state:

'With the introduction of general conscription [in March 1935], the Armed Forces again became the great school of national education. . . . The Wehrmacht owes its rebirth primarily to the Führer and Reich Chancellor, and to his political tool, the

NSDAP. The Wehrmacht, SA, SS, HJ, Labour Service, Police, etc., are the parts of the whole, which, in *separate* [author's italics] fields of activity, serve the same aim. Community of purpose and comradeship must link all of these organisations.'[18]

Von Blomberg, therefore, saw the Armed Forces as a central part of the general system that was National Socialist Germany, with tasks inseparable from those of the new régime, but nevertheless preserving a separate identity. As a direct consequence, the principles of National Socialism took a direct hold on much of service life. It took just fourteen months after Hitler's rise to power for special ideological instruction to be introduced into the Army, at the time when the crisis with the SA was at its height. On 4 April 1934, von Blomberg announced:

'The first year of the National Socialist government has laid the foundations for the political and economic reconstruction of the nation. The second year places the emphasis on the spiritual saturation of the nation with the principles of the National Socialist state. Instruction in accord with this end is therefore an important task for all organisations who support the new state with their will. This applies especially to the Armed Forces. . . . I therefore order that in the future, concerning instruction in current political matters in the Armed Forces, increased significance and greater attention are to be paid to these topics by all units . . . the content of the teaching will be issued twice monthly by the Defence Ministry as "Principles for Instruction in Current Political Matters." [These were nothing more than a distillation of National Socialist propaganda.]'[19]

In 1936, political instruction became more organised. On 30 January, von Blomberg ordered the introduction of a special course of indoctrination in all Officer Training Schools, Staff Colleges, and the Armed Forces Academy, and provided for the establishment of training courses, held in Berlin by Party progagandists, for all officers who were to become instructors. Special local courses were instituted for all other officers not at the various academies. In 1937 the Party organised courses similar to those in Berlin to be held in each Wehrkreis. Once-weekly instruction was now given by officers to all NCOs and men. Simultaneously with direct political education, the Reich Ministry for Propaganda and Public Enlightenment was authorised to disseminate 'educational' literature throughout the Armed Forces; reading rooms were provided for the troops, largely stocked with propaganda; units were given funds with which to purchase the Party newspaper *Völkischer Beobachter*; and books and pamphlets produced by the Ministry were made available free, or at very low prices. Restrictions were even placed on the newspapers allowed to be taken.

More disturbing however, had been von Blomberg's order of 26 May 1936, which directed that soldiers considered politically unreliable should be reported to the Gestapo. This was further extended, on 25 January 1938, by an order which required that especially difficult men be handed over to the Gestapo for the remainder of their period of service.

In religious matters, National Socialism at first made but little headway, although the strength of Christianity within the Armed Forces was gradually eroded. On 29 May 1935, in an 'Important Political Instruction,' von Blomberg reaffirmed that attendance of soldiers at church parades was voluntary, and in April 1937 the religious instruction known as Barrack Evening Hours ceased to be obligatory, being stopped altogether for reserve troops. Chaplains found themselves increasingly restricted: on 3 December 1935 von Blomberg made a point of stating that they must use no form of compulsion, either direct or indirect, to influence non-believers; on 14 February 1936 he banned the distribution of religious material within the Armed Forces, and specified that only nominated unit chaplins could minister to the needs of servicemen; on 3 March 1936 he forbade the collection of votes on the questions of the Evangelical church, maintaining that 'it is not in accordance with the strong reserve and impartiality of the Armed Forces in religious matters';[20] and individual Army commanders took steps to restrict the freedom to discuss religion, one of them, General Dollmann, ordering: 'The Armed Forces, as one of the bearers of the National Socialist state, demand of you as chaplains at all times, a clear and unreserved acknowledgement of the Führer, State and People.'[21]

On the issue of freemasonry, von Blomberg was fully in accord with National Socialist policy. The officer corps had a strong tradition of freemasonry, traceable back to Frederick the Great, but this made no difference to his attitude. On 26 May 1934 he ordered that no serviceman might belong to a Masonic lodge, and those who did so were either to resign or be dismissed; on 7

October 1935 he went further: former freemasons were not to be considered for selection as officers unless they had resigned from their lodges before 1 October 1932 and had not taken the Third Degree, and officer-candidates were to be made to sign an affidavit declaring they had never been freemasons. Later, however, because of the pressure of numbers, von Blomberg was forced to modify this order and consider applicants on their merits.

But it was on the Jewish question that the Armed Forces' acceptance of the tenets of National Socialism took on its most ominous form. The application of the Aryan Paragraph in February 1934 has already been noted, but in one of his very few interventions in internal service affairs, Hitler, in his role as Supreme Commander, emphasised the policy of racial selection within the Armed Forces in a decree dated 13 May 1936:

> 'The National Socialist concept of state demands the nurturing of the idea of race, and of a specially selected group of leaders from people of pure German, or similar blood. It is therefore a natural obligation for the Armed Forces to select its professional soldiers, hence its leaders, in accordance with the strictest racial criteria above and beyond the legal regulations, and so to obtain a selection of the best of the German people in the military school of the nation.'[22]

There then followed a detailed instruction as to the application of the policy to the forces, but, as the Aryan Paragraph was already in existence, this merely served to restate the policy rather than to exert any practical effect.

Discrimination had already been extended even further by von Blomberg's order of 15 July 1935, which prohibited servicemen from using Jewish shops. It ran: 'It conflicts with the duty of the Armed Forces as one of the responsible schools of the new state when soldiers shop in non-Aryan businesses. I ask that commanders will take care, by means of oral instruction in suitable form, that the basic National Socialist attitude in this regard also becomes generally current ... and that violations of this will be avoided in the future.'[23] After shopping came marriage. In an order dated 1 April 1936 von Blomberg stipulated that a soldier's bride must be of Aryan blood, and that if only one grandparent were Jewish, the marriage should not take place. This was confirmed by Hitler's above-mentioned decree of 13 May 1936, which expressly forbade the union of professional soldiers with non-Aryan stock.

Even in the serviceman's home life National Socialism intruded. In a decree of 6 September 1936 von Blomberg extolled the virtues of the Party's Block and Cell administration, a system whereby each and every family in the Reich came under the charge of a Party official who had the duties of propagating National Socialism, recruiting for the multitudinous Party organisations, investigating complaints or unreliable attitudes, and handling any general issue the Party might care to give him. Von Blomberg declared that he had no objection if the Party took on such an administration of soldiers' families, although he specified that one area of a soldier's life which must be left free from inquiry or influence was his official military duty.

By such means the German soldier, after 1935, became subject to National Socialist ideology wherever be might turn: his barracks were named after heroes of the NSDAP; Party officials were invited to all social functions; his reading was supervised; his political attitudes were, in theory at least, controlled, watched, and, if necessary, reported to the Gestapo; his ancestry could be the subject of close scrutiny; his choice of a wife was inhibited; and even his family home was not proof against the influences of political officialdom.

4

Independence

... a common basic attitude was lacking. Many methods of the Party ... did not appeal to us at all. ... We officers were fighting a continuous battle against the influences of the Party which strove for power over our soldiers, thereby to push aside the soldierly element which we represented.
    FIELD-MARSHAL ERICH VON MANSTEIN

By the beginning of 1938 it might have appeared as if the soldiers were already kissing Adolf Hitler's hands 'like hysterical women.' Not only was the Army, of necessity, in the forefront of the National Socialist policies of rearmament and national regeneration, but it had done everything possible to indicate its loyalty to the Führer. It had bound itself by an unconditional oath of obedience to his person; it had assisted in the eradication of his enemies, the SA leadership; it wore his emblem, the swastika, on its uniform; it openly lent its prestige to his government by appearing at rallies and commemorations; it officially accepted the basic tenets of his creed; and it recognised its role as the great educator of the youth of the Third Reich—Hitler's youth. Outward appearances, however, were deceptive; reality was somewhat different. The Army was far from being the subservient instrument of the dictator's will that it was later to become.

What, then, was the position of the Army within the Third Reich? At the time people said nothing had changed; that while Germany possessed a National Socialist Air Force, it still maintained an Imperial Navy and a Royal Prussian Army. While this was something of an exaggeration, there can be no doubt that the Army had abandoned to Hitler little or nothing substantial of its independence, had maintained considerable autonomy within the state, and was completely free from any Party supervision. According to paragraph 26 of the Defence Law, no soldier was allowed to undertake political activity, and this included being a member of the National Socialist Party or of its affiliated organisations. The only exceptions to this fundamental rule were minor ones: civilian members of the Armed Forces were allowed to hold Party office under certain conditions; participation in National Socialist welfare organisations was considered desirable; leading Party members could wear military uniform at Party functions during service, although they could not make speeches; and, although conscripts had to allow their membership to lapse, they could continue to pay their Party dues while in service. The Armed Forces retained full control over its own political instruction, and maintained the right to sole responsibility for its own publicity in the face of a serious challenge from the Propaganda Ministry. Just as important, the generals were successful in resisting the demands of Rudolf Hess, the Deputy Führer, for a Party Complaints Centre to be instituted within the Armed Forces to facilitate servicemen making complaints direct to the Party organisation. Furthermore, by the Army Law promulgated on 20 July 1933, the soldiers had been made independent of the jurisdiction of the civil courts. Nor was the Army responsible to any outside body for its application of the Aryan Paragraph, or of the marriage and freemasonry restrictions. And, when one of its soldiers was suspected of political unreliability, it was the Army and no other body that decided whether an investigation should be made, and, on its conclusion, whether the matter should be reported to the Gestapo.

If the Party's interference in service matters was negligible, so was Hitler's. In the later years of his rule he was often to imply that before 1938 his attitude towards the military leaders was dictated solely by his wish to undermine their hostility towards him and his creed. On one occasion he reminisced: 'Once that [conscription] was accomplished, the influx into the Armed Forces of the masses of the people, together with the spirit of National Socialism and the ever-growing power of the National Socialist movement, would, I was sure, allow me to overcome all oposition among the Armed Forces, and in particular in the corps of officers.'[1] It is on such sayings that many historians have fastened their attention, using them as proof of the thesis that, even before 1938, Hitler was scheming against his generals. But the Führer's memory was never the most truthful, and his reminiscences are usually marked by a high degree of fantasy, delighting, as he did, in conveying to those around him the idea that he was, and always had been, the all-seeing, all-powerful manipulator of the nation's destiny. Therefore it is necessary to look carefully at Hitler's actions in the five years in question, from January 1933 to January 1938, to discern whether or not he did in fact behave in a devious fashion towards the Army.

The evidence does not support the historians' contention. At no time did Hitler act against the interests of the Army's autonomy. What von Blomberg wrote in 1945 was the truth:

'In the early years of his régime, Hitler stressed his adherence to the historical tradition of which the *Tag von Potsdam* represented, and continued to represent, for the German people, a confession of faith. During these years we soldiers had no cause to complain to Hitler. He fulfilled hopes which were dear to all of us. If the generals no longer choose to remember this, it is obviously a case of deliberate forgetfulness. . . . Until Hitler entered upon the period of aggressive politics . . . the German people had no decisive reason for hostility to Hitler, we soldiers least of all. He had not only given us back a position of respect in the life of the German people . . . but by the rearmament of Germany, which only Hitler could achieve, he had given the soldiers a larger sphere of influence, promotion and increased respect. . . . Up until 1938 there was no sign of hostility. . . . We soldiers had no reason to complain. . . . To sum up, I would say that Hitler in the first period, which lasted up to 1938, strove to obtain the trust of us soldiers, with complete success.'²

Even though he was their Supreme Commander, on no occasion did Hitler interfere in the internal affairs of the Armed Forces against the advice of his military subordinates. Indeed, he revealed nothing but complete confidence in his generals. As Field-Marshal von Manstein later recorded: 'There is no doubt that when he originally came to power he had shown the military leaders a certain deference and respected their professional abilities.'³ Hitler's military adjutant, who was always close to the Führer, went further when he wrote:

'During this period Hitler adhered strictly to the boundaries of the area of responsibility of his military advisers. There is no substantial case in which Hitler intervened in military matters on his own authority and without previous consultation with his Minister of War. All directives and orders which required his permission, originated in the responsible places within the War Ministry, be it on the initiative of the Ministry or after consultation between Hitler and Blomberg, and were only shown to the former for his signature after countersigning by Blomberg, and, where necessary, by the commanders of the individual services. . . . No military authority, independent of the constitutional advisers, was exercised by the Head of State until the end of January 1938.'⁴

On one occasion, for example, Hitler abandoned his, and

Göring's, idea that the Army should adopt the National Socialist salute of raised arm, when Hossbach explained that it would be unpopular among the soldiers. In the light of this, it is easy to accept von Blomberg's assertion:

> '... Hitler on several occasions approached me with the idea of training the SA as a reserve formation. He gave in to my objections ... and the three regiments of the Waffen SS were not increased in my time—in spite of the heavy pressure on the part of Himmler. To what extent I was successful in keeping the Wehrmacht free from the influence of the Nazi Party, and from being linked up with it, has not been realised. ... In my time the Wehrmacht stood in no sense behind the Party, but took its stand independently alongside it. The Party often sought to change this situation but did not succeed, because Hitler listened to me in those days.'[5]

A number of actions on the part of Hitler form positive proof of his good intentions towards the military. In speeches he often publicly affirmed his belief in the importance of the Army. For example, in 1934, he declared: 'Our government is supported by two organisations: politically by the community of the Volk, organised in the National Socialist movement, and in the military sphere by the Army.'[6] The next year he pronounced that the Army was 'in war the nation's great defence, in peace the splendid school of our people. It is the Army which has made men of us all, and when we looked upon the Army our faith in the future of our people was always reinforced. This old glorious Army is not dead; it only slept, and now it has risen again in you.'[7] Nor was Hitler ungenerous in awarding influence and prestige to his military advisers. For example, on 21 May 1935, he appointed von Blomberg Commander-in-Chief of the three Armed Services in addition to his ministerial responsibilities, thereby raising him to a position of military authority surpassing that of any other peacetime general in German history. Such an elevation and concentration of powers was hardly indicative of any determined policy to undermine the influence of his military advisers, and it certainly confounded his policy of 'divide and rule,' which he was later to apply even to his most faithful followers. The next year, in 1936 on the occasion of his forty-seventh birthday, Hitler promoted von Blomberg to the rank of *Generalfeldmarschall*, von Fritsch (together with Göring, the Luftwaffe Commander) to *Generaloberst*, and Raeder, the Navy Commander, to *Generaladmiral*. By these promotions he was honouring 'the entire Wehrmacht, every individual officer and soldier.'[8] Hitler had wanted to bestow on his War Minister the new rank of *Reichsmarschall*, but the opinon of his military advisers was against it; instead, he had to be content with giving him the highest existing rank. Even so, von Blomberg was only the sixth German soldier to be thus honoured in peacetime, while Hitler's erstwhile political crony, Göring, had to be content with an inferior rank.

At that time, Hitler remained faithful to his declaration made in 1934, after his eradication of the SA challenge, that: 'For fourteen years I have stated consistently that the fighting organisations of the Party are political institutions and that they have nothing to do with the Army.'[9] As a result he took a leading role in protecting the military from the encroachments of Party formations. In 1933 he had ensured that the creation of the Reich Defence Council involved no opportunity to override the Army Commander-in-Chief's orders or directives. In early 1935, at the height of an SS campaign of vilification against von Fritsch and the Army, in which rumours of a military putsch were rife—Himmler had gone so far as to name the day on which the soldiers' revolt was to take place—Hitler had intervened and placed himself firmly on the side of his soldiers. The SS attacks ceased immediately, although only for the time being. A few months later, in April and May, on being told that listening devices had been found in Army telephones, and even in the *Abwehr* (military intelligence) offices, Hitler ordered that Gestapo authority should not for one moment encroach on Armed Forces' territory. In 1936, when Himmler and Heydrich again laid charges against the Army Commander, this time accusing him of homosexuality, Hitler rejected totally the bogus evidence on which they were based, and ordered the documents to be burnt. On this occasion a senior SS officer recorded: '. . . Hitler has said that, though von Fritsch was doubtless one of the strongest and most important opponents of National Socialism, he could not be dealt with in this fashion.'[10]

In other matters Hitler was equally on the side of his soldiers. In 1935 he rejected the National Socialist Reich Labour Service's requirement for a period of two years conscription, on the grounds that it would prejudice the Army's demands on the youth of the nation, which, also, would be two years. The same year he disbanded the Defence Policy Office of the Party, giving the reason that open rearmament had rendered it superfluous, thereby freeing the Army from one aspect of outside interest (although it had never been a controlling body). In compliance with the Army's opposition, he also omitted Party-orientated sections from the draft Defence Law of 1935. And in 1936, heeding the representations of von Blomberg and von Fritsch, he refused to have instituted a 'National Socialist Soldiers' Ring,' which officers and men would have been encouraged to join after their release from service. Hitler even expressed concern that von Blomberg was precipitating the introduction of National Socialist ideology into the Army; apparently he felt that 'the political permutation'[11] of the force was a matter of time and should be attempted only gradually.

Finally, some attention must be paid to Hitler's attitude to the armed SS formations being formed from 1933 onwards. In March of that year the first militarised SS unit was instituted, comprising a guard company numbering 120 men; twelve years later the armed SS contained within its order of battle some 600,000 soldiers. This, historians usually allege, is proof of the dictator's evil intent towards the military establishment, for, at the same time as he was making conciliatory, but worthless, gestures to its leaders, he was actively creating 'an élite and fanatical force, the SS, which, though ... in its infancy, was to challenge and humiliate the Army in its own field.'[12] They claim that Hitler deliberately went back on his promise to the generals that the Armed Forces would be 'the sole arms-bearers' in the defence of the nation, and that the creation of the armed SS was a conscious art of policy on his part, the aim of which was, firstly, to foster a spirit of rivalry and division within the Armed Forces which would strengthen his position, and, secondly, to act as a substitute for the Army by providing a politically reliable military force totally subservient to his will and to the tenets of National Socialism. Such conclusions are based on misleading interpretations of Hitler's role in the development of the armed SS. Possibly, it was the long-term aim of Heinrich Himmler, as *Reichsführer SS*, to create an SS force as an élite fourth arm of the Wehrmacht, which would rival and, perhaps, one day supplant the Army in its dominant position. But that vision was never shared by Hitler, and he was the final arbiter of the fate of the SS formations.

The key to an understanding of Hitler's ideas for the armed SS within the political and military structure of the Third Reich lies in the oath, first sworn by the Führer's personal guard, the *Leibstandarte SS 'Adolf Hitler,'* in November 1933, and subsequently by every man accepted into the ranks of the armed SS. It ran:

> *I swear to you, Adolf Hitler, as Führer and Reich Chancellor, loyalty and bravery. I vow to you, and those you have appointed to command me, obedience unto death. So help me God.*

Though not generally recognised at the time, this oath had considerable significance for the future of the German Army and for the nation as a whole. It was an important step in establishing the authority of Hitler as an independent factor in German public life, for he had now instituted a body of armed men pledged to him personally, with no defined status either within the state or Party. They were at his sole disposal for use as he alone thought fit. And just as Hitler, at the junction between Party and state, represented the hazy, ill-defined relationship between the two, so also did the élite force at his command, the armed SS. Furthermore, just as his political outlook was at first dominated by internal affairs and then by external expansion, so too was the role of his SS troops.

Despite all claims to the contrary, Hitler never intended to build up the armed SS to the point it ultimately reached, and it is probable that he was entirely sincere when he promised his generals in 1934 that the Armed Forces were to be the sole bearers of arms in the defence of the Fatherland. Even Himmler, never slow to seize an opportunity for expanding his domain, was prepared in 1936 to leave it to the Wehrmacht to guarantee 'the safety of the honour, the greatness and the peace of the Reich from the exterior.'[13] Thus, the first formations of the armed SS began as purely political instruments, one of the many aspects of the paramilitary organisations of the National Socialist movement. As the task of the SS was, in Himmler's words, to 'guarantee the security of Germany from the interior,' it was thought necessary that, to complement its activities in the areas of political education, secret police, counter-espionage and concentration camps, the SS should develop an armed force run on military lines for the purpose of anti-terrorist, heavy-police tasks during the periods of internal strife that were then thought likely to occur. Thus, an organisation of SS *Sonderkommandos* (Special Detachments, later renamed *Kasernierte Hundertschaften* [Barracked Hundreds] or SS *Politische Bereitschaften* [Political Readiness Squads] when they reached battalion strength) was instituted throughout Germany. In June 1934 some of these units, including the *Leibstandarte*, were sent against Hitler's internal enemies, the SA leaders.

By late 1934, the *Politische Bereitschaften* had reached such a size and state of military training that a new organisation and nomenclature was required. The Army leaders were apprised of the situation in August of that year, but they had to wait until 16 March 1935, the day Hitler announced the reintroduction of conscription, before the order officially establishing the new organisation was issued. The *Politische Bereitschaften*, consisting of three *Standarten* (regiments) modelled on the Army, made up of three battalions and motorcycle and mortar companies, each supported by a signals battalion, was henceforth known as the SS-VT, SS *Verfügungstruppen* (literally, For Disposal Troops, but better translated as Special Purpose Troops). From then on, as Hitler's attention turned from consolidating his position at home and became increasingly focused on foreign adventure, the SS-VT evolved a new role, transformed from a purely political police unit into a military force prepared to take action against its Führer's external, as well as his internal, enemies. It was a very short step from being equipped and trained for anti-terrorist duties to being organised for war. As Beck noted, 'it was interesting to observe that an organisation, which Hitler had categorically stated would never bear arms in military operations, was now taking part in every coup the Führer pulled off. Not only were they taking part, but they were, by 1938, wearing Army uniform instead of their own, except on ceremonial occasions.'[14] Units of the SS-VT took part in the occupations of the Rhineland, Austria, and the Sudetenland, and all the time their military aspect grew. From May 1935, membership of the SS-VT was officially regarded as military service with the Wehrmacht; in October 1936 the SS-VT Inspectorate, an armed SS

General Staff, was instituted under the command of Paul Hausser, a former Reichsheer General (this organisation was replaced in 1940 by the SS *Führungsamt* [the Operational Office); and by the summer of 1939 the SS-VT had completed its expansion to the strength of a division of 18,000 men with its own artillery and armoured car units. Even by November 1937 Himmler had felt confident enough to declare: 'the *Verfügungstruppen* are, according to the present standards of the Wehrmacht, prepared for war.'[15]

As a result of all this, the Army was highly suspicious of the SS-VT, viewing it as a distinct threat to its position as sole arms bearer. Von Fritsch voiced the fears of many when he wrote in early 1938: '. . . it is the *Verfügungstruppen* which, expanded further and further, must create an opposition to the Army, simply through its existence. . . . [It] develops itself totally apart, and, it appears to me, in deliberate opposition to the Army. All units report unanimously that the relationship of the SS *Verfügungstruppen* to the Army is very cool, if not hostile.'[16] Tension there was; perhaps inevitably. Relations between the SS and the Army, generally, were poor. The soldiers were indignant at what they considered to be the rivalry of political upstarts, and fearful of their future development, while the SS men were resentful of the Army's attitude, jealous of its undoubted overwhelming military superiority, arrogant of their own élite position within the Reich, and aggressive in their claims for further expansion. Both were contemptuous of each other. But it would be wrong to mistake this natural mistrust, fear, and enmity as indicative of any devious intent on the part of Hitler. The SS-VT was the Führer's force, in many ways independent of Himmler and his ambitions, and was not intended to rival, supplant, or even interfere with, the Army. This, Hitler made clear time and time again. As early as 24 September 1934 a circular had been sent to the leaders of the Armed Forces outlining the purpose of the SS-VT, and stating categorically that, although it was under the command of the Reichsführer SS, in time of war it would be placed at the disposal of the Army. This position never changed, and at no time was there ever any question of the Army losing operational control over the armed SS. However, in order to remove the existing doubt concerning the SS-VT, on 2 February 1935 Hitler issued a secret order, specifically stating that 'Directives for the material outfitting and recruitment for the SS-VT will be issued by the Defence Minister.' In time of war 'The SS-VT will be incorporated into the Army. They are then subordinated to military laws which also apply to matters of recruitment. . . . The preparation of the SS-VT for employment in war will proceed even in peacetime under the responsibility of the Defence Minister to whom they are subordinate in this respect.'[17] Later that year, heeding the advice given him by von Blomberg and others, Hitler excluded from the Defence Law the draft provisions concerning the status of the armed SS, thereby maintaining the Army's position as the military training school of the nation. On 17 August 1938 he issued a further, and more comprehensive, definition of the role of the SS-VT and its relationship to the Wehrmacht. He laid down that it 'forms no part of the Wehrmacht nor of the police. It is a permanent armed force at my disposal.' As 'a formation of the NSDAP' it was to be 'recruited and trained in ideological matters by the Reichsführer SS in accordance with the directives issued by me.' In cases of emergency 'the SS-VT will be used for two purposes:

(1) by the Commander-in-Chief of the Army within the framework of the Army. It will then be subject exclusively to military law and instructions; politically, however, it will remain a branch of the NSDAP.

(2) at home, in case of emergency, in accordance with my instructions. It will then be under the orders of the Reichsführer SS. . . .'[18]

Such, in 1938, was the position of the armed SS, which, in Hitler's view and in reality, presented no challenge to the Army.

Consequently, at the beginning of 1938, the German Army was as independent a military force as could be found anywhere in the west. Responsive to the political mood of the nation and to the policies of its legally constituted master, the Army was for all other purposes an autonomous power within the National Socialist state. The Minister responsible for it was answerable to no one but the Head of State, who, for his part, accepted the advice of his military advisers on service matters, and did not interfere with the running of the Armed Forces. The Army was, therefore, responsible for its own discipline, promotion, training, ideological instruction, and directives. No Party organisation had the slightest control over the Army whatsoever. Only Hitler, as its Supreme Commander, possessed any authority, but he chose not to use it. As the distinguished historian, Alfred

Vagts wrote in September 1935: '... the National Socialist Party has ceased to be a formidable rival of the Army.... The reign of the Party is over.'[19] Indeed, General Westphal noted that it was still possible for the professional soldier 'to be able to keep himself clear from politics. The older officers were particularly resistant to attempts to make them adopt the National Socialist outlook; they believed they could maintain their inner independence even under Hitler's dictatorship.'[20] He went on to record that: 'The healthy instinct of the people felt that the Army was striving to remain an oasis of simplicity, uprightness, and Christian service.'[21] It was particularly this preservation of old traditions, the most suspicious feature of all in the eyes of the Party, that the politically saner part of the populace found most comforting. It was not by accident that many fled into the Army simply to escape the influence of the National Socialists.

The Army's independence of the political structure of the Reich revealed itself in a number of ways. It was clear, for example, that the troops were addressing themselves too little to the ideological training ordered by their leadership. On 17 April 1935 von Blomberg felt himself forced to issue an exhortation to the troops to take seriously the programme of political instruction. He stated: 'It has come to my attention that the "Principles for Instruction in Current Political Matters" are not being given the attention which should be given them. I determine and authorise their contents, and they are just as binding as any other official instructions.'[22]

Even more disheartening to the Defence Minister was the strong and noticeable dissatisfaction felt by the officer corps for the Party, whose interference with the privacy of family life aroused special resentment. The soldiers were distrustful of its ambitions and disgusted by the arrogance and condescension which its dignitaries so often showed towards servicemen. A particular cause for complaint was that, on many occasions, former Party members serving in the Army made vindictive reports to NSDAP headquarters, complaining of matters ranging from the political unreliability of a certain officer to everday questions of military administration. Indeed, Party organisations such as the SA and SS positively encouraged their former members to report on their officers. Their activities were formally ended in 1937, after von Blomberg had made a number of strong complaints to Hess, although they continued illegally.

The Army refused to be overawed by the politicians. In 1935 Baldur von Schirach, the Reich Leader of German Youth, who was serving his time in the Army, was refused a commission, and then was threatened with detention for complaining about it to Party headquarters. There was also grave concern at the Party's attitude to religion, many officers feeling that it was doing all it could to force a break between church and state, and to render Christianity in Germany impotent. The arrest, on 1 July 1937, of Pastor Niemöller, widely regarded as a symbol of Christian resistance, profoundly shocked many within Germany and in the ranks of the Army (although a majority of officers were not displeased to see this man, who so constantly called for disarmament, out of the public eye). But even before then, there had begun a number of local battles to ensure that military chaplains were not compelled to accept National Socialist dogma. At least one Party official even went so far as to denounce an Army chaplain for high treason, and the whole subject aroused such ill-feeling that Keitel felt constrained to write in 1936: 'Church matters are so difficult that we only do any good if we leave them entirely alone. . . .'[23] There were many, however, including the Army Commander himself, who would not heed this advice, and, in the latter half of 1937, a wave of enthusiasm for church-attendance swept the Army, with church parades becoming unofficially obligatory in many garrisons. In November a memorandum from Protestant Army chaplains to the War Minister received much publicity, especially in the foreign press. Part of it read: 'The Party and the state today combat not only the churches. They combat Christianity. . . . The situation has become intolerable.'[24]

The National Socialist Jewish policy, too, received some resistance from the soldiers, this usually taking the form of patronising Jewish businesses, banning the vitriolic anti-Semitic paper, *Der Stürmer*, produced by Gauleiter Julius Streicher, and casting a blind eye on the non-Aryan ancestry of servicemen. Beck was one of those who attempted to assist Jewish soldiers dismissed from service, and von Fritsch, although revealing some anti-Semitic prejudice, nevertheless took action to ameliorate conditions for non-Aryan officers and their wives by prohibiting conjectures or rumours about possible ancestry. (Indeed, all von Fritsch's directives were written with a deliberate disregard for Party ideology. This was most apparent when he concerned himself with matters of the honour, the manner of living, the code of conduct, and the social responsibilities of the officers corps.) On several occasions von Blomberg pleaded with Hitler for a better treatment of Jews.

Other areas of friction were numerous. Party officials often publicly criticised the Army for being a centre of reaction, and demanded that the political attitudes of the officers be investigated. Complaints were made that soldiers did not donate enough to Party charities, such as Winter Help, and brawls in the street, even stabbings, were not unknown, Party members often overreacting to baiting by the servicemen. On one occasion soldiers shouted around the town of Braunsberg: 'First comes the Army, then nothing for a long while, then a large heap of shit, and then, perhaps, the NSDAP.'[25] On another, five young lieutenants at a dance in Neustadt gave a toast to Moscow, and received a battering for their foolishness. In particular, there was considerable vitriolic feeling between the Army and the SS and Gestapo, which arose out of the jealous and active competition of Himmler, Heydrich, and their followers against the most important and, as yet, entirely independent organisation within Germany.

The first determined onslaught by the SS against the Army's position began shortly after the events of 30 June 1934, when cooperation between the future rivals had been considerable. Every attempt was made to bring the political reliability of the Army's leadership into question, and the campaign, which had degenerated into open hatred, stopped only when Hitler personally intervened in early 1935. The truce did not last long, however, and by the summer the enmity was again marked. Von Fritsch recalled: '. . . there was scarcely a single senior officer who did not feel that he was being spied upon by the SS. Also, it became known again and again that, contrary to the expressed orders of the Deputy to the Führer [Hess], SS men who were serving in the Army had orders to report on their superiors.'[26] Gestapo surveillance penetrated the very depths of the Bendlerstrasse, even the offices of the intelligence service, and von Fritsch found himself constantly spied on, his forthrightness making him a prime target for suspicion. In Silesia, the Gestapo went as far as to undertake systematic enquiries into the political outlook of officers. In the streets, bars, cafés, restaurants, and clubs, personal relations between Army and SS were sour; SS men refused to salute officers, others attempted to exercise police authority over troops, and some even attacked lone or small groups of soldiers without provocation.

The state to which affairs had degenerated was such that a number of directives were laid down to regulate the relationship between Army and Party personnel. On 16 April 1935, in a decree, part of which has already been quoted, von Blomberg made clear that the servicemen were to be silent about any shortcomings of the Party:

> 'It would be a sign of lack of self-control and an absence of political instinct if annoyance over the defects of an individual led to derogatory criticism and remarks about institutions and organisations which are outside the Armed Forces. They ... incriminate him who states them.... Everyday friction and shortcomings, which can never be avoided completely, can easily be magnified to the status of prestige matters, but this is wrong. The Armed Forces do not need to pursue prestige politics.'[27]

This had little effect. On 28 January 1936, General

Dollmann, the commander of Wehrkreis IX, felt it necessary to issue a directive on Army-Party relations:

> 'In the Party, particularly in the lower ranks, some mistrust of the inner attitude and conduct of the officer corps exists. This mistrust is based on a series of incidents which are inclined to give the picture that the officer corps stood in opposition towards the concept of state and outlook represented by the Party. They believe that the officer corps inclines more to the circles who reject the present state, and hence are of the opinion that these circles regard the officer corps as their ultimate support. This is undesirable.... The officer corps must have confidence in the representatives of the Party. Party opinions should not be examined or rejected.'[28]

He then went on to illustrate how relations could, and should, be improved. These included the building up of social contacts with all levels of the Party, the ending of discrimination towards National Socialists in the selection of officers, the termination of functions disapproved of by the Party—such as celebrations on the birthday of the Kaiser—and the fostering of a friendly attitude towards the NDSAP at all times. Every attempt was made by von Blomberg to settle differences between Army and SS men out of court, and thereby prevent any increase in the rivalry. On 25 January 1938 he declared: 'I stress particularly that the relationship to the SS is, like that towards the other organisations of the movement, one of conscious comradeship. Shortcomings in this regard not only damage the appearance of the Armed Forces, but at the same time constitute a severe infringement of my expressed will. I request that attention be given to this thought in the allocation of punishment.'[29]

An indication of the degree of independence possessed by the Army had been revealed by its reaction to the murder of two of its retired generals, von Schleicher, the former Chancellor, and his assistant, von Bredow, both deliberately shot in their homes by the Gestapo during the bloody events of 30 June 1934. They were murdered partly out of revenge for their former intrigues against the National Socialists and partly from the unfounded fear that they were then plotting the overthrow of the new régime. The official version of the killing, to which Hitler assented, was given by von Reichenau in a communiqué:

> 'In recent weeks it had been established that the ex-Defence Minister, General (Retired) von Schleicher has maintained treasonable relationships with foreign powers and with SA leadership circles inimical to the state. It has therefore been proved that both in word and deed he has been acting against the state and its leaders. This meant that in connexion with the general purge now in progress, his arrest was essential. When police officers came to arrest him, General (Retired) von Schleicher offered armed resistance. There was an exchange of shots as a result of which both he and his wife, who placed herself in the line of fire, were mortally wounded.'[30]

Retired, and an unpopular 'political general' though von Schleicher was, his murder aroused considerable resentment within the Army. His few admirers believed the official pronouncement to be totally false, while many others held that the whole affair besmirched the honour of the Army and set a dangerous precedent. Despite the acceptance by the officer corps of the events of 30 June, reaction within the Army to the murder of the generals was immediate and not inconsiderable. Officers spoke out privately in von Schleicher's defence, one of them, Ludwig Crüwell, a future commander of the German Africa Corps, being made the subject of a Gestapo investigation as a result of his doing so; and von Hammerstein, still on the active list, ignored von Blomberg's order not to attend von Schleicher's funeral, even insisting on carrying the decorations of the deceased. Demands for the rehabilitation of the General's honour and the punishment of his murderers were strong. Von Hammerstein and the veteran and venerated Field-Marshal von Mackensen, representative of all that was admired in the old Imperial Army, submitted a long memorandum to President von Hindenburg, which, although intending to inform him of the whole sorry affair and to complain of von Blomberg's attitude to the murder, contained criticism of Hitler's foreign policy and proposed a reconstruction of Germany's government, which in effect meant the replacement of the National Socialist régime by a military dictatorship. This was nothing more nor less than the reassertion of von Schleicher's intention of making Hitler a prisoner of the Army and reorientating foreign policy towards a favourable understanding with Poland and Russia. The memorandum was signed by some thirty generals and senior staff officers. Although it was never received by von Hindenburg, the 'Blue Book of the

Reichswehr,' as it came to be known, was circulated throughout the Army with ever increasing effect. The clamour for rehabilitation rose, as did Hitler's disquiet. Such was the pressure from the officer corps, which the passage of time did nothing to diminish, that, after advice from von Blomberg, Hitler felt it necessary to make some concession towards the Army. This took the unusual, indeed unique, form of an admission by Hitler that he had erred, made to a gathering of top Army and Party officials in the Berlin Opera House on 3 January 1935. He conceded that the shootings of the two generals had been wrong, and that the derogatory statements made later by himself and Göring had been based on incorrect information. He promised that the names of the two innocent men would be restored to their regimental rolls of honour. This statement, although never formally announced publicly, was reported by Field-Marshal von Mackensen to the association of former General Staff officers, the *Verein Graf Schlieffen*, on 28 February. Although the Field-Marshal's move was regretted by von Blomberg, his action was well-received by the rest of the Army. Hitler had been forced to admit his mistake because of his soldiers' pressure.

But it was over rearmament and the nation's foreign policy that the independence of the German Army within the state became most noticeable and, from Hitler's point of view, most dangerous; for it was here that the Army's most vital interest—its military autonomy—was threatened. The political outlook of its soldiers was one thing, their capacity to wage war effectively, quite another. This, on no account, was to be endangered by the government without strong protests being mounted by the

Army's leadership.

Rearmament should have been the strongest link between the Army and Hitler. The soldiers rightly saw the new régime as providing the means by which they could regain their former might and ensure the defence of their homeland, while the Führer viewed the creation of a large and powerful Army as fundamental to the success of his foreign ambitions. Each was grateful for, or at the least cognisant of, the indispensable aid of the other. But here their identity of purpose ended, for Hitler proved incapable of understanding the almost unbearable strains imposed on the Army by his too rapid, and too vast, expansion. In five years the Army grew from 100,000 to 3,343,000 men. Although the size and pace of this rearmament were important in maintaining and extending the acceptance of Hitler by the officers of lower and middle ranks, it also proved to be a cause for considerable contention for the senior generals. As early as May 1934, Beck wrote in despair that the rearmament programme as then being undertaken was 'not a building-up of a peacetime army, but a mobilisation.'[31] Von Fritsch complained bitterly that the Führer's policy was 'forcing everything, overdoing everything, rushing everything far too much and destroying every healthy development.'[32] Von Blomberg, too, was deeply apprehensive, going as far as to be the sole voice in cabinet meetings speaking out against the policy. He described assurances from Hitler's foreign affairs specialist, von Ribbentrop, that there was no need to worry about foreign objections to rearmament as 'all stuff and nonsense!'[33]

The Army leaders wished to tread warily, for they feared the reaction of the major powers to Germany's efforts to establish herself as the greatest military state on the Continent, efforts in direct contradiction to the Versailles Treaty that had been established with such care just sixteen years perviously. In the event, they need not have worried. The naïvety of the great powers was matched only by their inaction, but this the generals could not foresee. Of equal concern was the potentially destructive effect on the Army of too much rearmament at too high a speed, which would strike at the very roots of Hitler's declared intention of creating 'an army of the greatest possible strength and internal compactness and homogeneity at the best imaginable level of training.'[34] In June 1936 von Fritsch ordered a study of the material, manpower, and financial requirements of rearmament, which came to the conclusion that military power was being pursued with such vigour that efficiency was declining; that the money required even to maintain the armaments industry in good order after 1940 would be crippling to the economy; and that, anyway, in a major war the Army would be capable of fighting for only seven consecutive months. But, despite frequent protests, nothing was done to ameliorate the situation; the generals' military advice was powerless against Hitler's political will.

The most fundamental parting of the ways between Hitler and his senior generals, however, came over the questions of foreign policy—grand strategy, the future employment of the Army in war. Hitler's plans were aggressive and expansionist, seeing military force as an integral part of their fulfilment. Those of his generals were the opposite, summed up in von Blomberg's directive of 24 June 1937, entitled 'Unified War Preparations of the Armed Forces':

'The general political situation justifies the supposition that Germany does not have to reckon on an attack from any side. This is due mainly to the lack of desire for war on the part of all nations, especially the western powers. It is also due to the lack of military preparedness on the part of a number of states, notably Russia. Germany has just as little intention of unleashing a European war. Nonetheless, the international situation, politically unstable and not exclusive of surprising incidents, requires readiness for war on the part of the German Armed Forces, (a) so that attacks from any side may be countered, (b) so that any favourable political opportunities may be militarily exploited.'[35]

Such an attitude permeated the whole High Command. Indeed, some generals were even more cautious in answer to a request in 1935 from von Blomberg, backed by von Reichenau, to undertake a detailed study of the possibilities of making a premature attack on Czechoslovakia in the event of war, Beck replied: 'After thorough consideration, I hold it to be my duty to declare this very day that if the memorandum of the Minister is not solely concerned with the purpose of operational studies, but is aimed at the practical introduction of preparation for war, then I must express the most dutiful request to be removed from my position at the Truppenamt, because I do not feel myself to be fitted for this latter task.'[36] After a brief exploration, the Czechoslovak plan was laid to rest until 1937.

The deployment plans drawn up by the Army leadership were primarily of a defensive nature, and much emphasis was placed on the building of fortifications and defensive systems in both the east (the Heibsberg Triangle and the Oder-Warthe line) and in the west (the West Wall). Apart from a series of plans for small-scale operations to counter any Polish invasion in the 1920s, no deployment plan was prepared until late 1935. Then, under the direction of von Manstein, the Operations Department of the General Staff drew up *Aufmarsch Rot* (Deployment Red), measures to be taken in the event of what was considered then to be the most likely scene for a future conflict: a two-front war in which Germany was faced by a major attack by the French in the west, assisted by the Czechs in the east. However, the plan depended on Czechoslovakia making the military mistake of remaining primarily on the defensive; no provision was made to counter the Czechs if they chose to do the sensible thing and use their large local superiority to make a quick thrust over the 120 miles to the Reich's capital, Berlin. Therefore, in 1937, another plan, *Aufmarsch Grün* (Deployment Green) was ordered to be drawn up, this aiming to concentrate Germany's forces for a pre-emptive strike at Czechoslovakia to secure the east, before turning to deal with the French invasion which, it was expected, would by then be underway in the west. (It was the 1914 Schlieffen plan in reverse.) Beck still regarded this as militarily unsound, for the same reasons as he gave in 1935: '. . . I can regard such an operation as an act of desperation by which the German Army, as well as surrendering German soil itself, excludes itself from the direct defence of the nation, in all likelihood to find an inglorious end in a foreign land, while at home the enemy dictate their own conditions.'[37] He also believed that any invasion of Czechoslovakia would inevitably bring Britain and France together in united action against Germany. This was an attitude with which many other generals, including von Blomberg, concurred. As a result of his opposition, both *Aufmarsch Grün* and two other plans authorised by von Blomberg, *Sonderfall Otto* (a special case designed to prevent the restoration of the Habsburgs in Austria) and *Sonderfall Erweiterung Rot/Grün* (a special case enlargement of plans Red and Green aimed at checking as far as possible the intervention of Britain, Poland, and Lithuania, a situation that was regarded as fatal) were never completed. Such was the nature of the German Army's preparation for war before 1938: defensive, and fearful of the consequences of aggressive action.

Hitler, however, never for one moment agreed with this purely defensive attitude. From the beginning he enunciated his plans to his generals in terms that could leave them in no doubt of his intentions. On 3 February 1933, some thirty days after assuming power, Hitler told a meeting of the senior commanders that the only answer to Germany's long-term problems was the acquisition of suitable living space through armed struggle. Some were impressed; a few, like von Fritsch, apprehensive; most were thoroughly cool in their response, a reaction which Hitler did not fail to perceive. General von Leeb remarked: 'A businessman whose wares are any good, does not need to boost them in the loudest tones of a market crier.'[38] The generals thought that the realities of Germany's situation would prevent such dangerous dreaming from ever being transferred into action. But a year later, on 28 February 1934 before a gathering of senior SA and Army leaders, Hitler again returned to this theme. One of those listening, General von Weichs, recorded the contents of his address, which included: 'The NSDAP has overcome the unemployment. These blossoms would last only for about eight years, however, as an economic recession must ensue. This evil could be remedied only by creating living space for the surplus population. However, the western powers would not let us do this. Therefore, short, decisive blows to the west and then to the east could be necessary.'[39] Again, the reception to such remarks was cool, if not unbelieving. Von Weichs noted: '. . . one did not take at face value these war-like prophecies, which were certainly in sharp contradiction to the protestations of peace which otherwise filled the air. The soldier was accustomed not to take the words of politicians too seriously. They often chose points of view which did not have to correspond with their true intentions, in order to achieve political ends. Thus these gloomy prognostications were probably soon forgotten.'[40] But Hitler did not forget them, nor the silence of his generals.

Despite von Weichs' complacency, there was by now growing disquiet over the new Chancellor's foreign policy. On 14 October 1933 he had surprised and shocked his generals by announcing, unbeknown even to von Blomberg, Germany's withdrawal from the League of Nations and from the Geneva disarmament conference. While German diplomats were fairly sure that no counter-action would be taken by the French, the Army leadership was alarmed to read in secret orders prepared by Hitler that the Führer was quite ready to defend the Reich's borders against expected League's sanctions. As the generals knew only too well, the German Armed Forces were totally inadequate to meet these. Moreover, the fact that Hitler was prepared to run such a risk without even consulting them, quite unnerved them. This was followed ninety days later by an unexpected and dangerous development in German policy in the east. The response of the Chancellor to the threat posed to Germany by a preventive war undertaken by Poland, plans for which were known to exist in early 1933, was to reverse the foreign policy that had formed the basis of the Army's strategic thinking since the early 1920s. On 26 January 1934, Hitler signed a ten-year non-aggression pact with the Poles, and, as a consequence, the German-Soviet military pact of 1926 was allowed to lapse. The implications for the Army and the nation of abandoning the distant friendliness of Germany for the Soviet Union, and embarking on a line of rapprochement with Poland, were considerable. Not only was this pact distasteful to the generals, who continually echoed von Seeckt's pronouncement that 'Poland's existence is intolerable and incompatible with the survival of Germany.... With Poland collapses one of the strongest pillars of the Peace of Versailles, France's advance post of power';[41] it was also dangerous, for it would lead eventually to conflict with the USSR and—if, as seemed likely, that country were joined by the western powers (France and Czechoslovakia at the very least)—to a war on two fronts. Thus, in both the west and the east, it appeared to the Army that Hitler was courting disaster, with Germany lacking totally the military capacity with which to guarantee the success of his policies.

The first open conflict between Hitler and the Army came over the question of the military reoccupation of the Rhineland. Both regarded this as necessary for securing the vital strategic, economic, and communications centers of the Ruhr and the Rhine valley, but there their agreement ended. In March 1936 Hitler believed the time to be opportune for such a move, while his generals feared the worst. It was inconceivable to them that Britain and France would not resist such a violation of their foreign policy, one that was in direct contradiction not only to the provisions of the Versailles Treaty and the Locarno Pact, but also to the continued security of France and the stability of Europe. There had been warnings that, if such a reoccupation were attempted, both France and Britain would act; Germany would be hopelessly outnumbered and ill-prepared for a war, and would have to concede to the Allies' demands. Her emerging political strength would then be halted, her rearmament policy shattered. Hitler, however, took no heed of his generals' warnings and pressed ahead with his plans, basing all hopes of success on a gigantic bluff which would test the willingness of the signatories to the Locarno Pact to act. He believed they would not move. His generals thought differently; Jodl described the atmosphere in the General Staff at that time as 'like that of a roulette table when a player stakes his fortune on a single number.'[42] The military advisers made efforts to have their alternative policies accepted; Beck even submitted a solution to Hitler, designed to allay Allied fears, which proposed that the occupation should be accompanied by an undertaking that the Rhineland would not be fortified. Von Blomberg, on behalf of the General Staff, suggested that a bargain be made with the French whereby, in return for the Germans withdrawing their few battalions after the occupation, the French, for their part, should withdraw four or five times as many from their borders. But all opposition came to nought. On 2 March von Blomberg issued the directive for the reoccupation entitled *Winterübung* (Winter Exercise), to be followed a few days later by the date of Z day, which was set for the 7th.

At first, only three battalions of German infantry were sent across the Rhine on that day, to a jubilant reception, although by the afternoon four divisions had been raised from the well-trained *Landespolizei* of the demilitarised zone. Hitler later recorded: 'The forty-eight hours after the march . . . were the most nerve-racking in my life. If the French had then marched into the Rhineland we would have had to withdraw with our tails between our legs.'[43] But the Führer held fast to his intentions; the French did not march; no one reacted. Nevertheless, the generals were far from confident, and on 9 March, at the behest of von Fritsch and Beck, a panicky von Blomberg urged Hitler to withdraw the troops from Aachen, Trier, and Saarbrücken for fear of a strong French attack. On that day the Führer's military adjutant was summoned no less than three times to the War Minister in order to impress on Hitler the urgency of the situation, only for the dictator to dismiss these requests and, after a tense meeting with his Minister, declare that von Blomberg possessed weak nerves. He later compared him to a 'hysterical maiden.'[44]

These hesitations and fears expressed so forcibly to Hitler over the Rhineland reoccupation, however reasonable they might have been, proved fatal to the future relationship between the Führer and his generals. Hitler had proved to his own satisfaction that his will-power and intuition were immeasurably superior to the combined professional expertise of his military advisers, a 'fact' which he was often to use later in justification of his acts. More important, he was convinced that, in the field of foreign adventure, his generals were not the compliant creatures he wished for, instead holding ideas far more cautious than, and in direct contradiction to, his own. This was the beginning of a disillusionment which in 1941 he expressed thus: 'Before I became Chancellor I thought the General Staff was like a mastiff which had been held tight by the collar because it threatened all and sundry. Since then I have had to recognise that the General Staff is anything but that. It has consistently tried to impede every action that I have thought necessary. . . . It is I who have always had to goad on this mastiff.'[45]

The generals' reluctance to countenance an aggressive foreign policy became ever more apparent to Hitler. Von Manstein remembered that 'It was the War Minister, von Blomberg, who first opposed general conscription. . . . It was also von Blomberg who at the time of the march into the Rhineland advised Hitler . . . to recall the German garrisons from the left bank of the river when the French ordered a partial mobilisation.'[46] On 15 March 1935, von Blomberg distinguished himself at a cabinet meeting by being the only person present to speak out against rearmament. This continued to concern him for a long time to come. As Keitel, von Reichenau's successor as Chief of the Ministerial Office, wrote later: 'What we and von Blomberg earnestly feared at the time was the possibility of sanctions of which we had become aware from Italy's Ethiopian campaign [which began on 5 October 1935]; they continued to hang over us like the Sword of Damocles all the time our rearmament programme was still only at the organisational stage; it must be remembered that we no longer had even a seven-division army on a war-footing, as it had been split up throughout the Reich since 1 October 1935 to provide the nuclei for the formation of the new thirty-six division army.'⁴⁷ For such reasons von Blomberg took great exception to German involvement in the Spanish Civil War, which lasted from mid-1936 to March 1939. As General Warlimont recorded: 'It is . . . not generally known that . . . he [von Blomberg] had been so vigorous in his opposition to increased involvement of the Army in the Spanish Civil War that it was hardly necessary for the Commander-in-Chief of the Army to intervene.'⁴⁸ Indeed, von Blomberg was generally expressing his dissatisfaction openly, without too much regard for who heard of it. He was active against the demands of Göring for his Air Force; he was critical of von Ribbentrop, a man well-regarded by Himmler, when ambassador to London; and he was contemptuous of the Italian Army, something that upset both the head of the Luftwaffe and the chief of the SS. Unfortunately, however, von Blomberg had weakened his position when, in August 1935, he sent his closet confidant, von Reichenau, to command Wehrkreis VII, hoping thereby to give his junior additional experience in troop command in preparation for his eventual succession to the post of War Minister. In his place, von Blomberg chose Wilhelm Keitel, an easy-going, efficient subordinate, but one who lacked the personality to provide any kind of driving force for new ideas, or for opposition to the Führer's policies.

The next direct confrontation between Hitler and his military advisers occurred on 5 November 1937, at a conference at the Reich Chancellery attended by the War and Foreign Ministers and the heads of the three services. Hitler repeated the basic principles of his future policy: 'The only, perhaps dreamlike solution as it appears to us, lies in winning a greater amount of living space, an endeavour which at all times has been the cause of the building of states and of the movement of peoples.'[49] Germany would have to begin this outward movement by 1943 at the latest, for by that time her war capacity might be declining relative to that of her future enemies, and the pressure of population and economics would force direct action. If the western powers would not permit this move east, they would have to be dealt with first. History had proved that such expansion as was an essential for Germany's survival could not be achieved without risk or force. It remained only to ask 'when?' and 'how?' Hitler's adjutant, Friedrich Hossbach, records the generals' reaction, one first of astonishment and then of objection:

> 'The discussion took a very sharp form at times, above all in the differences between Blomberg and Fritsch on the one hand, and Göring on the other, and Hitler participated mainly as an attentive observer.... I do remember exactly that the sharpness of the opposition, both in content and in form, did not fail to make its impression on Hitler, as I could see from his changing expressions. Every detail of the conduct of Blomberg and Fritsch must have made plain to Hitler that his policies had met with only direct impersonal contradictions, instead of applause and agreement. And he knew very well that both generals were opposed to any warlike entanglement provoked from our side. It is a sin of omission before history on my part that the opinions of Blomberg and Fritsch at the conference

of 5 November 1937 have not been recorded in greater detail....'[50]

At best, both feared that Hitler underestimated the strength of the Czech defences, and at worst they could see nothing but disaster in any conflict in which Britain and France were Germany's enemies. On 9 November, the anniversary of the abortive Munich putsch, von Fritsch again attempted to persuade Hitler of the unpalatable military realities of the course of action he proposed, but to no avail. Such was the Führer's anger at being thus opposed, that afterwards he refused to see von Neurath, the Foreign Minister and von Fritsch's ally on this question, until mid-January 1938. Von Blomberg, however, despite his fundamental disagreement with Hitler, which was expressed in such an unexpectedly severe manner on 5 November, proceeded, as was his duty, to carry out his Supreme Commander's wishes, ordering his staff to revise the plans for the invasion of Czechoslovakia, *Aufmarsch Grün*, so that they would correspond more closely with the recently declared policy. On 13 December, von Blomberg gave Hitler a report on the military preparations in which he laid great emphasis on Germany's inability to wage war and the inadequacies of the Armed Forces, especially in their reserves of ammunition. Warlimont wrote later that 'his real reason for stressing this factor was undoubtedly opposition to this dangerous type of policy.'[51] Furthermore, Beck, fully aware of Hitler's intentions, drew up a memorandum in which he contradicted every one of the military, political, economic, and moral bases of the Führer's plans.

By the beginng of 1938, then, Hitler had become

thoroughly disillusioned with his 'mastiff.' He made one further attempt to obtain the voluntary assent of the military at a meeting on 22 January at the War Ministry, directing his appeal over the heads of von Blomberg, von Fritsch, and Beck to the senior Army officers. But he was so unsure of his audience that his speech was badly delivered and his reception was unenthusiastic. Talk of the replacement of Christianity by National Socialism, of the serious plight of the Reich being solvable only by the acquisition of living space, of the domination of the world by pure-blooded nations, made little impact on the assembled generals. Frustrated abuse aimed at the audience, castigating them for their reactionary nature and their lack of foresight and positive thinking, produced nothing but antipathy. At the end, Hitler was aware he had failed to win the voluntary consent to the policies he so earnestly desired.

5

Crisis

The German officer has an abundance of pride and honour. But what use is that in these uncertain times? Politics now dominates all.

                      GENERAL LUDWIG BECK
                      Chief of the General Staff, 1933-38

By 1938, it was clear that Hitler's senior generals, who had always afforded him the loyalty owed to a legally constituted Head of State and Supreme Commander, and who had voluntarily allowed National Socialist ideology to enter the Army, were opposing the fundamentals of his future policy. Worse still, it was on their professional expertise that the success of this policy was based. Not unnaturally, Hitler's consternation, and irritation, must have been immense, although there is no evidence of any plan to rid himself of such opposition. Relations between the politician and the soldier in the Third Reich were at a stage when, in democracies, resignations would be obligatory and, in dictatorships, purges begun. The problem for Hitler, however, was not what to do—that, surely, was clear; it was how to do it. How could he eliminate the obstructions of his generals without bringing on himself the undying enmity of the instrument on which he was to rely for the success of his aims? Indeed, would not such action carry with it the very real risk of inducing an armed reaction from the Army? Was it, then, possible to get rid of his opponents at all? Contrary to the assertions of historians, the Führer was quite unprepared to take action against them. But, at this point fortune intervened, presenting to Hitler the solution of his dilemma. It took the murky guise of an unfortunate marriage to a prostitute, a case of mistaken identity with a homosexual, and the overweening ambition of two of the Führer's most ruthless political subordinates.

By 1938 the Army had reached a position broadly similar to that of the SA in 1934: both could be considered as the most powerful organisations within the National Socialist state; both were independent of the Party leadership; both were the objects of jealousy and ambition; and, most crucial of all, both had forfeited Hitler's confidence. The SS had intrigued against the Army since 1934, Himmler and his associates seeing it not only as the one important section of German society remaining free from their influence and control, but also as a powerful check to their military ambitions, then finding expression in the establishment of the SS-VT. Göring, in his capacity of Commander-in-Chief of the Luftwaffe, had long considered the generals as his rivals. He was angered by their limitation of the size and role of his Air Force, and resentful of their condescending treatment. Von Fritsch had once accused him of being a dilettante! Von Blomberg and von Fritsch made him feel small; he was their junior and, worse still, they blocked his path to the coveted post of War Minister. Consequently, at the beginning of 1938, powerful forces around Hitler were ranged against the Army leaders. All that was required was the pretext on which to act decisively.

Von Blomberg was the first to toss his fate unwittingly to fortune. On 12 January 1938, the widowed War Minister married Erna Grühn, a shorthand typist from the Reich Egg Marketing Board, who was already pregnant with his child. How von Blomberg first met her was a mystery—possibly it had been on one of his jaunts to Berlin's night-club area—but clearly he was aware that she was a girl 'with a past.' But the past, unbeknown to him, included prostitution and posing for pornographic photographs. Such a revelation, should it become public, would utterly ruin von Blomberg's career. As it was, his marriage to a mere typist outraged the officer corps; should she turn out to be a prostitute as well, his resignation or dismissal would be inevitable.

While Field-Marshal and Frau von Blomberg were happily on their honeymoon, a certain Curt Hellmuth Muller of the Reichskriminalpolizei was engaged in identifying lewd pin-up females, when he came across a photograph of the unclad body of the War Minister's wife. A further search revealed that she appeared in police records for morality crimes. From there the file on Frau von Blomberg quickly found its way onto Keitel's desk via the Berlin Police President, Count von Helldorf. But Keitel, an old friend and confidant of von Blomberg, whose daughter his son was to marry, refused to take any responsibility for the information now in his possession, and pleaded that, as he had not seen the woman in question, von Helldorf should take the matter to Göring, who, with Hitler, had acted as witness to the wedding. This the Police President undertook to do, little knowing what the result would be. The move was fatal: Göring now held the means by which to destroy his rival, and thereby to advance his own position. To secure von Blomberg's dismissal, however, was not enough; he must assure himself of the succession. Von Fritsch, the senior general in the Armed Forces, and a brilliant soldier, was von Blomberg's natural successor, and his appointment to the War Ministry would have been consistent with the tradition of installing an Army officer as the Head of State's highest military adviser. But Göring already had at hand the means by which von Fritsch could be eliminated. He had planned a brilliant double-stroke against the military leadership; one, to all outward appearances, based not on dubious political motives but on moral principles. Hitler would not refuse; the generals could not object; the public would applaud; and Göring would become War Minister. It was all so simple.

Von Fritsch's hostage to fortune was, like von Blomberg's, sexual, but, unlike the War Minister's, totally without foundation. As a middle-aged man who had never married, he was an easy target for charges of homosexuality. Both Himmler and Heydrich were eager to exploit such an opportunity, and in August 1936 had placed before the Führer an eight-page document purporting to prove von Fritsch a homosexual. Hitler, however, sensing instinctively that the allegation was utter nonsense (as did all who knew von Fritsch) and that it must have been based on false evidence (which it was), dismissed it out of hand and ordered the file to be burnt. The case of the SS revolved around a statement made under interrogation in 1935 by one Otto Schmidt, a labourer of many previous convictions who specialised in the petty blackmail of homosexuals. One cold evening in November 1933 in Berlin, near the Wannsee Station, Schmidt had witnessed a homosexual act between a man with a monocle and a youth. Masquerading as a detective he had ascertained the man's name and title from his identity card. It was, he remembered, General von Fritsch. Schmidt then proceeded to blackmail the man for a couple of thousand reichsmarks. Such was the substance of the allegation against the Army's Commander-in-Chief, and it was this that Göring had asked to be reconsidered in mid-December 1937. This was no idle speculation on the part of the Air Force Commander; his interest in the matter followed hard on von Blomberg's visit to him to ask for advice concerning his proposed marriage to Erna Grühn, when the War Minister had pointed out that not only was she a child of the people but that she also possessed a 'certain,' undefined past.

Now began between Göring and Himmler an unholy alliance whose sole object was the downfall of the Army's leaders and, thereby, an end to the indepence of the military. The Gestapo, who had long had von Fritsch under surveillance, keeping his file up to date, initiated a watch on Erna Grühn and detailed two agents to shadow the Army Commander on his trip to Egypt. The trap was set; all that was required was positive proof against von Blomberg. This arrived with von Helldorf on Saturday 22 January, 1938, and, on the 24th, Göring, weeping crocodile tears and lamenting his role as the bearer of bad tidings, placed the allegations against Germany's two principal generals on Hitler's desk.

There can be no doubt that the evidence against his chief military advisers hit Hitler hard. While he was clearly dissatisfied with his generals, he was totally unprepared for this blow, and, although he probably never believed the charges against von Fritsch, the scandal concerning von Blomberg's marriage bitterly revolted him. He had attended the wedding as a witness and had even shaken the bride's hand. One of his aides, Wiedemann, wrote: '... thoughout the whole four years during which I served him, I have never seen him so downcast. He paced slowly up and down his room, bent and with his hands behind his back, mumbling that if a German Field-Marshal could do something like this, then anything in the world was possible.'[1] General von Rundstedt found the Führer 'in a fearful state of excitement such as I had never seen before. Something had cracked in him; he had lost all confidence in men.'[2] Hitler was thrown off balance, and was as yet unaware of the opportunity fate had presented him.

Indeed, it took him some time to grasp the potential of what has come to be known as the 'Blomberg–Fritsch affair.' His shock, hesitation, and indecision are proof enough that he was completely unprepared for the replacement of his generals. It is evidence, too, of his hitherto well-intentioned attitude towards them. Deviousness was lacking completely. Hitler was not even convinced immediately of the necessity of his War Minister's dismissal, and at first thought of a divorce as the answer to the problem. But Göring's machinations continued, his most effective ruse being not to inform von Blomberg of the extent of the charges brought against him, thereby ensuring Hitler's rage at what he took to be the War Minister's inability to comprehend the heinous nature of his offence. Göring then emphasised the outrage of those in the officer corps who were aware of the scandal, an outrage expressed later by Beck who declared that the Field-Marshal was not fit to command a regiment, and that he must straightway divorce his new wife or else be struck off the officer list. In any event, his career as War Minister was finished. It was bad enough that Germany's highest-ranking general should have married a typist; it was unthinkable that she should turn out to be a prostitute too. It was an insult to the very tradition of the officer corps, an affront to its honour, and a weakening of its prestige. Furthermore it would provide the Party with a subject for much criticism and mirth. To bring home to the generals the enormity of the whole affair, prostitutes throughout Germany were constantly phoning them to announce the elevation of one of their members. Von Fritsch was one of the few to take a calmer view, preferring to wait until his superior's guilt was proven, while all the time the clouds were gathering over his own future.

But, although as last convinced of the need for dismissal, Hitler had no thought of taking over von Blomberg's position himself. Indeed, from 24 to 26 January, the day of the removal, Hitler spent much time searching for a successor. On the morning of the 26th, for example, on hearing from Hossbach of von Fritsch's complete rejection of the homosexuality charges, Hitler declared with an air of relief: 'Why, then things are in order and von Fritsch can become Minister.'[3] The Army adjutant, however, replied that von Fritsch had no wish to have this honour bestowed on him, and the discussion turned to other possibilities. Finally Hitler seized on the idea of having the elderly Count von Schülenberg as his new Minister, a 'safe' man with a distinguished war record, who, as a Party supporter, held high honorary ranks in both the SA and SS. Von Schülenberg was even ordered to attend on the Führer in expection of his appointment. Later that same morning, having informed von Blomberg of his dismissal, Hitler, still valuing his ex-Minister's advice on such matters, asked him to nominate a likely successor, excluding von Fritsch. The former War Minister suggested Göring as the most senior of those remaining, but Hitler would not for one moment entertain the idea, von Blomberg later recalling that he made 'one or two unpleasant remarks about Göring; he was too easy going—the word idle may even have been used—and in any case there was no question of him.'[4] (Hitler had already firmly decided on this point, having told his aide, Wiedemann, the day before that there was 'No question of it. That fellow Göring does not understand even how to carry out a Luftwaffe inspection.')[5] But who else? Perhaps out of spite for his former military colleagues whom he believed were now treating him so badly, or perhaps even because he genuinely believed it, von Blomberg suggested that Hitler himself should take over the post of War Minister and Commander-in-Chief of the Armed Forces. To this, Hitler made no reply.

This advice of von Blomberg was among the most significant ever given in the short history of the Third Reich, and certainly was of immense importance to the future of the Army. Hitler was presented with the solution to his problems with the military leaders, a solution which, in his five years of office, he had never seen fit to even contemplate, let alone scheme for seizing the opportunity. He immediately gave up the search for other men. The new direction his mind took was indicated by his next question to von Blomberg: whom could he suggest to head the staff? Obtaining no satisfactory answer, Hitler asked him who was in charge of his own staff. Von Blomberg replied that it was Keitel, but added 'He's nothing but the man who runs my office.' Hitler recognised immediately that he had found a man who would be an efficient *chef de bureau,* and at the same time totally subservient to his leader, possessing no independent ideas of his own. 'That's exactly the man I am looking for,'[6] the director exclaimed, and with that, von Blomberg, having performed his greatest service for his Führer and his greatest disservice to the Army, disappeared into oblivion.

During the meeting with von Blomberg, there had been no trace of bitterness on Hitler's part. Jodl was told by Keitel that the Führer had discharged the unpleasant duty of dismissal with 'superhuman kindness' and that he had even given the Field-Marshal the promise, unfulfilled as it turned out, that 'as soon as Germany's hour comes, you shall be at my side.'[7] Hitler had told von Blomberg that he should go into voluntary exile from Germany for a year while the storm blew over, and that for this the Reichsbank would be directed to give him 50,000 reichsmarks in foreign exchange. Furthermore, as was the tradition for field-marshals, von Blomberg would continue to draw full salary and, nominally, remain on the active list. Hitler even summoned him to the Reich Chancellery for the last time on the morning of 27 January to wish him well before his exile to Italy.

For the rest of his life, von Blomberg remained faithful to his wife, only once giving any indication that he would be prepared to renounce her for a return to active duty. But till the end he was ostracised by his fellow generals, even when he lay dying in captivity after the Second World War. Surprisingly, it was Hitler who did most to ensure that his former War Minister lived out the rest of his life peacefully, and he never gave in to the Army's demand that the Field-Marshal should be brought before a specially constituted Court of Honour, the verdict of which would have been predictable and, moreover, would only have strengthened Hitler's position.

Von Blomberg's suggestion to Hitler on the morning of the 26th not only undermined the semi-autonomous position of the Army within the Reich; it also sealed von Fritsch's fate. Till then Hitler had been undecided about his Army Commander, telling Hossbach that he was aware of von Fritsch's great services and had no desire to part with him. Von Fritsch sensed this, believing the Führer would realise the allegations were false and punish their perpetrators, Göring and Himmler. With Hitler, remembering the SS attack on von Fritsch in 1936, far from convinced of his guilt, there was some justification for this hope, though it turned out to be unrealised. Furthermore, the firmness and confidence with which many of the military dismissed the evidence as false did not fail to impress the Führer. However, von Blomberg's suggestion, with all its potential, far outweighted such feelings. Now he possessed within his grasp not just the nominal control of the Wehrmacht, but its actual direction as well; he could ensure it would provide no opposition to his policies in the future. For this to become a reality, though, it was vital to have a compliant Army Commander. Von Fritsch had to go, and on what better pretext than homosexuality. Could not people believe such a charge of the bachelor Army Commander? Furthermore, if von Fritsch were removed for such a reason it would, Hitler believed, avoid any interpretation that the dismissal arose from a clash of personalitites or from his own ambition to humble his military advisers.

As a result, by the afternoon on 26 January, Hitler, without any further provocation or proof, had set himself firmly against von Fritsch; by early evening he had decided that legal action would be taken against his Army Commander, not by the usual form of a military tribunal, but by a special court under the auspices of the Gestapo. There was to be no chance of von Fritsch avoiding conviction. Immediately after this decision, Hitler saw Keitel and told him that, whatever happened, he wanted a new Army Commander. Later that day, in his last act renouncing von Fritsch, Hitler called him to the Reich Chancellery, and at the meeting Göring and Himmler seized the opportunity to illustrate their allegations in a most startling manner. The blackmailer Schmidt was produced to identify von Fritsch in Hitler's presence, and the Army chief, confronted so unexpectedly by his accuser, became inarticulate with rage, a show of emotion which did much to lower him in the Führer's eyes. Göring was so well-satisfied with the outcome of the incident that all he could do was collapse on a sofa shrieking: 'He did it, he did it.'[8] Hitler asked von Fritsch for his resignation 'for reasons of health,' but this was refused, and the Führer had to wait another four days before it was given.

The trial of von Fritsch opened more than a month

later, on Thursday 10 March, with proceedings suspended for a week owing to the occupation of Austria. On the 18th the court returned the verdict of 'acquitted on the grounds of proven innocence.' Thus, despite all his attempts to direct the course of events against von Fritsch, even by the appointment of Göring as court president, Hitler was unable to prevent a few intrepid men, led by Count von der Goltz, the defence counsel, and Dr. Carl Sack, the official attorney, from demonstrating that the accusation was false. They proved that, from almost the beginning, the Gestapo had been aware that the accusation was based on a case of mistaken identity; that the man Schmidt blackmailed was not the Army Commander, von Fritsch, but a retired Army captain called von Frisch, who even spelt his name differently; and that Himmler, Heydrich, and their subordinates had done all in their power to hide these facts. Only Göring, through his clever manoeuvrings, escaped open condemnation.

In the particular battle that revolved around the specific issue of von Fritsch's innocence, the Army triumphed over the Party. But in the generals' wider, and more serious, conflict against political interference, the military were soundly beaten. On 4 February the two new Commanders-in-Chief of the Armed Forces and the Army were announced, as well as a radical reorganisation of the high command structure. The new Commander of the Wehrmacht was Hitler. On that day the subjection of the German Army to the will of the Führer began.

Why did the Army not take direct action during the 'Fritsch crisis' to preserve its traditional autonomy and prestige? As von Fritsch himself noted bitterly: 'No nation ever allowed the Commander-in-Chief of its Army to be subjected to such a disgraceful treatment. . . . Such treatment is not only undignified for me, at the same time it dishonours the whole Army.'[9] If its leaders were reluctant to act against Hitler because, despite all, they still maintained their previously justified belief in his good intentions towards them, could they not have moved against the evil influences surrounding him and perverting his judgement? It would not have been the first occasion in history when men had sought to save a ruler from his advisers. At that time, a united Army taking concerted action throughout the nation would almost certainly have been successful. Its only opponents would have been the Luftwaffe, still in its infancy and vulnerable to surprise occupation of the airfields, and the SS, which then possessed only 10,000 men under arms. Moreover, there were strong indications that, had the Army taken the initiative, the SA, then numbering some two and a half million men, would have joined it to exact revenge on their hated SS rivals for the events of 30 June 1934. In the event the crisis passed; the Army made no move.

At first glance it appears that such inaction was inexcusable on the part of the Army's leaders, fully justifying their condemnation by historians. Wheeler-Bennett wrote: 'The Fritsch–Blomberg crisis awakened many to the realisation of their true position, but of that many there were all too few who were prepared to take action in the cause of their own emancipation. The majority—some because of ambition, some because of the fatal mystic spell of their own oath of loyalty, some through fear—elected to continue to support the Führer, to submit to the dictates of his "intuition" and to follow in his train.'[10] But this judgement implies a certain freedom of action possessed by the military leaders which, in reality, was not available to them. The Army found itself unable to react otherwise than submissively, despite the aggressive intentions of a few of its members; once again, it was the prisoner of its heritage.

It should not be forgotten that, for most of the officers, the Blomberg–Fritsch affair was characterised only by their complete ignorance of the events. Such was the veil of secrecy surrounding the dismissals that, outside Berlin, few officers had even the slightest indication before the beginning of February of the troubles besetting their leadership. Colonel Warlimont, for example, then an artillery regiment commander at Düsseldorf, heard not a hint of the momentous decisions being taken until Hitler's announcement on 4 February, and even by the autumn, when he was in an important post in the newly formed Armed Forces High Command, he was not much better informed. Indeed, many of those who turned up to hear the Führer deliver his speech on the 4th had heard of the reorganisation only through the morning's papers. In short, the officer corps as a whole was presented with a fait accompli of which it knew little or nothing of the facts that lay behind it. As General Guderian remarked, 'blame can be apportioned only to the few individuals in authority at the top,' because for 'the majority, the true state of affairs remained obscure.'[11]

What, then, of the Army leadership referred to by Guderian? Why did it make no attempt to thwart Hitler's moves? The reasons are not hard to discern. As has been shown, the officer corps possessed none of the political experience and expertise with which to comprehend and counter the skilful machinations of the Führer during that particular period. As Westphal remarked: 'For centuries Germans had never had to suffer an internal tyranny, such as other countries had often experienced, and the Prusso-German Army had never placed itself at the disposal of a revolution. Only one famous rebel had ever risen in its ranks, General von Yorck; and he had revolted only against foreign domination.'[12] Nor were the generals personally equipped for rebellion. This, the Italian ambassador, Attolico, recognised: 'The Germans are not given to conspiracy. A conspirator needs everything they lack: patience, knowledge of human nature, psychology, tact. . . . To fight conditions here, you ought to be persevering and a good dissembler like Talleyrand and Fouché. Where will you find a Talleyrand between Rosenheim and Eydtkuhnen?'[13]

The naïvety of the generals is perhaps best illustrated by Guderian's reactions. After the Second World War he referred to 4 February as 'the second blackest day of the Army High Command' (the first, he believed, was 30 June 1934), and went on to record that 'The Fritsch case did prove the existence of a serious lack of trust between the Head of the Reich and the leaders of the Army; I was aware of this, though I was not in a position to understand what lay behind it all.'[14] This, however, contrasts strongly with what he wrote at the time. In a letter to his wife written on 7 February, Guderian stated categorically: 'The report to Hitler has provided me with the insight into things which would better not have happened. The Führer has acted, as usual, with the finest human decency. It is to be hoped that he will be approved by his colleagues.'[15] Other generals were equally credulous. They simply could not believe that Hitler, the friend and ally of the Army in the struggles against Party interference, could have turned so suddenly, and so bitterly, against his military advisers. The reversal of his attitude was too complete, and too sudden, to comprehend. As Guderian recalled: 'These serious allegations against our most senior officers, whom we knew to be men of spotless honour, cut us to the quick. They were quite incredible, and yet our immediate reaction was that the first magistrate of the German state could not simply have invented these stories out of thin air.'[16]

The general feeling was that, at worst, the Führer was the dupe of an SS intrigue, and that, once the facts were known, a full and proper rehabilitation of the former Army Commander would take place. Even von Fritsch himself had no other thought except that Hitler was acting only out of ignorance of the truth. As he later recounted: 'Yet if I had known how wholly this man is without scruple and how he gambles with the fate of the German people, I should have acted differently and taken on myself the odium of having acted through egotistic motives.'[17] As it was, von Fritsch, the one central figure in the crisis around whom the Army would have rallied, refused to take any decision. He was no political general and was incapable of acting like one; he saw the matter primarily as a personal attack on him by the Party, in accordance with past events, and had no intention of causing bloodshed for his own sake alone.

A highly sensitive man, von Fritsch was in such a state of shock at the enormity of the charges against his person that he was rendered unable to take action, whether or not he believed it correct to do so; indeed, so submissive was he, that he even gave himself to Gestapo interrogation, and unheard of thing for an Army officer to do.

Beck, as Chief of the General Staff, was perhaps the only other man in a position to speak for the Army, but he was inhibited by his sense of duty, his decision to await events, and his belief in the importance of maintaining his position as a counterbalance to Hitler and his associates in the controversy over foreign policy. Furthermore, the strain on Beck was immense: his health was failing and now he had added to his already strenuous duties those of Acting Commander-in-Chief until 4 February. Gerd von Rundstedt, too, the senior Army general after von Fritsch, a most respected man who was far from being full of ardour for National Socialism, declared that he was quite assured of Hitler's (and Göring's!) sincerity and good intentions. So convinced was he that everything was satisfactory that he purposely failed to present von Fritsch's challenge of a duel to Himmler, an occasion which might have given an opportunity for wider action against the SS.

An even greater impediment to concerted Army action came from the new Army Commander-in-Chief, von Brauchitsch. For personal reasons he was the creature of his master, Adolf Hitler, and his acceptance of the post before von Fritsch's trial implied recognition and approval of the Führer's actions. His equivocal attitude towards the whole affair made it impossible for the Army to present a united front, and his only positive action during the whole period was to protest against the Gestapo's intrusion into Army barracks to interview former servants of von Fritsch. After von Fritsch's innocence had been proved, von Brauchitsch refused to lay before Hitler demands from certain senior officers calling for a reinstatement of von Fritsch, a public explanation of why he had been forced to retire, and several changes in senior SS and Gestapo appointments, including those of Himmler and Heydrich. This, too, was a missed opportunity which might have led to greater things. Nevertheless, whatever the personal and political shortcomings of these men, none of them possessed that degree of independence from his military heritage which enabled him to take decisive action against his legally constituted Head of State.

In the west, the reaction of an Army to the removal of its Commander-in-Chief had, traditionally, been one not of revolution but of obedience. Usually, every attempt was made to understand the reasons that lay behind the government's action. Indeed, the year before, Stalin had begun, unhindered, his great purges of the Red Army leadership that make Hitler's 1938 reorganisation look ridiculously mild in comparison; and the British Secretary of State for War had dismissed both the Chief of the Imperial General Staff and the Adjutant-General without fear of reaction. Few German officers would have questioned the legally constituted executive's authority in this sphere, and, certainly, von Fritsch had no quarrel with the principle. His oath of loyalty had been given. On 25 January, he declared as soon as he heard of the charges against him: 'If Hitler wants to get rid of me then he has only to say the word and I will resign.'[18] As it was, it took him four days to do so, but this was not because he disagreed with Hitler's right to order his dismissal, but because he found the method by which he had done so distasteful, and feared that his resignation would be taken as a confession of guilt. In the end, however, von Fritsch's overriding sense of duty guided his actions. Nor could Beck find any reason for overturning the authority of the state simply because it conflicted with the interests of the military establishment. Dissatisfied as he was with the turn events had taken, Beck nevertheless found himself forced to admit: 'Mutiny and revolution are words that do not exist in the lexicon of the German soldier.'[19]

After 26 January, Hitler's handling of the Fritsch crisis was brilliant, thoroughly confounding the politically inept generals. He made every effort to avoid any issue which would unnecessarily alarm the officer corps, cause it to close ranks and enter into a direct confrontation with himself. Therefore, he did not dismiss von Fritsch instantly but allowed him several days in which to decide to resign. He submitted to fierce military opposition to the idea of a special Gestapo court to try von Fritsch, and, instead, instituted a normal military Court of Honour, making every effort to convey the impression that the crisis was not of his making and that his sole desire was simply to render justice. Indeed, Hitler did all he could to allay military suspicion of his actions: to Beck, on 26 January, he promised that he would do nothing without first consulting him; to von Rundstedt he gave assurances as to the future integrity of the Army; and to the assembled generals, on 4 February, he declared that all talk of Himmler being the future Commander-in-Chief of the Armed Forces was nonsense (as, indeed, it was) and that at some future date this post might once again be occupied by a senior Army officer.

Furthermore, there were two major distractions, one connected with, the other external to, the crisis, that diverted the attention of the senior generals away from the crucial issues at stake. First, much effort was expended on the narrow 'details' of von Fritsch's trial, his innocence and rehabilitation, and, as Guderian noted: 'Even in [this] case ... which from the very beginning seemed not only improbable, but unthinkable, it was necessary to wait for the promulgation of the court's findings before any serious steps could be taken.'[20] Secondly, the preoccupation with the von Fritsch crisis was made to seem of little importance in the affairs of state in comparison with the momentous occupation of Austria decided on on 10 March and put into effect on 12–13 March. All thoughts were immediately turned from the postponed trial to the successful action; all eyes were now centred on the Führer in his latest glory. His popularity had never been greater; his position seemed unassailable; and the generals could bask in the reflected glory of his achievement. The best, and perhaps the only, time for action was over.

What if Germany's military leadership had been capable of ordering concerted action against Hitler and his advisors during the Fritsch crisis? Would the Army have obeyed? Some believed so. Captain Engel remembered: 'We in the Army have missed out on everything it was imperative to do. In February 1938 I was with the troops. The fury of the officers was tremendous. At that time the troops would still have obeyed us.'[21] A number advocated strong action, even force, in support of their Commander-in-Chief, including a few within the higher circles of military leadership—Halder, Beck's deputy, Hossbach, Hitler's military adjutant, von Hammerstein, the former Commander-in-Chief, Canaris, head of the Abwehr, and von Witzleben, Commander of the Wehrkreis covering the important Berlin area. Throughout the Army there was considerable feeling that things were going on that ought not be accepted. For example, General von Viehbahn was so horrified when he heard of the Gestapo interrogation of von Fritsch that he asserted that if the troops knew of it there would be a revolution—and he was far from being an ardent anti-National Socialist. It also seems quite clear that a number of units would have moved into action had they received orders to do so, among them the 9th Infantry Regiment at Potsdam, the 48th Infantry Regiment at Döberitz, the 2nd Panzer Regiment at Eisenbach, and the 9th Cavalry Regiment. The soldiers' antagonism towards the SS was considerable; Halder believed that all ranks would have risen against the 'black ones' had the word been given, and certainly the SS men themselves were terrified at the prospect of an Army revolt. One senior SS officer recorded: 'Before the sitting of the Court of Honour that was to try General von Fritsch, I was told to report to Heydrich and to arm myself with a service pistol and an ample supply of ammunition. . . . After dinner he [Heydrich] took a large number of aspirins. Then suddenly he said, without any preamble, "If they don't start marching from Potsdam during the next hour and a half, the greatest danger will have passed."'[22]

Others, however, have expressed themselves differently. They believed that neither the soldiers nor the nation would have risen against Hitler, and that only when the dictator had suffered a significant reverse, perhaps from England and France in war, would it have been the right psychological moment to strike. They also maintained that it was impossible to move solely against the SS, and that, from the beginning, it would have been a revolt against the person and the power of the Führer, because in the last resort Hitler stood or fell by the support of his Party and its organisations. Such is the view of men of the calibre of von Manstein, von

Manteuffel, Warlimont, Geyr von Schweppenburg, and Heusinger, as well as of von Fritsch. Even Hossbach later came to confess that he had been wrong in advocating force as a solution. By 1938, the political complexion of the Army had altered considerably. No longer was it the tightly knit body of professionals it had been in 1933; instead, it was a loosely structured formation, undergoing fast expansion, with several years of National Socialist indoctrination and political success behind it. Gone even was the homogeneity of the officer corps, which was in the process of experiencing what was to be a twenty-five-fold increase in number by 1939. National Socialist rearmament had opened up a career to talent and ambition, which had been recognised by the mass of new lieutenants, large numbers of whom had passed through the ranks of the Hitler Youth. The considerable expansion of the Army, and break-up of the old regiments during the reorganisation had particularly shattered the unity and the conservatism of the officer corps that had existed since the days of Frederick the Great, and which had formed the cornerstone of the Prusso-German military tradition. Gentlemen of the Imperial Army, former NCOs, Austrians, one-time police and SA officers, and young men fresh from the Hitler Youth rubbed shoulders one with another. Commanders complained that it was impossible to weld these heterogeneous elements together, a task which was made immeasurably more difficult by the continued expansion and reconstruction of units. 'Dilution' was the term used by the professional officers to describe the process. This is illustrated by the changing social composition of the officer corps. In the Reichsheer, the aristocracy on average had held twenty per cent of all commissions.

During the Weimar Republic the proportion of aristocrats among newly commissioned lieutenants rose from twenty-one per cent in 1922 to thirty-six per cent in 1932, and occupied sixty-one per cent of the generalships. By 1936, however, only some twenty-five per cent of generals were aristocrats, and during the war the top ranks came almost exclusively from the middle class. Although the aristocrats maintained their dominance in the *Generalfeldmarschälle*, the middle class composed twenty-one out of the twenty-six *Generalobersten* and one hundred and forty-six out of one hundred and sixty-six *Generäle der Infanterie*. Moreover, the reintroduction of conscription had brought the Army into close contact with, and dependence on, the masses, and the masses had, as yet, experienced only the benefits of National Socialism and none of its drawbacks. Gone were the days when, before 1933, the other ranks had been composed mainly of conservative peasants, and when the more radically minded townsmen were the exception. Conscription had made the Army truly representative of the people, and, as von Fritsch claimed: 'Ninety per cent of all Germans run after this man [Hitler].'[23] It also had to be considered what the Army would do after a successful revolt. For this it was totally unprepared, realising, as did von Fritsch, that 'It was not possible to rule a people like the Germans with bayonets,'[24] above all people who knew little of the generals, and had no enthusiasm for a coup, especially one which would overthrow their idol, Adolf Hitler. Obscurity and unpopularity were not the best qualifications for embarking upon a period of military rule, certainly one for which no preparations had been made.

Such, then, was the position of the Army leaders in

February and March 1938, the crucial period during which the German Army was subjected to Hitler's will. What else could they have done but submit to the dictates of their Führer? The generals did not possess the historians' advantage of hindsight, nor were they blessed with the political understanding and skill required to counter a man like Hitler. They were still as much the prisoners of their heritage as they ever had been: politically naïve, unaware of Hitler's true intentions, lacking the means to stop him, and constrained by their tradition of obedience to the Head of State. When to this is added the realisation that a majority of the soldiers would not have obeyed their orders to act against Hitler, it is understandable that the generals behaved as they did. Just as in 1933, it would have been remarkable had they done anything else.

For one group of Army officers, however, the Fritsch crisis had entailed a complete and lasting break with the traditions of the Army. For those men, it was now clear that opposition to Hitler through official, constitutional channels was impossible, and that only an underground conspiracy, prepared to use violence, would suceed in ending his menace to both Germany and the world. Before 1938 most of them, while being opposed to the Party, had wondered only how to control the Führer; now they sought to remove him altogether. Perhaps the first of the military conspirators was General Erwin von Witzleben. Born in December 1881 at Breslau, he served in the First World War as an infantry battalion commander and a General Staff officer, becoming commander of Wehrkreis III, which included Berlin, in February 1934. Although lacking the intellectual breadth of a man like

Beck, he was a good, unpretentious soldier with a fund of commonsense. To von Witzleben, National Socialism was an abomination, Hitler a national disaster, the military oath a crime. On this he was prepared to act. It did not need any crisis such as the Fritsch or the later Czechoslovak affairs to make him commit himself unreservedly to conspiracy. His first moves in this direction came in the summer of 1937, when he began organising a circle of associates perpared to assume the burden of opposition, prominent among whom was General Count Erich von Brockdorff-Ahlefeld, a divisional commander. Between them, these two men undertook a careful check of all officers in command of formations, perferably those strategically placed to mount an armed coup. By 1938 their efforts were beginning to show some reward.

At the same time as von Witzleben was forming his circle in the provinces, others were at work closer to the corridors of power. This conspiracy centred on the Abwehr, the German military intelligence (part of the Armed Forces High Command after 4 February 1938), and was due primarily to the convergence of three men: Admiral Wilhelm Canaris, Head of the Abwehr, Colonel Hans Oster, his deputy, and Hans Bernhard Gisevius, an official in the Reich Ministry of the Interior.

A career naval officer who had commanded a submarine for a period in the First World War, Canaris was forty-seven when he took command of the Abwehr. A small, unassuming man of variable temperament and strange phobias (he usually disliked robust men, for example), he possessed a quick brain and a remarkable ability to judge character. A master of dissimulation, he, alone of all opponents of Hitler, managed to conceal from the dictator his real feelings. His genuine and deep goodness and humanity led him to abhor, both emotionally and intellectually, every aspect of National Socialism. By 1937 he was convinced of the necessity for its downfall and had begun to make contact with others, especially corps intelligence officers throughout Germany. His toast at the dinner table among friends was: 'We are thinking of the Führer—to rid ourselves of him.'[25]

Oster was in many ways the opposite of his master, although they got on well together. Handsome, elegant, talkative, rash, a man of the world, he was born in 1888, the son of a Dresden cleric. Although he had been dismissed from the service because of a love-affair with the wife of a fellow officer, he was able to return to the Army in 1934 on the intercession of Halder, although he was never allowed to regain his former full General Staff status. Like that of Canaris, his opposition to the National Socialist régime was that of a right-wing nationalist. The third in the triumvirate was Gisevius, a big, impetuous man with strong likes and dislikes, who had been dismissed from the Gestapo because of his ill-concealed distaste for its methods. A friend of Oster, he shared with him a disgust for the SS and the gangster methods of the régime.

As time went on, the Abwehr group enlarged the number, and improved the nature, of its contacts. Prominent among them was Arthur Nebe, Chief of the Criminal Police Office and an associate of Heydrich, Count Wolf von Helldorf, Police President of Berlin and a former SA leader, Hjalmar Schacht, former Reich Minister of Economics, Erich Schultze, a close friend of Heydrich, and Carl Goerdler, Lord Mayor of Leipzig and former Reich Price Commissioner. Contact was made also with von Witzleben. The network was beginning to spread.

The Fritsch crisis, which lasted some six weeks, acted as a catalyst among opposition circles, and was especially important in consolidating the Abwehr group, strengthening its ties with other strands of dissatisfaction, and providing it with valuable experience, especially in matters of organisation. The whole affair showed the need, and provided the opportunity, for action against the régime. It was, however, a frustrating experience. All that the Abwehr group found itself able to do was to collect information vital for the defence of von Fritsch and the proving of his innocence, being quite unable to organise any form of resistance to the régime among the Army. There were a number of reasons for this. The Abwehr group by itself commanded no one and possessed negligible influence within the Army; it was, therefore, vital for it to have not just the support, but also the leadership, of senior officers of respected authority. Von Fritsch was the obvious choice, for he alone could count on a wide, even universal, response to his appeal for action, as, to a lesser extent, could Beck. But neither would move. Weeks were wasted in the vain hope that they would be persuaded that it was not merely their own future, but the fate of the nation, that was at stake. Neither, however, possessed insight enough for the role, and while the opposition waited expectantly, the opportunity for action slipped quietly by. Time was on Hitler's side.

What of von Witzleben, whose command of the forces around Berlin placed him in a better position than all other troop commanders? He was regarded as the only one who would have a full understanding of the issues at stake. But at this critical point, von Witzleben lay ill in a Dresden sanatorium. Thus, in order to circumvent what appeared to be near paralysis at the centre of military affairs, an attempt was made to gain support from the soldiers in the provinces. Selected corps commanders were visited to get them to put pressure on von Fritsch for action and, at the same time, to rouse their colleagues. Collective resignation by the twelve corps commanders was proposed, but came to nothing. Typical of the reaction from the generals was that of General Alexander Ulex, commander of the 11th Army Corps. Personally loyal to von Fritsch, devoted to the traditions of the Army, and suspicious of the National Socialists, he refused to take part in the movement to save his chief, using as his excuse the fact that it was impossible to attain a united front, as von Reichenau and Dollman, at the very least, among the corps commanders would support Hitler. Days later his troubled conscience forced him to remark: 'It is a great burden to me to have the feeling of having failed at the decisive moment.'[26] The most rewarding feature of the conspirators' work during this period, apart from producing the evidence that proved von Fritsch's innocence, was the growth of contacts. Many were brought within their network, including Beck who had become convinced that the Fritsch crisis had 'opened up a chasm between Hitler and the officer corps . . . which can never be closed again.'[27] Even more important for the future was the fact that Beck's deputy, Halder, had now joined the conspirators. The question was, could these men, a tiny minority in the Army and the nation, hope to achieve in the future what the military establishment had signally failed to attempt—the downfall of Adolf Hitler and the destruction of National Socialism?

The final act in the Fritsch affair revolved around the struggle for the former Army Commander's rehabilitation. The energy with which many generals pursued this matter exemplifies their inability to see the wood for the trees, thereby expending their effort on periphera, in this case the honour of von Fritsch, rather than on fundamentals such as the independence of the Army. On 30 March Hitler wrote to von Fritsch in a manner which appeared to express satisfaction at the outcome of the trial, but which contained no expression of apology for the affair. The Führer had no thought of rehabilitation; it was not in his nature to trouble himself for someone who had opposed him. It has been recorded by those close to him that Hitler used to become unpleasant and bitter as soon as von Fritsch's name was mentioned. The Army, however, felt differently, seeing the issue of their former Commander-in-Chief's rehabilitation as a question not simply of his personal integrity but of the honour and integrity of the officer corps as a whole. It would also be an indictment of the SS. The rehabilitation was seen as vital for the restoration of the traditional balance between the political and the military, a balance which had been lost, irretrievably as it turned out, during the crisis.

Pressure mounted: von Brauchitsch was so besieged by troubled officers urging him to exert his influence on Hitler that he was reduced at times to seeking refuge in the house of a cousin; the venerable Field-Marshal von Mackensen sent a barrage of letters and telegrams to Hitler and prominent Army officers; and Army commanders down to regimental level were continually beset by their troubled subordinates. By May it was becoming clear that the generals might stage a collective strike. General Ulex, repenting of his previous faint-heartedness, gave written notice of his resignation from the Army should von Fritsch not receive satisfaction. He was followed by General von Kluge, whose letter of intent, though it was suppressed by Keitel (an old regimental comrade), may well have been shown to Hitler as a warning of what might happen. Even General Eugen Ritter von Schobert, commander of Wehrkreis VII and one of the generals more devoted to Hitler, announced that he was contemplating resignation. By June, according to von Kluge, no fewer than twelve Wehrkreis commanders had threatened collective resignation if their 'sharp protest' to Hitler were not heeded. It was now clear that the time was approaching when decisive action must be taken. The only question was, who would take it? In the event it was Hitler, who, sensing the danger of allowing matters to drift further, realised it was vital to direct events to his advantage. This, by brilliant timing and a superb performance, is precisely what he achieved at a meeting on the afternoon of 13 June, when he addressed Army Corps and Wehrkreis commanders at Barth on the Pomeranian coast.

Hitler was helped considerably by von Brauchitsch. The ambivalent and pusillanimous Commander-in-Chief of the Army so far had successfully managed to ward off the strongest of the military protests without giving in. On the morning of the 13th he proved himself of further inestimable value by presenting his views on the rehabilitation issue to the assembled officers at Barth.

(Fortunately for him, Beck was not among them, for he would certainly have disagreed with what he had to say.) He stressed that the affair had caused him much concern, and that he had been on the point of resigning in protest at von Fritsch's treatment. By this he won his audience's sympathy; his next ploy was to shatter their nerve with a bombshell. The Führer, he informed them, had announced that there was to be an unavoidable military clash with Czechoslovakia in the near future. In such circumstances, when nothing less than national survival was in question, he could not honourably resign, and he begged his audience to follow his example. The generals were caught, off balance, on the horns of an apparently insoluble dilemma—military honour or national security.

Nor did Hitler give them time to resolve their difficulty for themselves. That same afternoon he stepped in and provided them with the solution, enabling them to reconcile the apparently irreconcilable and to set at rest their consciences. Hitler's performance was brilliant; to the Navy Commander-in-Chief, as well as to the majority of those present, he appeared 'unequivocal and convincing.'[28] Only to the few, like Ulex, who knew the intricacies of the affair, was it obvious that 'some things he concealed, some he distorted, on some he lied.'[29] In a masterful speech lasting for an hour and a half, full of pathos, Hitler played on his audience's emotions, hopes, and fears. He asked for their sympathy: he had been the victim of a shameless deception. He elaborated on the position in which the revelation of the charges against the Army Commander had placed him, charges that had shaken him to the very core, and that had been made worse by the confrontation of von Fritsch with his accuser Schmidt. He pointed out that his predicament had been made even more difficult by the man's complete exoneration 'as the result of a fortunate accident.'[30] He asked for their understanding: how could he combine compensation for von Fritsch's personal tragedy with reasons of state? For the Army's sake he had given 'bad health' as the reason for von Fritsch's retirement, and he could hardly disavow that now by contradiction. Was it not better that the public remained in ignorance of the whole sordid affair, for von Fritsch's sake as well as for the Army's? And in any case, he could not expect von Fritsch to work with him again after all that had happened. Therefore he had decided that, for the time being, the only possible way to rehabilitate the former Army Commander was to appoint him to the honorary colonelcy of his old artillery regiment, the 12th. In the future, he assured them, he would seek every way to indicate his respect for this 'irreproachable man of honour.'[31] He gave them hope: they could rest assured that such a thing would never happen again; any attack on the Armed Forces from outside their ranks would be out of the question; and changes in military personnel would be undertaken only for internal reasons and not under external pressure. He played on their vanity: he was waiting only for the next convocation of the Reichstag to compliment the Army on its fine performance during the occupation of Austria. He gave them blood: he had ordered the shooting of the blackmailer Schmidt, the real villain of the whole affair. And he concluded by asking for their support: he appealed to them not to abandon the service of the nation at such a critical time. Was not his entire confidence placed with the Wehrmacht? He begged them to place a similar trust in him. They did so.

Hitler had successfully convinced the majority of his generals of his good intention; at the very least he had shown them the need to stay at their posts. As Ulex said to a sceptical and discontented Beck: 'Neither you nor Brauchitsch can in the existing situation do anything else than stay.'[32] Von Fritsch found the honorary colonelcy offensive, believing it to be a deliberate slight; Beck was horrified at the frivolity of it all. But nevertheless, on 11 August, at the Gros Born exercise ground, von Fritsch was invested with his new appointment at an elaborate military ceremony presided over by von Brauchitsch. Hitler, unable to avoid a public congratulation, wrote a letter.

The promises made at Barth were soon forgotten. Von Fritsch received no further honour from his Führer, and his personal fate ceased to be an issue. Not for one moment did Hitler consider returning him to a post in the High Command. Instead, von Fritsch lived quietly in a house built for him by an Army subscription, attending the occasional military exercise, taking part in one or two hunts, and making rare visits to Berlin; he did little else. Retiring ever more within his shell, he became increasingly depressed at his treatment, at the same time resigning himself to his nation's future. His view is summed up in his oft-quoted phrase: 'This man [Hitler] is Germany's destiny for good or ill, and this destiny will run its course to the end; if it leads us into the abyss he will take us all with him—there is nothing to be done about it.'[33] Feeling strongly that he must share in his country's fate, he accompanied his regiment into the field against Poland, where, on 22 September 1939, he was struck dead by a sniper's bullet. A memorial was erected on the spot, only to be destroyed later in the war, as also was his grave. The news of his death was given to Hitler on the evening of the 22nd, when General Jodl began his daily report with the words: 'Today there fell one of the finest soldiers Germany has ever had, Generaloberst Baron von Fritsch.'[34] Hitler gave a start, but said nothing. He later refused to attend the funeral.

Even after his death, von Fritsch still maintained some influence. The veneration that the General Staff and the whole Army felt towards this man came once more to the fore, and the indignation about his ignominious treatment was revived. Hitler condemned the obituary that von Brauchitsch issued on the occasion, and personally supervised the details of all further ceremonies in von Fritsch's honour. The German General Staff, however, mourned a man whom it had never ceased to respect. Thereafter, General Staff officers who had been especially close to General von Fritsch were regarded with particular suspicion by the Führer—as, for instance, General von Funck, who was at least twice during the war kept out of important commissions, something that would have been unheard of before January 1938. That date was, indeed, the turning point in the relationship between Hitler and his Army.

6

The First Shackles

Few realised at the time the complete break with the past that these events represented. The Army, quite unprepared, embarked on a new experience. It was not to be a happy one.

GENERAL FRANZ HALDER
Chief of the General Staff, 1938-42

Friday, 4 February 1938 had been a day of immense importance both to the Army and to Germany: it was the day on which Hitler had revealed to the world a profound shift in the distribution of power within the Third Reich, and thus began the concentration of the nation's military leadership into his hands, a process which was to be carried still further four years later with his assumption of the active command of the Army. At midnight of 3–4 February, the Führer's decree was read over German radio:

> 'From henceforth I exercise personally the immediate command over the whole Armed Forces. The former Wehrmacht Office in the War Ministry becomes the High Command of the Armed Forces [OKW], and comes immediately under my command as my military staff. At the head of the Staff of the High Command stands the former chief of the Wehrmacht Office [Keitel]. He is accorded the rank equivalent to that of Reichs Minister. The High Command of the Armed Forces also takes over the functions of the War Ministry, and the Chief of the High Command exercises, as my deputy, the powers hitherto held by the Reich War Minister. The task of preparing the unified defence of the Reich in all fields, in accordance with my instructions, is the function of the High Command in time of peace.'[1]

In addition, the resignation and dismissal of von Fritsch and von Blomberg were announced, together with the appointment of von Brauchitsch. Consequent on this came a drastic and sweeping removal of senior officers from their posts, and some from active service altogether. Sixteen high-ranking generals were relieved of their commands and forty-four others, with a number of senior field-officers, were transferred. Among those of the Army High Command who went into the military wilderness of troop commands were von Schwedler, head of the Personnel Office, and two of his departmental cheifs, Colonels Küntzen and Behlendorff, and von Manstein, Beck's Head of Operations in the General

Staff. Some of the most prominent among these sent into retirement were: Kress von Kressenstein, a senior Wehrkreis commander; von Porgrell, Inspector of Cavalry; von Niebelschutz, Inspector of Training; and Lutz, Inspector of Mobile Troops. At the same time was announced the retirement of von Neurath, the formerly complacent, now conservative, Minister for Foreign Affairs, his replacement by the subservient von Ribbentrop, and the removal of the German ambassador in Rome, Ulrich von Hassell, an advocate of restraint known as *Il Freno*—the brake. By so many simultaneous blows, Hitler's opponents were stunned into submission. The ambitious Göring, although he had not realised his aim, was placated by being given the rank of *Generalfeldmarschall*, which, with von Brauchitsch only a *Generaloberst*, made him the senior officer of the Armed Forces. Ironically and shamefully, on this day, on the same occasion that von Fritsch's resignation was made public, Hitler announced the elevation of Walther Funk, Goebbels's Secretary of State, to the post of Minister of Economics. Funk was a notorious homosexual.

Thanks to the opportunities presented him by the foolish indiscretion of his former War Minister, by a case of mistaken identity in a sordid blackmail case, by the craven ambition of his political associates, and by the gross political naïvety of his generals, Hitler had achieved an unexpected coup of considerable importance, and had laid the basis for his career as a war lord. Without any previous scheming, he had eliminated the last of the restrictions placed on his foreign policy and rearmament; he had taken direct control of the Armed Forces and, by the new command organisation and its change of personnel, had ensured their compliance to his will. Most important of all, he had humbled the Army, bringing it more fully within his sphere of influence. Thus, von Seeckt's dictum that 'The Army is the first instrument of power in the Reich'[2] was no longer true.

At first sight, the new appointments of 4 February might have seemed not unfavourable to the Army. Admittedly, Hitler was now Commander-in-Chief of the Armed Forces, but his record as Supreme Commander in the past had not been disastrous. Rather, on the contrary, his interference in service matters could hardly have been less, and the situation was better than if Göring had been appointed, a move that had been feared. As for Keitel— well, he was harmless enough; and the aristocratic von Brauchitsch, no doubt, would do what was necessary— after all he was no National Socialist and his military qualities were beyond criticism. Yet it was soon to become apparent that such hopes were ill-founded; the degree to which Hitler managed to subordinate the Armed Forces in general, and the Army in particular, may be seen in the personalities of those who now came to the leadership.

The manner by which the new Army Commander-in-Chief was chosen revealed much of Hitler's new attitude towards the military. The search was begun on 26 January and, at the beginning, the Führer's own candidate was von Reichenau, the obvious man—able, progressive, and, to all appearances, a safe 'Party general.' But Keitel, to whom Hitler turned for advice, regarded such a choice as potentially disastrous: it would provoke strong resistance from the military hierarchy, possibly even leading to mass resignation; it would also create the unfortunate, if correct, impression that there was to be a sweeping change in military policy. Keitel regarded von Reichenau's personality, too, as unsuitable, believing him to be slothful, superficial, inordinately ambitious, and unpopular with his colleagues. Instead, Keitel proposed von Rundstedt, who was thought too old by Hitler; von Leeb, of whom he did not think highly enough; and von Brauchitsch, a name put forward also by von Blomberg at his fateful meeting with the Führer on 26 January, to whom Hitler made no objection. Not only was von Brauchitsch an excellent soldier, Keitel argued, but he was well thought of in the Army and possessed no political ambition. What could be better? Later, when von Rundstedt was asked for his opinion, his immediate and complete rejection of von Reichenau made a considerable impression on the Führer; his suggestion that Beck should take command received instant and cold dismissal from Hitler, but his subsequent confirmation of the general acceptability of von Brauchitsch was listened to thoughtfully. It appears that, from that time on, the idea of von Brauchitsch as his future Army Commander gained ascendancy in Hitler's mind. Von Reichenau, from the Führer's point of view, was now seen as too much of a risk: he would needlessly antagonise the Army, and his independence of mind and political ambition might one day pose a threat to Hitler himself. Certainly he was no longer considered, the expressions of Hitler's further support for him being merely a tactical manoeuvre designed to gain the maximum concessions from von Brauchitsch in the bargaining over his appointment.

Negotiations were entered into with speed and were kept strictly secret—Keitel, for example, was not allowed to go to the Reich Chancellery other than in civilian clothes. There, he and Hitler would confer on the terms to be accepted by any future Army Commander, and Keitel would then take these proposals to von Brauchitsch, who was staying at the Hotel Continental. From time to time Keitel, occasionally accompanied by von Brauchitsch, would visit Göring at the Air Ministry. Hitler himself had three meetings with the favoured candidate. Beck, however, was furious that he was not consulted and that Keitel, an outsider, should be acting as the adviser of the new appointment; it was, however, an indication of things to come.

As it turned out, Hitler was infinitely better off having von Brauchitsch as his new Commander-in-Chief than von Reichenau. Whereas the latter was of strong personality, active, independent, and ambitious, von Brauchitsch, brave and able soldier though he might have been, was personally vulnerable, and submissive to Hitler. The impression was soon gained that he was 'ready for anything,' and, indeed, the price he was forced to pay for his elevation to the command of the Army was high—the loss of his freedom of action. Three conditions were imposed on him by Hitler: he must lead the Army to a closer union with the state and its philosophy; he must, if necessary, choose a more suitable Chief of Staff (Hitler by then had come to dislike and fear Beck); and he must endorse a new structure for the Armed Forces high command. Although he took a little time to agree to the last, von Brauchitsch accepted these conditions, together with the need to remove a number of senior Army officers, prominent among whom were those directing the Army Personnel office. By 3 February the deal was settled; Hitler had gained all he wanted, and the Army, in whose name von Brauchitsch had mistakenly surrendered its most vital concerns, had lost its autonomy. The heavy load on von Brauchitsch's conscience was lightened only by the erroneous belief that by his actions he had saved the Army from a worse fate—command by von Reichenau. Silently, he was to carry in office a burden from which there was no escape.

The new Commander-in-Chief of the Army, Walter von Brauchitsch, came of a Silesian family which had provided Prussia with a dozen generals over the previous 150 years. Born in 1881 in Berlin, he possessed an aristocratic background which met with the full approval of such men as von Rundstedt—he had even been page to the Empress Augusta Victoria before entering a Guards artillery regiment. His bearing, too, was pleasing, for, as von Manstein recorded, he was 'a man of elegant appearance who . . . was never anything but dignified. . . . He was correct, courteous, and even charming, although this charm did not always leave one with an impression of inner warmth.'[3] Certainly his military record was worthy of his new position: during the First World War he had won the coveted Hohenzollern House Order; as a departmental head in the Troop Office he had distinguished himself by his experiments with aircraft and mechanisation; and while Director of Army Training and Inspector of Artillery he had pursued his profession with great energy, which continued during his command of Wehrkreis I and Fourth Army Group.

His character, however, appears to have been regarded as something of an enigma. Von Manstein remembered that: 'Just as he lacked the aggressiveness that commands an opponent's respect, or at least compels him to go warily, so did he fail to impress one as a forceful, productive personality. The general effect was one of coolness and reserve. He often appeared slightly inhibited, he was certainly rather sensitive.'[4] But Adam, not a poor judge of men, spoke of him as 'an intelligent man of determined and self-willed character.'[5] However, his record in dealing with Hitler bears eloquent testimony to the veracity of von Manstein. Von Brauchitsch was as ill-suited as any person could be to oppose or to moderate the damaging demands of the dictator. The new Army Commander-in-Chief was little more than the moral hostage of his Führer, and choosing him was the climax of Hitler's manoeuvres in 1938 to destroy the Army's independence.

The reason for this sad state of affairs goes back to 1926, when von Brauchitsch, already married, had fallen in love with a certain Charlotte Ruffer, the divorced wife of a brother officer. His wife, however, steadfastly refused to grant a divorce without raising a scandal that would have been ruinous to his career, unless a financial settlement were made which would have been well beyond his means. By 1938 von Brauchitsch had not been living with his spouse for more than five years, and he was in a mood to sacrifice his career in order to free himself from his emotional and domestic problems. Resignation was uppermost in his mind. But, just at the point when his despair was total, he was offered the glittering prize to which all professional soldiers aspire— the command of his army. Furthermore, when he told Hitler of his marital affairs, the Führer replied that if money were the only hindrance to the divorce, then money would be provided. Göring also promised that von Brauchitsch would be shielded from criticism within the officer corps. Von Brauchitsch was undoubtedly aware of the problems such a solution might present for his future freedom of action, so beholden would he be to Hitler, who was to provide out of his own pocket a capital settlement of some 80,000 reichsmarks; but he now had within his grasp the promise of avoiding resignation and obscurity and, instead, of obtaining his divorce, marrying the woman he loved, and rising to the height of the military profession, while at the same time being protected from scandal by the most powerful men in the state. His choice was one many men would have made.

After 4 February 1938, Hitler had as his Army Commander a man under great personal obligation to him, guilty of adultery, and married to a lady with a certain past. (She had had several protectors and a husband who had died in a bath tub!) His moral probity was hardly of the highest. Nor was von Brauchitsch ever to be rid of the spectre of von Blomberg's fate; it was not for nothing that a senior British Foreign Office official, Sir Robert Vansittart, could discern: 'Hitler has a stranglehold on von Brauchitsch of some private and discreditable kind.' To make matters worse, von Brauchitsch's disposition, origin, and upbringing were not conducive to standing up to the Führer. He was often bewildered in the presence of Hitler, whose occasional coarse style of speech unnerved him, and when he did manage to summon up enough nerve to argue, he often did so in a curt, impetuous, even condescending, tone which was greatly resented. Furthermore, his new wife, a domineering woman to whom he was devoted, was, in the words of his fellow officers, '200 per cent National Socialist.' Thus, as Halder remarked, the Commander-in-Chief of the German Army stood before Adolf Hitler 'like a little cadet before his commandant.'[6] General Warlimont noted how he 'often appeared practically paralysed.'[7] Von Brauchitsch was painfully aware of this; it was a failing which greatly embarrassed him. He confessed to Halder: 'Please do not hold it against me. I know you are dissatisfied with me. When I confront this man, I feel as if someone were choking me and I cannot find another word.'[8]

From the beginning of his period in office, von Brauchitsch found himself beset by the conflict between his commitment to Hitler and his duties to the Army, and never was he able to reconcile his enslavement to the Führer with his need to gain the confidence of his colleagues. As a result, he received the respect of neither. He realised at once the impossibility of his situation when confronted with the question of von Fritsch's rehabilitation. The Army demanded he take action, but Keitel warned him that he 'should not straightway put a burden on his prestige with Hitler in this delicate matter.'[9] All he could do was make vague promises that 'There can be no talk of a reinforced influence of the Party in the internal affairs of the Armed Forces,'[10] and at the same time salve his conscience towards his much-abused predecessor by placing adjutants, horses, and a car at his disposal and by authorising a collection for a house to be made among the officer corps. Von Brauchitsch managed to retain Beck as his Chief of Staff until the autumn, pleading that this was necessary because of his own unfamiliarity with the Army High Command. However, he received no recognition for this from Beck, who was continually annoyed by his chief's weakness before Hitler, and only dissatisfaction from the Führer, who became impatient at what he considered to be the continual objections to his policies still emanating from the Army Command.

Certainly von Brauchitsch maintained the resistance to any attempt by the Party organisation to interfere in military matters, and in this he was aided by Hitler who, seeing the Armed Forces now as his own inviolable province, wished to see no encroachment on his territory by anyone else. But at the same time, National Socialist doctrine became more evident in the directives and orders of the new Army Commander than it had been under von Fritsch. For example, on 18 December 1938, von Brauchitsch issued an order containing a number of Blombergesque passages: 'Adolf Hitler, our leader of genius, who has recast the great lessons of the front-line soldier in the form of the National Socialist philosophy. . . . The Armed Forces and National Socialism are of the same spiritual stem. . . . The officer corps must not be surpassed by anybody in the purity and genuineness of its National Socialist outlook . . . the officer must handle any situation in accordance with the views of the Third Reich.'[11]

The fundamental change in the relationship between Hitler and the Army was also evident in the change in the nature of the important post of the Armed Forces Adjutant to the Führer, and in the creation of a new office, Army Adjutant to the Führer. Until 1938, the Armed Forces Adjutant had been one of the most important military personages in the Army, and a far from negligible figure in the counsels of the Reich. As the Armed Forces representative to the Führer, he also possessed a special responsibility for the Army, and it was taken as automatic that he would speak for its interests. The other two services had their own separate adjutants, but not the Army. Always at Hitler's hand, he was often called on to give his Führer advice, which was usually acted on. In some ways, his influence was as great as that of the War Minister, but, as it was always behind the scenes, it was never apparent. From 2 August 1934, the post had been held by Colonel Friedrich Hossbach, a man much respected and liked by the officer corps and with considerable influence over an impressionable Hitler. Nicknamed 'the old Fritz,' after his namesake, Frederick the Great, or 'the last Prussian,' because of his unbending principles and martinet's devotion to regulations, Hossbach was extremely important to Hitler because of his high standing in the military profession. He was immune from intimidation, and gave unfailing support to von Fritsch during the crisis. On 25 January 1938, the day after the Führer had received the accusation against the Army Commander, Hossbach spent some ten hours in vehement debate with Hitler and Göring, afterwards telling von Fritsch of the charges, although strictly forbidden to do so. However, his very independence proved his downfall. Hossbach was clearly a liability on the course Hitler had now set himself, and so, on the 28th, he was dismissed from his post amid tears of rage and protestations that no German officer should be treated in such a manner.

Hossbach's successor was Major Rudolf Schmundt, a man who represented as well as anyone the type of officer with whom Hitler was determined to surround himself from that time on. Basically decent and amicable, he was nevertheless weak-willed, an insecure man who needed ideals and a hero on whom to depend. Unfortunately for his reputation, it was to Hitler that he gave his devotion (previously it had been Beck), and thus, unlike Hossbach, he ceased to function as the representative of the Wehrmacht and of the Army, becoming instead yet another docile executive instrument of the Führer's will. As his hero began to lose his majesty and infallibility, Schmundt increasingly found solace in alcohol, his personality disintegrated, and his death in the Bomb Plot of 20 July 1944 came as a merciful release.

For the Army, the loss of Hossbach and the emergence of Schmundt was a severe setback which was exacerbated by the role of Wehrmacht Adjutant changing with Hitler's assumption of the post of Commander-in-Chief. It was now reduced to a mere link between the offices now incorporated in the person of the Führer, and it was an indication of the Army's loss of status that it now felt necessary to create the new and separate post of Army Adjutant to the Führer. For his part, Hitler, not unreasonably, felt the generals were now sending someone to watch over him. The man the Army leaders chose to serve them in this important role was Captain Gerhard Engel, a talented and energetic artillery officer with an esteem for von Fritsch which was warmly reciprocated. Although no supine creature like Schmundt, Engel nevertheless was held in high opinion by Hitler, who had been briefed by him during army manoeuvres in 1937. However, although he was to prove an ardent exponent of the Army's interests, his influence was severely curtailed by the soft-cushioning that surrounded Hitler, and by the lowered prestige of the Army in the dictator's eyes.

But the greatest importance of the announcement of 4 February 1938 lay in the implications it contained for the reorganisation of the High Command. The new Armed Forces of the 1920s and early 1930s, which rose out of the ruins of the old imperial force, had been given a concentration and coordination of command not seen since the days of Frederick the Great. Its titular head was the Head of State, the Reich President, who, as *Oberste Befehlshaber der Reichswehr* (Supreme Commander), was limited in his prerogative to protocol and making the most senior appointments. Responsible to him was the *Reichswehr Minister* (Reich Defence Minister) who had charge of the overall administration of, and policy regarding, the Armed Forces and national defence. The Reich Defence Minister's executive office was the *Ministeramt* (Ministerial Office), which was renamed the *Wehrmachstamt* (Armed Forces Office) on 13 February 1934 and *Wehrmachtamt* in October 1936. Next in the hierarchy, and arguably the man who wielded most effective power, was the *Chef der Heeresleitung* (Chief of the Army Leadership), in whose office was concentrated the entire direction of the Army, including operations, discipline, promotion, training, and equipment. Von Seeckt viewed this as the revival and continuation of that tradition of personal command on which the cohesion of the old Army had rested, and through which the independence and influences of the Army within the state were assured. The executive instrument by which this control was exerted was the *Heeresleitung* (Army Leadership), a camouflaged Army High Command which, under the provisions of the Versailles Treaty, was denied to Germany. In the event of war, it was envisaged that the Chief of Army Leadership would take the main decisions on the overall direction of the nation's effort, as did the Supreme Commander of the Army in the years 1914–18. Such was the position in 1933, one that left little room for direct interference on the part of Hitler as Reich

Chancellor, even should he so wish.

As has been indicated earlier, in the first five years of his régime Hitler showed no desire to bring any direct authority to bear on the Army; his influence over von Blomberg as a member of the Reich Cabinet was sufficient for his needs at that time. Nothing was substantially altered by his assumption of the powers of Reich President with von Hindenburg's death on 2 August 1934, or by his official adoption of the title *Oberste Befehlshaber der Wehrmacht* (Supreme Commander of the Armed Forces), on 21 May 1935. Of greater significance for the future was the alteration in the status of the Reichswehr Minister. On the same day, 21 May, his post was renamed *Reichskriegsminister* (Reich War Minister) and was linked with the new title of *Oberbefehlshaber der Wehrmacht* (Commander-in-Chief of the Armed Forces). His executive instrument, the Wehrmachtamt, remained untouched. At the same time, the *Chef der Heeresleitung* became the *Oberbefehlshaber des Heeres* (Commander-in-Chief of the Army) and the *Heeresleitung* the *Oberkommando des Heeres* (Army High Command).

The significance of these changes was considerable. Through his title of Commander-in-Chief of the Wehrmacht, the War Minister could lay claim to assume responsibility for the coordinated direction of the organisation, intelligence, war propaganda, economic warfare, and, most important of all, operations of all three services. This was a claim which had been in existence ever since von Blomberg's appointment as Defence Minister in 1933, but which was further extended by this new post. Not only had the individual service chiefs to give up an important part of their prerogatives in his favour, but, for the first time, there was a superior commander interposed between the Army Commander and the Supreme Commander and Head of State. No longer would the Army Commander-in-Chief have authority to direct all fighting services, and several departments under his control in peacetime were to pass to the Wehrmacht Commander in the event of war. It was argued that the development in warfare on land, sea, and in the air that had taken place since 1918 demanded the institution of a combined Wehrmacht High Command to coordinate and direct operations in all three elements. Such a reorganisation was supported most vigorously by von Reichenau and his successor Keitel, but was hotly opposed by most of the senior Army leadership, led by Beck backed up by von Fritsch. They saw quite clearly that such a development would give increased power to the group who admired Hitler and a corresponding increase in the Führer's influence, as well as a considerable reduction in the authority of the Army, which had hitherto possessed complete autonomy in its own spheres, especially in its operations. Never, even in the Kaiser's days, had there been a superior operational command exercising authority over the Army; now the Army Commander-in-Chief was expected to hand over to a new, higher commander, interposed between him and the Head of State, a substantial part of his prerogative and freedom of action, as a consequence of which he would find himself degraded in the military hierarchy.

Apart from this loss of authority and autonomy, the creation of a unified Wehrmacht High Command was disliked by the Army leaders on purely military grounds. In a long memorandum to von Blomberg, dated August 1937, von Fritsch emphasised that the three services were not equal partners, that the Army comprised eighty per cent of the Armed Forces, and that, in the final analysis, land warfare was the decisive factor in Germany's overall strategy. The structure of the High Command ought to reflect this, and, in his words: 'Since the commands of the Army and the Armed Forces are inseparable, their separation should not consciously be caused by the creation of an Armed Forces High Command as an independent command staff.'[12] Such a creation would, in time of war, lead to considerable conflict. For the future, von Fritsch proposed that the authority of the War Minister be limited to the organisation of the whole nation in time of war, and that the Commander-in-Chief of the Army should 'be the principal adviser of the Head of State in all matters concerning the conduct of war, including naval and air matters, and must be his sole adviser on questions of land warfare.'[13]

However, the years before 1938 had seen some progress in the direction of an Armed Forces High Command, and the Wehrmachtamt had been expanded to include an embryo staff for the unified direction of the three services. How far, if at all, this was at the insistence of Hitler, it is impossible to tell; certainly no evidence has been traced that points one way or the other. Nevertheless, it may be safely assumed that the dictator was unperturbed at seeing a part of the Army's autonomy and authority taken from it and given to a higher command better disposed to his person. But this process, gradual though it was, did not proceed without considerable opposition from all three services. An Armed Forces Academy, set up in 1935 with the aim of providing suitably trained officers for such a command, was disbanded after only two years; and the practice of a new command organisation through war games, study periods, skeleton exercises and Wehrmacht manoeuvres (held in 1937), caused criticsm to reach, in Warlimont's words, a state of 'well-nigh open rebellion—a most unmilitary state of affairs.'[14] So appalled was von Fritsch in early 1937 at the suggestion of forming Wehrmacht Territorial Commands to replace the Army Wehrkreis that he immediately offered his resignation, thus forcing Hitler to turn down the proposal. In June, matters were made worse by von Blomberg's directive, 'On Unified War Preparation of the Wehrmacht,' over which he threatened to resign if von Fritsch protested to Hitler. Personal relationships began to suffer, and the gap between the two groupings around von Blomberg and von Fritsch widened even further.

However, the events of January 1938 brought to an abrupt halt the argument between the two men. The announcement of 4 February, although its implications were by no means immediately realised, presented the Army leaders with a fait accompli, and the reality of a considerable extension of Hitler's authority over them. With the dismissal of von Blomberg and the elimination of the post of War Minister and Commander-in-Chief of the Wehrmacht, Hitler, as Führer and Supreme Commander, assumed personal, sole, and direct command of the Armed Forces. The Wehrmachtamt became the *Oberkommando der Wehrmacht* (High Command of the Armed Forces) which also assumed both the duties of the former War Ministry and the functions of the Supreme Commander's general staff. The *Chief der Oberkommando der Wehrmacht* (Chief of OKW) was to fulfil the duties of a high-level Chief of Staff to the Supreme Commander and exercised the authority of the former War Minister. He was accorded the rank of Reich Minister and given a seat in the Reich Cabinet, the Ministerial Council for the Defence of the Reich, and the Secret Cabinet (which never met). No representative from the Army was a member of these bodies, although the Commander-in-Chief of the Luftwaffe held positions in all three, and the Commander-in-Chief of the Navy held a seat in the Secret Cabinet.

The creation of the OKW represented a fundamental change in the structure of the High Command. Previously, the War Minister and his executive arm had been primarily a military authority determined to defend its professional interests against the pressures of the politicians, and fully capable of acting on its own authority. Now it was replaced by a body which was nothing more than the military bureau of the Head of State, Supreme Commander, and Commander-in-Chief —Hitler—serving simply to carry out his wishes. As one of the OKW's functionaries, General Warlimont, wrote, those who now composed the highest echelons of the OKW '... made it clear that their conception of their overriding duty was to carry out Hitler's wishes and where required smooth the path for him in the military sphere. This was clearly a very different objective from that which Blomberg had set himself.'[15] From such men the Army could expect little sympathy or support in any controversy with Hitler. The character of General Staff officers had changed fundamentally. Blind, unquestioning obedience had never been one of the characteristics of the General Staff, for, while the Prussian tradition repudiated political disobedience, it nevertheless allowed for the rejection of a military order under extreme circumstances. As a general once told one of his officers: 'Sir, the King of Prussia made you a staff officer so that you should know when you ought not to obey.' Indeed, a staff officer had a responsibility to make known his objections to an order when he believed it to be misguided. Unthinking obedience in the military sphere had always been held to be inconsistent with responsibility and conscience; now, however, it was regarded as an essential. In the autumn of 1938 Hitler embodied this new principle in a special order. As Guderian records:

> '... there [had] existed within the Army a system by which the chiefs of staff, down to and including the chief of staff of an army corps, shared the responsibility for the decisions taken by their respective commanding generals. This system, which involved the forwarding of a report by the chief of staff should he disagree with his commander, was discontinued on Hitler's orders. ... The system of joint responsibility ... was one inherited from the old Prussian Army. ... In accordance with the "leader principle" which he propagated, Hitler now logically ordered that the man who was in command must bear the entire and undivided responsibility; by this decree he automatically abolished the joint responsibility of the Chief of the Army General Staff [and of the OKW, too] in relationship to himself in his capacity as Supreme Commander of the Armed Forces.'[16]

As Keitel later recorded: 'For the execution of his [Hitler's] plans, which were unknown to us, he needed impotent tools unable to inhibit him.'[17] It was not for nothing that it was said that OKW stood for 'Oben kein Widerstand'—no resistance at the top. Its members chose to ignore the traditions of the Army, and their elevation destroyed the powerful bond of professional outlook within the senior ranks of the officer corps. Germany's generals now included a caste apart—Hitler's men.

The Führer's new military right-hand man was, from the Army's point of view, the worst possible choice. Wilhelm Bodewin Johann Gustav Keitel was born in 1882 of a middle-class Hanoverian family of landowners, to whom military traditions and tendencies were alien. Tall, good-looking, occasionally sporting a monocle, an excellent horseman with a penchant for hunting, Keitel possessed an enjoyment of the good life that was often marred by his extreme correctness and his nervousness. Conscientious, loyal, and with an insatiable appetite for work, especially of a detailed kind, he was an able staff officer whose flair for organisation was invaluable in a period of such considerable expansion. Ambitious, but lacking in exceptional talent, shrewd, but not highly intelligent, he had found promotion within the Army relatively slow until, in October 1935, von Blomberg, with the approval of von Fritsch, selected him to become his subordinate in succession to von Reichenau. The War Minister thought well of Keitel, but realised he had climbed as far up the military ladder as his capabilities would allow. Certainly he never envisaged him as a future Field-Marshal. But then came Keitel's golden opportunity with the Blomberg–Fritsch crisis. Hitler turned to him, saying: 'I rely entirely on you. You are my trusted and only counsellor in the problems of the Wehrmacht.'[18]

Only in Hitler's eyes was Keitel suitable for the post of Chief of OKW—even Keitel himself felt embarrassed by his feeling of inadequacy for the job, once declaring aloud: 'I am no Field-Marshal.'[19] His problem was that he was inordinately weak in character, infinitely preferring to serve than to dictate, so that he quickly earned for himself the nickname *'Lakaitel'* (Lackey), and he often resembled a footman running to attend to his master's every need. He was also known as the 'nodding ass.' A cynical adjutant once remarked: 'See that Field-Marshal scurrying past, with his adjutant bringing up the rear with measured tread.'[20] His insecurity was revealed in a hasty and faltering gait. Speer records his first impression of Keitel as 'a general who seconded his chief's [von Blomberg's] every word by an approving nod of his head.'[21] When he had known him for some time, his opinion became more definite: 'Basically Keitel hated his own weakness; but the hopelessness of any dispute with Hitler had ultimately brought him to the point of not even trying to form his own opinion.'[22] On more than one occasion Hitler expressed his satisfaction with the way the Chief of OKW conducted himself; Speer recorded: 'Hitler said that he could not do without Keitel because the man was "loyal as a dog" to him. Perhaps Keitel embodied most precisely the type of person Hitler needed in his entourage.'[23] As a result, Keitel exerted no influence at all on the course of operations: his function was purely executive, to carry out his master's decisions. As he himself admitted at Nuremberg after the war: 'Far from the Chief of the OKW advising Hitler, it was Hitler who advised him.'[24] Indeed, the Führer, with no respect for his military ability, was known to set little store by his judgement, often using him as little better than a doormat. Whenever Keitel raised an objection to Hitler's schemes the reply was always the same: 'I don't know why you are getting so het up by this. You are not answerable for this, the responsibility is mine alone.'[25] No wonder Keitel could call his position 'an abortion of an office.'

For the Army, Keitel was a disaster. He gave his loyalty not to his own caste but to Hitler, and thus he was unresponsive and, indeed, antagonistic to its interests. Warlimont wrote: 'He was honestly convinced that his appointment required him to identify himself unquestioningly with the wishes and instructions of his Supreme Commander, even though he might not personally agree with them. . . . He worked conscientiously to this end and apparently to no other; he was a tireless worker but had no very firm personal convictions and was therefore inclined always to seek a compromise; in his position these characteristics were fatal.'[26] The last comment may be given by Guderian: 'Field-Marshal Keitel was basically a decent individual. . . . It was [his] misfortune that he lacked the strength necessary to resist Hitler's orders. . . . He paid for this with his life at Nuremberg. His family were not permitted to mourn at his grave.'[27]

The man who was to become Hitler's foremost military adviser was Alfred Jodl, although, as Chief of the OKW *Wehrmachtführungsamt* (Operations Office), he was Keitel's subordinate. A highly gifted staff officer, Jodl, born in Aachen in 1890 of a distinguished Bavarian family, served with the artillery and the General Staff during the First World War, being wounded in the right leg in 1914. An able, ambitious, but exceptionally reserved man, he was far from being a weak nonentity; on the contrary he displayed a strong and intelligent personality in all his dealings with Hitler and his subordinates. His lack of experience of command in the field, however, was a severe drawback, and he was often unaware of the effect of his orders on the troops in the field.

Jodl was probably closer to Hitler than any other general, for not only did he brief him every day on progress in the OKW theatres of war, but, for three years after the Norwegian campaign, in which he played a leading role, he sat next to the Führer at meals. So close was his association that Jodl was regarded as the only reliable source of information on Hitler's thoughts and intentions. Unlike Keitel, however, he was not an uncritical admirer of Hitler. By 1942, Jodl was convinced that the Second World War was lost, but believing that internal dissension within the Reich had caused the defeat of the Armed Forces in the First World War, he always strove to keep his criticisms in check. As he wrote in his cell at Nuremberg: 'I made it a guiding principle to do everything in my power to combat every division, every indication of a breakdown—in short, all domestic conflicts in so far as they might affect the Wehrmacht.'[28] To Jodl, loyalty was an integral part of military high command. However, this did not mean he would never pursue the dictates of his own logic. Speer records that Jodl 'rarely contradicted Hitler openly. He proceeded diplomatically. Usually he did not express his thoughts at once, thus skirting difficult situations. Later he would persuade Hitler to yield, or even to reverse decisions already taken. His occasional deprecatory remarks about Hitler showed that he had preserved a relatively unbiased view.'[29] Indeed, on rare occasions, he could lose his patience with his Führer and, in Westphal's words, give 'free vent to his resentment.'[30]

Like his chief, though, Jodl was remarkably unsatisfactory from the Army's viewpoint. Ironically, he had been posted by Beck to von Blomberg's empire in the hope that there he would champion the Army's cause. Quite the opposite resulted. Jodl became such a staunch supporter of the idea of an Armed Forces High Command that in 1937 he refused the post of Luftwaffe Chief of Staff in order to remain at the post in which he believed so much. As a result, he became cool, if not openly hostile, towards the Army establishment, believing its criticism of the OKW and of Hitler to be infinitely damaging. An entry in his diary for 10 August 1938 described most vividly his attitude:

> 'I was summoned to the Berghof with senior officers of the Army. After dinner the Führer talked for nearly three hours explaining his line of thought on political questions. Thereafter certain of the generals tried to point out to the Führer that we were by no means ready. This was to say the least unfortunate. There are a number of reasons for this pusillanimous attitude which is unhappily fairly widespread in the Army General Staff . . . [it] is obsessed with memories of the past, and, instead of doing what it is told and getting on with its military job, thinks it is responsible for political decisions. It does get on with its job with all its old devotion, but its heart is not in it, because, in the last analysis, it does not believe in the genius of the Führer. . . . As sure as fate the result of all this belly-aching will be not only enormous political damage—for all the world knows about the differences of opinion

between the generals and the Führer—but also some danger to the morale of the troops.'[31]

The third of the OKW triumvirate was Walther Warlimont, Head of Branch L—*Landesverteidigung* (National Defence)—until September 1939, when he became Deputy Chief of the Operations Staff, a man whose character differed widely from that of both Keitel and Jodl. A Rhinelander, born in 1895, he was strikingly handsome, possessing an easy, graceful manner and obvious intelligence, and was thus the social asset of the OKW, playing host to numerous military attachés and foreign diplomats. Extremely able (for nine months from November 1938, at the age of only 43, he was responsible also for the duties of the Chief of the Operations Staff while Jodl was absent), an expert in war economy, and a first-class staff officer, he was firmly convinced of the desirability of an organisation such as the OKW—so much so, indeed, that in 1937, as a Colonel in the Wehrmachtamt, he had submitted a memorandum direct to the Führer on the necessity for a unified command, without even showing it to his chiefs, Keitel and von Blomberg. However, his acute mind ensured that, while he was adamant about the advantages of an Armed Forces High Command, he was no admirer of Hitler and, by the outbreak of the war, had come to oppose his policies.

During the invasion of Poland, intense dissatisfaction with the workings of the OKW, as it was then constituted, set in, and Warlimont found himself sympathising with the position of the Army Command. In this he was not alone, for, as he afterwards wrote, 'there was a split right through OKW, and no fewer than two Chiefs of Sections, Admiral Canaris [Intelligence] and General Thomas [Economics], together with the vast majority of their officers, were on the side of the Army.'[32] But against Keitel and Jodl they could do little. Jodl, in particular, saw the OKW not as containing officers and 'colleagues who had the right to think for themselves, to make suggestions and to advise, but as a machine for the elaboration and issue of orders'[33]—orders that came from Hitler himself.

The theory and the practice of the German High Command were two very different things. The theory was unification, centralisation, and coordination; the practice was disunity, fragmentation, and improvisation. The United States War Department *Handbook on German Military Forces*, published in 1941, noted: 'The outstanding characteristic of German military operations in the present war has been the remarkable coordination of the three sister services, Army, Navy, and Air Forces, into a unified command for definite tasks. These services do not cooperate in a campaign; rather their operations are coordinated by the High Command of the Armed Forces.'[34] This is the picture of Germany's military command structure that has been generally accepted until the present day, but one man who worked in a senior position within that High Command has given posterity a very different picture. Warlimont wrote: 'When the Second World War broke out no established headquarters existed capable of undertaking the overall direction of the German war effort.'[35] There lies the truth.

Immediately before mobilisation for war, the structure of the German High Command was headed by Adolf Hitler, Supreme Commander and effective Commander-in-Chief of the Wehrmacht; directly below him was the coordinating agency, the OKW, the head of which, Keitel, exercised the authority of the former Minister of War. The OKW consisted of the following. First, and most important, was the Armed Forces Operations Office concerned with plans, operations, communications, transport, and propaganda for the Armed Forces as a whole, whose chief, Jodl, was also Keitel's deputy. (By far the most important of its branches was the National Defence Branch in which the details of the operational planning were worked out and sent to the high commands of the three individual services.) Second in the structure of the OKW came the *Allgemeines Wehrmachtamt* (the General Armed Forces Office), concerned with matters of administration, welfare, pensions, vocational training, science, and prisoners of war. Third was the *Amt Ausland/Abwehr* (Foreign and Counter-Intelligence Office) under Canaris. Fourth came the *Wehrwirtschaftsamt* (Military Economics Office); fifth the *Wehrmacht Zentralabteilung* (Armed Forces Central Branch), concerned with mobilisation, personnel, and administration; sixth the *Wehrmachtsabteilung* (Armed Forces Legal Branch); and seventh, and last, was the *Wehrmachthaushaltsabteilung* (Armed Forces Budget Branch).

Directly beneath the OKW in the chain of command came the three service high commands—*Oberkommando des Heeres* (OKH), *Oberkommando der Kriegsmarine* (OKM) and *Oberkommando der Luftwaffe* (OKL). The Army High Command was under the direction of the Army Commander-in-Chief, and consisted firstly, and by far the most important, of the *Generalstab des Heeres* (Army General Staff), which was concerned with operations, training, supplies, fortifications, and intelligence on foreign armies. The Chief of General Staff possessed five deputies: Assistant Chief of Staff for Operations *(Oberquartiermeister I*—Head Quartermaster I); Assistant Chief of Staff for Training *(Oberquartiermeister II)*; Assistant Chief of Staff for Organisation and Technical Matters *(Oberquartiermeister III)*; Assistant Chief of Staff for Foreign Armies *(Oberquartiermeister IV)*; Assistant Chief of Staff for Military Science *(Oberquartiermeister V)*. The second office in the OKH was the *Heeres Personalamt* (Army Personnel Office). Third came the *Allgemeines Heeresamt* (General Army Office), concerned with publications, budget, law, replacements, clothing, punishment, ordnance stores, and inspectorates of arms and services. Fourth was the *Heeres Waffenamt* (Army Ordnance Office), fifth the *Heeres Verwaltungsamt* (Army Administration Office), sixth the *Inspektion der Kriegsschulen* (Inspectorate of Military Training Schools), and seventh the *Chief der Schnellen Truppen* (Chief of Mobile Troops).

Such an intricate organisation may seem confusing, but only one salient feature need be remembered; the operational ideas of the Führer and Supreme Commander were to be transmitted to the OKW Operations Office and its National Defence Branch, whence, in a detailed form combining the activities of all three services, they were to be forwarded to the various high commands, foremost among which was the OKH, where the General Staff would turn the OKW directive into operational orders for the whole of the Army. At least, such was the theory. In practice, all was confusion. At the centre of the Reich's military direction after 1938 there was only one reality: Hitler. He was the sole political authority from which all power in the Reich emanated; General Guderian wrote:

> 'Up to this time Hitler had been receptive to practical considerations, and had at least listened to advice and been prepared to discuss matters with others; now, however, he became increasingly autocratic. One example of his change in behaviour is furnished by the fact that after 1938 the Cabinet never again met. The Ministers did their work in accordance with instructions issued by Hitler to each of them singly. There was no longer any collective examination of major policy.... The national administration was emasculated.'[36]

Departmental ministers were given no opportunity to make their reports to Hitler for months and, finally, for years on end. Even the Party suffered, from 1937 there being no further meetings of Reichsleiters and Gauleiters. In the military sphere Hitler disregarded totally the command structure he himself had instituted. Even the OKW and its operations staff was by-passed, and, as Warlimont bitterly recorded, 'it found itself confined to an ill-defined sphere of activity, floating between the intuitive political initiatives of the dictator and their military consequences—on the one it was totally without influence, on the other its possibility of action depended on the degree of recognition accorded it by the high commands of the three services.'[37] Indeed, only a few weeks after promising he 'would never take a decision affecting the Wehrmacht without first hearing the views of his Chief of Staff,'[38] the Führer decided on the invasion of Austria without even having the courtesy to inform Keitel of his plan. The long-suffering Chief of

OKW learnt of it only through a member of Hitler's personal staff. It was clear that, in Warlimont's words, the OKW 'had no authority other than that which Hitler was occasionally willing to lend.'[39]

What, then, of the position of the Army High Command during the final years leading to the outbreak of the Second World War? Although the generals' opposition to Hitler's policies had been made impotent by the events of early 1938—revealed strikingly by their failure to make even the slightest impact on the Führer's plans for the occupation of Austria and for the attack on Czechoslovakia—there was still a considerable degree of direct contact between the Army Commander, his staff, and the dictator. This became evident during the preparations for the invasion of Poland. In March 1939, Hitler first dropped a casual hint to von Brauchitsch that he was prepared to use force against Poland, and the Chief of the OKW learnt of his intention only some days later. Once the Operations staff of the Armed Forces High Command had brought up to date the mobilisation procedure, it became nothing more than a registry for assembling the plans already drawn up by the three services. The various Commanders-in-Chief avoided the OKW and cultivated a personal planning relationship with their Supreme Commander, while the Chief of OKW degenerated into a go-between, 'a whipping boy who had thrust upon him . . . all those jobs which . . . no one else . . . wished to handle.'[40] The Führer dealt directly with his Army chiefs. Warlimont remembered that 'By the middle of August [1939], by which time Hitler had long been established in the Berghof, he began to give signs of increased activity in military matters; this consisted almost exclusively of the issue of a stream of new demands and requirements concerning the Army's plans for the move forward.'[41] Neither Keitel nor Jodl took any part in this.

Consequently, at the outbreak of the war it might have appeared as if, despite the February 1938 reorganisation, the Army had retained its position as the sole director, under the Supreme Commander, of military operations. But the portents for the future were ominous. There now existed an instrument, wholly under Hitler's control and occupying, in theory, the central position of the Reich's military command, which, should the dictator so wish, could wrest from the Army General Staff its traditional role as the nation's supreme operational authority. This is exactly what occurred: the OKW became one of the main instruments by which Hitler was to subject the Army to his own will as a war lord.

The two Commanders-in-Chief: von Blomberg talking with von Fritsch at the Nuremberg Party Rally in September 1937, only a few months before their downfall.

The oath being sworn to Adolf Hitler on his assumption of the office of Reich President and Supreme Commander in August 1934.

Above: The growing military pretensions of the SS: men of Hitler's bodyguard, the Leibstandarte SS 'Adolf Hitler', who formed part of the SS Verfügungstruppe. *Below:* The occupation of the Rhineland: infantry marching out of their barracks prior to moving into the demilitarised zone, March 1936.

Above: Hitler with his commanders-in-chief: from left to right, Göring, von Brauchitsch and Raeder. *Below:* The incorporation of Austria within the Reich: soldiers of the Austrian Army, with the German national eagle already on their right breasts, march past Hitler in Vienna on 14th March 1938.

Top left: General Ludwig Beck, Chief of the General Staff, 1934–1938, shortly before his resignation over the proposed invasion of Czechoslovakia. *Top right:* Field Marshal Wilhelm Keitel, Chief of the Wehrmacht High Command, 1938–1945. *Bottom left:* One of the first of the military conspirators: Field Marshal Erwin von Witzleben, who was hanged in 1944. *Bottom right:* General Alfred Jodl, Deputy Chief of the Wehrmacht High Command.

Above: The glorification of rearmament: the Army displaying its newly acquired might in the Nuremberg stadium during the National Socialist Party Rally of 1938. The anti-tank gun in this picture, however, was so ineffective that it was nicknamed the 'door-knocker'.
Left: Early experiments: cardboard tank structures mounted on motor cars moving into the attack accompanied by infantry.

Left: The man to whom the German panzer force owed so much: General Heinz Guderian. In 1944 he became the third Chief of the General Staff during the war. *Below:* The PzKw I training tank, shown here on manœuvres in the Nuremberg Stadium, September 1938. By the time manufacture of these machines ended in 1941, 1,500 had been produced.

7

Road to War

War came upon us by stealth; only when we looked back, could we clearly see how it had come: by Hitler.
FIELD-MARSHAL ERICH VON MANSTEIN

The Austrian adventure took place in the middle of the Fritsch crisis. On 9 March 1938, the Austrian Chancellor announced that a plebiscite would be held on Sunday, 13 March, on terms disadvantageous to the National Socialists, in which the people were to declare whether they were in favour of a free, independent Austria. That evening Hitler tood advice, not from his Army chiefs, nor, indeed, from the heads of OKW, but from an intimate circle consisting of Göring, von Reichenau, and two other generals known to him personally. On the 10th he summoned Beck and von Manstein, the former Chief of Operations, and, without asking for their opinion, ordered them to prepare for an immediate invasion of Austria. This they did reluctantly, having first expressed their belief to the dictator that the Army was not prepared for such a task. But, as Keitel remarked, 'their objections were summarily brushed aside by Hitler.'[1] On the 11th, OKW issued a directive which included the announcement that the Führer himself would take charge of the operations. And, on the 12th, German troops proceeded to incorporate a recalcitrant Austria into the Greater German Reich.

Both Beck and von Brauchitsch were bitterly opposed to this rushed occupation, fearing, above all, western intervention. They chose to express their main opposition through the Chief of the OKW, but, as Keitel himself recalls, they had chosen the wrong avenue of approach:

'The night [10–11 March] that followed was sheer purgatory for me: one telephone call followed another from the Army General Staff and from Brauchitsch; finally, at about four o'clock in the morning there was a call from the then Chief of the [OKW] Military Operations Staff, General von Viebahn [who was dismissed in 1938 and succeeded by Jodl]; all adjured me to persuade the Führer to call the operation off. I had no intention of asking this of the Führer even once; of course I promised them I would try, but I called them back a short time later (having made no attempt to contact him) and told each one that he had rejected their protests. This was something of which the Führer never learnt; if he had, his verdict on the Army's leadership would have been devastating, a disillusionment I wanted to spare both parties.'²

Against such odds, the Army leaders had little chance.

By the coup in Austria, Hitler had confirmed and consolidated his new position in the military structure of the Reich. He had demonstrated that he alone was capable of decisive leadership (although his extreme nervousness during the operation led him at one point even to cancel the march); that the opposition from the officer corps was both reactionary and groundless; and that the role of the Army leadership was merely to supply the force he required, without question.

A month later, Hitler turned his attention towards Czechoslovakia. On 21 April, the Führer summoned Keitel and explained to him the reasons why Czechoslovakia was considered to be a danger to the Reich, as well as the political principles that would be followed as preliminaries for the attack. The crux of the matter was that Czechoslovakia lay in a position that was strategically very difficult for Germany when the time came for the great reckoning with the east; the country could be used as a springboard for the Soviet forces to plunge deep into the heart of the Reich. Nevertheless, Hitler rejected the idea of an unprovoked attack because of 'hostile world opinion which might lead to a critical situation; instead they preferred lightning action based on an incident (for example, the murder of the German minister in the course of a demonstration).'³ Hitler then placed in the hands of the OKW the task of drawing up *Aufmarsch Grün* for the attack on Czechoslovakia, plans that the OKH had previously opposed so strongly that they had never been completed. The operation, drawn up by the OKW planning staff under Jodl, was ready for

Hitler's signature on 20 May. It opened with the words: 'It is not my intention to smash Czechoslovakia by military action in the immediate future without provocation. . . .'[4]

At this point plans were overtaken by events. On that same day, 20 May, the Czech government, alarmed at rumours of a German attack and at reports of troop concentrations near the frontier, ordered a partial mobilisation of its armed forces. The British and French governments at once made strong representations to Berlin, warning of the possibility of a general war should Czechoslovakia be invaded, while France and the Soviet Union reaffirmed their promise of immediate support for the Czechs. Outraged rather than frightened at such accusations and reactions (they were, after all, groundless at that time), and unwilling to accept any loss of prestige, Hitler took a fateful decision: to solve the Czechoslovakian issue that same year, even if he thereby risked a European war. The plan for the invasion was recast, and, on 28 May, Hitler gave his signature to the new, and last, version of *Aufmarsch Grün*. Its first sentence ran: 'It is my unalterable decision to smash Czechoslovakia by military action in the near future.'[5] The date for the execution of the plan was set for 1 October.

The reaction of the Army leaders was one of utter dismay. They had always been opposed to any idea of an invasion of Czechoslovakia, and Beck had already expressed strong reservations to von Brauchitsch about the first OKW plan, which, he argued, would render a general war inevitable, a war that Germany would be bound to lose. Now that direct action had been decided on, to take place within four months, the generals' reaction was heated. At the conference of 30 May, at which Hitler communicated his decision to his Army leaders, their oppostion was far from muted. Jodl noted in his diary: 'The whole contrast becomes acute once more between the Führer's intuition that we must do it this year and the opinion of the Army that we cannot do it yet as most certainly the western powers will interfere and we are not yet equal to them.'[6] But the generals faced an extreme difficulty: the plan had been drawn up by OKW without any help from them, and they were now presented with a fait accompli with no chance of reversing or, indeed, of amending it. Furthermore, their opposition was against a background of military preparation for the invasion. Events were running away from them. Beck, the leader of the opposition, produced a new memorandum for his chief on 3 June, followed by yet another on 16 July. Both were designed to convince von Brauchitsch of the disaster Germany was facing. The July document contained the following summarised sentiments that may be held to be common among the generals:

> 'There was no doubt that an attack on Czechoslovakia would bring France and Britain into the conflict at once . . . the outcome would be a general catastrophe for Germany, not only a military defeat. The German people did not want this war, the purpose of which they did not understand. Similar thoughts were also abroad within the Army. . . . Military preparations had attracted foreign attention. . . . Any hope of achieving surprise had thereby been dashed.'[7]

Beck ended with the following exhortation:

> 'I now feel in duty bound . . . to ask insistently that the Supreme Commander of the Wehrmacht should be compelled to abandon the preparations he has ordered for war, and to postpone his intention of solving the Czech problem by force until the military situation is basically changed. For the present I consider it hopeless, and this view is shared by all my Quartermasters-General and departmental chiefs of the General Staff who would have to deal with the preparations and execution of a war against Czechoslovakia.'[8]

At the same time Beck urged von Brauchitsch to organise some form of collective military, although peaceful, resistance to Hitler's policy.

Beck's attitude could hardly have been more definite. Von Brauchitsch, however, was equivocal. Although he undoubtedly shared the prevalent professional view of Hitler's plans, his political incapacity and character weakness prevented him from making anything but purely nominal appeals to the Führer. He had no desire to place himself at the head of any opposition to Hitler, for, as he later recorded: 'Why, in heaven's name, should I, of all men in the world, have taken action against Hitler? The German people had elected him, and the workers, like all other Germans, were perfectly satisfied with his successful policy.'[9] Furthermore, his relationship with Beck, strained from the beginning, was now reaching a crisis in mutual confidence; von Brauchitsch took to bypassing Beck and dealing directly with his deputy, the new Chief of Army Operations Staff, Halder, while the Chief of Staff, for his part, repeatedly offered his resignation to the Army Commander.

Von Brauchitsch, nonetheless, was worried. Although he consistently refused to convey to Hitler the generals' opposition, he did, at Beck's insistence, call a secret conference of the Army leaders on 4 August. All were in agreement that any Czechoslovak venture would be militarily foolish, and von Brauchitsch closed the meeting with the prophecy that a European war would mean the end of German culture. However, no plan of action was agreed on: Beck wanted the Army Commander to lead his generals to demand that Hitler should reverse his policy; von Reichenau believed that it would be far more effective if individual officers went to see the Führer, who would be indignant at a mass confrontation; von Rundstedt wanted von Brauchitsch to tread warily in his opposition and not to court dismissal, thereby allowing von Reichenau to take over his position; and Busch, although convinced of the folly of playing with general war, advanced the argument that this was not the province in which the soldier should interfere. In the event, it appears that when the Army Commander conveyed to Hitler the fears of his generals, albeit somewhat half-heartedly, he came up against an indignant and unbending reception. Once again, von Brauchitsch yielded to his Führer's will.

Hitler immediately mounted a counter-offensive against his discontented generalship, flatly denying the need for any anxiety. He began with a flanking movement by inviting their chiefs of staff to a dinner on 10 August to explain to them his political views. But he met with scepticism, and the occasion ended on a discordant note when, in response to an assertion that it was impossible to hold the western fortifications for more than three weeks, the enraged dictator rounded on the assembled officers, accusing them of defeatism and a lack of morale. Next, he executed a surprise manoeuvre of appeasement by formally rehabilitating von Fritsch on the 11th. His last action was a frontal attack on the 15th, when, after field manoeuvres, he informed his generals of his firm and final resolve to smash Czechoslovakia that autumn, at the same time reminding them of his prophetic gifts which, despite all advice to the contrary, had so often proved right in the past. The generals remained silent; their protest was over.

Beck, alone, was prepared for one more, final, attempt. After the meeting on the 15th, he demanded an audience with his Army Commander. Von Brauchitsch, at the end of his patience, could take no more from his Chief of Staff and had him informed that he could not meet his request as he was just going off on a few days' leave. Beck was enraged. On the 18th, on von Brauchitsch's return, he had a stormy interview with his chief, in which he was informed of Hitler's latest order which prohibited political interference by the Army and demanded nothing less than unconditional obedience from all generals. Beck could go no further. He resigned, calling on von Brauchitsch to do likewise. The Army Commander refused, 'hitched his collar a notch higher, and said: "I am a soldier; it is my duty to obey."'[10] On the 21st, a thankful Hitler agreed to the resignation, and on 27 August Beck attended his office for the last time.

By his resignation, Beck had finally burst free of the rigid confines of the Prussian military tradition: the oath, the code of obedience to the Head of State, and the ingrained notion that the soldier was above politics, were now cast aside. He had set his reasons on paper a month previously:

> 'History will burden these [Army] leaders with blood-guilt if they do not act in accord with their specialised political knowledge and conscience. Their military obedience has a limit where their knowledge, their conscience, and their sense of responsibility forbid the execution of a command. If their warning and counsel receive no hearing in such a situation, then they have the right and duty to resign from their offices. If they all act with resolution, the execution of a policy of war is impossible. By this they have saved their country from the worst—from ruin. It is a lack of greatness and of recognition of the task if a soldier in the highest position in such times regards his duties and tasks only within the limited framework of his military instructions without being aware of the highest responsibilities towards the nation as a whole. Extraordinary times demand extraordinary measures.'[11]

Beck's act was honourable and courageous, but there it ended. Although he believed that the time had come to free Germany (and even Hitler himself) from the tyranny of the Party and secret police, and that this was possibly the last occasion on which it could be attempted, his subsequent moves ensured that his resignation would not be the catalyst for this action. Ordinarily, such a move on the part of a distinguished and respected Chief of the General Staff in the midst of a national crisis would have had a resounding impact, not only on the officer corps but on the wider, political world, both at home and abroad; disillusion and resignations would have followed. Yet Beck's action signally failed to achieve any such effect. He was supported by none of even his closest colleagues, and his act did nothing more than bring to an end his resistance to Hitler through the normal official channels. One of the reasons for this failure lies in the fact that, on Hitler's orders, Beck's resignation was not communicated either to the public or to the Army, 'for reasons of foreign policy,' until the end of October, although his successor, Franz Halder, took over his duties on 1 September. Beck, out of loyalty to his country in time of crisis, accepted this condition; he made no attempt to turn his resignation into a burning issue around which the opposition could focus. A man of principle, he was not yet one of action. Furthermore, there were a number of men in the Armed Forces, besides Hitler, who were only too glad to see Beck leave the field. Of these Keitel was understandably one. He wrote later: 'I wept no tears over Beck in view of the shameless way he had treated me.'[12] Nor could support be expected from the Army Commander, his relationship with his Chief of Staff having long since become unworkable. Beck always looked back to this time bitterly and complained: 'Brauchitsch left me in the lurch.'[13]

As for the other generals, united resistance against Hitler was impossible. Despite their knowledge of the dangerous follies inherent in his present course of action, their political naïveté held them rigidly to their oath of obedience. Unlike Beck, they had no conception of any higher duties or wider responsibilities to the Army and to the nation, nor did they possess Beck's awareness of the nature of the régime they served, a régime in which the Army was, at that time, the only possible counterbalance to Hitler and the Party. As a result, putting their doubts firmly behind them, they immersed themselves in their work, tried to forget the vexed question of conflicting principles, breathed a sigh of relief when Germany, once again, triumphed on the international scene, and gratefully basked in the reflected glory of Hitler's success. Such was their reaction—a human one which has shaped the course of history since time began.

Beck's successor as Chief of the Army General Staff, the fifty-four year old Franz Halder, was a man who exemplified von Moltke's saying: 'Genius is diligence.' Born in 1884 to a well-known Bavarian military family, the son of a distinguished general, Halder enjoyed an outstanding career as a staff officer, rising to become, on 10 February 1938, Beck's deputy and Chief of Operations. His elevation to Chief of the Army General Staff meant a severe break with the longstanding Prussian tradition of that office, for he was a Southerner, a Bavarian. Indefatigable and cautious by nature. Halder was a man of conservative outlook, although by no means rigid or hide-bound. Dedicated to his duty as a soldier, he personified the General Staff motto: 'Achieve much, appear little,' and saw himself as the 'Guardian of the Grail,' declaring on one occasion: '... we shall not depart by one hair's breadth from this spirit of the German General Staff.... He to whom the mantle of honour has no more meaning than a badge of rank or an increase in pay, lives on a different plane to that on which the Prussian General Staff was founded and has grown great.'[14] Even his physical appearance denoted the ideal staff officer: his hair close-cropped, his piercing eyes made all the more noticeable by his habit of wearing pince-nez, his whole aspect, unprepossessing though it was, reflecting quiet intelligence, shrewdness, and diligence. Nor was he a colourless administrator of the mould of Keitel. On the contrary, Halder possessed wide intellectual interests, with a special liking for mathematics and botany. An unexpected vehemence destroyed any impression of a phlegmatic personality, his emotions causing him to be moved to tears on many an occasion. In addition, he possessed the independence of mind, which, contrary to the accepted view, had always characterised the German staff officer in military affairs. As von Manstein recorded: 'He was incorruptibly objective in his utterances, and I myself have known him put a criticism to Hitler with the utmost frankness. On the same occasion one also saw how fervently he stood up for the interests of the fighting troops and how much he felt for them when wrong decisions were imposed on him.'[15]

It has been said that Halder took the post of Chief of the Army General Staff only so he could best continue his opposition to Hitler, whom he detested. His beliefs and actions seem to bear out this view. During the Blomberg–Fritsch affair he was one of the few who advocated strong action, even revolt; advice that Beck rejected. When relinquishing his post to Halder, Beck admitted: 'I now realise that you were right at the time. Now all depends on you.'[16] Indeed, the changeover between the two men took on the aspect of the senior bestowing his heritage of opposition to the Führer on the junior. According to Gisevius, one of the conspirators, 'Beck had assured us . . . that he would leave a successor who was more energetic than himself, and who was firmly determined to precipitate a revolution if Hitler should decide on war. . . . on taking office, General Halder immediately took steps to start discussions on the subject with Schacht, Goerdeler, Oster, and our entire group . . . he considered that we were drifting towards war, and that he would undertake an overthrow of the government.'[17]

However, despite his deep abhorrence of all that Hitler and his régime stood for, the new Chief of the General Staff was confronted with an irreconcilable dichotomy between his role as a conspirator and his duty as a highly placed soldier. This has been sympathetically described by von Manstein:

'Now, although it may be given to a politician to play the dual role of responsible adviser and conspirator, soldiers are not usually fitted for this kind of thing. . . . As Chief of the General Staff, it was Halder's duty to strive for the victory of the Army he was jointly responsible for leading—in other words, to see that the military operations of his Commander-in-Chief were successful. In the second of his roles, however, he could not desire such a victory. There cannot be the least doubt that Halder, when confronted by this difficult choice, opted for his military duty and did everything to serve the German Army in its arduous struggle. At the same time, his other role demanded that he should at all costs hold on to the position which, he hoped, would one day enable him to bring about Hitler's removal. To that end, however, he had to bow to the latter's military decisions, even if he did not agree with them. The conflict was bound to wear him down inwardly and finally led to his downfall. One thing is certain: it was in the interest of what was at stake, and not of his own person, that . . . Halder stuck it out for so long as Chief of Staff.'[18]

As Jodl discerned, despite the removal of Beck there still remained 'a strong current of resistance to Hitler's intentions and plans . . . within the Army General Staff.'[19] The very generals in whose hands the execution of Case Green had been placed, von Reichenau and von Rundstedt, expressed their apprehension to von Brauchitsch and urged him to attempt once more the conversion of Hitler. The Army Commander's interview with the dictator and Keitel on 3 September achieved nothing more than a further opportunity for more abuse from Hitler. This was followed on the 9th, during the Nuremberg Party rally, by another meeting, this time with Halder in attendance (he shared Beck's views on the Czech venture), which lasted from 10.00 p.m. to 3.30 a.m. the next morning. The protesters again achieved nothing, and, according to Keitel, Hitler, 'who wished to bring these recalcitrants round by calmly and patiently lecturing them . . . lost his patience [and] . . . coldly and sullenly . . . dismissed the gentlemen from his presence.'[20] The strained relationship between Hitler and his Army leaders was summed up by Jodl in his diary:

'. . . the Führer is aware that the Commander-in-Chief of the Army asked his commanders to support him in his attempt to make the Führer see sense on the subject of the adventure into which he seems determined to plunge. The Commander-in-Chief himself, so he said, unfortunately had no influence with the Führer. The atmosphere in Nuremberg was consequently cool and frosty. It is tragic that the Führer should have the whole nation behind him with the single exception of the Army generals.'[21]

However much the Army leadership might have opposed Hitler's intentions, they remained loyal to his wishes and faithful to their conception of duty. The western defences were strengthened; the plans for the deployment of five armies (36 divisions) against Czechoslovakia were expedited and presented to the Führer on 18 September; and all preparations were undertaken so that the attack could begin on 1 October.

Nevertheless, for one group within the Army, the Czechoslovak affair did serve to act as a catalyst for direct action against Hitler, action which, if successful, would have resulted in his deposition, and possibly in his death. It was a conspiracy set afoot by Canaris and Oster of the Abwehr group, and supported by a number of senior Army officers: Halder, von Witzleben, still commander of the vital Wehrkreis III, von Brockdorff-Ahlefeld, divisional commander of the Potsdam garrison, General Erich Hoepner, commander of 1st Light Division in Thuringia (a man who refused to have the statutory picture of Hitler hanging in his office), General Karl-Heinrich von Stülpnagel, Halder's successor as head of the Operations Department of the Army General Staff, von Hammerstein, and Beck. The plan was simple: Hitler would be arrested as soon as the final order for the invasion of Czechoslovakia had been given, and would later be put on trial on the charge that his activities constituted a grave danger to Germany; the Army would deal with all opposition and, unknown to him, von

Brauchitsch would issue a decree to the effect that he was the supreme authority of government pending the formation of a civilian caretaker administration which would proceed to determine a new form of government acceptable to the majority. Such a scheme rested on two fundamental factors: first, that the putsch would take place at the best psychological time—the moment Hitler gave the order to attack (it was Halder's task to communicate this information as soon as he knew it); and, second, that the thesis that the Czechoslovakian adventure would escalate into a major European conflict must be shown to be correct. (To ensure foreign intervention, the conspirators sent a number of envoys to London to warn of Hitler's intentions, but they achieved nothing.) By mid-September their plans were ready, in Halder's words, 'to the last gaiter-button,'[22] so carefully were they laid.

The political preparation for the invasion proceeded apace. Hitler based his aim of crushing Czechoslovakia on demands for the incorporation of the Sudetenland (that part of Czechoslovakia in which there was a large ethnic German population) into the Reich, and issued an ultimatum to that effect on 26 September. It was to expire at two o'clock on the afternoon of the 28th. Europe braced itself. Hitler announced to the British ambassador on the 27th: 'I am prepared for every eventuality. It is Tuesday today, and by next Monday we shall be at war.'[23] In Berlin, massed armour paraded down the Wilhelmstrasse; in London, trenches were dug; in Paris, there was panic. It was just as the generals had predicted: the Czechs had massed a well-trained, 800,000-strong field army behind strong defences; the French had partially mobilised and were capable of placing sixty-five divisions to face twelve of the Germans on the frontier; the British mobilised their fleet; the Soviets stated they would honour their treaty obligations; the Italians did nothing. Germany now faced the real possibility of a war on two fronts; her troops were outnumbered by those of France and Czechoslovakia alone by two to one. Perhaps even more shattering to Hitler than the prospect of facing such enemies was the painful awareness that his own people were, at best, apathetic to war. At the Berlin military parade, an American correspondent noted that the populace 'refused to look on, and the handful that did, stood at the kerb in utter silence. . . . It has been the most striking demonstration against war I've ever seen. . . . Hitler looked grim.'[24] In western Germany people rushed to leave the cities, such was the fear of air attack. Von Brauchitsch made his final attempt through Keitel to avert war, but to no avail.

But, as so often in the career of Adolf Hitler, just as Europe teetered on the edge of a general war, fate presented the German dictator with the means not only to avoid almost certain and catastrophic failure, but also to gain at least part of what he had demanded, with the prospect of the rest to come. The governments of France and Britain were still not convinced of the necessity for war, and, through the mediation of Mussolini, Hitler was persuaded to accept Chamberlain's proposal for a four-power conference on the Czechoslovak question. (Ironically, the country most concerned, Czechoslovakia, was not invited to attend.) The result of the meeting of the four leaders, Hitler, Mussolini, Chamberlain, and Daladier, which took place at Munich on 29 September, was the total acceptance of the Führer's demands. Military blackmail had worked. While Chamberlain fluttered his scrap of paper and declared 'peace in our time,' German troops prepared to march, unopposed, into the Sudetenland on 1 October.

Hitler's triumph at Munich spelt ruin for the military conspirators. Their ostensible reason for undertaking the coup had been denied them: instead of the Führer appearing as the great war-monger, he now was likened to a noble statesman, ensuring Germany's rights while still maintaining the peace of Europe. Even before Munich, it had been doubtful whether the mass of the Army would have followed the lead of a few officers and shed its loyalty to Hitler in the face of external aggression; but now, amid the overwhelming rejoicing that met the Führer's achievement, an attempted coup by a few relatively unknown and obscure men would have had no chance of success. In the foreseeable future there was little hope for the conspirators. The west's surrender at Munich had made Halder extremely wary, and, despite the urgings of Beck, Goerdeler, Canaris, and Oster, who were certain that Britain and France would act the minute Hitler occupied the rest of Czechoslovakia (had they not entered into a guarantee with the Czechs?), the Chief of the General Staff refused even to plan a putsch until the intervention had actually taken place. If war were declared over Czechoslovakia he would move, but not otherwise. Likewise von Brauchitsch, who, reportedly, before Munich was becoming sympathetic to the idea of a coup, was no longer prepared even to entertain the idea. Moreover, a great blow was dealt to the conspirators' plans by the routine removal of von Witzleben from the crucial Wehrkreis III around Berlin to command Army Group 2 based at Frankfurt-am-Main.

For the time being, at least, there could be no action from this quarter.

As was predicted by the conspirators, Hitler's occupation of the Sudetenland was only a preliminary to greater things. Just three weeks later he gave the order to plan the move against the rest of Czechoslovakia, and, after a few months of political preparation, the unhappy country was occupied on 15–16 March on the pretext of safeguarding the order and peace of central Europe. Czechoslovakia ceased to exist, being replaced by the Protectorate of Bohemia and Moravia. On 23 March, the Memelland was also placed under German rule. Halder's fears were proved justified: the world looked on; not a finger was lifted to aid the Czechs. Hitler was confident that 'in two weeks not a soul will bother to talk about it.'[25] But on this point he was wrong; his intuition failed him. The day following Hitler's entry into Prague, Chamberlain spoke to a meeting in his constituency. 'Is this,' he said, 'a step in the direction of an attempt to dominate the world by force? . . . no greater mistake could be made than to suppose that because it [Great Britain] believes war to be a senseless and a cruel thing, this nation has so lost its fibre that it will not take part to the utmost of its power in resisting such a challenge if it ever were made.'[26] Fifteen days later, the Prime Minister told a packed House of Commons: 'In the event of any action which clearly threatened Polish independence and which the Polish government accordingly considered it vital to resist with their national forces, His Majesty's government would feel themselves bound at once to lend the Polish government all support in their power. . . . I may add that the French government have authorised me to make plain that they stand in the same position. . . .'[27]

Just as the Czechoslovak affair marked a turning-point in the relations between Germany and her European neighbours, so, too, did it signify the final collaspe of the mutual trust and reliance between Hitler and the Army leaders. It was gone forever; one year had served to shatter it completely. Hitler now revealed a contempt for, and mistrust of, his generals not evidenced before the Blomberg–Fritsch affair. Certainly before 1938 Hossbach had detected in him a certain disillusionment with the Army leaders and their 'everlasting hesitations,' and there was a noticeable decline in his consideration for Army affairs and a greater readiness to entertain suspicions and complaints from the Party. But never would he previously have said, as he did now, that all generals were cowards. The ease with which he had humbled the once-proud *Generalität* during February and March 1938 had aroused in him a deep contempt which found its outlet through continual, and ever-increasing, insulting remarks. Men who allowed themselves to be dominated like Keitel, inhibited like von Brauchitsch, and rendered impotent like von Fritsch could never hope to regain his earlier respect and deference. What he saw as their vulnerability and weakness of character made him disdainful of their whole caste. At the meeting at the War Ministry on the afternoon of 4 February 1938, Hitler had concluded by saying: 'After such sorrowful experiences I must consider anyone capable of anything. The 100,000-man Army has failed to produce any great leaders. From now on I shall concern myself with personnel matters and make the right appointments.'[28] Not a word of protest was raised at this. For the first time the generals were feeling thoroughly intimidated and shamed by Hitler. As General Curt Liebmann wrote later:

'We all had the feeling that the Army—in contrast to the Navy, the Luftwaffe, and the Party—had suffered an annihilating blow and that in future any measure directed against it would be defended with a certain justice on the plea that the generals did not deserve any confidence.'[29]

Now, with the Army leadership shown to have been so mistaken over Czechoslovakia, added to their already miserable record over rearmament, the Rhineland, and Austria, Hitler's respect for the professional competence of his advisers reached a new low, forcing him to exclaim: 'What kind of generals are these whom I as the Head of State may have to propel into war? By rights, I should be the one seeking to ward off the generals' eagerness for war. . . .'[30] From then on his view was: 'I do not ask my generals to understand my orders but only to carry them out.'[31] He regarded the Army as an uncertain element in the state, even worse than the Foreign Office and the Judiciary. Westphal wrote: 'Hitler . . . saw in the General Staff . . . the "Public Enemy No. 1" or, as he and Göring were fond of saying, "the last Freemasons' Lodge in Germany."'[32]

In May 1938 Hitler transferred the supervision of the building of the West Wall from the Army to the Todt Organisation, abusing the military for having been too slow and accusing the General Staff of sabotaging his requirements. Outbursts became common. On hearing from Adam, then earmarked for Commander-in-Chief in the west, that more troops were needed to hold an attack from the French, Hitler lauched into a tirade, the butt of which was Keitel, who later wrote: 'I was obliged to stand there and listen to him ranting at me that this general had been a bad disappointment to him, and he would have to go; he had no use for generals like those who had no faith in their mission from the very outset.... Brauchitsch had the same lecture from him, and this outstanding soldier [Adam] was pensioned off.'[33] This incident had a sequel on 30 January 1939, when, at a meeting with senior officers, Hitler roundly condemned this spirit of faintheartedness, declaring 'I want no more warning memoranda from anybody.'[34] He announced that it was to be von Brauchitsch's task to give the officer corps a new purpose and select only those who had faith in the Führer. This spirit of contempt showed itself in other National Socialist leaders. In August 1938, Göring berated an assembly of officers, telling them: 'In this building [the War Ministry] lives the spirit of faintheartedness. This spirit must go.'[35] Von Manstein recorded the Luftwaffe Commander's address to a group of high-ranking military leaders six months later: 'In the course of his speech he quite brazenly upbraided the Army, as distinct from the other two services, for maintaining an outlook that was steeped in tradition and did not fit in with the National Socialist system. It was a speech which... von Brauchitsch, who was among those present, should on no account have tolerated.'[36] But he did, and there lay the rub. Even the leaders of the OKW found it in themselves to criticise the caste from whence they sprang. Jodl, for example, denigrated the men of the OKH for 'their pusillanimity and smugness,'[37] and, according to Warlimont, the heads of OKW 'openly expressed their displeasure that von Brauchitsch, supported by Halder, should try to put over his point of view even in matters of purely military policy. They once more made it clear that their conception of their overriding duty was to carry out Hitler's wishes and where required smooth the path for him in the military sphere.'³⁸

For their part, the Army leaders, with the exception of those fundamentally opposed to the Hitler régime, were humiliated and cowed. They, the professionals, had time and time again been shown up by an amateur; they had expended their capital of goodwill with the Führer for nothing. His intuition had proved right all along. The outcome of the Czechoslovak episode stunned them. It appeared as if Hitler had achieved everything he had aimed at without firing a shot: he had saved the nation from war, and had given it to additional glory and security. To the Germans, and to the Army, this was incontrovertible proof of his consummate skill as a statesman. Jodl summed it up: 'The genius of the Führer and his determination not to shun even a world war have again achieved victory without the use of force. One hopes that the incredulous, the weak, and the doubters have been converted, and will remain so.'³⁹ It seemed that, yet again, the generals' expertise had been proved wrong and Hitler's instinct right. That this was almost entirely due to factors outside the Führer's control, on chance and on the weakness of Germany's enemies, was not apparent; that their worst fears had come within an ace of being fulfilled mattered not at all. Hitler's successes told a different story. As von Brauchitsch told his captors after the war, the principal point was that all foreign countries had come to recognise Germany as an equal partner, which she certainly had not been before 1933.

As a result, the majority of generals resigned themselves to the Führer, to his intransigence and dominance. The reasons were many: Hitler's achievements in foreign policy, his obvious concern to expand the Reich's military capabilities, and his belief in the soldierly virtues (even though this was limited by his own convenience) had gone far to dissipate the evil impressions gained during the crisis of the previous February. His 'genius' was clear for all to see; the 'facts' proved it, and his 'glory' was bright enough for all to bask in; the Army was, after all, the prime instrument of his successes. Of his internal policies, the success in assuaging inflation, reducing unemployment, improving economic health, building roads, raising standards of public health, maintaining order, stimulating pride in country and creating enthusiasm for military affairs, overrode those more unpleasant aspects of the regime— the bullying of the Church, the increasing persecution of the Jews, which came to a head in the 'Chrystal Night' Pogrom of November 1938, and the maintenance of the concentration camps, from which the occasional death was by then being reported. Furthermore, the continual and hectic activity entailed in the rapid and large-scale rearmament and in the frequent occurrence of foreign ventures ensured that the Army was kept off-balance, its leaders' policies degenerating into rushed improvisations, its officers' energies concentrated on military affairs. Hitler had begun with the initiative; he kept it, and exploited it. Thus, in 1939, when the clouds of war began again to gather over Europe and Hitler embarked on yet another venture that risked armed conflict, the generals did nothing. Their opposition, for a time at least, was over. On 3 April 1939 Hitler issued a top-secret directive to his service chiefs which opened thus: 'The present attitude of Poland requires . . . the initiation of military preparations to remove, if necessary, any threat from this direction for ever.'⁴⁰ The operation was to be codenamed 'Case White,' and the plans were drawn up so that the attack could be undertaken at any time from 1 September. On 7 May the Army submitted its estimate of the situation; the preparations for the attack on Poland had begun. On 23 May, the day after the signing of the Pact of Steel with Italy (a military alliance, the military terms of which were kept secret from the Army), Hitler announced his future foreign policy to fourteen senior officers from all three services. He was unequivocal about his aim: it was war. 'Further successes can no longer be attained without the shedding of blood. . . . Danzig is not the subject of the dispute at all. It is a question of expanding our living space in the east. . . . There is no question of sparing Poland and we are left with the decision: to attack Poland at the first suitable opportunity. We cannot expect a repetition of the Czech affair. There will be war. Our task is to isolate Poland.' But he was quite prepared to take on the west: France and Britain, if they did not remain neutral, and, if need be, the Soviet Union as well. Declarations of neutrality would be ignored if they got in the way of military operations. 'The aim must be to deal the enemy a smashing or a finally decisive blow right at the start. Considerations of right or wrong, or of treaties, do not enter into the matter. . . . Preparations,' he announced, 'must be made for a long war as well as for a surprise attack, and every possible intervention by England on the Continent must be smashed.'⁴¹ Not one word of dissent was heard. By 15 June Hitler had in his hands the OKH plans for the Army's operations against Poland.

Preparations for the war proceeded calmly. Few made any attempt to save Germany from the impending catastrophe. Von Brauchitsch complied with Hitler's every wish, promised him to bring the war against Poland to a conclusion within a few weeks, and even threatened to arrest Schacht if he set foot in the OKH, so infuriated was he by the man's attempt to persuade him that his former oath to the constitution did not permit the declaration of war without the consent of the Reichstag. Halder, although approached by the underground opposition, would have nothing to do with their plans, and was, in any case, anxious that Germany's strategic position be improved by reacquiring Danzig and the Corridor before discarding the Führer. The OKH, generally, worked diligently to perfect their preparations. Men of Beck's calibre were lacking: one of the very few voices raised in protest was that of General Georg Thomas, head of the OKW Economics Department, who, together with Schacht, wrote a memorandum exposing the fallacies behind the idea of a quick war and explaining that Germany lacked the resources for a long conflict. This was presented to Keitel, but the only reaction it elicited was the assurance that Hitler's genius would overcome all problems. Colonel Rudolf Gercke, head of the Transport Department of the General Staff, added his note of pessimism when he reported: 'As regards transport, Germany is at the moment not ready for war.'[42] Such warnings went unheeded. The generals, indeed the Germans as a whole, had disliked and distrusted Poland since its inception in 1919, believing that a war against that country was 'a sacred duty though a sad necessity'[43] in order to eliminate once and for all the threat of a Polish attack on East Prussia and Silesia, and to remove the desecration involved in the creation of the Polish Corridor and the inclusion of two million

Germans within the Polish borders. Furthermore, the majority of the generals were confident of victory over a Poland which, they were sure, would stand alone, deserted by her allies as Czechoslovakia had been, against a Germany guided by the genius of Adolf Hitler, the victor of Munich. News that a pact was to be established with the Soviet Union was of considerable reassurance to the officers, especially to those nurtured in the Seeckt doctrine, for they believed that the removal of this potential enemy would guarantee also the neutrality of France and Britain.

Indeed, such was their confidence that neither OKW nor OKH drew up contingency plans in case of intervention from the east or the west. Despite Hitler's warlike speech of 23 May, the generals had at that time little fear of a European war. Von Manstein wrote later:

> 'We had watched Germany's precarious course along the razor's edge to date with close attention and were increasingly amazed at Hitler's incredible luck in attaining... all his overt and covert political aims. The man seemed to have an almost infallible instinct. Success had followed success.... All those things had been achieved without war. Why, we asked ourselves, should it be different this time? Look at Czechoslovakia.... we recalled Hitler's assertion that he would never be so rash as to unleash a war on two fronts.... That at least implied a man of reason. Raising that coarse voice of his, he had explicitly assured his military advisers that he was not idiot enough to bungle his way into a world war for the sake of Danzig or the Polish Corridor.'[44]

In such a climate of optimism and willing submission to the Führer's will, the military conspirators had no chance of organising a coup before war broke out. This they realised, and instead looked ahead to the time when the loyalty of the people and of the Army waned under the impact of the first disaster. Consequently, they restricted themselves to sending a number of emissaries abroad, whose purpose was to stiffen the resolve of the west through a complete exposé of Hitler's aims. They had to ensure that there would be no more Munichs; someone had to stand up to the dictator and now it could only be the democracies.

Hitler's last meeting with his senior officers before the outbreak of the European war took place on 22 August, the day von Ribbentrop flew to Moscow to sign the vital pact of non-aggression with the Soviet Union. The Führer's mood was uncompromising: 'Essentially, all depends on me, on my existence, because of my political talents.' War must come; there was no time to lose. 'Our economic situation is such that we cannot hold out more than a few years. . . . We have no other choice, we must act. . . . the political situation is favourable to us; in the Mediterranean, rivalry among Italy, France, and England; in the Orient, tension. . . . England is in great danger. France's position has also deteriorated. . . . Yugoslavia carries the germ of collapse. . . . Romania is weaker than before. . . . Turkey has been ruled by small minds. . . . All these fortunate circumstances will not prevail in two or three years.' It was highly probable that the west would not fight, but the risk had to be taken. Had this not been done before with spectacular results? Over Czechoslovakia he had carried his point when the generals had lost their nerve. The pact with the Soviet

Union had rendered western intervention most unlikely. It seemed impossible that Britain and France would risk a long war alone. It was now necessary to 'test the military machine. The Army must experience actual battle before the big final showdown in the west.' The dictator ended with the words: 'Close your hearts to pity! Act brutally! Eighty million people must obtain what is their right. . . . The stronger man is right. . . . Be harsh and remorseless! Be steeled against all signs of compassion. . . . Whoever has pondered over this world order knows that its meaning lies in the success of the best by means of force. . . .'[45] The generals remained silent; only one, von Wietersheim, chief of staff of Army Group Command 2, summoned enough courage to ask questions of his Führer. Keitel, who was present, believed that Hitler realised 'he was confronted with an iron phalanx of men who inwardly refused to be swayed by any speech they thought was just propaganda . . . it was a bitter disappointment to him.'[46] Von Manstetin, however, gained a more favourable impression of the whole affair and wrote: 'As a result of Hitler's address neither von Rundsetdt nor I—and presumably none of the other generals either—concluded that war was now inevitable . . . there would be an eleventh hour settlement.'[47] The attack was scheduled to begin at 4.30 a.m. on 26 August.

The only setback Hitler received to his plans came not from the Army, but from abroad. On the 25 August, Great Britain, undeterred by the signing of the German–Soviet pact, gave her guarantee to Poland; France followed suit. Almost simultaneously came news from Italy that in the event of a European war she could not fulfil her part of the Pact of Steel without substantial help from Germany in the form of military supplies. Hitler, faltering, ordered a temporary postponement of the invasion while he attempted to ensure the neutrality of the west. 'The Führer is finished,'[48] declared a delighted Oster, while Canaris announced: 'Peace has been saved for the next twenty years.'[49] But their high hopes came to nought. Hesitation turned to hate, and by the 28th, Hitler, anxious for revenge, had decided on armed conflict, even if it should be a two-front war. Late on the 30th he issued the order for the attack to begin at 4.45 a.m. on 1 September. Receiving this order early on the morning of the 31st, von Brauchitsch passed it to Halder who, through the efficient machinery of the Army General Staff, alerted the Army. That evening, under cover of darkness, a million and a half German troops began their final movement towards the Polish border.

PART TWO

The Battle of Ideas

However praiseworthy it may be to uphold tradition in the field of soldierly ethics, it is to be resisted in the field of military command. For today it is not only the business of commanders to think up new techniques which will destroy the value of the old; the potentialities of warfare are themselves being continually changed by technical advance. Thus the modern army commander . . . must be able to turn the whole structure of his thinking inside out.

ERWIN ROMMEL
The Rommel Papers

8

The Myth

Catchwords ... are necessary for all those who are unable to think for themselves. ... The following observations have no other object than to stimulate someone ... to think for himself and, whenever a catchword is uttered, to confront him with the question: Is this true?

HANS VON SEECKT
Commander-in-Chief of The German Army, 1920–26

In September 1939 the Germans overran Poland. In April 1940 they seized almost the whole of Norway. The following May they broke through Belgium and France and reached the coast. In June they took Paris, defeated France, and turned their attention on Great Britain. The impression on contemporary minds made by these fast and devastating victories was immense; the contrast with the bitter and lengthy deadlock of the previous World War seemingly inexplicable. Writing a number of years after the event, Churchill managed to convey the atmosphere of those 'dark and evil days':

'Now at last the slowly gathered, long-pent-up fury of the storm broke upon us. Four or five millions of men met each other in the first shock of the most merciless of all the wars of which record has been kept. Within a week the front in France, behind which we had been accustomed to dwell through the hard years of the former war and the opening phase of this, was to be irretrievably broken. Within three weeks the long-famed French Army was to collapse in rout and ruin, and our only British Army to be hurled into the sea with all its equipment lost. Within six weeks we were to find ourselves alone, almost disarmed, with triumphant Germany and Italy at our throats, with the whole of Europe open to Hitler's power....'[1]

How was this to be explained? How could the once-mighty and confident Allied Armies find themselves torn asunder in a matter of days, brushed contemptuously aside by a German Army, which, six years previously, had been only 100,000 men strong and denied all modern instruments of offence such as tanks and heavy artillery? At once the answer was believed to lie in a new form of warfare. A bewildered and fearful President of the Ministerial Council of France, Reynaud, explained on 21 May 1940, the day after the Germans had reached the Channel: 'The truth is that our classic conception of the conduct of war has come up against a new conception. At the basis of this ... there is not only the massive use of heavy armoured divisions or cooperation between them and aeroplanes, but the creation of disorder in the enemy's rear by means of parachute raids. ... We must think of the novel type of warfare which we are facing and take immediate decisions.'[2]

Military theorists, professionals and journalists on both sides of the Atlantic rushed immediately into print, to analyse, interpret, and catalogue the inexplicable; books, pamphlets, and articles appeared, one after another, each purporting to account for the reasons for these overwhelming victories by the Germany Army. Very quickly a coherent new theory of warfare was discerned and described in the fullest detail by the Allies. One of the best known of the contemporary writers was F. O. Miksche, an officer serving with the Free Czechoslovak Army, who wrote in 1941:

'Tactics have now been remade again. The new methods have been worked out and applied by German theorists. They are methods of "total war," first brought to the world's attention by Ludendorff's book of that name [published 1920]. ... Using machines instead of masses of men, they attack the whole of the forces of the enemy throughout all the territory held by that enemy; or rather they threaten and disrupt those forces by penetrating deeply into the territory. And they have introduced this same method into the spheres of economics, politics, and diplomacy.'[3]

Two years later, in 1943, J. R. Lester, in his book *Tank Warfare*, wrote:

'What the Germans did accomplish, though, was to reduce these theories [of the military theorist and historian, Liddell Hart, and others] to definite plans, to develop them to their logical conclusions with ruthless efficiency, to set up the necessary organisations to put the plans into operation, to lay the necessary foundations of metal, to create a large body of highly trained men with the necessary spirit to attempt the tasks, and the skill to accomplish them.'[4]

From such expositions emerged three basic elements fundamental to the new German system: first, that it was revolutionary, a complete break with the past, especially with the First World War, relying on the most recent developments in mechanisation, armour, and air-power to achieve the speedy disruption and demoralisation of the enemy's command and communications, thus allowing his disorganised and bewildered troops to be easily captured or destroyed; second, that it was a coherent theory, consciously adopted by the German High Command as its strategic and tactical basis for the prosecution of the war; and, thirdly, that the Armed Forces of the Third Reich were organised and equipped to meet the requirements of this new, and demanding, form of warfare.

Since 1945, although some have questioned the degree to which the German Army was equipped to undertake this new strategy, the historians of the Second World War have but echoed the conclusions of writers such as Miksche, Wintringham, and a host of others. Sir Basil Liddell Hart, whose military writings spanned half a century, beginning in the 1920s, asserted in his *History of the Second World War* that '... the German High Command had, rather hesitatingly, recognised the new theory of high-speed warfare, and was willing to give it a trial,'[5] and he described the battle of France as 'one of history's most striking examples of the decisive effect of a new idea, carried out by a dynamic executant.'[6] Major-General J. F. C. Fuller, also a renowned military theorist, wrote in his *Decisive Battles of the Western World:*

> 'The tactical policy of Germany was based on the offensive, and designed to overcome the linear defensive of her opponents by means of the attack by paralysation. Her army was fashioned into an armour-headed battering-ram which, under cover of fighter aircraft and dive-bombers—operating as flying field artillery—could break through its enemy's continuous front at selected points. The soul of German policy was mobility—a sharp, rapid, and short war on one front only.'[7]

And so a new form of warfare was born in the minds of men, one conceived out of bewilderment and the desire to rationalise the reasons for defeat; nurtured by those such as Liddell Hart and Fuller, who were flattered by the thought that the novel theories they had developed in the 1920s had been adopted and practised, albeit by the enemy; and wholeheartedly accepted by large numbers of historians only too glad to make use of a seemingly incontrovertible fact on which to base a whole series of assumptions about the war. To this child of the imagination, they gave the name *Blitzkrieg*.

Blitzkrieg (Lightning War) is a term inevitably linked

with the German Army and the Second World War. From a convenient way of explaining the unknown, it evolved into a strict definition of a new form of warfare believed to be the basis for the devastating early victories of Hitler's Germany. The essence of *Blitzkrieg* was seen to lie not so much in the use of airborne units, which was, in any case, limited and of a purely tactical nature, nor in the activities of the dive-bomber, which were designed essentially to support the ground forces, but in the handling of the new armoured formations. As Liddell Hart wrote in a letter to Guderian: 'The secret of *Blitzkrieg* lay partly in the tactical combination of tanks and aircraft, partly in the unexpectedness of the stroke in direction and time, but *above all* in the *"follow through"*—the way that a breakthrough (the tactical penetration of the front) was exploited by a deep strategic penetration carried out by an armoured force racing ahead of the main army, and operating independently.'[8] This is a concept which, remaining intact and unquestioned for the past thirty-five years, has been raised to the status of a self-evident truth. But *Blitzkrieg* is a myth. It is a word devoid of any meaning, having substance not in fact but in fiction, serving only to mislead and to deceive. For Hitler and the German military establishment, the High Commands of the Army and the Wehrmacht, did not espouse a new, revolutionary idea of war; the German Armed Forces were not organised, equipped, or directed according to new, revolutionary principles; and the German form of war in the years 1939 to 1942 was the product not of one new, revolutionary strategy, but of two strategies—one well-defined and traditional, the other ill-expressed and novel—whose mutual conflict went far to hamper the practice of the mode of warfare popularly imagined to be *Blitzkrieg*.

The etymology of the word *Blitzkrieg* is interesting, providing good reason for regarding the idea behind it with some suspicion. As if to point to the false impression it conveys, *Blitzkrieg*, although a German word, was not a German expression. German military manuals both before and during the war may be scoured in vain for any mention of it, and it is seldom found in even the post-war memoirs of the generals who were supposed to have evolved and practised its methods. As an expressive description, 'lightning war' extends back at least as far as the fourteenth century, when the Sultan Bayazid was known as *Yilderim* (The Thunderbolt) because of his method of rapid attack. It was with that meaning in mind that the word *Blitzkrieg* was adopted in 1939 and 1940. *Time* magazine of 28 September 1939 appears to have been the first to use the expression, in an article which referred to events in Poland as 'no war of occupation, but a war of quick penetration and obliteration—*Blitzkrieg*—lightning war.'[9] As a piece of journalese the word was a great and immediate success, being highly evocative of the fast and furious campaigns then being waged by the Germans on the continent of Europe. Guderian later recorded: 'As a result of the successes of our rapid campaigns . . . our enemies coined the word *Blitzkrieg*. . . .'[10] Its future was assured, and *Blitzkrieg* quickly evolved from a purely descriptive term into a whole new theory of strategy and tactics, a concept which, ever since, has pervaded all thought and writing on the Second World War. Indeed, so powerful was it that even the Germans came to use the word, Hitler believing: 'the expression *Blitzkrieg* is an Italian invention; we picked it up from the newspapers.'[11]

A further illusion, in part resulting from the idea of *Blitzkrieg*, also remains prevalent: it is that the German Army of 1939 was a well-trained force of overwhelming numbers possessing the best of modern weapons, fully prepared for a modern, mobile European war. At the time, military commentators were advancing the belief that 'The German Army is a new type of army. . . . Compared with German Army of today the armies of the western powers are terribly deficient both in numbers and equipment. Everything in the German Army today makes for mobility, striking force, and fire-power. In 1939-40 the military revolution in Germany will be complete, and by the doubling of its war material the German Army will be prepared to take the field at full strength.'[12] The same writer, Max Werner, had previously estimated German tank strength at between 6,000 and 7,000 machines, more than twice as many as they actually possessed. Such illusions before and during the war are easy to understand; they arose from the impression of overwhelming power and thorough preparedness shown by the Reich's Armed Forces through their outwardly impressive rearmament and decisive early victories, and were fostered by skillful propaganda, mass parades, and the general militarisation of society under National Socialism. Even after the war, when the reality of the Army's state in 1939 was revealed for all to see, these beliefs remained. For example, in 1956 a French writer, who had been taken prisoner in 1940, wrote of Germany as 'A nation straining at the leash, convoys of motorised troops tearing along autobahns, and an industry whose factories were working round the clock to create the most powerful war machine that Germany had ever possessed.'[13]

Nothing, however, could be further from the truth. The outbreak of a general war in 1939 took the German military leaders by surprise; the Army that marched triumphantly into Poland was one constituted not for war but for peace, and had still to be reorganised into a well-equipped, well-trained instrument of aggression. Four more years of tranquillity were required for the expansion of the period from 1933 to 1939 to be transformed from a purely numerical factor into a qualitative basis for military endeavour. Hitler's war abruptly interrupted this progression, and ensured that the Army was never to overcome the major defects with which it began the conflict. Consequently, the reasons for the German Army's initial victories lay not so much within itself, but in the weakness of its enemies. Perhaps never before in history had the countries of Europe been so ill-prepared for war.

'*Heerlos, Wehrlos, Ehrlos*'—disarmed, defenceless, dishonoured—was the constantly echoed, bitter catchphrase of the years 1919 to 1935. By the terms of the Treaty of Versailles, signed in the palace of the same name on 28 June 1919, the Allied peacemakers had attempted to ensure that never again would Germany possess the capacity to wage aggressive war. The total military force allowed her was restricted to 100,000 long-term volunteers, of whom 4,000 were officers, organised in seven infantry and three cavalry divisions, the armament and disposition of which were minutely specified. Weapons of offence such as tanks, heavy artillery, and aeroplanes were prohibited, the army being allowed light arms and field-guns only. The General Staff and the Military Academy were both disbanded, military schools and armament factories drastically reduced in numbers, and all preparations for mobilisation, such as the maintenance of secret lists of trained military personnel, were forbidden. Strict adherence to these provisions was to be ensured by the rigorous inspection of the Inter-Allied Control Commission. But perhaps even more serious than the imposed numerical and material restrictions were the humiliations of defeat and the uncertainties of internal disruption that attended the birth of the new German Army of Peace—the *Reichsheer* (National Army). There were few soldiers who, in 1919, could have looked to the future with much confidence; and yet, by 1933, the Reichsheer, still only 100,000 strong and still without tanks and heavy artillery, was one of the most efficient military machines on the continent of Europe, and formed the nucleus, however insufficient, of the greatly expanded German Army which, within seven years, was to reach the verge of world domination.

Ironically, it was the severe restrictions imposed on the Reichsheer that contributed greatly to such an unexpected development. Thanks to the peacemakers' action, Germany's Army, freed of the dead-weight of unprofessional masses and of ageing, cumbersome equipment, was able to transform itself into a dedicated military élite, ambitious for future development and desirous of regaining lost honour and prestige. Plans for the expansion of the Reichsheer were accepted unquestioningly, and the small 100,000 strong force was regarded as *Nicht ein Soldnerheer, sondern ein Führerheer* (an army not of mercenaries but of leaders), the kernel of a greatly enlarged force within the shell of an unduly restricted one. The Reichsheer recruited only those with the highest physical attainments; it accepted and encouraged men of good education; it greatly improved the relationship between officers and other ranks, a relationship based on confidence and comradeship, which in no way prejudiced strict discipline, instead of on authority and a harsh penal code; it encouraged the closest possible cooperation between all branches within the Army, fostered by a spirit of teamwork and the development of an effective system of communications between all levels, and types, of command; it embarked on the study and development of new equipment, which included exercises with dummy tanks, the institution of such bodies as the Inspectorate of Transport Troops, the illegal establishment of fighter, reconnaissance and bomber squadrons as part of the Army's aerial capability, and general military cooperation with the Soviet Union, involving experiments with armour and heavy artillery; it represented the unification of the various German armies, the Prussian, Bavarian, Saxon, and Württembergian, which had previously been coordinated by treaty, into a single federal force; and it created the first centralised directing authority in German military history, the *Chef der Heeresleitung*—supported by the *Truppenant*, the executive organ concerned with operational and training matters—who was directly responsible to the Reichswehr Minister, a system which replaced the previous confusion of War Minister, Head of the Military Cabinet, Chief of the General Staff, and Inspector-Generals.

The man mainly responsible for these developments was General Hans von Seeckt, Chief of the Army Leadership from 27 March 1920 to 6 October 1926. His achievement, according to Sir Basil Liddell Hart, was 'in starting a train of ideas which revitalised the German Army, turned it into a new line of progress, and enabled it to add a qualitative superiority to the quantitative recovery that the victors' inertia permitted it to carry out. He gave the Reichswehr a gospel of mobility....'[14] In short, von Seeckt's name has been indissolubly linked with the rising of the German Army, phoenix-like, from the ashes of impotence and defeat, and the establishment of that force on the principles of *Blitzkreig*. As such, it was he 'who had the primary influence on the Second World War.'[15]

However, such a high estimate of his importance, which gives von Seeckt a place in German military annals ranking with that of von Moltke and von Schlieffen, mistakes not only the nature of his work but the product for which he was given responsibility. A guardsman and a brilliant staff officer—he had been the architect of significant victories over the French and the Russians in the First World War—von Seeckt was fifty-four when appointed to command the Army with the mission of neutralising 'the poison contained in the disarmament clauses of the Treaty.'[16] But however energetic he was in pursuing this objective, von Seeckt remained a conservative by inclination, and was determined to shape the Reichsheer according to the best traditions of the Imperial Army. On his assuming office, his first words to his soldiers were that they should 'salvage what is of value from the past and put it to work in the present for a brighter future.'[17]

The traditions to which von Seeckt and his Army were grateful heirs were those that spanned the centuries. From Frederick the Great, King of Prussia in the mid-eighteenth century, was inherited a sense of individual honour and pride in the regiment which not only inspired courage under fire but also made retreat unthinkable, unless it was militarily expedient. From Gerhard von Scharnhorst, the great military reformer of the Napoleonic era, came the idea of intensive training, together with the concept of discipline as the willing, intelligent, but unquestioning subordination of the individual to his superiors in the efficient exercise of the military art. From von Moltke, von Schlieffen, and the Imperial Army came the strategic doctrine of decisive manoeuvre that aimed at the total destruction of the enemy through the massive encirclement of his forces, and the acceptance of new developments in weapons and machines in the achievement of that aim. Such were to be the principles that inspired the regeneration of the German Army. But they provided no basis for any radical change in direction.

Preparations for German rearmament had begun well before Hitler's accession to power in 1933. Two five-year economic plans were adopted in 1928: the first, to be concluded by 1933, called for the provision of an Army of sixteen divisions for defence against Poland; the second envisaged equipping a force of twenty-one divisions (an Army of 300,000 men) by 1937-38, to be trebled on mobilisation, for defence against France. Owing to the shortage of raw materials, the first programme was never begun, and although the second was initiated on 7 April 1933, progress was unexpectedly slow. However, by 1932 military plans for rearmament had begun to bear fruit. At the end of the year the Reichswehr Minister had ordered that, as from 1 April 1933, the Reichsheer would be enlarged by 2,500 men in a cautious reaction to the Five-Power Declaration of 11 December, which stated that the disarmament clauses of the Versailles Treaty should be replaced by a convention in which Germany would possess equality of rights in an arrangement that would provide security for all nations. Such was the state of world opinion at that time it only required the emergence in Germany of a political system pledged to rearmament to set the nation once again on the road to military strength.

Nonetheless, at the moment when hopes of rearmament were on the point of being realised, there was no common agreement as to the form this expansion should take. At the beginning of 1933, opinion on that point was far from uniform, von Seeckt by no means having enjoyed a monopoly of the argument. Some, a minority, wished merely to expand the Reichsheer as it stood; others, a high percentage, inclined towards von Seeckt's idea, and envisaged an extension of the Army to a small force of 200,000 effectives, fully equipped with the modern instruments of war, and a reduction in the terms of service from twelve years to six, together with a force of 20,000 officers and non-commissioned officers to train and command a large defensive militia. Such, too, had been the idea of von Seeckt's successors, Generals von Heye and von Hammerstein. And a few, led by Generals Gröner and von Schleicher, energetically supported the creation of a militia on the Swiss model, with long-service volunteers only for the armoured and technical forces. In the event, all three plans were rejected, and in their place was firmly established the traditional Continental concept of the mass army based on universal conscription. Von Seeckt had lost the argument; the ideas that had dominated the Reichsheer for the previous fourteen years were abandoned. Manpower, rather than quality, was the keynote for the future.

The reasons for the re-establishment of a mass Army along the lines of the old imperial force could be found in the new leadership that, in 1933, came to dominate Germany's military development. The new Defence Minister, von Blomberg, was an ardent admirer of Ludendorff, possessing nothing but admiration for his leadership during the First World War, and espoused, uncritically, his theories of mass armies and total warfare. He believed, as Ludendorff expressed it, that 'the fighting forces can never be . . . too strong. It is a fact that victory "goes to the big battalions" . . . numbers are only too often the decisive factor. It is a mistake to forget this. . . . The totalitarian war demands the incorporation in the Army of every man fit to bear arms. . . .'[18] But, more important, von Seeckt's idea found no favour with Adolf Hitler, whose political aims and preference called for large numbers of men under arms. In 1932 he made a speech which included the sentence: 'For whether Germany possesses an Army of 100,000 men or of 200,000 or 300,000 is in the last resort completely beside the point: the essential thing is whether Germany possesses eight million reservists whom she can transfer into her Army without any fear of falling into the same *Weltanschauliche* catastrophe as that of 1918. . . .'[19] Germany's enemies, Hitler reasoned, possessed massive armies: France had 600,000 men under arms in peace and a potential war strength of 5,000,000, while Czechoslovakia and Poland could each mobilise some 1,000,000 men. Against such odds, his argument ran, what could 100,000 men, or even 250,000 as was proposed at the Geneva Disarmament Conference, hope to achieve? Equality of numerical strength, at the very least, was seen as the only answer. Furthermore, Hitler called for a mass conscript army so as to complete the education of German youth by giving them discipline and training in the soldierly ideals that were supposed to form the basis of National Socialism. Thus, Hitler's first contribution to the future downfall of the German Army was to decide on rapid and considerable expansion as the basis of the Reich's military policy.

9

The War Lord

The value of a whole army—a mighty host of a million men—is dependent on one man alone: such is the influence of spirit.

SUN TZU
The Art of War

The advent of Hitler and National Socialism was bound to have a great impact on the German Army; the new movement provided it not only with the means, but also with the reason, for its existence. 'Armies for the preparation of peace do not exist,' Hitler had declared in 1930, 'they exist for triumphant exertion in war'; and war was to be the dynamic of his foreign policy, the principles of which were established in the mid-1920s and tragically put into practice in the late 1930s and early 1940s. It was a policy derived from his concept of

Social Darwinism, of biological determinism summed up in the phrase: 'Might is right; the stronger nation masters and thrives on the weaker.' The future, Hitler believed, belonged to the *Herrenvolk* (the master race), 'the militant Nordic section which will rise again and become the ruling element over these shopkeepers and pacifists, these puritans and speculators and busybodies.'[2] Although no detailed plan of conquest was ever propounded, the National Socialists nevertheless possessed a general strategy which might be summed up in three concepts: *Grossdeutschland*, *Lebensraum*, and *Weltmacht:* A 'greater Germany' with sufficient 'living space' would inevitably acquire 'world power.'

In *Mein Kampf* Hitler wrote prophetically:

'The foreign policy of a People's State must first of all bear in mind the duty of securing the existence of the race which is incorporated in this state. And this must be done by establishing a healthy and natural proportion between the number and growth of the population on the one hand and the extent and resources of the territory they inhabit on the other.... What I call a healthy proportion is that in which the support of a people is guaranteed by the resources of its own soil and subsoil.... Our movement must seek to abolish the present proportion between our population and the area of our national territory, considering national territory as a source of our maintenance and as the basis of political power.... The confines of the Reich as they existed in 1914 were thoroughly illogical, because they were not really complete, in the sense of including all the members of the German nation.

Nor were they reasonable, in view of the geographical exigencies of military defence.... We National Socialists must stick firmly to the aim that we have set for our foreign policy: namely, that the German people must be assured the territorial area which is necessary for it to exist on this earth.'3

How was this to be achieved? Hitler never possessed, nor fostered, any illusions as to this. In the second paragraph of *Mein Kampf* he wrote for all the world to see: 'the tears of war will produce the daily bread for the generations to come.'4 Eight years later he was to state: 'It is impossible to build up an Army and give it a sense of worth if the object of its existence is not the preparation for battle.'5 Thus the German Army of the Second World War was one developed by its political master for the specific purpose of waging war; it was intended primarily as an instrument of aggression.

'Hitler was a statesman. He was a dictator. He was Supreme Commander of the Armed Forces and, from 1941, Commander-in-Chief of the Army as well. He had unleashed the war, and it was up to him and no one else to conduct it. He did in fact lead the war.'6 So wrote General Jodl while a prisoner at Nuremberg, shortly after being sentenced to death by hanging for complicity in waging his Führer's battles. As he indicated, the 1935-45 conflict was in a unique way Hitler's own; he began it and, until 1943 when the initiative passed to the enemy, it was he who determined its course; he was the last of the warlords, the prime, and often the only, political and military mover of his country's destiny. Hitler, the former corporal of the trenches, was the force around which Germany's war machine revolved, ultimately to such an extent that it came to be a bitter, if apposite, jest among the officer corps that not a single private could be moved from door to window without his approval. Germany's Army became Hitler's Army, an instrument primarily moulded and directed according to his principles and attitudes, with the result that his failings and weaknesses as a military commander were reflected in its development and in its deployment in the field.

There have been conflicting views as to Hitler's military ability. Was he, as he himself once declared, 'the greatest strategic genius of all time,'[7] or, as Halder believed, 'a demoniac man [who] was no soldier-leader in the German sense. And, above all, he was not a great general.'[8] Military matters fascinated Hitler, and he was captivated by the power of modern armies. As an Austro-German he had immense pride and respect for the traditions of the nation's army; as a former infantry corporal, whose bravery on the Western Front won him the Iron Cross First Class, a high distinction for one of his rank, he possessed considerable sympathy for ordinary soldiers as well as an understanding of their hopes, fears, and deprivations; and as a national leader whose future policy was geared to military success, he maintained considerable interest in the force upon which his fortunes depended so greatly. One of his physicians, Dr. von Hasselbach, noted that 'The officers who had contact with him were continually astounded how precisely Hitler was informed about the calibre, mechanism, and range of a field piece. . . . When new weapons or vehicles were demonstrated, Hitler showed astonishing intuition concerning the advantages and flaws of their construction, and he often made helpful suggestions for improving them.'⁹

But Hitler's considerable technical knowledge, learnt somewhat parrot-fashion, was no guarantee of his ability in the wider field of military strategy. There, his inexperience, his self-education, and his amateurism were most noticeable and most fatal. His character was deficient of the application and the self-discipline necessary for acquiring anything more than a superficial military knowledge. Not that this worried the Führer; indeed, he maintained that it was a strength on his part, and, until the end, he liked to emphasise that his was a feeling, an intuition, for war, one that was immeasurably superior to the professional, but restrictive, attitude of his officers. The result was a uniquely individual approach to war-making. Percy Schramm, the Führer's official war-diarist from 1943 to 1945, summed it up:

> 'Will-power was to Hitler the dominating factor everywhere. . . . He thought that if he had ever learnt to think in the terms of a General Staff officer, at every single step he would have had to stop and calculate the impossibility of reaching the next. Consequently, he concluded, he would never even have tried to come to power, since on the basis of objective calculations he had no prospect of success in the first place. Once in power he remained a revolutionary no less in his way of acting than in his way of thinking. He regarded it as self-evident that his initial successes had created the prospect of further triumphs, insofar as they encouraged his followers and intimidated his adversaries. The Führer regarded it as proper in his military leadership, as he had in his political

activity, to establish goals which were so far-reaching that the objective professionals would declare them impossible. . . . A good many of the military successes during the first part of the war had, after all, been achieved despite the predictions of the General Staff. . . . Perhaps the most decisive of all the problems of the supreme German leadership in the war was that Hitler, because of his initial successes, could say that he, and not the General Staff, which on the basis of its calculations had not established such far-reaching goals, was the true realist. He had foreseen actual developments more clearly, precisely because he had taken the incalculable into account. But then the situation changed again, and in the end the General Staff was correct in its calculations.'[10]

Acute though Schramm's observations usually were, he failed to perceive that, despite the repeated protestations to the contrary, Hitler felt his lack of training in, and familiarity with, military affairs, and that he was ever insecure in the presence of the ability and specialist knowledge displayed by his generals. As a man who was inordinately fearful of his own deficiencies, he was haunted by the ever-present spectre of failure, unable and unwilling to come to terms with the brutal facts of his own existence, with the reality behind the façade. He therefore sought refuge in the creation of visions of himself as a supreme warlord, the spiritual successor to Frederick the Great and Attila the Hun, the manipulator of powerful armies sweeping across the face of the Continent, the purveyor of mass destruction. He hid behind the self-conscious adoption of 'will-power,' which, as von Manstein recognised, was the 'decisive factor in Hitler's military leadership.'[11] He was continually attempting to prove to himself, his associates, and the German people that he, above all others, possessed a nerve of iron, that his will-power alone would ensure final victory even in the face of desperate odds. His conversation was littered with such sentiments. In August 1944, for example, he embarked on a lengthy justification of his actions: 'For the past five years I have cut myself off from the other world. I have neither visited the theatre, heard a concert, nor seen a film. I live only for the single tasks of leading this struggle, because I know if there is not a man in there behind it who by his very nature has a will of iron, then the struggle cannot be won. . . .'[12] It was with such words that Hitler continually strove to bolster himself; perhaps after his early successes he even came to believe in them for a while. But during the war, when he was starkly confronted with failure in the form of devastating military reverses, the façade began to crack and the inadequacies reveal themselves. Fits of violent rage, which indicated total frustration and despair, even insanity, became common, and, his health steadily deteriorating, his nerves visibly faltering, Hitler withdrew further into a fantasy world of moving non-existent armies about out-of-date fields of battle, a lone, suspicious creature surrounded by nothing but desertion and defeat. What he had sought to conceal for so long, so successfully, now became a reality for all to see.

What of Hitler's understanding of the conduct of war? In 1933 he summed up his ideas as follows:

'I have the gift of reducing all problems to their

simplest foundations. War has been erected into a secret science and surrounded with momentous solemnity. But war is the most natural, the most everyday matter. War is eternal, war is universal. . . . Let us go back to primitive life: the life of the savages. What is war but cunning, deception, delusion, attack, and surprise? . . . The place of artillery preparation for frontal attack by the infantry in trench warfare will in future be taken by revolutionary propaganda, to break down the enemy psychologically before the armies begin to function at all. . . . When the enemy is demoralised from within, when he stands on the brink of revolution, when social unrest threatens—that is the right moment. A single blow must destroy him. Aerial attacks, stupendous in their mass-effect, surprise, terror, sabotage, assassination from within, the murder of leading men, overwhelming attacks on all weak points in the enemy's defences, sudden attacks, all in the same second, without regard for reserves or losses: that is the war of the future. A gigantic, all-destroying blow. I do not consider consequences; I think only of this one thing. . . . I do not play at war. . . . I shall make war. I shall determine the correct moment for attack. . . . Gentleman, let us not play at being heroes, but let us destroy the enemy. . . . I have made the doctrines of revolution the basis of my policy. . . . The next war will be unbelievably bloody and grim. But the most inhuman war, one which makes no distinction between military and civilian combatants, will be at the same time the kindest, because it will be the shortest. . . . My motto is: Destroy him by all and any means. I am the one who will wage the war.'[13]

From such superficial, egocentric bombast, historians have attempted to discern a coherent, revolutionary policy of war, the basis of *Blitzkrieg*. One of the earliest, Major-General Fuller, wrote of Hitler in 1943 as 'one of the most, if not actually the most, original soldiers in all history,'[14] and in 1961 he claimed: 'As a tactical theorist, Hitler was as clairvoyant as he was astute as a politician. He had watched the last war closely and had absorbed its tactical lessons—a remarkable thing for a corporal to do. But what was more remarkable, he projected them into the future and built his military power on them. In 1939, the superiority of the German Army [lay] . . . in its tactics, which, if not devised by Hitler himself, were forced by him upon his reluctant General Staff.'[15] Such a thesis, however, is untenable. Hitler was no military theorist; he possessed no coherent, detailed strategy, and his utterances reveal no revolutionary insight into the future workings of war. For what was new or original about them? Speedy manoeuvre certainly wasn't; nor was the use of modern technology, nor the emphasis placed on psychological warfare, a weapon of war as old as mankind and which had been used systematically in the 1914–18 War. It is worth remembering that, despite his boastful predictions, Hitler never succeeded in using 'revolutionary propaganda, to break down the enemy psychologically before the armies began to function . . . ,'[16] and that during the invasion of the Soviet Union, when its use would have served German interests well, he conspicuously failed to exploit its potential.

Thus, instead of a revolutionary doctrine, Hitler possessed only the vaguest philosophy of war. His approach was very much that of the military illiterate and the political street-fighter: the former with his fascination for numbers, destructive power, and speed of operations; the latter with his belief in the importance of deception, brute force, and propaganda. In the place of a coherent theory of strategy and tactics, Hitler formed a pseudo-philosophy of war, the product of an amalgam of the ill-assorted, half-formed ideas so typical of National Socialism. He viewed warfare in Hobbesian terms of force and fraud, possessing the romantic vision of himself as a reincarnation of the *Furor Teutonicus*, a modern *Feldherr*, a warlord in the traditions of Attila the Hun. As such, Hitler's military thinking was limited to high-sounding, but empty, phrases. While he could state, quite unexceptionally, that 'The next war will be quite different from the last world war. Infantry attacks and mass formations are obsolete. Interlocked frontal struggles lasting for years on petrified fronts will not return, I guarantee that. They were a degenerate form of war . . . ,' he could also, in the next breath, indicate an alarming ignorance and misapprehension when pronouncing: '. . . strategy does not change, at least not through tactical interventions. . . . Has anything changed since the battle of Cannae? Did the invention of gunpowder in the Middle Ages change the laws of strategy? I am sceptical as to the value of technical inventions. No technical novelty has ever permanently revolutionised warfare. Each technical advance is followed by another which cancels out its effects.'[17] That such a man came to exert so decisive a control over the fortunes of the Army in the field of battle was a disaster. As a military commander, Hitler bore out to the full Gröner's warning: 'Unfortunately, strategy is a contagious disease which by preference affects heads which are not exactly filled with wisdom.'[18]

Many historians have seen in the combination of Hitler's foreign and economic policies further evidence of the existence of *Blitzkrieg*, this time as a grand strategic principle. They argue that Hitler realised that, in common with the Wilhelmine Empire, the Third Reich was incapable of winning a great war of the proportions of the 1914–18 conflict; that it simply did not possess the manpower, the raw materials, or the economic resources necessary for total war, and that, as a result, he based his grand strategy on a series of consecutive, separate, local wars which achieved their objectives in single, short, but decisive campaigns. Thus, the historians continue, Hitler's Army was consciously organised and equipped, and his economy geared, for limited lightning wars, each of no more than three months' duration. But, however attractive this thesis might be as an explanation of the unusual events of 1935–42, it possesses no basis in reality. It is true that Hitler realised that Germany could not undertake a conflict of the magnitude of the First World War, and that wars between large coalitions were to be avoided if possible. But in this he was far from being alone among the statesmen of Europe. Furthermore, no special significance should be attached to his desire to gain territorial objectives through conflicts of the shortest possible duration, for few national leaders have wished, or planned, otherwise. Indeed, it was an accepted and well-established German policy to base preparations for war on such a precept, the famous Schlieffen Plan for the attack against France and Russia in 1914 being the prime example, founded as it was on a lightning victory being achieved in the west before turning east.

Such awareness and hope, alone, provides no proof of any detailed policy of *Blitzkrieg*, while even the most cursory glance at the German economy will reveal the total absence of any such systematic planning. For the German preparations for war were nothing but a chaos of competing interests and makeshift administrative methods, one of the distinguishing features of National Socialism. The Third Reich's economic resources, far from being organised according to a national plan, let alone to a well-thought-out strategy for war, were 'up for grabs,' to use a colloquial expression which so well describes the highly competitive struggle between industrial and commercial interests, the various departments of state, the party and its organisations, especially the Labour Front, and the Armed Forces, the individual services of which were as disregarding of the others' interests as were the civilian agencies. Such a chronic condition was rendered worse by the personal nature of Hitler's dictatorship, which took little notice of the written word (the Führer was bored by paper work), but which was fairly receptive to those who had the ear of the Führer. Therefore, the Party functionaries such as Göring, Goebbels, Himmler, von Ribbentrop, and Ley had a considerable advantage over the Army and Navy chiefs in gaining support for their own schemes. This economic chaos was further complicated by the fact that the National Socialist leaders, ever fearful for their popularity, demanded, simultaneously with the large sums being spent on rearmament, the maximum prosperity for the civilian economy. Unemployment was to be eradicated, output of consumer goods greatly increased, services such as railways and roads improved, and construction of public buildings considerably expanded. Guns *and* butter, to paraphrase Göring's famous remark, was their aim. But this the economy proved incapable of providing. This result was that, while the German economy was in part geared *to* war, it was not geared *for* war. It was not until March 1940 that the Ministry of Armaments and Munitions was created, and it was 1942 before that body began to acquire the wide-ranging and overriding powers necessary for a coordinated policy of war production. The miracles of output that were then achieved are adequate proof, if proof were needed, of the gross inadequacy of the Third Reich's economic planning for war.

Thus, while Hitler and National Socialism gave the German Army the most potent reason for its existence—war—it failed miserably to provide it, at the same time, with the means necessary for its successful execution. Not only did the dictator fail to understand the strategic realities behind the Army's operation in the field, but he proved utterly incapable of ensuring that it possessed, in adequate quantities, even the most fundamental material resources essential for its tasks. Furthermore, Hitler's personal character was to ensure that his close union with the Army was not likely to be a happy one. The ancient Chinese believed that a commander in war stood for the virtues of wisdom, sincerity, benevolence, courage, and strictness; Hitler possessed none of these. His personal failings, his ignorance, and his neglect were largely the cause of the Army's struggle being hard and, ultimately, fruitless.

10

Strategic Tradition

Mobility is the keynote of war.
NAPOLEON

On 16 March 1935, Hitler announced to the world that Germany was rearming. In the fulfilment of Article 22 of the National Socialist twenty-five-point programme, which demanded the 'abolition of a mercenary army and the formation of a national army,' he declared that 'service in the Wehrmacht is based on compulsory military service.'[1] This was the conclusion of the long campaign against the Versailles restrictions, and the culmination of a surreptitious expansion undertaken since 1933. Over the past two years rearmament had been proceeding apace: during 1933 the size of the Army had been increased by some ten to 20,000 men; in December of that same year the decision was taken to treble the numbers to 300,000; and, on 1 October 1934, a new organisation for the future expansion was introduced, allowing for the establishment of twenty-one infantry and three cavalry divisions, and the enlargement of Wehrkreis headquarters to army corps size. On that date, 70,000 additional men entered the Army, bringing the total of men under arms to 240,000. And then, in March 1935, seven days after the existence of the German Air Force was declared, the most decisive step was taken, one that marked a considerable extension in the rearmament policy as it had been understood by the Army until that time. Twelve months' service in the Armed Forces became compulsory for the youth of Germany, and the Army was increased to the size of thirty-six divisions. The cry that had been on the lips of nationalists for sixteen years—*'Wir wollen wieder Waffen!'* (We will have arms again)—was heard no more.

Hitler's decision, taken without any proper consultation with his military advisers, meant that the Third Reich would possess an active force of some 450,000 men, a more than four-fold increase on the number allowed by the Versailles Treaty, and half as much again as the figure regarded by the Army as tolerable for training purposes at that time. The first knowledge most of the generals had of this decision came from their radios on the morning of 16 March 1935. All were surprised. Von Manstein remembered that 'The General Staff, had it been asked, would have proposed twenty-one divisions.... The figure of thirty-six ... was due to a spontaneous decision by Hitler.'[2] However, there was no sign of their misgivings the next day when, at celebrations to mark the Heroes Memorial Day, the military fervently welcomed the rebirth of their tradition, the re-establishment of the mass army. At Hitler's side in the State Opera House sat Field-Marshal von Mackensen, the aged representative of the old Army, attired in his uniform of the Death's Head Hussars, and behind them, under a massive silver and black Iron Cross, stood representatives of the new Army clad in their field grey and holding upright the war flags of the nation. It was a memorable occasion, symbolising the unity of the old and the new, manifested in the emergence of the conscript mass Army of National Socialist Germany. And on 1 June, as if to signify the complete break with the unlamented, immediate past, the Reichswehr was renamed *Die Wehrmacht* and the Reichsheer became simply *Das Heer*—the Army.

But the expansion to thirty-six active divisions announced in March 1935 was not the limit of the German peacetime army. By mid-1939, it contained no fewer than fifty-two active and fifty-one reserve divisions, which amounted to 730,000 men under arms, with another 1,100,000 in reserve. (The incorporation of Austria into the Reich in 1938 ultimately gave six active divisions to the German Army.) The 1939 peacetime figures represent a staggering 500 per cent increase in active formations in only six years, and a thousand per cent increase in total mobilised strength. In seven years, a force eighteen times the size of the original body had been trained. After mobilisation for war in September 1939, the German Army possessed 3,706,104 men under arms.

In terms of numbers, German rearmament in the six years until September 1939 had been a sizeable achievement. Indeed, it was little short of a military miracle that such a grossly expanded force could have achieved the degree of efficiency required to dominate the continent of Europe in two years of war. But numbers alone do not compose an Army. Without training, equipment, organisation, and command, the men are nothing but an ill-assorted group instead of a well-coordinated force of soldiers, finely trained to the efficient practice of warfare. At the basis of an army lies its *Kriegsführung* (war direction), the strategic doctrine that may be defined as the art of distributing and applying military means to fulfil the ends of policy. An army's strategy is the system of large-scale measures whereby its forces in the field are manoeuvred so as to bring the war to a conclusion, and it is this that gives an army its particular soul, its distinctive, unique character without which it would be just an incoherent, inanimate mass. Thus, a twentieth century force which bases its training, equipment, organisation, and command on a defensive strategy of interlocking trench and fortification systems will be radically different in composition from one which relies on an aggressive doctrine of decisive manoeuvre. On the quality of its strategic direction, then, is based the fortune of the army and, consequently, of the entire nation. An army's *Kriegsführung* is its most treasured possession.

Hitler's Army, although unmistakably a creature of the twentieth century, had the roots of its strategic direction firmly embedded in its imperial past. It was dominated by a well-established tradition extending back to the 1850s, a tradition which was to prove a greater source of strength to the commanders and troops in the field than were the numbers and quality of their equipment or the questionable tenets of their political creed. As has been seen, the link that bound the Army to its history was both immutable and indissoluble, strong enough to overcome the humiliation of defeat and the ravages of the peace treaties in 1918 and 1919. From two men in particular, Helmuth von Moltke and Alfred von Schlieffen, both renowned Chiefs of the General Staff, the German Army owed the principles that determined the nature of its wars—with only a short break—from the years 1861 to 1942, principles that placed emphasis on fast, decisive manoeuvre aimed at the encirclement and the destruction of the mass of the enemy.

Few men can have been as receptive to the opportunities presented by modern developments as von Moltke, Chief of the Prussian General Staff from 1857 to 1871. It was he who established the German military practice of exploiting the material resources and technological innovations of the age. In the mid-nineteenth century it was this readiness to use the new, and explore the unknown, that made possible not only the establishment of the Prussian Army as Europe's foremost military instrument, but also the creation by the northern state of Prussia of a united Imperial Germany. The application of the power of the industrial revolution enabled the Prussians, stimulated as they were by the desire for expansion, to spearhead the transformation of warfare from the napoleonic to the modern, leaving to subsequent generations of German soldiers the task, not of creating any new strategy, but of improving and exploiting the form already elaborated and practised to such effect. For Germany, and for the rest of the world, the revolution in war came not with the emergence of the tank or the aeroplane in the 1900s, but with the appearance of the railway, the telegraph, and the rifled weapon in the previous century. These inventions, coupled with improved standards of health, the mass production of goods, and the energy of capitalist organisation, permitted the rapid mobilisation and movement, the systematic supply, and the centralised command of considerably increased numbers of troops armed with weapons of greater accuracy and range than ever before. At first, even with the lessons of the first and terrible test of the new technology during the American Civil War in the early 1860s before them, European commanders had little idea of the impact that these developments would have on tactics and strategy. An exception, however, was von Moltke, who, with his officers, evolved new principles to suit these changed conditions—principles which, having evolved with time, were applied by his successors in the German High Command during the Second World War.

Central to this German idea of war was the concept of rapid, decisive manoeuvre. Von Moltke and his contemporaries saw that new armaments, in particular the breech-loading rifle, had made defensive fire-power the strongest single factor on the battlefield. In 1869 he wrote: 'It is absolutely beyond all doubt that the man who shoots without stirring has all the advantage of him who fires while advancing, . . . and that, if to the most spirited dash one opposes a quiet steadfastness, it is fire-effect, nowadays so powerful, which will determine the issue.'[3] As a consequence, any aggressor would have to make both time and space his servants in order to possess any chance of victory; the enemy might have more men and better guns, but speed and movement would master them. Von Moltke argued that 'Little success can be expected from a mere frontal attack, but very likely a great deal of loss. We must therefore turn towards the flanks of the enemy's position.'[4] Furthermore, the significant advances in communication and transport allowed a mobilisation and a concentration of large forces much faster than anything ever experienced before, thereby laying the enemy open to be caught off-balance before his preparations were complete. This, von Moltke saw as the means by which the dreaded result of the coalition system then gripping Europe, a war on two fronts, could be avoided. It was now possible, he argued, to deploy the main body of the army on one front, there to arrive at a speedy victory, before turning to effect a decision on the other front by an equally deft stroke. The quick concentration of force at the decisive point was indispensable, the grand sweeping movements of encirclement basic, and the total destruction of the enemy paramount.

However, von Moltke was careful not to transform his ideas about warfare into a rigid doctrine. For him the art of war lay in a combination of calculation and daring, each new conflict bringing with it new circumstances that invalidated any attempt to impose on it strict, preordained strategic principles. In his words: 'Strategy is a system of ad hoc expedients; it is more than knowledge, it is the application of knowledge to practical life, the development of an original idea in accordance with continually changing circumstances. It is the art of action, under the pressure of the most difficult conditions.'[5] It was left to von Schlieffen, the Chief of the General Staff from 1891 to 1905, to develop von Moltke's principles into well-established doctrines. Von Schlieffen's rejection of the strategy of attrition was total. For him, the only method of war was decisive manoeuvre, the extension of von Moltke's precepts to their limit. He coined the expression *Vernichtungsgedanke* (the idea of annihilation), which conveyed in a single striking term what he believed to be the end of all military endeavour—the total destruction of the enemy's forces, not by means of relatively slow, costly frontal attacks, but of swift, decisive blows from the flanks and the rear. Victory was seen to lie in strategic surprise, in the concentration of force at the decisive point, and in fast, far-reaching concentric encircling movements, all of which aimed at creating the decisive *Kesselschlachten* (cauldron battles) to surround, kill, and capture the opposing army in as short a time as possible. In his service regulations, von Schlieffen wrote: 'How is the enemy's wing to be attacked? Not with one or two corps, but with one or more armies, and the march of these armies should be directed, not against the flank, but against the enemy's line of retreat. . . . This leads immediately . . . to disorder and confusion which gives an opportunity for a battle with inverted front, a battle of annihilation, a battle with an obstacle in the rear of the enemy.'[6] Such, von Schlieffen agreed, were the lessons to be derived from history, especially from the great Carthaginian victory at Cannae in 216 B.C., a battle won by the speedy double envelopment of the numerically superior Romans, and from the Prussian success at Leuthen in 1757, when Frederick the Great's army decisively defeated an Austrian force twice its size, in what Napoleon was to call 'a masterpiece of movements, manoeuvres and resolution.' Likewise, the Germans of the nineteenth and twentieth centuries were to find their victories on the flanks and rear of their enemies. Double envelopment became their theme, *Vernichtungsgedanke* their watchword.

When compared with what had gone before, the new form of warfare as practised by the Germans was swift and efficient in the extreme. Indeed, the epithet *Blitzkrieg* might well be applied to their wars from 1866 to 1914 with as much justification as to their 1939–41 campaigns. The 1866 war against the Austro–Hungarian Empire, then generally believed to possess one of the best Continental armies, with France poised in the background, lasted just seven weeks, while the outcome of the campaign against the French in 1870–71 was decided in little more than six, although the fighting continued for another three months owing to the fierce resistance of Paris. The battle of Sadowa in 1866 had been conceived by von Moltke as one of encirclement, but there his generals failed him; the battle of Sedan four years later showed that the Prussian military establishment had learnt its lesson, and Napoleon III was forced to surrender with 104,000 men, till then the largest field force captured in modern times. In 1914 the Germans, confronted with a war on two fronts, put into practice a modified version of von Schlieffen's brilliant plan of 1905, comprised, first, of a wide manoeuvre aimed at turning the French rear which would result in the total defeat of France in a couple of months, and, then, of a switch of the armies to the east, there to face the slow but massive 'Russian Bear' with sufficient forces to bring about its death. The Germans came close to achieving this; in fewer than six weeks they advanced to within thirty miles of Paris and expected to end the campaign within a further week. But faulty decisions by their commanders both before and during the invasion, and the physical and material exhaustion that such a rapid advance occasioned, enabled the Allied armies to halt the German onslaught on the Marne.

It is at this point in the history of the German Army, in mid-September 1914, that mobility of operations temporarily gave way to a static form of war—a war of attrition in which victory would belong to the side possessing numerical and material superiority. The breakdown of the invasion plan, and the apparent failure of the all-pervasive strategy of manoeuvre, stunned the General Staff, and led to the fatal resolve to abandon, at least temporarily, the offensive, and stand on the defensive. Thus, the German Army surrendered their advantage of mobility and gave the Allies time to recover and reinforce. The resumption of the offensive came too late, and the subsequent race to the Channel in an attempt to outflank the opposition ended in stalemate. Once the deadly trio of trench, wire, and machine-gun was established in one unbroken line from the Channel coast to the Swiss border, all attempts to re-establish the strategy of swift, decisive manoeuvre failed. Their possession of time and space gone, the Germans learnt the power of the defensive that von Moltke and von Schlieffen had feared. Four weary years of deadlock and ultimate defeat were the result, a painful time made more bitter by the constant reminder of the open warfare that continued in the east until peace was made with Russia in 1917. Ironically, the superiority of German mobile strategy was never more evident than in the two whirlwind campaigns in the autumns of 1915 and 1916, by which Serbia and then Romania were humiliated, their armies swept away, and all danger from them eliminated. Thus, despite the unpleasant experience on the Western Front, *Vernichtungsgedanke* remained a principle of German strategy until the end of the war.

In the crisis of uncertainty and doubt that understandably pervaded German military thinking immediately after the bitter and humiliating defeat in 1918, the traditional strategy of decisive manoeuvre came in for some questioning. Was it still possible? If so, was it even desirable? Some feared that the 1914-18 War had shown that its days were numbered, that fire and fortification rather than movement now irrevocably dominated the battlefield. Others wanted to copy the French doctrine of the offensive, which, although slow, was safe. It presented no vulnerable flanks to the enemy and, supported by massed tanks and artillery, possessed considerable fire-power which was valuable in defence as well as in attack. But the majority remained firm—even buttressed—in their allegiance to the strategy that the Germans had rightly come to regard as their own special reserve. They believed that the experience of the war had shown the need for greater mobility, not less, and that the failure of the German Army was one of command and instrumentation rather than of doctrine. Foremost among them was von Seeckt. In a much-quoted phrase he summed up his strategic principles: 'In brief, the whole future of warfare appears to me to lie in the employment of mobile armies, relatively small but of high quality, and rendered distinctly more effective by the addition of aircraft, and in the simultaneous mobilisation of the whole force, either to feed the attack or for home defence.'[7] The army of the future, he claimed 'must satisfy three main demands: first, high mobility, to be attained by the employment of numerous and highly efficient cavalry, the fullest possible use of motor transport, and the marching capacity of the infantry;

second, the most effective armament; and third, continuous replacement of men and material.'

At the centre of von Seeckt's idea was the abandonment of mass armies and the adoption, instead, of small but highly mobile and well-trained striking forces to carry out the strategy of decisive manoeuvre. He argued that the past had shown that 'Mass becomes immobile: it cannot manoeuvre and therefore cannot win victories, it can only crush by sheer weight . . . A conscript mass, whose training has been brief and superficial, is "cannon fodder" in the worst sense of the word, if pitted against a small number of practised technicians on the other side.' In its place, von Seeckt wished to see a professional army possessing a higher mobility, a stronger and more flexible logistical system, and a greater degree of independence from civilian reserves, one which was capable of mobilising rapidly, taking the initiative, and moving decisively to annihilate the enemy before his preparations were complete. At the same time there would be a large-scale militia which, 'though unsuited to take part in a war of movement and seeking a decision in formal battle, is well able to fulfil the duty of home defence, and at the same time to provide from its best elements a continuous reinforcement of the regular, combatant army in the field.'[8]

Enlightened though von Seeckt's ideas were, they were by no means revolutionary. Reliance on a military mass had never been a central part of the German military tradition, but emphasis on manoeuvre and the implementation of new technology had. Von Seeckt went no further than this. His concept of war differed not at all from that of von Moltke and, especially, of von Schlieffen. In the 1920s he wrote:

'Graf Schlieffen is no concept for us; he typifies in head and heart the continuous life of the German General Staff, the German soldier, the German nation. We will not allow him to become a more petrified concept . . . but we will seek in him and learn from him, in new and clear form, the old eternal rules of war. Let us condense them into three sentences: The destruction of the enemy is the goal of war. . . . Every operation must be dominated by one simple clear idea. Everybody and everything must be subordinated to this idea. Decisive force must be thrown in at the decisive point; success is to be purchased only with sacrifice. Let us take to heart these doctrines of Schlieffen, the man, and then the concept "Schlieffen" will be synonymous with Victory.'[9]

Imbued with such beliefs, von Seeckt possessed no vision of any revolutionary strategy and, while he appreciated the importance of ground-support aircraft, he did not envisage the future in terms of armoured warfare. Indeed, the tank figured little in his writings, and he even wrote that 'the days of the cavalry, if trained, equipped and led on modern lines, are not numbered. . . . its lances may still flaunt their pennants with confidence in the wind of the future.'[10] Von Seeckt, in drawing his strength from the past, had failed to realise the potential of the future.

In the 1920s and 1930s, the strategic basis of the German Army for the forthcoming decade was decided. The successors to von Moltke and von Schlieffen were the victors; the idea of *Vernichtungsgedanke* predominated, and Hitler's force was imbued with the belief in the power of the strategic initiative, manoeuvre, encirclement, and annihilation. As von Manstein, one of Germany's foremost field-marshals, wrote to Liddell Hart:

> 'Not only the German strategical but also the tactical thinking was influenced by the Schlieffen theory that a decisive success would be only reached in outflanking the enemy in connection with a frontal attack which alone would seldom lead to such a success.... The Schlieffen theories were also much studied in the German Army between the wars and had great influence on the strategical and tactical thinking. The idea to outflank and to encircle the enemy governed the German strategy and tactics.'[11]

The Army of the Third Reich retained its imperial heritage. The official statement of military strategic doctrine was set out in *Die Truppenführung* (the Troop Command) produced between 1931 and 1933 by a committee of officers under the chairmanship of Beck, and issued for the first time in the autumn of the latter year. *Die Truppenführung* was well-written and cogently argued, and was far from being hide-bound in its principles. On its first page was declared unequivocally: 'Even war undergoes a constant evolution. New arms give ever new forms to combat. To foresee this technical evolution before it occurs, to judge well the influence of these new arms on battle, to employ them before others, is an essential condition for success.'[12] On the question of tactics *Die Truppenführung* was a brilliant exposition of modern principles, and drew sound lessons from

Germany's terrible experience in the 1914-18 War. Throughout, it emphasised the fundamental tactical role of combat teams of battalion strength composed of all arms employing every known method of the infiltration technique. Initiative, decisive manoeuvre, and envelopment were the keynotes of the German tactical doctrine, and its success in the war years was to prove it immeasurably superior to the methods of its enemies. Strategically, too, *Die Truppenführung* was far from reactionary, not only advocating the use of tanks and motorised transport to achieve the decisive destruction of the enemy, but doing so in a manner which contrasted with prevalent foreign doctrine. Instead of restricting the role of the armour merely to supporting the infantry, it emphasized that 'if tanks are too closely tied to the infantry, they lose the advantage of their speed and are liable to be knocked out by the defence.'[13]

Nevertheless, such ideas, although adapted to modern developments, were not revolutionary. The official strategic doctrine of the German Army as expressed in *Die Truppenführung* contained nothing that departed from the train of thought initiated by the first Chief of the Army General Staff some seventy years earlier. Infantry divisions, with their marching troops, horse-drawn guns, and waggons, would remain the deciding factor of the strategy of decisive encirclement, and the motorised infantry and armour would be subordinated to their needs. The new formations would serve as the 'cutting edge' of the infantry's flanking thrusts, using their superior speed, flexibility, and striking-power to penetrate the enemy's front line, destroy his artillery positions, rout his nearby reserves, and, finally, close the pincers around the opposing forces. But the emphasis would still lie on the infantry as the 'mass of decision,' the means by which the ring round the enemy would be drawn tight and consolidated, and his resistance overcome. This is a theme continually expressed in the Army training manuals. The German Army *Leadership and Battles of the Infantry*, published in January 1940, proclaimed that 'The infantry is the main arm. All other arms are subsidiary to it,'[14] and, in 1942, an OKW treatise on strategy in the war up to that date (the years commonly associated with the success of the panzer divisions) contained a chapter entitled 'Infantry, the Queen,' in which it was claimed that the infantry still dominated the battlefield. It ended with the following paragraph:

> 'Each new weapon, so say the wiseacres, is the death of the infantry. The infantryman silently pulls on his cigarette and smiles. He knows that, tomorrow, this new weapon will belong to him. There is only one new factor in the techniques of war which remains above all other inventions. This new factor is the infantry, the eternally young child of war, the man on foot, even as Socrates himself was, the only and the eternal, who sees the whites of the enemy's eyes.'[15]

As before, and still part of their strong tradition, the Germans were eager to make full use of the development of modern weapons in order to exploit the potential of their *Vernichtungsgedanke*. Motorisation was seen as the only effective counter to increased fire-power. As one German manual put it: 'The task of military motorisation is to strive for a maximum tactical and operational mobility and speed, so that the army may be able, in the shortest possible time, to develop a maximum fighting strength at the fulcrum of the battle, in order that it may thus prove superior at the decisive point [*Schwerpunkt*], even if inferior as a whole.'[16] As far as it went, this was all to the good, for the subsequent German victories were largely the result of the happy combination of traditional strategy and modern armament. But it did not go far enough. The High Command and the senior generals failed to recognise what von Moltke had understood in the 1860s: that contemporary inventions may revolutionise the form of warfare, that they may offer possibilities, not only for the strengthening of traditional strategy, but also for its complete transformation—as with the railway, the telegraph, and the rifled weapon in the mid-nineteenth century, so with the lorry, the tank, and the aeroplane in the early twentieth century. Out of these was to emerge a new idea of war so revolutionary in its implications that few could comprehend it, and even fewer dared to use it. There was all the difference in the world between a traditional strategy using modern weapons to further its precepts, and a novel strategy based on the potential offered by those weapons to revolutionise war. This new concept may be called the 'armoured idea.'

11

Strategic Revolution

Attacking does not merely consist in assaulting walled cities or striking at an army in battle array; it must include the act of assaulting the enemy's mental equilibrium.

SUN TZU
The Art of War

Vernichtungsgedanke and the armoured idea had much in common, a fact that has obscured their differences and aided their obfuscation under the all-embracing myth of *Blitzkrieg*. Both rejected any policy of attrition, both relied on rapid, decisive movement, and both laid emphasis on the concentration of force at the crucial point. But here the similarity ended. For the armoured idea arose not from the historic tradition of the German Army but from the unique experience of the terrible years of deadlock on the Western Front, and from the recognition of the revolutionary possibilities presented by the combustion engine, the tracked weapon-platform, and the aeroplane.

The trench warfare of the years 1914-18 was both alien and distasteful to the Germans: it was alien because a static strategy ran directly counter to their tradition of manoeuvre, and it was distasteful because they were painfully aware that the high cost of a struggle of attrition against an enemy with greater resources in men and material would surely lead to ultimate defeat. Therefore, from the beginning, every attempt was made to overcome the stalemate; massed infantry assaults, heavy bombardments, gas and mines were tried, but all failed; it was only with the development of a new system of organisation and tactics that, by 1918, the Germans finally found the method that would permit large scale breakthroughs on the Western Front. It became known as 'infiltration.' Of it, a French staff officer wrote: 'This terrible word, which expressed the latest moves of the enemy and his method of fighting, was feared on account of the striking light it would throw on our present inferiority in the country and in the Army. Not only has the word a suggestion of cunning, it expresses a treacherous action impossible to avert, of a kind to cause alarm.'[1]

The essence of infiltration lay in the surprise, speed, and flexibility of heavily armed groups of 'storm-troops,' at any level of command up to battalions, who, in addition to the light machine-guns, flamethrowers, and light mortars of the infantry, were closely supported by light artillery. No attempt was made to achieve a wide breakthrough at once, but instead, immediately after an intense, relatively short artillery bombardment, the storm-troops were sent forward to make narrow but deep penetrations in the enemy's lines, avoiding any contact with opposing strong-points. More troops were pushed, or infiltrated, through these gaps, and the remaining isolated centres of resistance, such as machine-gun nests, were then attacked from the flank and rear. Meanwhile, the original storm-troops continued to advance into the enemy's rear to pierce his vital nerve-centres—his headquarters, communications, and supply lines. General confusion and paralysis resulted, and this, coupled with the effect on morale of the uncertainty and fear induced by the rapid and deep attack, led inevitably to the collapse of the opposition. The narrow penetration had been turned into a wide breach through which the rest of the army could advance to begin, once again, the traditional German mobile strategy. It was this method that enabled Ludendorff to achieve such success in his March–April 1918 offensives, success which, had its momentum been kept up, might well have caused the Allies to suffer total disaster.

Just as the tactics of infiltration were novel in action, so the military technical developments of the early twentieth century were revolutionary in potential. Mechanisation and air-power together permitted the addition of a new dimension to warfare, for those far-seeing enough to use it. Until the very end of the First World War, the German Army's mobile strategy had been shackled by the limited speed and endurance of its infantry, and, more fundamentally, by the restricted capacity and length of its logistical system. An advancing army could go no faster than its most important, but, at the same time, its slowest troops—the infantry. Normally, a corps could cover fifteen miles a day for three days, followed by one day of rest, but for the strategy of decisive manoeuvre this could prove woefully inadequate. Von Schlieffen's plan for the invasion of France had required of the crucial right-flanking armies a ruinous rate of continuous marching at not less than fifteen miles a day for three weeks; even more disastrous than this was the inflexible system providing for the constant supply of food, ammunition, and equipment that significantly limited the huge armies to a relatively short striking range. The size of the problem may be understood by a brief look at the logistics of the German First Army on the all-important German right wing in France in 1914. Consisting of 260,000 men, 784 artillery pieces, and 324 machine-guns, it required in fodder for its 84,000 horses, 1,848,000 pounds a day. The result of such a burden was that a corps could not operate with full efficiency over twenty-five miles from the nearest railroad, and that the horse and waggon transport system failed completely at a distance of more than fifty miles. Consequently, because of the inadequacy of the horse as a means of mass, fast transport, the Germans were forced either to restrict their range of action to the route and capacity of their enemy's railway system, which they had to repair if necessary, or to build new railroads fast enough to keep them within close operating range of the advancing armies. Von Moltke was fully aware of this restriction, recognising that, had the nature and the dispositions of the enemy in the 1866 and 1870 campaigns been different, these limits might well have spelt ruin for the doctrine of decisive manoeuvre. This is precisely what might have happened during the great 1914 advance. Even had the German generals not made their mistakes of command, and had they found the retreating enemy's flank and rear, it is highly possible that the von Schlieffen plan, whether in its original or modified form, would have failed simply because the masses of men and horses that composed the invading armies had outdistanced their supplies and had marched themselves to exhaustion. Certainly such restrictions continually prevented the Germans from achieving the complete annihilation of the Russian armies in the east, where the enormous distances, the poor roads, and the inadequate railway system made difficult any deep penetrations or large encirclements of the enemy. In the spring offensive of 1918, too, the same limits of endurance and supply robbed the Germans of ultimate success. No mobile operation could be continued for long in the face of such harsh realities.

The advent of the lorry, the tracked-vehicle, and the aeroplane altered all this. The army now possessed the means to overcome the severe restrictions imposed on strategy by the speed and endurance of men and animals. No longer would the advancing forces be limited to a distance of between twenty-five and fifty miles from a railhead; no longer would speed and distance be dictated by marching feet or horse-drawn waggon. The motor engine and the propeller shaft would change all that. Certainly the new transport brought its own inherent difficulties, such as the necessity for a constant flow of petrol and an efficient repair system, but these were by no means insuperable, especially with the advent of air transport. Distances of thirty or forty miles a day over several weeks were now possible, and relative independence from the once-inhibiting problems of logistics presented itself. Now, the only check on the fullest exploitation of a mobile strategy would be the dispositions and the quality of the enemy.

This was a development of considerable potential, which, when allied to the tactics of infiltration, produced a strategy of revolutionary proportions—the armoured idea, or, to use a term current at the time, the 'indirect approach,' an expression coined by Sir Basil Liddell Hart in the 1920s. (The Germans possessed no comparable term.) The first exposition of the idea was by another Englishman, Major-General J. F. C. Fuller, as early as May 1918, when he wrote a long service memorandum entitled 'Strategical Paralysis as the object of the Decisive Attack' (later changed to 'Plan 1919'). To quote its author, its salient points were:

> 'The fighting power of an army lies in its organisation, which can be destroyed either by wearing it down or by rendering it inoperative. The first comprises killing, wounding, and capturing the enemy soldiers—body warfare; the second in rendering inoperative his power of command—brain warfare. To take a single man as an example; the first method may be compared with a succession of wounds which will eventually result in his bleeding to death; the second—a shot through the brain. The brains of an army are its Staff—Army, Corps, and Divisional Headquarters. Could they suddenly be removed from an extensive sector of the . . . front, the collapse of the personnel they control will be little more than a matter of hours. As our present theory is to destroy personnel, our new theory should be to destroy command, not after the enemy's personnel has been disorganised but

before it has been attacked, so that it may be found in a state of disorganisation when attacked. The means proposed were a sudden eruption of squadrons of fast-moving tanks, which unheralded would proceed to the various enemy headquarters, and either round them up or scatter them. Meanwhile every available bombing machine was to concentrate on the supply and road centres. Only after these operations had been given time to mature was the enemy's front to be attacked in the normal way, and, directly penetration was effected, pursuit was to follow.'[2]

In this, Fuller was echoing an idea centuries old, one expressed thus by Sun Tzu: 'To fight and conquer in all your battles is not supreme excellence; supreme excellence consists in breaking the enemy's resistance without fighting.'

Such theories from abroad coincided with much of the experience gained by the German Army during the years of the First World War, and for some officers, a tiny minority, they came together to produce a new concept of war. From their past tradition they understood the importance of decisive manoeuvre as the basis of strategy; from their tactics of infiltration they learnt the effectiveness of offensive action by well-armed, highly-trained mixed groups of men at any level of command attacking with vigour, speed, and flexibility to paralyse the enemy; from their failures they were forced to appreciate the necessity of full cooperation and communication between all arms of an attacking force; from their neglect, and the Allies use, of the tank, they became aware of the potential of a vehicle which possessed the unique combination of fire-power, protection, and mobility; from the developments in mechanisation and in air-power they recognised the means by which the considerable restrictions of physical exhaustion and limiting supply lines could be overcome, and a significant measure of operational freedom achieved; and from the British military theorists they found ideas that were important in broadening and welding together elements already present in their thinking. The result of this combination was a revolutionary theory seldom put into words and often inadequately presented, but which was sometimes expressed through unhesitating action in the field: action taken by men firm in the belief that they possessed within their grasp a new and potent means of victory—the armoured idea.

In the German Army, Heinz Guderian was the driving force behind the expression of this new strategy. As General von Manteuffel, who was in close touch with him from 1936, recorded:

> 'Guderian favoured from the beginning the strategic use of panzer forces—a deep thrust into the enemy—without worrying about a possible threat to his own unprotected and far-extended flanks. . . . It was Guderian—and at first he alone—who introduced the tank to the Army and its use as an operative weapon. It was certainly not the General Staff. . . . In peacetime he at first stood alone when he insisted that the breakthrough of tanks should be pressed long and deep, and at first without regard to the exposed flanks.'[3]

Although he cannot be credited with the introduction of

tanks, Guderian certainly revolutionised strategic thinking within the Army. On 1 April, 1922, as a thirty-four-year-old *Jäger* (Rifleman) signals specialist who knew nothing about armoured vehicles, he was posted to the Motorised Transport Department of the Inspectorate of Transport Troops. At first he was reluctant to continue in his job, even asking to be returned to his regiment, but soon he came to recognise the potential that motorisation offered Germany's then limited forces. He understood that mobility could offset numerical inferiority. Although this was no new revelation, his interest was awakened, and his attention on the lorry broadened to take account of the tank. By 1929 he had evolved the idea of strategic penetration by armoured forces, and, in his own words, had become 'convinced that tanks working on their own or in conjunction with infantry could never achieve decisive importance. . . . what was needed were armoured divisions which would include the supporting arms needed to allow the tanks to fight to full effect.'[4]

Guderian committed his new ideas to paper in the form of a number of articles in military periodicals, to be republished in 1937, when there appeared his first book, *Achtung! Panzer!*, a collection of the best of his lectures and writings over the previous decade. The quality of his argument was never profound, but the ideas behind it were expressed with vigour. In an article in the *Militärwissenschaftliche Rundschau* of December 1935, for example, he wrote:

'One night the doors of aeroplane hangers and Army garages will be flung open, motors will be tuned up, and squadrons will swing into movement. The first sudden blow may capture important industrial and raw-material districts or destroy them by air attack so that they can take no part in war production. Enemy government and military centres may be crippled and his transport system disorganised. In any case, the first strategic surprise attack will penetrate more or less deeply into enemy territory according to the distances to be covered and the amount of resistance met with. The first move of air and mechanised attack will be followed up by motorised infantry divisions. They will be carried to the verge of the occupied territory and hold it, thereby freeing the mobile units for another blow. In the meantime the attacker will be raising a mass army. He has the choice of territory and time for his next big blow, and he will then bring up the weapons intended for breaking down all resistance and breaking through enemy lines. He will do his best to launch the great blow suddenly so as to take the enemy by surprise, rapidly concentrating his mobile troops and hurling his air force at the enemy. The armoured division will no longer stop when the first objectives have been reached; on the contrary, utilising their speed and their radius of action to the full, they will do their utmost to complete the breakthrough into the enemy lines of communication. Blow after blow will be launched ceaselessly in order to roll up the enemy front and carry the attack as far as possible into enemy territory. The air force will attack the enemy reserves and prevent their intervention.'[5]

To Guderian and his followers, armour, mobility, and speed were all-important. In 1937, he wrote:

'... until our critics can produce some new and better method of making a successful land attack other than self-massacre, we shall continue to maintain our belief that tanks—properly employed, needless to say—are today the best means available for a land attack.... Everything is therefore dependent on this: to be able to move faster than has hitherto been done: to keep moving despite the enemy's defensive fire and thus to make it harder for him to build up fresh defensive positions: and finally to carry the attack deep into the enemy's defences. The proponents of tank warfare believe that, in favourable circumstances, they possess the means for achieving this.... We believe that by attacking with tanks we can achieve a higher rate of movement than has been hitherto obtainable, and—what is perhaps even more important—that we can keep moving once a breakthrough has been made.... We no longer believe that other formations have the fighting ability, the speed and the manoeuvrability necessary for full exploitation of the attack and breakthrough.'[6]

The degree to which the German armour enthusiasts were inspired by the military theorists abroad was considerable. In the English edition of his memoirs, Guderian wrote selflessly:

'It was principally the books and articles of the Englishmen, Fuller, Liddell Hart and Martel, that excited my interest and gave me food for thought. These far-sighted soldiers were even then [the early 1920s] trying to make of the tank something more than just an infantry-support weapon. They envisaged it in relationship to the growing motorisation of our age, and thus they became the pioneers of a new type of warfare on the largest scale. I learned from them the concentration of armour.... Furthermore, it was Liddell Hart who emphasised the use of armoured forces for long-range strikes, operations against the opposing army's communications, and also proposed a type of panzer division.... Deeply impressed by these ideas I tried to develop them in a sense practicable for our own Army. So I owe many suggestions of our further development to Captain Liddell Hart.'[7]

Fulsome praise indeed, although in the original German language edition of Guderian's work there was no mention of Liddell Hart in this context, and in the bibliography of his pre-war *Achtung! Panzer!*, no inclusion of the Englishman's works. Guderian's son remembered that it was Fuller, rather than Liddell Hart, who had possessed the greater influence on his father before the war (and yet Guderian specifically rejected Fuller's 'all tank' theory, and adopted Liddell Hart's solution—the armoured division as a team of all arms). Nevertheless, wherever the emphasis lay, there was no doubt of the significant impact made by the British military writers on the panzer generals, an impact which may even have been greater than that of the German theorists themselves. One of Rommel's chiefs of staff in the desert war, Fritz Bayerlein, noted:

'In his [Rommel's] opinion, the British could have avoided most of their defeats if only they had paid more heed to the modern theories expounded by those two writers [Liddell Hart and Fuller] before the war. During the war, in many conferences and personal talks with Field Marshal Rommel, we discussed Liddell Hart's military works, which won our admiration. Of all military writers it was Liddell Hart [not Guderian] who made the deepest impression on the Field-Marshal, and greatly influenced his tactical and strategical thinking. He, like Guderian, could in many respects be termed Liddell Hart's "pupil."[8]

The theory and practice of the armoured idea, or the strategy of indirect approach, which developed from 1918 to 1942, may be considered as follows:

Breakthrough. The armoured force concentrates its power at the enemy's weakest point and, enjoying a local superiority in men and material, attacks with the fullest advantage of surprise. The resulting breakthrough is on a narrow front, and all opposing strong points are left for the rest of the army, which follows through, widening the gap and consolidating the gains.

Penetration. The armoured force, independently of the rest of the army, drives deep into the enemy's rear, searching not for his troops but for his line of least resistance. The main thrust is obscured by constantly developing and fading decoy threats. The speed and flexibility of the attack are of prime importance; considerations such as the security of flanks are only secondary. The unpredictability and momentum of the force now become its primary weapon, for they not only cause considerable disarray in the opposing command, but also prevent the enemy from concentrating sufficient formations to put up an effective opposition.

Aim. The aim of the attacking force is to turn a tactical advantage into a strategic one. This is achieved by means of the indirect approach. The enemy's capacity to resist is destroyed not by the direct killing or capture of his troops, but indirectly, by the rendering inoperative of his power of command. Action without direction loses coordination; troops without headquarters, or with one that is bewildered and panic-stricken, are reduced to a mob. Just as damaging is the psychological impact—the perplexity, doubt, consternation, and sheer terror brought about by the lack of any definite appreciation of the situation, fear of the unknown, and the prospect of imminent death. The heart, as well as the head, becomes atrophied. The paralysis is complete, the victory total.

Such was the armoured idea. Throughout, it was the specialised and relatively small attacking force that set the pace of the campaign, unhindered by the slower mass of the field army, to which was given the task of mopping up the isolated pockets of resistance and capturing the large numbers of disorganised and demoralised enemy troops. This was achieved, preferably, by means of the traditional encirclement manoeuvres, made so much easier by the armoured troops' deep penetration.

The basic military organisation required to implement this new form of war was the armoured division. The division would, in theory, consist of a balanced team of all arms—tank, anti-tank, infantry, artillery and engineer—which together produced the combination of maximum striking power, high speed across country, and complete flexibility in response to enemy action demanded by the rapid, independent thrusting movements of the new concept. Modern inventions would be fully employed to give maximum freedom and speed to the force's operation, and these would include motorised transport, tracked self-propelled artillery, mechanised infantry, and aeroplanes for the dropping of supplies. As Guderian wrote in 1936:

> 'The armoured branch will include all other arms. Infantry, artillery, and engineers are necessary to the development of its action, but it will impose upon them its own methods of combat by making them dependent on the motor. Supporting infantry, artillery, and engineers will be motorised and partially armoured within the framework of the armoured division and the motorised infantry division. They will adjust their new tactical programme and employment to their new speed. An important role will be played by the engineers, who will have abundant material for crossing gaps, and who will be trained to use it rapidly and to oppose the action of enemy tanks by the rapid construction of anti-tank obstacles. The desire to protect the armoured weapon against the counter-attack of its most dangerous enemies, the tank and the plane, will require the incorporation of numerous and powerful anti-tank and anti-aircraft weapons into the panzer division. Thus the armoured arm—minutely trained on the other hand for cooperation with the air arm—will be able to fight its own battle.'[9]

There was to be no set formula as to the relative strength of the armoured to the non-armoured forces within the field army, perhaps twenty-five per cent of the total would have been adequate, but certainly the rest of the Army, although consisting largely of infantry formations, was intended to be well-motorised and capable of swift action to consolidate the achievements of the armoured force. However, the main emphasis was to be placed upon the proper equipping and organising of the panzer arm. There lay the key to victory, which was to be gained thus: 'The attack by tanks,' wrote Guderian in 1936, 'must be conducted with maximum acceleration in order to exploit the advantage of surprise, to penetrate deep into enemy lines, to prevent reserves from intervening, and to extend the tactical success into a strategical victory. Speed, therefore, is what is to be exacted above everything else from the armoured weapon.'[10] Nothing was to prevent the achievement of speed; the armoured formations were to reign supreme. This, Guderian made clear in 1937:

'We conclude that the suggestion that our tanks be divided among infantry divisions is nothing but a return to the original English tactics of 1916–17, which were even then a failure, for the English tanks were not successful until they were used in mass at Cambrai. By carrying the attack quickly into the enemy's midst, by firing our motorised guns with their protective armour direct into the target, we intend to achieve victory. It is said: "The motor is not a new weapon: it is simply a new method of carrying old weapons forward." It is fairly well-known that combustion engines do not fire bullets; if we speak of the tank as a new weapon, we mean thereby that it necessitates a new arm of the service, as happened for example in the Navy in the case of the U-boat; that, too, is called a weapon. We are convinced that we are a weapon and one whose successes in the future will leave an indelible mark on battles yet to be fought. If our attacks are to succeed, then the other weapons must be adjusted to fit in with our scale of time and space in those attacks. We therefore demand that in order to exploit our successes the necessary supporting arms be made as mobile as we are, and that even in peacetime those arms be placed under our command. For, to carry out great decisive operations, it is not the mass of the infantry but the mass of the tanks that must be on the spot.'[11]

Few proponents of armoured warfare, however, could have expressed their beliefs thus; to most, the panzer division presented only a hitherto undreamed-of potential of power and velocity which provided them with an idea of war based on speed and daring. Although such men could represent their theories only inadequately, they felt strongly that any strategic heritage, however well-founded on the idea of mobility, was an anathema if it imposed restraint on the new instrument of war and thereby failed to recognise that 'speed, still more speed, and always speed'[12] was the secret. They placed their faith in the words of an old German proverb: 'He who dares, wins.'

The similarities of the strategy of *Vernichtungsgedanke* and of the armoured idea have been noted: decisive manoeuvre was common to both. But here all affinity ended, and the two concepts found themselves in direct conflict one with another. Physical destruction in one was supplanted by paralysis in the other as the primary aim; well-coordinated flanking and encirclement movements were replaced by unsupported thrusts deep into the enemy's rear areas as the method; guarded flanks and unbroken, if strained, supply lines gave way to velocity and unpredictability as the basic rules of operation; centralisation of control was superseded by independence of action as the first condition of command; and the mass infantry armies, whether or not supported by tanks and aircraft, made way for the relatively small powerhouses of the armoured divisions as the primary instrument of victory.

So fundamental were the differences between the two ideas that it is hardly surprising that the overwhelming majority of Germany's General Staff and officer corps, a body of men not noted for their radical outlook, viewed the revolutionary concept with less than favour. But could they be blamed for not recognising its potential and validity? It was, after all, a complete reversal of the rules of warfare as they knew them—extended flanks, deep, unsupported thrusts by relatively small formations which left the mass of the army in a secondary role, and which were aimed at the paralysis and not at the physical destruction of the enemy. The tradition and method of *Vernichtungsgedanke* simply could not be thrown overboard in favour of so novel a strategy as the indirect approach, centred around the actions of the, as yet, untried armoured divisions. Nevertheless, it was against this official doctrine of manoeuvre that a minority of German officers rebelled. The role they sought for armour and motorisation was one not merely of importance but of domination, to which the rest of the army was to be subordinate. As Guderain wrote in 1936: 'In the zone of action of the armour, the action of the other arms is to be based on that of the armour.'[13] The revolutionaries rejected *Vernichtungsgedanke*, and saw the dangers inherent in being shackled to a tradition which did not take full account of the potential of new developments. The controversy naturally enough centred around the fortunes of the armoured force. As one of the leading revolutionaries, Guderian, later recorded:

> '... tradition is not always regarded as simply supplying ideals of behaviour, but rather as a source of practical example, as though an imitation of what was done before could produce identical results despite the fact that meanwhile circumstances and methods have completely altered. Hardly any mature institution can avoid this fallacious aspect of tradition. The Prusso-German Army and its General Staff were not immune from making this mistake in a number of ways. In consequence there was inevitably a certain internal stress between misunderstood tradition and the new tasks that had to be performed ... so when it was a matter of setting up an independent, operational air force, or of developing the newly conceived armoured force within the Army, the Army General Staff opposed these innovations. The importance of these two technical achievements insofar as they affected the operations of the combined Armed Forces was neither sufficiently studied nor appreciated, because it was feared that

they might result, in the one case, in a decrease in the importance of the Army as a whole and, in the other, in a lessening of the prestige of the older arms of that service.'[14]

As a result, the history of the German Army from the 1930s to the middle years of the Second World War became essentially the record of the unresolved conflict between the protagonists of a new strategy founded on the revolutionary use of armoured, motorised and air forces engaged in a mission of paralysis, and the adherents of the traditional strategy based on mass infantry armies, with the new arms at best treated only as equal partners, the cutting edge of the old decisive manoeuvre of encirclement and annihilation. This came to an end only in 1943 with the German loss of the initiative, their renouncement of the superiority of manoeuvre, and the return to a more or less static strategy of attrition with, as its consequence, failure on the field of battle. This was the result of the stranglehold of tradition that, together with the ineptitude of the Supreme Commander, Adolf Hitler, was to ensure the total military defeat of the much-vaunted German Army.

The battle between the two sides of German strategic thought was both bitter and unevenly matched. In conversation with Liddell Hart, General von Thoma recorded:

'It may surprise you to hear that the development of armoured forces met with much resistance from the higher generals of the German Army, as it did in yours. The older ones were afraid of developing such forces fast—because they themselves did not understand the technique of armoured warfare, and were uncomfortable with such new instruments. At the best they were interested, but dubious and cautious. We could have gone ahead much faster but for their attitude.'[15]

Rommel went further than this, his last writings before his death in 1944 revealing that his dream of armoured warfare was not a thing of the past, but still remained to be realised in the future:

> 'Nevertheless, even the German officer corps was by no means completely free of the old prejudices. There was a particular clique that still fought bitterly against any drastic modernisation of methods and clung fast to the axiom that the infantry must be regarded as the most important constituent of any army. This may be true for Germany's eastern army as it is fighting today in Russia, but it will not be true in the future, which is where our attention should be concentrated— when the tank will be the centre of all tactical thinking. The African campaign and the new aspects of warfare which it brought were never understood by men like General Halder. They stuck to their established methods and precedents, even though these often showed themselves to be outdated and hence false.'[16]

The main opponents of the new strategy were, according to Guderian, Generals Beck and Halder. Placing the blame for the rejection of his ideas squarely on the shoulders of the two Chiefs of the General Staff,

Guderian condemned them for being men of the old school and dismissed them and their officers as 'Gentlemen of the Horse Artillery.' Unfairly, he criticised Beck for having 'no understanding of modern technical matters.... He was a paralysing element wherever he appeared.'[17] Halder he characterised as 'an officer of routine.... He did the inevitable, but nothing more. He did not like panzer divisions at all. In his mind infantry divisions played the leading role now and for ever.'[18] They, for their part, regarded Guderian as a mere 'technician,' obsessed with modern developments to the exclusion of sober strategic realities, and thus wholly unfit for the higher operational posts that demanded a wider, more mature vision. He was not, it was constantly asserted, a 'War Academy soldier,' for, although he had entered its portals in 1914, the outbreak of war had abruptly terminated his course after only a short time. His nickname, *Brausewetter* (Hothead) aptly summed up the prevailing attitude towards his person among the Army High Command, an attitude hardly conducive to the advancement of either his career or his ideas.

However much Guderian might inveigh against such 'reaction,' he was condemned to prosecute a frustrating and, ultimately, a frustrated advocacy; the dominance of the traditional strategy was too deep-rooted within the military establishment for it to be overturned. None of those who dominated the Army's leadership could comprehend the full implications of Guderian's theories. Von Fritsch, for example, who, Guderian believed, was 'always ready to try out new ideas without prejudice and, if they seemed to him good, to adopt them,'[19] was very much in agreement with Beck as to the employment of armour, and they both planned to strengthen the infantry by assigning to it packets of tanks and assault-guns, thereby contradicting Guderian's idea of the concentration of all armour within the framework of the panzer division. Of the Army Commander, General Westphal wrote: 'Fritsch was in favour of motorising parts of the Army, but, like Beck, he considered it first necessary to gain experience before deciding finally the make-up and number of mobile divisions that were desirable. Above all it was considered necessary to bear in mind the limit imposed by the fuel factor.'[20] Von Fritsch's successor was little better, for, as Guderian recorded: 'In regard to armoured forces Field-Marshal von Brauchitsch already showed understanding before the war—from the time when he became commander of Army Group 4, in Leipzig, which embraced the motorised and mechanised forces of the Army. He had his own ideas of mechanised operations and tactics—without, however, making full use of these.'[21] The two successive Chiefs of the General Staff, although they did not, as Guderian and others have asserted, advocate the French doctrine of tying down the tanks to close support of the infantry, nevertheless possessed considerable reservations about what they saw as the indiscriminate use of armoured divisions. Certainly Guderian was correct when he recorded that since Beck 'inevitably chose men with much of his own attitude to fill the more important General Staff posts, and even more so to form his own close circle, as time went on he erected—without wishing to do so—a barrier of reaction at the very centre of the Army which was to prove very difficult to overcome.'[22] Even Hitler, fascinated as he was by the power of the panzers, proved an unstable ally in the fight for the armoured arm; General George Thomas was of the opinion that 'Hitler attached much importance to the possession of much heavy artillery, many mechanical weapons, and anti-tank weapons. The great importance of the tanks was not recognised until the success in the Polish campaign.'[23]

Just as deadening to the hopes of the armour enthusiasts was the resistance to radical change that came from the established arms. Foremost among these was the artillery, which, because of the higher intellectual quality of gunners and the lower mortality of artillerymen compared with that of infantrymen and cavalry-men in the First World War, came to dominate the top posts of the Army: von Fritsch, von Brauchitsch, Beck, Halder, Fromm, Keitel, Jodl and Warlimont were all from its ranks, and, by the end of the Second World War, of Germany's generals, forty per cent had begun their career in that arm (including six of the nineteen Field-Marshals). The artillery formed a closely knit fraternity, highly protective of its interests—interests that did not always coincide with those of the armour. The new idea led, in Guderian's words, to 'a demand for self-propelled artillery mounts as early as 1934; but the artillerymen did not believe in such fast-moving combat. Accustomed for five hundred years to draw their guns with the muzzle pointing backwards and to unlimber for action, they successfully opposed this proposal until the bitter experience of war taught them to follow the suggestions . . .'[24] Furthermore, as their traditional role had always lain in the provision of close support for the infantry on a basis which made them equal partners with the 'queen of the battlefield,' the gunners were inclined to look with suspicion on any theory that detracted from this. Further opposition, naturally enough, came from the cavalry, whose very existence was threatened by motorisation and armour. The horse and the tank in the 1930s were uneasy bed-fellows.

The opposition to the armoured idea in the German Army was anything but unthinking or irrational. Conservative its detractors might have been, but they were far from being merely 'hide-bound.' Cogent arguments were put forward to refute the novel theories of Guderian and his associates, to meet point by point their new principles. Representative of these was an article in the *Militär Wochenblatt* of October 1934. In analysing the new factors of warfare, it pointed to the quite reasonable belief (held in all European Armies) that modern developments, while they had made weapons of offence far more effective, had also strengthened the methods of defence, thus making favourable the chances of holding up the attack with comparatively small forces. It also asserted that modern armies conducting an offensive would be much more dependent on a steady supply of munitions, material and, above all, fuel-oil than were the armies of 1914, and that, therefore, they would be very sensitive to every dislocation of supplies, dislocation made all the more likely by any deep thrusts of the armoured forces with their long, unprotected flanks and supply lines. A few weeks later, the same military magazine carried an article which stated: 'A strategic raid is a very delicate matter, because although it offers a tempting chance it also represents a great and terrible risk. We must remember in particular that the loss of prestige that would result at the very beginning of a war for any country which carried out such a raid unsuccessfully would be incalculable.'[25] Such arguments gained additional force when it was realised that the German Army simply did not possess the material resources required to implement the armoured idea at a time when it was undertaking expansion into a mass conscript army along traditional lines. After all, a panzer division cost around fifteen times as much to equip and to maintain as an infantry division, and before 1939 there was no proof that the former's efficiency in battle would warrant such expenditure during a time of costly expansion.

Furthermore, the supporters of the new strategy suffered from one great weakness: they proved themselves incapable of communicating their ideas to their brother officers. They were men of action, not of the word, impatient of, and unresponsive to, what they considered shortsighted opposition. As Rommel recorded: 'My staff and I gave no regard whatsoever to all this unnecessary academic nonsense, which had long been overtaken by technical development. Consequently, many officers of the academic type, steeped in their ancient theories, failed to understand us and so took us for adventurers, amateurs, and the like.'[26] And General von Manteuffel was to admit of his much-beloved chief, Guderian, after the war: 'He may not, on some occasions, have stressed this point [the strategic use of armoured forces] very emphatically—simply because many of the older officers could not get used to these new methods, and he may not have tried to present them in a more favourable form.'[27] Moreover, these men were denied free expression of their views in the official manuals of the Army, and the few who bothered themselves to propound their messages were forced to limit themselves to professional magazines and the occasional book, none of which contained a truly lucid exposition of the new idea to equal the eloquent arguments of *Die Truppenführung*. Nor was Guderian's own character an asset in this battle of ideas. Although possessing considerable originality, energy, intelligence, determination, and tenacity, those very traits that made him a highly gifted soldier ensured that he would be, at the same time, a difficult man with whom to work. One of his former subordinates remarked later that 'He lacked the psychological faculty of feeling and sensing his way which a "leading personality" ... should possess. ... He had not the gift of listening calmly to his subordinates or men of his own rank. ... He was a strong "rider," and successful as such, but he lacked the mind and psychological insight into the spirit of the "horse" which are essential in a good rider.'[28] Critical, frank, and acerbic, Guderian was not the type of man to present his argument tactfully to his superiors and persuade them of his sagacity through a combination of charm and logic. On the contrary he often appeared to be nothing other than an arrogant firebrand. This impression was forcefully expressed by Halder, who noted: 'Guderian will not tolerate any Army commander, and demands that everybody up to the highest position should bow to the ideas he produces from a restricted view point. ... I will not give way to Guderian.'[29] Such a man was not the best person to advance a cause which was in such direct opposition to so traditional, established, and highly successful a form of war as *Vernichtungsgedanke*.

Against such odds, the outcome of the battle was a foregone conclusion. Guderian and his supporters failed; the military establishment triumphed. Although the years up to 1939 were to witness the formation of a German panzer arm, it was not one ordered to the specifications of the armour enthusiasts. By 1933 the *Inspektion der Kraftfahrtruppen* (Inspectorate of Transport Troops), under General Oswald Lutz, with Guderian as his chief of staff, had taken over from the cavalry its important reconnaissance functions; plans had been drawn up for the development of tanks, and some machines had actually been made (armoured cars had appeared); attempts were being made to establish motorised anti-tank battalions in each infantry division; and large-scale exercises had been held involving mock tank battalions and infantry regiments to test the concept of the armoured formation. In June 1934 the *Inspektion der Kraftfahrkampftruppen* (Mechanised Troops Inspectorate) was created, again with Lutz at its head and Guderian as his chief of staff, and in October the first tank unit was formed, Panzer Brigade I, equipped with light training tanks. In May 1935 a General Staff exercise studied the use of an armoured corps in the field, and in July an improvised panzer division undertook a highly successful exercise which revealed to all that the movement and control of a team of all arms, including tanks, was possible. Clearly the time was ripe for the birth of the new force, and on 27 September the *Kommando der Panzertruppen* (Armoured Troops Command) was instituted, with Lutz as its Chief, followed on 15 October by the establishment of three panzer divisions. In 1938 two more armoured divisions were formed, and on 20 November Hitler appointed Guderian *Chef der Schnellen Truppen* (Chief of Mobile Troops), a newly instituted post which had authority over the development and training of all Germany's mechanised and mounted troops, an authority denied to the former Armoured Troops Command, which had possessed control over tank-equipped units only. Finally, before the outbreak of the war, Germany's sixth armoured division, 10th Panzer, was insituted in April 1939.

The importance of Guderian and his supporters in the development of this panzer arm should not be underestimated, for it was largely through their efforts that the force that was raised from virtually nothing in 1935 had reached such a high state of readiness by 1939 that it could demonstrate to the world an unequalled degree of military proficiency on the field of battle. But such an achievement should not for one moment be represented as the triumph of the armoured idea. In the German Field Army after mobilisation, only roughly one in twenty of its division was panzer, and just one in ten was fully motorised (this included four light divisions and four motorised infantry divisions). Furthermore, even the existing panzer force, small as it was, suffered from neglect and misunderstanding. Despite Guderian's efforts, the German Army failed to organize its limited armour in such a way as to exploit its potential to the full. Guderian had argued that 'there could be no question for the time being of even approaching [the enemies'] standard of equipment either in quality or in quantity. We had, therefore, to attempt to compensate for these deficiencies by means of superior organisation and leadership. A tight concentration of our limited forces in large units, in divisions to be precise, and the organisation of those units as a panzer corps would, we hoped, make up for our numerical inferiority.'[30] This was not to be. In October 1937, as a result of a long-thought-out policy of the General Staff, the 4th Panzer Brigade was formed, made up of two tank regiments, a quarter of the total of such formations. This brigade, intended to provide infantry support, was followed by a second, the 6th, in 1938. That same year saw the establishment of three light divisions to add to the one incorporated from the Austrian Army. Formed in place of further armoured divisions, they were basically motorised infantry formations each with a tank battalion and a reconnaissance regiment. Therefore, although Guderian later managed to have the 4th Panzer Brigade turned into the 10th Panzer Division, out of the thirty-three tank battalions and 3,195 tanks in existence by September 1939, nine battalions and 1,251 tanks were outside the framework of the armoured division.

Equally as disturbing for Germany's armoured force was the fact that in September 1939 ninety per cent of its tanks were obsolete. The outbreak of war had interrupted the long-term plan decided on in 1932—and subsequently carried out with little sense of urgency—for the equipping of the panzer division with two main battle tanks, a light machine to form the main striking force and a medium one in support. Because of design and production problems it had been necessary to introduce a stop-gap training tank, and there emerged in 1934 a very light, six-ton machine, the PzKw I (*Panzerkampfwagen*—armoured fighting vehicle), armed with only two machine-guns. Yet it was out of date even before it made its appearance, and further delays caused another, improved, short-term, light tank, the nine-ton PzKw II, to appear. This too was inadequate, and by 1939 not only was its 2cm armament outclassed by similar foreign machines, but its armour was no longer proof against anti-tank weapons.

The first production models of the intended main battle tanks, the twenty-ton PzKw III and PzKw IV, were completed only in 1936, the former being armed with a 3.7cm anti-tank gun, the latter with a short-barrelled 7.5cm weapon capable of firing both high-explosive and anti-tank rounds, but at low velocity. The choice of armament for the PzKw IIIs had been the subject of much controversy; Guderian recalled that he was 'anxious that they be equipped with a 5cm weapon since this would give them the advantage over the heavier armour plate which we soon expected to see incorporated in the construction of foreign tanks. Since, however, the infantry was already being equipped with 3.7cm anti-tank guns, and since, for reasons of production simplicity, it was not considered desirable to produce more than one type of light anti-tank gun and shell, General Lutz and I had to give in.'[31] The Army Weapons Department and the Artillery Inspectorate had won the day; the needs of the panzer force were neglected. This was a story often repeated. In 1938 the Weapons Department came to realise its mistake and ordered that the PzKw III be fitted with the 5cm gun, but it was not until the middle of the French campaign that the tanks so armed made their first appearance.

After 1936, the re-equipping of the panzer units with these main tanks proceeded only slowly. In 1939, for example, output of the PzKw IV was even greatly reduced, so that only forty-five were built the whole year. Indeed in September, the month war began, only fifty-seven tanks of all types were produced. Such was the state of the panzer arm at the time of the campaign against Poland that its main battle tank, the PzKw III, which was intended to provide three-quarters of Germany's total tank strength, in reality composed only one thirty-second. Of a total of 3,195 machines on 1

September 1939, 1,445 were PzKw Is, 1,226 PzKw IIs, 215 PzKw I Command tanks, and only 98 were PzKw IIIs and 211 PzKw IVs. Germany's panzer force was committed to battle equipped mainly with training tanks.

In addition, scarce and much-needed equipment was denied to the panzer divisions and dissipated throughout the Army. Therefore, although the development of assault-guns for the infantry, the motorisation of all infantry anti-tank gun companies, and the creation of four light divisions were no doubt of value to the Army as a whole, the damage to the armoured force was considerable. As Guderian records:

'The development of tracked vehicles for the tank supporting arms never went as fast as we wished. It was clear that the effectiveness of the tanks would gain in proportion to the ability of the infantry, artillery, and other divisional arms to follow them in an advance across country. We wanted lightly armed half-tracks for the riflemen, combat engineers, and medical services; armoured self-propelled guns for the artillery and the anti-tank battalions; and various types of armour for the reconnaissance and signals battalions. The equipment of the divisions with these vehicles was never fully completed.'[32]

This is an understatement. In 1939, of the 2,060-odd motor vehicles in a panzer division (not including the tanks or the 200 motorcycles), not one was wholly tracked, few were half-tracked, and only one type was armoured—the SdKfz 251 (*Sonderkraftfahrzeug*—special purposes motor vehicle) half-track personnel carrier, and this was still extremely rare. Thus, by the outbreak of war, fewer than one-fifth of all vehicles in the panzer division were partially tracked and possessed a cross-country mobility approaching that of the tanks. Road-bound, unarmoured trucks did not lend themselves to the full exploitation of armoured warfare.

Lastly, the panzer troops were not given a command of sufficient status to justify their claim to supremacy. The Armoured Troops Command under Lutz, instituted in 1935, had been refused equal status with the infantry, cavalry, and artillery, and, as Guderian stated, was responsible only for looking after tank-equipped units' interests with the Chief of the General Army Office. Furthermore, a few days after its formation, Guderian was posted from his influential post as chief of staff to Lutz to become the first commander of the 2nd Panzer Division, which virtually ensured that he took little part in policy making for almost two and a half years. The fortunes of armoured and mechanised development came in 1937 to lie elsewhere, in the hands of von Brauchitsch and his successor, von Reichenau, who, as the commanders of the newly instituted Army Group Command 4, possessed operational and training control over all motorised units—the XVI Army Corps under Lutz (from 4 February 1938 under Guderian), consisting of the three panzer divisions; the XV Army Corps, made up of the light divisions; and the XIV Army Corps formed from the motorised infantry divisions.

The creation of the Chief of Mobile Troops in late 1938 did mark a theoretical improvement in the situation, for it brought the development of all mechanised and cavalry troops under the authority of one organisation. Guderian had even been given the Führer's assurance that

'Together, we'll see that the necessary modernisation is carried through.'[33] However, it was not long before Guderian and his small staff found that the powers of the new command were illusory; some even saw in his appointment a plot to deny an influential role to the protagonists of the armoured idea. Certainly Guderian himself felt that he could have been more effective had he continued as Commander XVI Army Corps. He made no use of Hitler's promise of an alliance, believing it either worthless or improper to enlist the Führer's aid in internal Army affairs, and he was forced to expend much of his time and energy in futile battles with the traditionalists. Guderian met with obstruction from the Training Department to his draft training manuals, his proposals to modernise the cavalry received direct rejection by the General Army Office, and he failed to obtain the necessary priority for the equipping of his panzer divisions. Although the very existence of an independent command for mobile troops gave some support to the arguments of the armour enthusiasts, it was short-lived. On mobilisation in 1939, Guderian's post was dissolved, and he himself transferred to a field command as a motorised corps commander. (At one point in 1939 he had even been given a mobilisation appointment with a reserve infantry corps, and it was only with great difficulty that he managed to get it revoked.)

The interests of the panzer force came to lie with the *Inspekteur der Schnellen Truppen* (Inspector of Mobile Troops) who, along with eleven other arm and service inspectors, was directly subordinate to the Commander of the Replacement Army, General Fritz Fromm, a man not noted for his sympathy with the armoured idea.

Furthermore, the Inspector possessed no command functions and little influence, his duties being merely to keep records and publish orders, directives, training manuals, and other material on behalf of the mobile troops. The Inspector, who was, until June 1942, the little-known General Kühn, was served by the *Abteilung für Panzertruppe, Kavallerie, und Heeresmotorisierung* (Department of Armoured Troops, Cavalry and Army Motorisation) in the General Army Office, an organisation which underwent several changes before its abolition in 1943. In the Army Ordnance Office the technical concerns of the armoured force were represented by the *Kraftfahr und Motorisierungsabteilung* (Department for Motor Transport and Mechnisation), a body wholly incapable of dealing with the specialities of tank design. And, although after 10 October 1939 the three fighting arms of infantry, artillery, and engineers and fortifications troops possessed representatives, known as *Waffengeneräle* (Arm generals), attached to the General Staff in order to advise the Army Commander-in-Chief and the Chief of the Army General Staff on the organisation, training, and tactical employment of their respective branches, it was not until 5 March 1940 that a representative was appointed for the armoured troops. He was given the title *General der Schnellen Truppen beim Oberbefehlshaber des Heeres* (General of Mobile Troops with the Commander-in-Chief of the Army). The first holder of the office was General Wilhelm Ritter von Thoma, a future commander of the German Africa Corps. It was only after three years of war, when the panzer arm was on the verge of complete collapse, that a command with anything approaching sufficient authority was instituted to safeguard its interests and advance its requirements. By then it was too late; the German armoured force was broken.

Thus, at no time was the German panzer arm given the status and the special attention by the military establishment that indicated they had accepted it as the most important component of a new form of warfare. Indeed, even the creation of the first three panzer divisions in October 1935 did not differ much from contemporary developments in other European countries. The previous year, the same type of organisation, based on a tank brigade supported by an infantry brigade, had been adopted by the French in their Division Légère Mécanique, and had also been tried during the 1927-28 British Army manoeuvres. Until the outbreak of war, as well as after, the men who dominated the Army High Command kept strict control over the development of the mobile arm and took steps to ensure that the tenets of the armoured idea found no expression in the composition and employment of the panzer troops. Revolutionary reorganisation had no place in the German Army. Instead, the Third Reich's mechanised force was subordinated to the requirements of the traditional strategy of decisive manoeuvre by a mass army; the proponents of the strategy of indirect approach, whether or not they were conscious of the full implications of the theory, had lost the battle.

12

Unreadiness

Because of the many difficulties under which it laboured, the more astounding were the great successes which the Army achieved in the first years of the war.
GENERAL SIEGFRIED WESTPHAL

While the battle for the armoured divisions was being fought and, in part, lost, the formation of the mass of the Army was quietly proceeding apace. Here lay the real task of the generals, a task whose very magnitude tended to push any proper consideration of the armoured idea into the background. Out of a defence system consisting of a small professional force devoid of 'weapons of aggression,' a new Army would be formed, based on universal conscription, full armament, and the utilisation of modern technology. Welcome though this must have been to the generals, they were faced, nonetheless, with the fact that it was not they who directed the pace and nature of this expansion. Just as before 1933 it had been the restrictions of the Versailles Treaty that had largely determined the size, organisation, and quality of the Army, after that year it was the policies of Adolf Hitler. In numerical terms his achievement was that, by September 1939 the peacetime Army of 730,000 men and fifty-two active divisions could be increased in a matter of a few weeks to a wartime force of 3,706,104 men and 103 divisions.

Remarkable though this was, behind the impressive facade of numbers of divisions lay certain grave weaknesses. No military force could undergo such a considerable numerical expansion without experiencing dangerous strains. In 1934, for example, there had been eighty-four infantry and twenty-four artillery battalions in existence; by 1 September 1939 there were 885 and 439 respectively. Perhaps the most serious weakness was the inability of the 100,000-man Reichsheer to provide the masses of commissioned and non-commissioned personnel necessary for the constantly expanding formations. There had been only 4,000 active officers in 1933, and of these 450, more than one in ten were medical and veterinary personnel. Of the 3,550 actual troop and staff officers, some 500, one-seventh, were released for service in the new Air Force. This meant there were only 3,000 officers to provide the nucleus of a corps which was to expand to more than 100,000 by the outbreak of war.

To meet the new Army's requirements, several expedients were used in addition to normal recruiting. The period of training required to gain a commission was shortened; 1,500 non-commissioned officers were given commissions; some 2,500 police officers from the militarised *Landespolizei* were transferred to the Army, among whom were many pre-1918 officers (the *Landespolizei* had always been used as a source of military training); officers who had been discharged since 1918 were brought back into service; the grade of *Ergänzungs-Offiziere* (officer on the supplementary list) was established for officers who, although no longer fit for duty with line units, were recalled because of their experience or specialist knowledge, and employed within the High Command, high-level staffs, the Armed Forces Recruiting and Replacement Organisations, the *Grenzwacht* (frontier guard) and the *Landwehr* (territorials); some 300 legal officials were drafted from the Ministry of Justice; about 1,600 former Austrian officers came into the Army after the occupation of Austria; and, finally, an unspecified number of former SA leaders, many of whom had served in the First World War, were commissioned after only a few months' military training. Thus, by September 1939, only about one in six officers was a fully trained professional. Standards inevitably deteriorated, for five-sixths of the officer corps had neither the knowledge, nor, more important, the experience required. General Wolf, commander of the 21st Infantry Division, wrote to Beck in 1935:

'The draft of new officers (they call them "buyers" here in East Prussia) and the bulk of the new arrivals need a great deal of "settling in," for all the good they will show. In addition we get many here who come from "small garrisons." It rather worries me to think of next winter. How are we going to inspire these officers with an intelligent interest in their profession and keep them away from the local custom of sitting night after night in the café or in the beer hall . . .'[1]

It was even feared that the abilities of many officers were being overtaxed by being given rank beyond their capabilities; as a consequence, von Leeb went so far in 1939 as to describe the new Army as 'a blunt sword.'[2]

However, the social dilution of the officer corps possessed certain benefits. The admission of other-rankers tended to break down artificial distinction and allow good leaders to make their way in the Army. Furthermore, there was a considerable lowering of the barriers between officers and men, both on and off duty, and there were frequent meetings on equal terms on the playing fields and in the cafés, which fostered a general spirit of easy comradeship within a framework of discipline. This was to become important in the forthcoming years in maintaining morale under extremely trying conditions.

Just as there was a shortage of commissioned officers, so there was of NCOs, despite the fact that many in the Reichsheer could be used in that capacity. The situation had become so alarming by 1938 that the military authorities were forced to improve the conditions of a non-commissioned officer's career, increasing the chances of his obtaining a commission in the course of ordinary routine. Indeed, during the war, the proportion of NCOs given commissions in some regiments was as high as seventy-five per cent. Nevertheless, the desire of some to seek glory on the field as a means of self-advertisement, and their social insecurity, which often caused them to court popularity, sometimes by engaging in drinking bouts with the other ranks, were not welcomed by their subordinates and superiors alike.

Another aspect of the rapid expansion of the Army was the detrimental effect it had on the coherence of units. This was summed up by General Westphal:

> 'Even when it is taken into consideration that in peacetime each division contained on the average only one-half to two-thirds of the number of battalions and batteries provided for, it can be seen that the demands on the Army were extraordinary. By 1937 the strength had been quadrupled. Every company and battery had therefore had to split up at least twice in four years so that new units could be formed from its parts. This multiple dismemberment damaged very seriously not only the coherence of the Army but also its training.'[3]

Furthermore, the Army, even expanded so greatly, proved unable to provide military training for approximately 3,250,000 men eligible for service between the ages of twenty and forty. Only thirty-eight per cent of the manpower available to the German Armed Forces was fully trained by September 1939, 1,830,000 of the 4,250,000 of the age group from twenty-one to forty-five; and even more distressing to both Hitler and the Army leadership was that this lack of training was especially high among men between the ages of twenty-one and and thirty-five. Expedients thus had to be found to strengthen national defence. A frontier guard was formed from members of the border population who had received military training and were fit for service, and was given the task of border duty and manning of fortifications. On the outbreak of war this frontier guard constituted a security screen only, possessing no artillery whatever. In addition, in 1936, twenty-one Landwehr divisions were formed throughout the Reich, composed of the older age groups of reservists, from thirty to forty-five, who received summer and weekend training. These formations were, however, of poor quality by the time war broke out, for Hitler had not waited until they had been improved by the addition of trained 1914 class conscripts who would normally have left the peacetime Army and gone into the reserve.

One of the most distressing aspects of the rapid rearmament, therefore, was this shortage of trained reserves, which was further exacerbated by the extension of the period of military service from one to two years decreed on 24 August 1936 in the interests of improved training, and by the low birth-rate in the years after 1920. In September 1939, the Army possessed only 500,000 fully trained Class I reservists, and another 600,000 partially trained Class II reservists, to reinforce the 730,000 men already under arms. To provide short-term reservists, special replacement units were formed of men eligible for military service, but who were not subjected to the two-year term of service, being given instead training for three months only. The severe problems in acquiring enough officers were made more difficult by the impossibility of providing intensive training, neither the time nor the resources being available to retrain those who had seen service in the previous war, and whose assistance in the event of another could not be dispensed with. There was a shortage of instructors even for the active Army formations, and the reserve units were forced to take only what few were left. Consequently, there were 1,700,000 reservists between the ages of thirty-five and forty-five who had received no exercise in the military art since 1918. As Westphal recorded: 'For this reason it was possible to detect even in peacetime a degree of improvisation which is normally reached only in an advanced stage of a war. . . . A warworthy army cannot be improvised. . . .'[4]

The circumstances in which the 'army troops' found themselves were poor. Although they were relatively well-provided with motorised transport (for example, in the artillery, of the two regiments and thirty-five heavy artillery battalions, only one was unmotorised), their development still had a long way to go. General Westphal wrote after the war:

> 'Apart from the large formations, a considerable number of special troops were needed outside the divisional units. The 100,000 man Army had no need of these "army troops" without which no modern army can exist, and it was therefore necessary to build them up from scratch. They consisted of heavy and very heavy artillery, sappers, railway troops, chemical warfare troops, signallers, transport, and motor transport troops. The development of these forces was only in its infancy when war broke out, and as it could not be properly completed during the war, the German Army suffered serious deficiencies in these specialised forces right up to 1945. Particularly embarrassing was the shortage of sappers. . . .'[5]

Lastly, and perhaps most important of all, the German Army in 1939 suffered from an acute shortage of military equipment, especially motorised transport. The German economy, with its desultory system of planning, had failed to keep pace with the vast numerical expansion in the size of the Armed Forces. The inadequacies of the armoured divisions have already been noted, but those of the infantry divisions were just as bad. Only four infantry divisions were fully motorised; the eighty-six others possessed fewer than one-quarter of the trucks and passenger cars necessary for their transport, and, on mobilisation, fifty-one of them were equipped largely with requisitioned civilian vehicles. Horses, therefore, played a significant role in the German Army. Even the best infantry divisions each required 4,842 of the animals to supplement their 394 passenger cars and 615 trucks, while the weakest needed about 6,030 and only 330 passenger cars and 248 trucks. On 1 September 1939, the eighty-six non-motorised infantry divisions had a total of 445,500 horses. Divisional artillery, and a high percentage of the supply services, all depended on the horse, while the infantrymen had to rely on their own feet. In the infantry formations, only the anti-tank, infantry gun, signals, headquarters, medical staffs, and some pioneer units were fully motorised, and just fourteen divisions from a total of 103 within the German Army were totally independent of the horse. In this, the force committed to battle in 1939 differed little from its predecessor in 1914. During the First World War, 1,400,000 horses had passed through the German Army; in the Second, it was to be almost double that number—2,700,000.

The quality of the equipment of the German Army at the beginning of the war left much to be desired. It had a variety of weapons of old design and numerous variants which went far to impair efficiency in the field. The lamentable condition of the tanks has already been described, but the infantry and artillery were little better off. The standard infantry weapon was the Type 98 rifle based on a design first drawn up by Mauser in 1898. The long Karabinier 98a, and its successor, the 98b, were adequate weapons but no more, and it was not until October 1941 that the Gewehr 98/40 rifle, intended to become standard, was introduced. The German soldiers were equipped with at least five types of machine-pistol—the MP 18 and 34 (Bergmann), and MP 28 and 38 (Schmeisser), and the MP 34 (Steyr-Solothurns and Ermas) prior to the general issue of the MP 38 (Schmeisser), which was to appear in 1940 in an improved, modified form, the MP 40. It was not until 1942 that the old variants were finally withdrawn from service. The machine-guns, too, were outdated. The war began before the Army was fully equipped with a standard weapon, the MG 34, and many of the soldiers were still armed with the MG 18, MG 08/15, and MG 15 light machine-guns, and the SMG 08 and ZB 26 Czechoslovak weapons. It was not until March 1941 that all these older types could be withdrawn from front-line service. The anti-tank rifles were the ineffective 7.92mm Panzerbüchse PzB 38 and 39. There was a complete absence of heavy mortars, except those used for firing smoke bombs; the only ones in existence being the 5cm Granatwerfer 36 and 8.1cm Granatwerfer 34 models, and it was not long before the lighter of both these was found to be relatively ineffective. The infantry was also provided with infantry guns for close support, weapons peculiar to the German Army, of both light and heavy variety—the 7.5cm le.IG18 and the 15cm s.IG33. The only anti-aircraft weapons issued to the Army formations were the light 2cm Flak 30 and 38, and the only anti-tank gun was the 3.7cm Pak 35/36, which came to be nicknamed the 'Army's doorknocker,' so ineffective was it against contemporary armour. Furthermore, German artillery was almost uniformly competent but uninspired, the result of years of neglect. The divisional artillery of light and medium field-howitzers were modified developments of those used in the previous war—the 10.5 le.FH18 and the 15cm s.FH18. The guns (Kanonen) used by the 'army troops' were the standard 10cm K 18 (also used by the panzer divisions), the 15cm K 18, the 17cm and 21cm howitzers (termed 'mortars' by the Germans), which also dated back to the First World War. The famed 8.8cm Flak 18, 36, and 37, and the 3.7cm Flak 18, 36, and 37 were solely under Luftwaffe control, although they were used in the field to accompany the armoured formations and to protect certain vital sectors of the front.

Furthermore, there were serious shortages in arms and munitions. For example, fifty infantry divisions were without machine-pistols, light or medium mortars, 2cm anti-aircraft guns, and heavy infantry guns, while thirty-four possessed no armoured cars. Most of the formations selected for service on the Western Front as a holding force while the invasion of Poland took place, suffered from an acute lack of anti-tank and artillery guns, and many of the low-quality infantry divisions were provided with old, out-of-date equipment. But perhaps the most serious deficiencies lay in the munitions required to make the weapons effective. The Army High Command based its stocks on a forecast of requirements for four months of fighting—little enough, it might be imagined. However, at the outbreak of war there was an ammunition shortage of some seventy per cent of this requirement. It lacked, for example, forty-five per cent of heavy field howitzer ammunition, sixty-five per cent of heavy infantry gun shells, seventy per cent of pistol bullet and 2cm Flak ammunition, seventy-five per cent of light infantry gun and heavy artillery ammunition, eighty-eight per cent of light and heavy artillery ammunition, eighty-eight per cent of light and ninety per cent of medium mortar shells, and a staggering ninety-five per cent of 2cm ammunition for tank guns.

The Army leadership, painfully aware of the inadequacies of the reserves of equipment and trained manpower, took steps to overcome the latter, tackling the problem with some skill. At the outset they saw before them two alternatives: either a small but highly qualified and well-equipped wartime army, or a mass army in which numbers compensated for deficiencies in material and training. Hitler, however, left them with little choice, his obsession with numbers forcing them in 1938 to adopt a compromise solution for the organisation of the wartime force. On mobilisation the Army would be divided into two: the *Feldheer* (Field Army), consisting of the divisions of the peacetime active and reserve force only slightly weakened by detaching some cadres; and the *Ersatzheer* (Replacement Army), which was organised on a broad basis without regard to the deficiences that would develop, and which was intended not only to provide trained replacement for the Field Army formations, but also to form additional field units to be committed to battle. Thus, the wartime Army of 1939 was composed of a Field Army of 2,321,266 men (plus another 426,798 construction troops formed from the Reich Labour

Service) and a Replacement Army of 958,040, making a grand total of 3,706,104.

As a further aid to the solution of the problems of the wartime Army's organisation, a graduated structure of infantry divisions was formed. This was known as the *Welle* (Wave) mobilisation plan. The First Wave would consist of the thirty-five active infantry divisions that had existed in peacetime, replenished mainly from Class I reservists of the youngest age class (mountain divisions were rated as qualified for the First Wave). Second Wave divisions, which would not be activated until mobilisation had begun, but would be ready for action within some four days, would consist of sixteen reserve divisions made up of Class I reservists with a cadre, six per cent of their strength, from active divisions; they would be equipped with motor vehicles requisitioned from the national economy. Third Wave divisions, the weakest of all, which would take from four to eight weeks to become operational, were twenty-one in number and were composed only of reservists mainly from Class II and the Landwehr; somewhat deficient in armament and equipment, most would be selected either for the West Wall defences or for training centres. Lastly, the fourteen Fourth Wave divisions would also be composed mainly of reservists, but with some nine per cent of active personnel; and they would not take to the field for several weeks. The advantages of this Wave system of mobilisation were considerable, for, although complete mobilisation was no faster than that of Germany's enemies, it did allow partial mobilisation without improvisation, and ensured that the most powerful formations, the peacetime, active divisions, could mount an attack almost at once without having to wait for the completion of any lengthy process.

The Field and Replacement Armies possessed between them a grand total of 3,706,104 troops, of whom 105,394 were officers, 29,495 officials, 481,009 NCOs, and 3,090,206 men. Apart from the Army, Germany possessed other ground troops in the SS and Luftwaffe formations. At the outbreak of war the SS-VT consisted of four motorised infantry regiments (one of which had not completed its training), an artillery regiment, and independent signals, pioneer, reconnaissance, anti-aircraft machine-gun, and anti-tank battalions (one of each), together with supply and replacement units, to a total of some 23,000 men. Immediately on mobilisation, most of these units were dispersed among Army field formations. The Luftwaffe, too, contributed towards Germany's total number of ground troops in the form of the Flak Regiment Hermann Göring and the 1st *Fallschirmjäger* (Paratroop) Regiment (2 battalions), as well as numerous anti-aircraft field units. The 400,000 servicemen in the Air Force, and 50,000 in the Navy, brought the total of servicemen in the Wehrmacht on mobilisation to around 4,179,000.

But numbers were not everything. As has been shown, the paper figures, the massed parades, the manoeuvres, all served only to obscure from the world the lamentable condition in which the German Army found itself on the outbreak of the European war. Owing to the wide variety and enormous size of the tasks involved in the five-year expansion, the problem of transforming the Army onto a war-footing had been relegated to the background; Indeed, the formation of even the peacetime Army was incomplete. Of the thirty-five First Wave divisions, one whole infantry regiment and thirty-one infantry battalions (a total of forty battalions out of 315—twelve per cent) had still to be formed, as well as five artillery battalions, twelve artillery observation batteries, and other divisional services. Of the units that took to the field in September 1939, only between five and six per cent were fit for modern, mobile war, and even these were woefully ill-equipped. Only fourteen of the Field Army's 103 divisions were fully motorised, the other eighty-nine being dependent to a large extent on their feet, the horse, and the railway, and being hampered by serious logistical limits similar to those experienced by the old Imperial Armies. Independence from the restricting umbilical cord of supply was not granted to eighty-five per cent of the Field Army. Moreover, because of deficiencies in training and equipment, the Third and Fourth Wave divisions, which formed forty per cent of the infantry and thirty-four per cent of all field divisions, were ill-suited to the demanding conditions of a war of manoeuvre of any sort.

Such was the state of the German Army at the outbreak of the Second World War. This Army, which had expanded so rapidly since 1935, was, within two years, to be embroiled in an ever-intensifying conflict in both the east and the west, as well as in North Africa. In the early years of victory it was to prove so spectacularly successful, and in the years of defeat so tenacious in defence, that its high place in the history of warfare is assured. However, from the very beginning it possessed deficiencies so fundamental that they were never overcome—indeed, they only increased with the passage of time. Neither in its strategic basis, nor in its organisation and equipment, was the German Army prepared to adopt any new concept of war, and its imperial character—its reliance on old-fashioned infantry divisions hampered by logistical limitations, unrelieved by any thorough use of mechanisation, and directed according to the precepts of von Moltke and von Schlieffen—was not consonant with the belief that it was fashioned according to any revolutionary theory, even one so firmly founded in the imaginations of men as *Blitzkrieg*.

A Note on Sources

I have relied upon a wide range of sources, both original and secondary, and have drawn as much on many of the well-known works on the period as on the fine collections of documents found in the archives of the Imperial War Museum (IWM), the Public Record Office (PRO) and the Liddell Hart Papers (LHP). Of particular use have been the collection of captured German documents found in the IWM, and the interrogation reports and translations of documents prepared for the War Crimes Military Tribunal in 1945 and 1946, found in the LHP.

I have made extensive use of quotations, and would like to place on record my indebtedness to the following published works which must be regarded as basic texts for all students of the German Army:

Heinz Guderian, *Panzer Leader*, Michael Joseph, 1952.
Wilhelm Keitel, *Memoirs*, with introduction and epilogue by Walter Görlitz, William Kimber, 1965.
Albert Kesselring, *Memoirs*, Kimbler, 1953.
B. H. Liddell Hart, *The Other Side of the Hill* (revised),

Cassell, 1951.

Erich von Manstein, *Lost Victories*, Methuen, 1958.

Erwin Rommel, edited by B. H. Liddell Hart, *The Rommel Papers*, Collins, 1953.

Walter Warlimont, *Inside Hitler's Headquarters*, Weidenfeld and Nicolson, 1964.

Siegfried Westphal, *The German Army in the West*, Cassell, 1951.

My quotations from men such as Halder, Jodl and Zeitzler come from translations of captured documents and interrogation reports.

I also owe a great deal to the information contained in books by the following authors: B. H. Liddell Hart, J. F. C. Fuller, R. O'Neill, J. Wheeler-Bennett, K. Demeter, H. Deutsch and H. Rosinski.

I should also like to thank two Americans, John Calder and Otto Kuhn, for making available to me their, as yet, unpublished manuscripts on the German Army 1933 to 1939; although much of their material can be found in published works, their compilations are of considerable value to a researcher.

Notes

PART 1 The Political Destiny of the German Army, 1933–39

1 Political Heritage

1. Gordon Craig, *The Politics of the German Army 1640–1945*, London, 1955, p. 229.
2. *Official Record of the Trial of the Major War Criminals before the International Military Tribunal*, Nuremberg, 1947–49, Vol. 22, p. 522.
3. Walter Warlimont, *Inside Hitler's Headquarters 1939–45*, London, 1964, pp. ix–x.
4. B. H. Liddell Hart, *The Other Side of the Hill*, London, 1951, p. 51.
5. LHP, files on German generals.
6. Ibid., quoted from Wolfgang Forster, *Ein General Kämpft gegen der Krieg*, Munich, 1949, p. 39.
7. John Wheeler-Bennett, *Nemesis of Power*, London, 1964, p. 9.

8. Plato, *Laws XII*, taken from OKW, *Glückhäfte Strategie*, Berlin, 1942.
9. Karl Demeter, *The German Officer Corps in Society and State, 1650–1945*, London, 1965, p. 168.
10. Berghahn, *The Approach of the First World War*, London, 1973, p. 10.
11. Author's collection, Gestapo interrogation of Hans Oster, 1944 (also in Demeter).
12. Demeter, p. 165.
13. Author's collection, Oster interrogation.
14. Herbert Rosinski, *The German Army*, New York, 1966, p. 165 (quoting Seeckt).
15. Demeter, p. 357.
16. Hans von Seeckt, *Thoughts of a Soldier*, London, 1930, pp. 79–80.
17. Author's collection, Oster interrogation.
18. Siegfried Westphal, *The German Army in the West*, London, 1951, p. 4.
19. Demeter, p. 358.
20. Ibid., p. 357.
21. Westphal, p. 3.
22. Author's collection, Oster interrogation.
23. Wilhelm Keitel, *The Memoirs of Field-Marshal Keitel*, London, 1965, p. 243.
24. Demeter, pp. 195–6.
25. Rosinski, pp. 131–2.
26. LHP, files on German generals.
27. Author's collection, Oster interrogation.
28. Craig, p. 388.
29. Wheeler-Bennett, p. 200.
30. Ibid., p. 213.
31. Ibid., p. 225.
32. Ibid., pp. 285–6.

2 First Years

1. LHP, extracts from Hitler's speeches etc.
2. Adolf Hitler, *Hitler's Secret Book*, New York, 1952, p. 85.
3. Hermann Rauschning, *Hitler Speaks*, London, 1939, p. 20.
4. Ibid., p. 16.
5. Ibid., p. 20.
6. Heinz Guderian, *Panzer Leader*, New York, 1957, p. 384.
7. Ibid., p. 387.
8. Joachim Fest, *The Face of the Third Reich*, London, 1972, p. 362.
9. Ibid., p. 358.
10. Ibid., p. 358.
11. Wheeler-Bennett, p. 291.
12. Craig, p. 470.
13. Friedrich Hossbach, *Zwischen Wehrmacht und Hitler*, Hanover, 1949, p. 103.
14. Robert O'Neill, *The German Army and the Nazi Party, 1933-39*, London, 1966, pp. 141-2.
15. Ibid., p. 93.
16. Adolf Hitler, *My New Order* (Speeches), New York, 1941, p. 397.
17. Fest, p. 358.
18. Unpublished manuscript, Otto Kuhn, dated 1973, concerning the SA and SS 1920-39; also quoted in Heinz Höhne, *Order of the Death's Head*, London, 1969.
19. Ibid.
20. Ibid.
21. Ibid.

22. O'Neill, p. 63.
23. Demeter, p. 202.
24. O'Neill, pp. 66–8.
25. Höhne, p. 96.
26. O'Neill, p. 70.
27. Ibid., p. 81.
28. Ibid., p. 138.
29. Hossbach, p. 76.
30. Telford Taylor, *Sword and Swastika*, London, 1953, p. 154.
31. Warlimont, p. 10.
32. LHP, files on German generals; also quoted by O'Neill.
33. O'Neill, p. 48.
34. Harold Deutsch, *Hitler and his Generals*, Minneapolis, 1974, pp. 25–6.
35. O'Neill, p. 50.
36. Westphal, p. 45.

3 *Alliance*

1. Taylor, pp. 117–8.
2. Westphal, p. 7.
3. Fest, p. 360.
4. Demeter, p. 203.
5. Ibid., p. 203.
6. O'Neill, p. 76.
7. Wheeler-Bennett, p.394.
8. Demeter, pp. 152–3.
9. O'Neill, p. 86.
10. LHP, files on German generals.
11. O'Neill, p. 90.

12. Ibid., p. 96.
13. Ibid., p. 96.
14. Unpublished collection, dated 1970, of Reichswehr and Wehrmacht Orders and Decrees, by John Calder; also quoted by O'Neill.
15. Ibid.
16. Ibid.
17. Demeter, p. 210.
18. Calder; also quoted by O'Neill.
19. Ibid.
20. O'Neill, p. 112.
21. Ibid., p. 113.
22. Calder; also quoted by O'Neill.
23. Ibid.

4 *Independence*

1. Adolf Hitler, *Hitler's Secret Conversations*, 1941-44, New York, 1953, p. 403.
2. Taylor, pp. 117-8.
3. Erich von Manstein, *Lost Victories*, London, 1958, p. 77.
4. Hossbach, p. 77.
5. Taylor, pp. 153-4.
6. Alan Bullock, *A Study in Tyranny*, London, 1962, p. 405.
7. Ibid., p. 339.
8. Taylor, p. 119.
9. Bullock, p. 307.
10. Deutsch, p. 31.
11. Ibid., p. 23.
12. Wheeler-Bennett, p. 325.

13. Kuhn, unpublished manuscript.
14. Ibid.
15. George Stein, *The Waffen SS*, Oxford, 1966, p. 11.
16. O'Neill, p. 149.
17. Kuhn, unpublished manuscript.
18. Helmut Krausnick *et al.*, *Anatomy of the SS State*, Collins, 1968, pp. 262-3. (Chapter 2, by Hans Buchheim).
19. Taylor, p. 121.
20. Westphal, p. 6.
21. Ibid., p. 8.
22. Calder, unpublished manuscript; also quoted by O'Neill.
23. O'Neill, p. 112.
24. Calder, unpublished manuscript.
25. O'Neill, p. 253.
26. Ibid., p. 144.
27. Calder, unpublished manuscript; also quoted by O'Neill.
28. O'Neill, p. 101.
29. Calder, unpublished manuscript; also quoted by O'Neill.
30. LHP, files on German generals.
31. O'Neill, p. 127.
32. Fest, p. 363.
33. O'Neill, p. 129.
34. Fest, p. 363.
35. Calder, unpublished manuscript; also quoted by O'Neill.
36. O'Neill, p. 172.
37. Ibid., p. 172.
38. Ibid., p. 180.
39. Ibid., p. 180.

40. Ibid., p. 181.
41. Herbert Mason, *The Rise of the Luftwaffe*, London, 1925, p. 97.
42. Ibid., p. 210.
43. Bullock, p. 345.
44. Deutsch, p. 38.
45. Wheeler-Bennett, p. 290.
46. Manstein, p. 78.
47. Keitel, pp. 36–7.
48. Warlimont, p. 10.
49. Author's collection, Hossbach memorandum.
50. Ibid.
51. Warlimont, p. 10.

5 *Crisis*

1. Höhne, p. 243.
2. Ibid., p. 243.
3. Deutsch, p. 115.
4. Höhne, p. 245.
5. Ibid., p. 245.
6. Warlimont, p. 13.
7. Wheeler-Bennett, p. 367.
8. Höhne, p. 244.
9. Fest, p. 365.
10. Wheeler-Bennett, p. 694.
11. Guderian, p. 30.
12. Westphal, p. 24.
13. Fest, p. 557.
14. Guderian, p. 30.
15. Kenneth Macksey, *Guderian: Panzer General*, London, 1975.

16. Guderian, p. 28.
17. Deutsch, p. 417.
18. O'Neill, p. 199.
19. Deutsch, p. 420.
20. Guderian, p. 30.
21. Deutsch, p. 250.
22. Walter Schellenberg: *Schellenberg*, London, 1958, pp. 14–5.
23. Deutsch, p. 213.
24. Ibid., p. 417.
25. Harold Deutsch, *The Conspiracy against Hitler in the Twilight War*, Minneapolis, 1968, p. 62.
26. Deutsch, *Hitler and his Generals*, p. 254.
27. Wheeler-Bennett, p. 393.
28. Deutsch, *Hitler and his Generals*, p. 404.
29. Ibid., p. 403.
30. Ibid., p. 404.
31. Ibid., p. 405.
32. Ibid., p. 410.
33. Fest, p. 365.
34. Deutsch, *Hitler and his Generals*, p. 408.

6 *The First Shackles*

1. Wheeler-Bennett, p. 372.
2. Mason, p. 96.
3. Manstein, p. 75.
4. Ibid., pp. 75–6.
5. Deutsch, *Hitler and his Generals*, p. 221.
6. Ibid., p. 230.
7. Deutsch, *Twilight War*, p. 34.
8. Ibid., p. 34.

9. Deutsch, *Hitler and his Generals*, p. 280.
10. O'Neill, p. 207.
11. Calder, unpublished manuscript; also quoted by O'Neill.
12. O'Neill, p. 160.
13. Warlimont, p. 8.
14. Ibid., p. 9.
15. Ibid., p. 17.
16. Guderian, pp. 387–8.
17. Keitel, p. 52.
18. Deutsch, *Hitler and his Generals*, p. 132.
19. Ibid., p. 214.
20. Keitel, p. 15.
21. Albert Speer, *Inside the Third Reich*, London, 1971, p. 164.
22. Ibid., p. 339.
23. Ibid., p. 339.
24. Hugh Trevor-Roper, *The Last Days of Hitler*, London, 1952, p. 61.
25. Keitel, p. 28.
26. Warlimont, p. 13.
27. Guderian, p. 388.
28. Percy Schramm, *Hitler: The Man and the Military Commander*, London, 1972, p. 193.
29. Speer, p. 339.
30. Westphal, p. 52.
31. Jodl, KTB, 10 Aug. 1938.
32. Warlimont, p. 59.
33. Ibid., p. 46.
34. U.S. War Department, *Handbook of German Military Forces*, Washington, 1941, p. 15.
35. Warlimont, p. 3.
36. Guderian, pp. 364–5.

37. Warlimont, p. 17.
38. Ibid., p. 14.
39. Ibid., p. 17.
40. Ibid., p. 21.
41. Ibid., p. 25.

7 Road to War

1. Keitel, p. 58.
2. Ibid., pp. 58–9.
3. William Shirer, *The Rise and Fall of the Third Reich*, London, 1964, p. 437.
4. Bullock, p. 446.
5. Wheeler-Bennett, p. 398.
6. Ibid., p. 399.
7. O'Neill, p. 219.
8. Wheeler-Bennett, p. 401.
9. Ibid., p. 400.
10. Ibid., p. 404.
11. O'Neill, pp. 200–1.
12. Keitel, p. 66.
13. Shirer, p. 454.
14. Barry Leach, *German Strategy against Russia, 1939–41*, London, 1973, p. 33.
15. Manstein, p. 80.
16. Deutsch, *Twilight War*, p. 31.
17. Ibid., p. 34.
18. Manstein, pp. 80–1.
19. Warlimont, p. 18.
20. Keitel, p. 69.
21. O'Neill, p. 229.
22. Deutsch, *Twilight War*, p. 38.

23. Bullock, p. 464.
24. Shirer, p. 554.
25. Karl Bracher, *The German Dictatorship*, New York, 1970, p. 392.
26. Shirer, p. 554.
27. Ibid., p. 554.
28. Deutsch, *Hitler and his Generals*, p. 395.
29. Bracher, p. 489.
30. Ibid., p. 490.
31. Westphal, p. 23.
32. Ibid., p. 23.
33. Keitel, p. 73.
34. Ibid., p. 246.
35. O'Neill, p. 226.
36. Manstein, p. 77.
37. Warlimont, p. 16.
38. Ibid., p. 17.
39. Wheeler-Bennett, p. 425.
40. Shirer, p. 570.
41. Ibid., pp. 590–2.
42. Ibid., p. 605.
43. Wheeler-Bennett, p. 228.
44. Manstein, pp. 23–4.
45. Shirer, pp. 641–5.
46. Keitel, p. 87.
47. Manstein, p. 30.
48. Wheeler-Bennett, p. 451.
49. Ibid., p. 451.

PART 2 *The Battle of Ideas*

8 *The Myth*

1. Winston S. Churchill, *History of the Second World War*, Vol. 1, London, 1949, pp. 3–4.
2. Tom Wintringham, *New Ways of War*, London, 1940, p. 5.
3. F. O. Miksche, *Blitzkrieg*, London, 1941, p. 24.
4. J. R. Lester, *Tank Warfare*, London, 1943, p. 64.
5. B. H. Liddell Hart, *History of the Second World War*, London, 1970, p. 22.
6. Ibid., p. 66.
7. J. F. C. Fuller, *Decisive Battles of the Western World*, Vol. 3, London, 1956, pp. 381–2.
8. LHP, letter from Liddell Hart to Guderian, dated 7 Oct. 1948.
9. Larry Addington, *The Blitzkreig Era and the German General Staff*, New Brunswick, 1971, p. 234.
10. Guderian, p. 385.
11. Hermann Rauschning, *Hitler Speaks*, London, 1939, p. 182.
12. Max Werner, *Military Strength of the Powers*, London, 1939, p. 154.
13. J. Benoist-Méchin, *Sixty Days That Shook the West*, London, 1963, p. 43.
14. B. H. Liddell Hart, *The Other Side of the Hill*, London, 1951, p. 27.
15. Ibid., p. 23.
16. Mason, p. 90.
17. Demeter, p. 51.
18. Erich von Ludendorff, *The Nation At War*, London,

1936, pp. 87-9.
19. Adolf Hitler, *My New Order*, New York, 1941, pp. 116-7.

9 *The War Lord*

1. Wheeler-Bennett, p. 290.
2. Rauschning, p. 230.
3. Adolf Hitler, *Mein Kampf*, London, 1938, pp. 523-31.
4. Ibid., p. 11.
5. Wheeler-Bennett, p. 290.
6. Schramm, p. 197.
7. John Strawson, *Hitler as a Military Commander*, London, 1971, p. 241.
8. Franz Halder, *Hitler as Warlord*, London, 1950, p. 70.
9. Schramm, p. 103.
10. Ibid., p. 108.
11. Manstein, p. 276.
12. LHP, file on Hitler and his generals.
13. Hermann Rauschning, pp. 16-21.
14. J. F. C. Fuller, *Machine Warfare*, London, 1942, p. 28.
15. J. F. C. Fuller, *Conduct of War*, London, 1961, p. 244.
16. Rauschning, p. 17.
17. Ibid., pp. 15-6.
18. Craig, p. 441.

10 *Strategic Tradition*

1. Wheeler-Bennett, p. 338.

2. Shirer, p. 352.
3. Fuller, *Conduct of War*, pp. 117–8.
4. Ibid., p. 118.
5. Edward Mead Earle, *Makers of Modern Strategy*, London, 1948, p. 180.
6. Ibid., p. 183.
7. Liddell Hart, *The Other Side of the Hill*, p. 29.
8. Seeckt, pp. 63–4.
9. Ibid., p. 24.
10. Liddell Hart, *The Other Side of the Hill*, p. 29.
11. LHP, letter from von Manstein to Liddell Hart, dated 25 Jan. 1958.
12. OKH, *Die Trupenführung*, HDV 300, 1937, p. 1, para. 2.
13. Ibid., para. 339.
14. E. Middeldorf, *Taktik im Russlandfeldzug*, Berlin, 1956, p. 10.
15. OKW, *Glückhäfte Strategie*, Berlin, 1942, p. 92.
16. Fuller, *Machine Warfare*, pp. 39–40.

11 *Strategic Revolution*

1. Wintringham, pp. 28–9.
2. Fuller, *Conduct of War*, p. 243.
3. Liddell Hart, *The Other Side of the Hill*, pp. 65–75.
4. Guderian, p. 13.
5. Werner.
6. Guderian, 1937, reprinted in *Armor*, Nov.–Dec. 1952, pp. 54–6.
7. Guderian, p.
8. Erwin Rommel, *Rommel Papers*, London, 1953, p. 299.

9. Guderian, *Militär Wissenschaftliche Rundschau*, 15 Oct. 1936, p. 10.
10. LHP, Guderian, 1936.
11. Guderian, 1937, reprinted in *Armor*, Nov.–Dec. 1952, pp. 54–6.
12. Fuller, *Conduct of War*, p. 257.
13. LHP, Guderian, 1936.
14. Guderian, pp. 383–4.
15. Liddell Hart, *The Other Side of the Hill*, p. 122.
16. Rommel, p. 517.
17. Guderian, pp. 21–2.
18. Liddell Hart, *The Other Side of the Hill*, p. 69.
19. Guderian, p. 20.
20. Westphal, p. 37.
21. Guderian, p. 69.
22. Ibid., p. 21.
23. Macksey, p. 58.
24. Guderian, pp. 62–3.
25. Guderian, *Militär Wochenblatt*, 28 Oct. 1934.
26. Rommel, p. 517.
27. Liddell Hart, *The Other Side of the Hill*, p. 66.
28. Ibid., p. 71.
29. Halder, *Kriegstagebuch* (KTB), 27 Aug. 1941.
30. Guderian, p. 24.
31. Ibid., p. 17.
32. Ibid., p. 26.
33. Ibid., p. 44.

12 Unreadiness

1. Demeter, p. 107.
2. LHP, files on German generals.

3. Westphal, p. 36.
4. Ibid., pp. 36-9.
5. Ibid., p. 37.

Select Bibliography

ADDINGTON, LARRY H.: *The Blitzkrieg Era and the German General Staff, 1865-1941*. New Brunswick: Rutgers, 1971.
ALLEN, WILLIAM SHERIDAN: *The Nazi Seizure of Power*. New York: Watts, 1965.

BAUER, EDDY: *Panzer Krieg* (2 Vols.). Bonn: Offene Wörte, 1965.
BECKER, CAJUS: *The Luftwaffe War Diaries*. London: Macdonald and Jane's, 1967.
BELFIELD, E. and ESSAME, A.: *The Battle for Normandy*. London: Batsford, 1965.
BENOIST-MÉCHIN, J.: *Sixty Days that Shook the West*. London: Jonathan Cape, 1963.
BERNHARDT, WALTER: *Die Deutsche Aufrüstung, 1934-39*. Frankfurt am Main: Bernard und Graefe, 1969.
BLAU, GEORGE E.: *The German Campaign in Russia: Planning and Operations, 1940-42*. Washington D.C.: U.S. Department of the Army, 1955.

BLUMENSON, MARTIN: *Breakout and Pursuit*. Washinton D.C.: U.S. Army Military History Department, 1961.

BLUMENTRITT, GÜNTHER: *Von Rundstedt, The Soldier and The Man*. London: Odhams, 1952.

BRACHER, KARL: *The German Dictatorship*. New York: Praeger, 1970.

BRACKMANN, ALBERT et al.: *Unser Kampf in Polen*. Munich: Bruckmann, 1959.

BROSZAT, MARTIN: *German National Socialism 1919–1945*. Santa Barbara, California: American Bibliographical Center-Clio Press, 1966.

BULLOCK, ALAN: *Hitler, A Study in Tyranny*. New York: Harper & Row, 1964.

CARREL, PAUL: *Hitler's War on Russia*. London: Harrap, 1964.
    Scorched Earth. London: Harrap, 1970.

CECIL, ROBERT: *Hitler's Decision to Invade Russia 1941*. New York: David McKay, 1976.

CHAPMAN, GUY: *Why France Fell*. London: Cassell, 1968.

CHURCHILL, WINSTON S.: *History of The Second World War*. London: Cassell, 1949.

CLARK, ALAN: *Barbarossa*. London: Hutchinson, 1965.

COLE, HUGH M.: *Ardennes and the Battle of the Bulge*. Washington D.C.: U.S. Army Military History Department, 1965.

COOPER, MATTHEW, and LUCAS, JAMES: *Panzer, The Armoured Force of the Third Reich*. London: Macdonald and Jane's, 1976.

CRAIG, GORDON: *The Politics of the Prussian Army*

1650–1945. New York: Oxford University Press, 1964.
CREVELD, MARTIN VAN: *Hitler's Strategy 1940–41*. New York: Cambridge University Press, 1973.

DALLIN, ALEXANDER: *German Rule in Russia, 1941–45*. London: Macmillian, 1951.
DELARUE, JACQUES: *The Gestapo*. New York: William Morrow, 1964.
DEMETER, KARL: *The German Officer Corps in Society and State, 1860–1945*. London: Weidenfeld and Nicolson, 1965.
DEUTSCH, HAROLD: *The Conspiracy against Hitler in the Twilight War*. Minneapolis: University of Minnesota, 1968.
   Hitler and His Generals, The Hidden Crisis, January–June 1938. Minneapolis: University of Minnesota, 1974.
DÖNITZ, Admiral KARL: *Memoirs*. London: Weidenfeld and Nicolson, 1958.

EARLE, EDWARD MEAD: *Makers of Modern Strategy*. Princeton: Princeton University Press, 1943.
EBELING, Dr. H.: *The Political Role of the German General Staff between 1918 and 1938*. London: New Europe, 1945.
ELLIS, L. F.: *The War in France and Flanders*. London: H.M.S.O., 1953.
   Victory in the West (2 Vols.). London: H.M.S.O., 1968.
ERICKSON, JOHN: *The Road to Stalingrad*. New York: Harper & Row, 1975.
ESEBECK, HANNS GERT Von: *Afrikanische Schicksals-*

jahre. Wiesbaden: Limes, 1950.
ESSAME, H.: *Battle for Germany.* London: Batsford, 1969.

FEST, JOACHIM: *The Face of the Third Reich.* New York: Pantheon, 1970.
    Hitler. New York: Random, 1975.
FRANK, FRIEDRICH, *et al.: Unser Kampf in Holland, Belgien und Flandern.* Munich: Bruckmann, 1941.
FRIED, HANS ERNEST: *The Guilt of the German Army.* New York: Macmillan, 1943.
FULLER, Major-General J. F. C.: *Armoured Warfare.* London: Eyre and Spottiswoode, 1943.
    Conduct of War. New York: Funk & Wagnalls, 1961.
    The Decisive Battles of the Western World (3 Vols.). London: Eyre and Spottiswoode, 1956.
    Machine Warfare. London: Hutchinson, 1942.
    The Second World War. New York: Hawthorn, 1969.

GAULLE, CHARLES De: *The Army of the Future.* London: Hutchinson, 1940.
GEYR Von SCHWEPPENBURG, L.: *The Critical Years.* London: Allen Wingate, 1952.
GILBERT, FELIX: *Hitler Directs His War.* Hauppauge, N.Y.: Universal Publishing, 1971.
GOEBBELS, JOSEF: *The Goebbels Diaries.* (Ed. Louis P. Lochner). Westport, Conn.: Greenwood Press, repr. of 1948 ed.
GÖRLITZ, WALTER: *The German General Staff.* London: Hollis and Carter, 1953.
GREINER, E.: *Die Oberste Wehrmachtführung, 1939–*

1943. Wiesbaden: Limes, 1951.
GRUNBERGER, RICHARD: *A Social History of the Third Reich*. London: Weidenfeld and Nicolson, 1971; Penguin, 1974.
GUDERIAN, HEINZ: *Panzer Leader*. New York: Ballantine, 1957, abr. ed. 1976.
   Mit dem Panzern in Ost und West. Göttingen: Volk und Reich, 1942.

HALDER, FRANZ: *Hitler as Warlord*. London: Putnam, 1950.
   Kriegstagebuch, 1939-1942.
HARRISON, G. A.: *Cross Channel Attack*. Washington D.C.: Army Military History Department, 1951.
HEIDEN, KONRAD: *Der Führer*. New York: Howard Fertig, repr. of 1944 ed.
HEISS, FRIEDRICH: *Der Sieg im Osten*. Berlin: Volk und Reich, 1940.
HIGGINS, TRUMBALL: *Hitler and Russia*. London: Macmillan, 1966.
HILLGRUBER, ANDREAS: *Hitlers Strategie*. Frankfurt am Main: Bernard und Graefe, 1965.
HINSLEY, F. H.: *Hitler's Strategy*. Cambridge: Cambridge University Press, 1951.
HITLER, ADOLF: *My New Order* (Speeches). New York: Octagon Books, repr. of 1941 ed.
   Table Talk. (Ed. H. Trevor-Roper). London: Weidenfeld and Nicolson, 1953.
   War Directives, 1939-45 (Ed. H. Trevor-Roper). London: Sidgwick and Jackson, 1964; Pan, 1966.
HOFFMANN, PETER: *The History of the German Resistance, 1933-1945*. Cambridge, Mass.: M.I.T. Press, 1976.

HÖHNE, HEINZ: *The Order of the Death's Head.* New York: Coward, McCann & Geoghegan, 1970.

HORN, A.: *To Lose a Battle.* New York: Macmillan, 1969.

HOSSBACH, FRIEDRICH: *Zwischen Wehrmacht und Hitler.* Göttingen: Vardenhoek und Ruprecht, 1965.

HOTH, HERMANN: *Panzer Operationen.* (Die Wehrmacht im Kampf, vol. II) Heidelberg: Vowinkel, 1956.

HOWARD, MICHAEL: *The Mediterranean Strategy in the Second World War.* London: Weidenfeld and Nicolson, 1968.

HUNTINGTON, SAMUEL P.: *The Soldier and the State.* Cambridge, Mass.: Harvard University, 1957.

INTERNATIONAL MILITARY TRIBUNAL: *The Trial of the German Major War Criminals: Proceedings of the International Military Tribunal Sitting at Nuremberg, Germany* (23 Vols.). London: H.M.S.O., 1949–51.

IRVING, DAVID: *Hitler's War.* New York: Viking Press, 1977.

JACOBSEN, H. A.: *Dokumente zur Vorgeschichte des Westfeldzuges, 1939–1940* (2 Vols.). Göttingen: Musterschmidt, 1956.

Fall Gelb: der Kampf um den deutschen Operationsplan der Westoffensive, 1940. Wiesbaden: Steiner, 1957.

JACOBSEN, H.A. and ROHWER, J.: *Der Zweite Weltkriege in Chronik und Dokumentum.* Darmstadt: Wehr und Wissen, 1961.

JODL, ALFRED: *Kriegstagebuch 1938–1945*—fragments prepared by the International Military Tribunal.

KEILIG, WOLF: *Das Heer* (3 Vols.). Bad Neuheim: Podzun, 1956 and various dates.

KEITEL, WILHELM: *The Memoirs of Field-Marshal Keitel*, with an introduction and epilogue by Walter Görlitz. London: William Kimber, 1965.

KENNEDY, R.M.: *The German Campaign in Poland, 1939*. Washington D.C.: Department of the Army, 1956.

KESSELRING, ALBERT: *Kesselring*. Westport, Conn.: Greenwood Press, repr. of 1954 ed.

KRAUSNICK, HELMUT et al.: *Anatomy of the SS State*. London: Collins, 1968.

LAFFIN, JOHN: *Jackboot*. London: Cassell, 1965.

LEACH, BARRY A.: *German Strategy against Russia, 1939-1941*. New York: Oxford University Press, 1973.

LESTER, J. R.: *Tank Warfare*. London: Allen and Unwin, 1943.

LEWIN, ROLAND: *Rommel as a Military Commander*. London: Batsford, 1968.

LIDDELL HART, B. H.: *The Other Side of the Hill*. London: Cassell (revised and enlarged), 1951.

A History of the Second World War. New York: Putnam, 1971.

Strategy. New York: Praeger (revised), 1961.

The Tanks—The History of the Royal Tank Regiment 1914-45 (2 Vols.). London: Cassell, 1959.

LUDENDORFF, ERICH: *The Nation at War*. London: Hutchinson, 1936.

MACKSEY, KENNETH: *Guderian: Creator of the Blitzkrieg*. New York: Stein and Day, 1976.

MANSTEIN, ERICH Von: *Lost Victories*. London: Methuen, 1958.

MASON, H. M.: *The Rise of the Luftwaffe, 1918–1940*. New York: Dial, 1973.

MELLENTHIN, F. Von: *Panzer Battles*. Norman, Okla.: University of Oklahoma Press, 1972.

MIDDELDORF, E.: *Taktik im Russlandfeldzug*. Berlin: E. S. Mittler und Sohn, 1956.

MIKSCHE, F. O.: *Blitzkrieg*. London: Faber and Faber, 1941.

MILWARD, ALAN S.: *The German Economy at War*. Atlantic Highlands, N. J.: Humanities Press, 1965.

MÜLLER-HILLEBRAND, B.: *Das Heer, 1933–1945* (3 Vols.). Frankfurt am Main: E. S. Mittler und Sohn, 1954, 1956, 1969.

The Organisational Problems of the Army High Command and their Solutions, 1938–1945. U.S. Army, Europe, Historical Division, 1953.

MUNZEL, O.: *Die Deutschen Gepanzerten Truppen bis 1945*. Hertford: Maximilian, 1965.

Heinz Guderian—Panzer Marsch. Munich: Schild, 1955.

Panzertaktik. Heidelberg: Vowinkel, 1959.

NEHRING, W.: *Die Geschichte de deutschen Panzerwaffe, 1916 bis 1945*. Berlin: Propyläen, 1969.

OBERKOMMANDO DES HEERES: *Jahrbücher des deutschen Heeres, 1940, 1941, 1942*. Leipzig: Breitkopf und Härtel, 1940, 1941, 1942.

Die Truppenführung. HDV 300.

OBERKOMMANDO DER WEHRMACHT: *Glückhäfte Strategie*. Berlin: 1942.

Kriegestagebuch (5 Vols.). Frankfurt am Main: Bernard und Graefe, 1961-63.

Sieg über Frankreich. Berlin: 1940.

Der Sieg in Polen. Berlin: Andermann, 1940.

Sieg im Westen. Berlin: 1940.

Die Wehrmacht, 1940, 1941. Berlin: Die Wehrmacht, 1940, 1941.

OGORKIEWICZ, RICHARD M.: *Armour.* New York: Arco, 1970.

O'NEILL, ROBERT: *The German Army and the Nazi Party, 1933-39.* New York: Heineman, 1967.

ORLOW, DIETRICH: *The History of the Nazi Party.* Vol. 1—1919-33, Vol. 2—1933-45. Pittsburgh: University of Pittsburgh Press, 1969, 1973.

PHILIPPI, ALFRED, und HEIM, FERDINAND: *Der Feldzug gegen Sowjetrussland, 1941-45.* Stuttgart: Kohlhammer, 1962.

PIELALKIEWICZ, JANUSZ: *Pferd und Reiter im II Weltkrieg.* Munich: Sudwest, 1976.

PLAYFAIR, I. S.: *The Mediterranean and Middle East.* (4 Vols.). London: H.M.S.O., 1954.

RAUSCHNING, HERMANN: *Hitler Speaks,* London: Butterworth, 1939.

REITLINGER, GERALD: *The Final Solution.* London: Vallentine, Mitchell, 1953.

RICH, NORMAN: *Hitler's War Aims.* (2 Vols.). New York: Norton, 1973, 1974.

ROBERTSON, E. M.: *Hitler's Pre-War Policy and Military Plans, 1933-39.* London: Longmans, 1963.

ROHER, J. *et al.*: *Decisive Battles of World War II: The German View.* London: Deutsch, 1965.

ROMMEL, ERWIN: *Papers*. (Ed. B. H. Liddell Hart) New York: Harcourt Brace Jovanovich, 1953.

ROSINSKI, HERBERT: *The German Army*. New York: Praeger, 1966.

SCHRAMM, PERCY ERNST: *Hitler: The Man and the Military Leader*. New York: Watts, 1971.

SCHRAMM, WILHELM RITTER Von: *Conspiracy among Generals*. New York, Scribner, 1957.

SEATON, ALBERT: *The Russo-German War, 1941–45*. London: Barker, 1971.

SEECKT, HANS Von: *Thoughts of a Soldier*. London: Benn, 1930.

SENFF, H.: *Die Entwicklung der Panzerwaffe im deutschen Heer zwischen der beiden Weltkriegen*. Berlin: E. S. Mittler und Sohn, 1969.

SENGER und ETTERLIN, Dr. F. Von: *Die deutschen Panzer 1926–45*. Munich: Lehmanns, 1959.

Die Panzergrenadiere. Munich: Lehmanns, 1961.

SHIRER, WILLIAM L.: *Berlin Diary*. New York: Knopf, 1941.

The Rise and Fall of the Third Reich. New York: Simon and Schuster, 1960; London: Pan, 1964.

SHULMAN, MILTON: *Defeat in the West*. Westport, Conn.: Greenwood Press, repr. of 1948 ed.

SIEGLER, F.: *Die höheren Dienststellen der deutschen Wehrmacht, 1933–45*. Stuttgart: Deutsche Verlagsanstalt, 1953.

SPEER, ALBERT: *Inside the Third Reich*. New York: Macmillan; Sphere, 1971.

SPEIDEL, H.: *We Defended Normandy*. London: Jenkins, 1951.

STEIN, GEORGE H.: *The Waffen SS*. Ithaca, N.Y.:

Cornell University Press, 1966.
STRAWSON, JOHN: *Hitler as a Military Commander*. London: Batsford, 1971.

TAYLOR, A. J. P.: *The Origins of the Second World War*. New York: Atheneum, 1962.
TAYLOR, TELFORD: *Sword and Swastika*. Magnolia, Mass.: Peter Smith, repr. of 1953 ed.
TOLAND, JOHN: *Adolf Hitler*. New York: Doubleday, 1976.
TREVOR-ROPER, H. R.: *The Last Days of Hitler*. New York: Macmillan, 3rd ed. 1962.
    Hitler's War Directives. London: Sidgwick and Jackson, 1964; Pan, 1966.

U.S. GOVERNMENT PRINTING OFFICE: *Nazi Conspiracy and Aggression* (10 Vols.). Washington D.C., 1946.
U.S. WAR DEPARTMENT: *Handbook of German Military Forces*. Washington D.C., 1941.

WARLIMONT, WALTER: *Inside Hitler's Headquarters, 1939–45*. London: Weidenfeld and Nicolson, 1964.
WERNER, MAX: *The Military Strength of the Powers*. London: Gollancz, 1939.
WERTH, ALEXANDER: *Russia at War, 1941–1945*. New York: Dutton, 1964.
WESTPHAL, SIEGFRIED: *The German Army in the West*. London: Cassell, 1951.
WHEELER-BENNETT, JOHN: *The Nemesis of Power*. New York: St. Martin, 1964.
WILLIAMS, JOHN: *The Ides of May. The Defeat of France May–June, 1940*. London: Constable, 1968.

WILMOT, CHESTER: *The Struggle for Europe*. Westport, Conn.: Greenwood Press, repr. of 1952 ed.
WINTRINGHAM, TOM: *New Ways of War*. London: Penguin, 1940.
    Peoples' War. London: Penguin, 1942.

YOUNG, Brigadier DESMOND: *Rommel, The Desert Fox*. New York: Harper & Row, 1951.

ZESKA, Major Von: *Das Buch vom Heer*. Berlin: Borg, 1940.
ZIEMKE, E. F.: *The German Northern Theatre of Operations, 1940–45*. Washington D.C.: Department of the Army, 1959.
    Stalingrad to Berlin. Washington D.C.: Department of the Army Historical Series, 1968.

Index

Aachen, 104.
Abwehr, 79, 134, 190.
Achtung! Panzer! (Guderian), 261, 264.
Adam, General Wilhelm, 26, 151, 196.
Africa Corps *see* German Africa Corps.
Allies, 209.
Armaments and equipment, 282–5, 296–9.
Armaments and Munitions, Ministry of, 235.
Armed Forces Academy, 160.
Armoured idea, 253, 257–81, 288.
Armoured Troops Command, 280, 285.
Army *see under* German Army.
Army Ordnance Office, 287.
Army Weapons Department, 285.
Artillery, 276–7.
Artillery Inspectorate, 283.
Attolico, Ambassador Bernardo, 124.

Aufmarsch Grün, 99, 100, 108, 178.
Aufmarsch Rot, 99.
Austria, 129, 173, 176–8.

Balkans, *see under names of countries.*
Bayerlein, General Fritz, 264.
Beck, General Ludwig, 12, 42, 48–50, 55, 56, 60, 103, 136, 148, 176, 177, 187: *Die Truppenführung*, 49; and racialism, 89; criticises Hitler's foreign policy, 108; and the Blomberg-Fritsch affair, 126; as conspirator against Hitler, 137, 190; opposition to Czechoslovak invasion, 180–5; resignation, 186–190; and new strategies, 273, 294; *et passim.*
Behlendorf, Colonel, 145.
Belgium, 207.
Benoist-Méchin, J., 214.
Bismarck, Chancellor, 23.
Blitzkrieg see under Strategy and Tactics.

Blomberg, Field-Marshal Werner von, 39, 40-5, 55, 56, 62, 85, 94, 95, 98, 100, 103, 104, 112, 145: his attitude to relations between Army and state, 64-7; politicises the Army, 66-8; and racialism, 70; on Hitler and the Army, 75-7; becomes Commander-in-Chief Armed Forces, 78; and anti-Semitism, 89; in relations between National Socialist Party and Army, 92-5; and reoccupation of Rhineland, 104; speaks against rearmament, 105; and preparations for war, 108; marriage to a girl 'with a past,' and its sequel, the Blomberg-Fritsch affair, 112-7; his directive, 'On Unified War Preparation of the Wehrmacht,' 161; belief in mass armies and total warfare, 221; *et passim*.

'Blue Book of the Reichswehr,' 94-5.

Blumentritt, General Gunther von, 51; *et passim*.

Brauchitsch, Field-Marshal Walther von, 126, 139, 285: appointment as Army Commander, 126, 146-50; character and background, 150-4; attitude to Austrian invasion, 177; attitude to Czechoslovak invasion, 181-3, 189, 193; and new strategic ideas, 275; *et passim*.

Bredow, General Ferdinand von, 42, 93.

Britain and British Army, 100, 103, 194, 204, 288; *et passim*.

Brockdorff-Ahlefeld, General Count Erich von, 134, 190.

Brownshirts *see* SA.

Canaris, Admiral Wilhelm, 129, 134, 169-70, 190, 205.

Cannae, 243.

Case Green, Operation, 189.

Case White, Operation, 200.

Cauldron battles *see Kesselschlachten under* Strategy and Tactics.

Cavalry, 276.

Chamberlain, A. Neville, 193, 194.

Choltitz, General Dietrich von, 33.

'Crystal Night' Pogrom, 199.

Churchill, Rt. Hon. W.S., 208.

Communists, 28, 52-3.

Concentration camps, 53, 199.

Crüwell, General Ludwig, 94.

Czechoslovakia, 50, 98, 102, 108, 140, 174, 196: German plans for invasion of, 178-83, 190, 191, 194.

Daladier, Edouard, 192.

Danzig, 201; *see also under* Polish Corridor.

Delbruck, Hans, 10.

Department for Motor Transport and Mechanisation, 287.

Dollmann, General Friedrich, 91-2.

Enabling Act, 1933, 31, 59.

Engel, Captain Gerhard, 129, 156.

Epp, General Franz-Xaver von, 18.

France, 99–104 *passim*, 179, 204, 207, 288.
Frederick the Great, 218, 243.
Freikorps, 16.
Frisch, Captain von, 121.
Fritsch, General Werner von, 36, 42, 47–8, 56, 57, 79, 97, 100, 104, 112, 125, 145: becomes *Generaloberst*, 78; and racialism, 89; opposes Hitler, 107–8; accused of homosexuality, 113–4, 119–20; resignation and trial, 120–1; his reactions to his downfall, 125; ramifications of his downfall, 126–137; attempts at his rehabilitation, 138–42; his honorary colonelcy and death, 142; and armoured strategy, 274–5; *et passim*.
Fromm, General Fritz, 286–7.
Fuller, Major-General, J.F.C., 211, 231, 258–9, 263, 264.
Funck, General von, 143.
Funk, Walther, 146.

General Army Office, 286.
General Staff, 11, 23, 57, 99, 103, 162, 186, 215, 228, 237, 280, 287: resistance to Hitler, 189; in First World War, 244–6; reaction to the armoured idea, 270; *et passim*; *see also under names of officers*.
Gercke, Colonel Rudolph, 201.
German Africa Corps, 287.
German Army: moral responsibilities in relation to Hitler, 12–4, 26–9; political and social heritage of, 13–29; Hitler's early attitude to, 30, 31–4; and SA, 37–42; leadership's early attitude to Hitler, 42–55; Aryan Paragraph, 56-7, 69, 74; new oath of allegiance, 59–62; adapts to National Socialism, 62–6; political instruction in, 66–7; and racialism, 69–70; its position in 1938, 72–3, 86; Hitler's behaviour to, 1933–38, 74–81; its relations with National Socialist Party, 78, 85, 87–93, 153–4; and SS, 83–6; disagreements with Hitler, 94–109; rapid expansion of, 96, 236–8, 289–303; preparedness for war, 98–101; position of, 1938, 110, 130–3; and the Blomberg-Fritsch affair, 112–43; soldiers' hatred of SS, 130; major reorganisation of, 144-7; office of Wehrmacht Adjutant changed and office of Army Adjutant created, 154–6; creation and implications of OKW, 156–65; command structure, 170–2; position of High Command before Second World War, 174–5; reaction to plans to invade Czechoslovakia, 179–193; trust between its leaders and Hitler destroyed, 195–6; leaders resigned to Hitler's dominance, 198; military successes, 1939, 207; strength, 1939, 214; condition of between the Wars, 215–222; traditions of, 218, 239–51, 271–2, 274; effect of advent of Hitler and National Socialism on, 223–5; Hitler's failure to provide for its success, 234–5; *Leadership*

and Battles of the Infantry, 251; and mechanisation, 255-7; conflicts caused by new strategies, 272-9, 283, 286, 288; lack of resources and equipment, 277-8, 282, 287-8, 294, 296-9; motorisation of, 284; Mobile Troops Command formed, 285-6; expansion and weakness of before Second World War, 290-303; division into Field Army and Replacement Army, 299; structure of infantry divisions, 300-1; mobilisation, 301; strength, 1939, 302; *et passim*; *see also under* Armaments and Equipment, Hitler, Rearmament, Strategy and Tactics, *and under Army branches and commands.*
Forces engaged
    XIV Corps, 285.
    XV Corps, 285.
    XVI Corps, 285, 286.
    Africa Corps, 287.
    9th Cavalry Regiment, 130.
    9th Infantry Regiment, 130.
    48th Infantry Regiment, 130.
    see also under Panzer Forces.
Gestapo, 67, 71, 79, 90, 91; and the murder of von Schleicher and von Bredow, 93; its part in von Fritsch's and von Blomberg's downfall, 114-5, 120-1.
Gisevius, Hans Bernhard, 134, 197-8.
Goedeler, Carl, 135-6, 188.
Goltz, Count von der, 121.

Göring, Reich Marshal Herman, 41, 77, 78, 95, 106, 176, 234: rivalry with Army generals, and von Blomberg's and von Fritsch's downfall, 113-4, 119, 121; made *Generalfeldmarschall*, 146; abuses Army leaders, 197; *et passim*.
Grenzwacht, 291, 293.
Gröner, General Wilhelm, 10, 16, 18, 25, 220, 232-3.
Grühn, Erna, 112, 114.
Guderian, General Heinz, 25-6: his reaction to the Blomberg-Fritsch affair, 123-5; his strategic ideas, 260-4, 267-9, 271-2, 273-82; character, 279; appointed Chief of Mobile Troops, 280, 285-6; in development of Panzer arm, 281-2; becomes commander 2nd Panzer Division, 285-6; *et passim*.

Halder, General Franz, 129, 130: joins conspiracy against Hitler, 137; becomes Chief of General Staff, character, 185, 186-90; as conspirator, 190, 191, 194, 201; as opponent of new strategies, 273; *et passim*.
Hammerstein-Equord, General Curt von, 18, 24-5, 26, 32, 42, 49, 94, 129, 190, 220.
Handbook on German Military Forces, 170.
Hasselbach, Dr. Hans von, 226-7.
Hassell, Ulrich von, 146.
Hausser, SS General Paul, 84.
Heibsberg Triangle, 99.

Helldorf, Count Wolf, 112, 114, 135.
Hess, Deputy Führer Rudolf, 74, 88.
Heusinger, General Adolf, 131.
Heydrich, Chief of Security Services Reinhard, 41, 79, 90, 113, 130.
Heye, General Wilhelm von, 220.
Hierl, Colonel Konstantin, 18.
High Command of the Army, *see under* OKH.
High Command of the Luftwaffe, *see under* OKL.
High Command of the Navy, *see under* OKM.
High Command of the Wehrmacht, *see under* OKW.
Himmler, Reichsführer SS Heinrich, 41, 79, 82, 90: his part in von Fritsch's downfall, 113, 119, 121.
Hindenburg, President and Field-Marshal Paul von, 24, 26, 35, 42, 47, 57, 94: death of, 58.
Hitler, Führer Adolf: early opposition to from Army, 17-8; becomes Reich Chancellor, 26; early attitude to Army, 30-7; achieves absolute authority, 30-2; and SA, 37-42; becomes supreme head of Reich, 58; Decree 13 May 1936, 69; behaviour to Army, 1933-8, 74-80; attitude to SS, 80-6; makes concessions to Army, 95; disagreements with Army, 96-109; warlike intentions and foreign policy, 100-9; dissatisfaction with Army, 110-1; and the Blomberg-Fritsch affair, 112-128, 138-43; becomes Commander-in-Chief of Wehrmacht, 121, 144-7; changes Army's command structure and leaders, 144-7; achieves direct command of Armed Forces, 161; increasing involvement in military matters, 174-5; decision to invade Czechoslovakia, 178-9; conspiracies against, 133-8, 190-4, 203; success in Czechoslovakia, 194-8; his dominance over Army, 198-9; announces war aims, 200; orders attack on Poland, 205; his desire for a mass army, 221-2; statement of his principles of foreign policy, 224-5; his character as military leader, 223-33; his strategies for war, 233-5; promises effective modernisation of Army, 285-6; *et passim*.
Hoepner, General Erich, 190.
Hossbach, General Friedrich, 36, 44, 76, 77, 107, 129, 131, 155-6.
Hugenberg, Alfred von, 28.

Indirect Approach *see* Armoured Idea.
Infiltration *see under* Strategy and Tactics.
Inter-Allied Control Commission, 216.
International Military Tribunal, 10-1.
Italy, 200, 204-5.

Jodl, General Alfred, 178, 198: character, 168; *et passim*.

Kapp putsch, 16.
Keitel, Field-Marshal Wilhelm, 112-3, 139, 145, 147, 148, 149: becomes Chief of Staff, 118; and creation of OKW, 159; character and background, 163-6; *et passim.*
Kesselschlachten see under Strategy and Tactics.
Kharkov, 248
Kluge, Field-Marshal Gunther von, 139; *et passim.*
Kressenstein, General Kress von, 146.
Kühn, General Friedrich, 287.
Küntzen, Colonel Adolf, 145.

Landespolizei, 104, 291.
Landwehr, 291, 294, 300.
Leadership and Battles of the Infantry, 252.
League of Nations, 101.
Leber, Dr. Julius, 20.
Leeb, Field-Marshal Wilhelm von, 100, 148.
Lester, J.R.: *Tank Warfare*, 209.
Leuthen, 243.
Liddel Hart, Sir Basil, 210, 263-4, 272: quoted, 12, 211, 217-8, 258.
Lithuania, 100.
Locarno Pact, 103.
Lossow, General Otto von, 18.
Ludendorff, General Erich, 21, 221, 255.
Luftwaffe, 122, 171; *et passim.*
Lutz, General Oswald, 146, 280, 283, 285: appointed Chief of Armoured Troops Command, 280.

Memelland, 194.

Miksche, F.O., 209.
Mobile Troops Command, 285-6.
Moltke, General Helmuth von, 244, 245, 252, 256: his concept of warfare, 240-3; *et passim.*
Müller, Curt Hellmuth, 112.
Munich Agreement, 192-3.
Munich Putsch, 18, 62.
Mussolini, Benito, 192.

National Socialist Party, 10, 18, 22, 25, 34, 37, 39, 52, 131, 232: accession to power, 27-8; ideology and the Army, 62-71; its position, 1938, 73-4; relations with Army, 86-93; concepts of *Lebensraum, Grossdeutschland* and *Weltmacht*, 224; *et passim; see also* SS and SA.
Nebe, Arthur, 135.
Neurath, Konstantin von, 108, 146.
Niebelschutz, General von, 146.
Niemöller, Pastor John, 88.
Night of the Long Knives, 37, 41, 57.
Norway, 207.
NSDAP *see* National Socialist Party.
Nuremberg Laws, 53.
Nuremberg Rally, 37, 62.

Oder-Warthe Line, 99.
OKH, 178, 200, 201, 202: reorganisation of higher command, 156-63; position in command structure, 171; status of prior to outbreak of war, 174; criticised by Jodl, 197;

et passim; *see also* General Staff.
OKL, 171.
OKM, 171.
OKW, 145, 176, 197: creation of, 156–63; low status of, 173–4; and plans for Czechoslovak invasion, 178–9; treatise on strategy, 251; *et passim*.
Oster, Colonel Hans, 15–6, 17, 19, 22–3, 134, 135, 188, 190, 205.

Pact of Steel, 200, 204.
Panzer Forces, 260, 264, 269, 275–6, 281–2, 286: first tank unit formed, 279–80; armoured divisions formed, 280–1; armaments and strength, 1939, 283–5; status of command, 284–8; *et passim*; *see also* Tanks.
Forces engaged:
 2nd Panzer Regiment, 130.
Panzerkampfwagen, 282.
Papen, Franz von, 28.
Paris, 207.
Poland, 28, 94, 99, 102, 174, 194, 199–200: German plans for invasion, 199–200; German attack on, 204–5; *see also* next entry.
Polish Corridor, 201, 202.
Porgrell, General von, 146.
Prusso-German Constitutionalism, 14.

Raeder, Admiral Dr. Erich: becomes *Generaladmiral*, 78.
Rearmament, 31, 35, 54, 95–7, 219–22, 236–8.
Reich Defence Council, 32, 79.

Reich Defence Laws: 1935, 31, 80, 85.
Reich Labour Service, 79.
Reich War Minister, 158–9.
Reichenau, Field-Marshal Walter von, 36, 38, 42, 46–7, 51, 53–4, 93, 98, 147, 148, 176: composes new Army oath, 58; and creation of OKW, 159.
Reichsheer, 215–22 *passim*, 238, 290.
Reichstag, 35, 53, 201.
Reichswehr Minister, 157.
Replacement Army, 286, 299.
Reynaud, Paul, 208–9.
Rhineland, 102, 103.
Ribbentrop, Reich Minister Joachim von, 96, 106, 146, 203.
Röhm, SA Leader Ernst, 18, 37, 38, 39, 40, 41, 57.
Rommel, Field-Marshal Erwin, 206, 264–5, 273; *et passim*.
Rosinski, Herbert, 21.
Ruffer, Charlotte, 151.
Rundstedt, Field-Marshal Gerd von, 126, 148; *et passim*.
Russia *see under* Soviet Union.

SA, 25, 26, 28, 35, 36, 37, 38, 39, 40, 41, 56, 57, 58, 291.
Saarbrücken, 104.
Sack, Dr. Carl, 121.
Sadowa, 244.
Schacht, Hjalmar, 135, 188, 201.
Scharnhorst, Gerhard von, 219.
Schirach, Baldur von, 88.
Schleicher, General Kurt von, 18, 24–6, 42, 93–4: murder of, 93.
Schlieffen, Alfred von, 218, 240, 242, 245, 256: his concept of warfare, 242–3.

Schmidt, Otto, 114, 121, 141.
Schmundt, Major Rudolf, 155-6.
Schobert, General Eugen Ritter von, 139.
Schramm, Percy, 227-8.
Schülenberg, General Count von, 117.
Schultze, Erich, 135.
Schwedler, General Victor von, 145.
Schweppenburg, General Geyr von, 131.
Sedan, 244.
Seeckt, General Hans von, 16, 17, 20, 21, 147, 157, 207: his part in revitalising the Army, 217-9, 220; his strategic theories, 246-8.
Siegfried Line *see* West Wall.
Sonderfall Erweiterung Rot/Grn, 100.
Sonderfall Otto, 100.
Soviet Union, 43, 94, 102, 179, 202: non-aggression pact with Germany, 203; *et passim*.
Spain, 106.
Speer, Albert, 165, 167.
SS, 41, 79, 80: first militarised unit instituted, 80; Hitler's attitude to, 80-6; oath of, 81; its growing strength and relations with Army, 84; its attacks on Army, 90-3; soldiers' hatred of, 130; *et passim*; for *SS Panzer units*, *see under* Panzer Forces.
Kasernierte Hundertschaften, 82.
Leibstandarte SS 'Adolf Hitler,' 82.
Politische Bereitschaften, 83-4.

Sonderkommandos, 82.
SS-VT, 83-6.
Stalin, 127.
Strategy and Tactics: historical perspective, 236-53; development of new strategies, 254-88.
Blitzkrieg, 207-15, 231, 233, 234, 244, 254-88, 304.
Infiltration, 254-5, 259.
Kesselschlachten, 243.
see also Armoured Idea and *Vernichtungsgedanke*.
Streicher, Gauleiter Julius, 89.
Stülpnagel, General Karl-Heinrich, 190; *et passim*.
Sturm Abteilung see SA.
Stürmer, Der, 89.
Sudetenland, 191, 193.
Sun Tzu, 223, 253, 259.

Tactics *see* Strategy and Tactics.
Tanks, 260-1, 262-3, 267-8, 275, 276-7, 279-80: first tank unit formed, 280.
Types:
PzKw I, 284.
PzKw II, 284.
PzKw III, 284.
PzKw IV, 284.
SdKf, 284.
Territorials *see* Landwehr.
Thoma, General Wilhelm von, 272-3, 287.
Thomas, General Georg, 170, 201, 275-6.
Todt Organisation, 196.
Trier, 104.
Truppenführung, Die, 49, 249, 250.

Ulex, General Alexander, 137, 139, 140, 142.

USSR *see* Soviet Union.

Vagts, Alfred, 86-7.
Vansittart, Sir Robert, 152.
Verein Graf Schlieffen, 95.
Verfügungstruppen see SS-VT.
Vernichtungsgedanke, 243-53 *passim*, 269, 279.
Versailles, Treaty of, 54, 215-6, 220, 236, 290.
Viebahn, General Max von, 129.
Völkischer Beobachter, 57, 67.

Waldersee, Field-Marshal von, 23.
Warfare: change in conditions of in modern times, 240-2; mechanisation, 255, 257, 259; *see also* Strategy and Tactics.
Warlimont, General Walter, 123, 131, 161, 166: character and background, 169-70; on relations between Hitler and the Army, 44-5, 162, 173-4; *et passim*.

Wehrmacht High Command *see* OKW.
Wehrmachtsadler, 56.
Wehrmachtsamt, 157, 160: becomes OKW, 161.
Weichs, General Maximilian von, 100.
Weimar Republic, 16-7, 35.
Werner, Max, 214.
Westphal, General Siegfried, 124, 275, 295: on the Army and politics, 87; on expansion of Army, 293; *et passim*.
West Wall, 99, 196.
Wheeler-Bennett, Sir John, 27, 59, 122-3.
Wiedemann, Captain Fritz, 115.
Wietersheim, General Gustav von, 204.
Wilhelm II, Kaiser, 23.
Winterübung, 104.
Wintringham, Tom, 210.
Witzleben, General Erwin von, 129, 133-4, 136-7, 190, 193.

TRUE AND DOCUMENTED!
THE INCREDIBLE STRATEGIES, STUNNING VICTORIES, AND AGONIZING DEFEATS OF *THE SECOND WORLD WAR*

HITLER'S NAVAL WAR
by Cajus Bekker   (300, $2.25)
The incredible story of the undermanned Nazi naval force that nearly won WW II—Operation Underdog.

PACIFIC SWEEP   (332, $2.25)
by William N. Hess
They were a handful of heroes against a sky black with zeros spitting death!

HITLER'S GENERALS   (335, $2.25)
by Richard Humble
The incredible love-hate saga of the Fuhrer and his Commanders.

LINE OF DEPARTURE: TARAWA   (347, $2.25)
by Martin Russ
Man for man and inch for inch, the bloodiest battle ever fought in the Pacific War.

THE BOMBING OF NUREMBERG   (356, $2.25)
by James Campbell
The greatest single air battle of WW II—when the hunters became the hunted!

THE ADMIRAL'S WOLFPACK   (362, $2.25)
by Jean Noli
The spellbinding saga of Adm. Karl Doenitz's U-boats and the men who made these "gray wolves" the scourge of the seas.

THE LAST SIX MONTHS   (377, $2.25)
by General S. M. Shtemenko
The action-packed account of the Soviet Army's final drive into the heart of Hitler's Reich.

23 DAYS: THE FINAL COLLAPSE OF NAZI GERMANY   (400, $2.25)
by Marlis G. Steinert
An hour-by-hour retelling of the death-throes of Hitler's Reich.

Available wherever paperbacks are sold, or order direct from the Publisher. Send cover price plus 40¢ per copy for mailing and handling to Zebra Books, 21 East 40th Street, New York, N.Y. 10016. DO NOT SEND CASH!